His face and one arm were worked out of the earth. The house was invisible behind him, but he could feel its menacing presence. He hoped she wouldn't so much as glance out a window— Miriam had the eyes of a falcon. . . .

He lay beneath the sky of morning, feeling the hunger rising yet again. The house stood in its garden, somber to John's eyes. He looked high to its roof, to the tiny window of the room where Miriam kept her dead.

There was something he could do there, if he dared, if he could bear it. The house was silent. Taunting. Daring him to enter. He would, when the moment was right. If she captured him first, he would lose his revenge forever. And if she did not? Then it would not matter.

Whitley Strieber

PUBLISHED BY POCKET BOOKS NEW YORK

POCKET BOOKS, a Simon & Schuster division of
GULF & WESTERN CORPORATION
1230 Avenue of the Americas, New York, N.Y. 10020

Published by arrangement with William Morrow and Co., Inc.
Library of Congress Catalog Card Number: 80-21355

ISBN: 0-671-42737-7

First Pocket Books printing January, 1982

10 9 8 7 6 5 4 3 2 1

POCKET and colophon are trademarks of Simon & Schuster.

Printed in the U.S.A.

For M.A.

Man comes and tills the field and lies beneath,
And after many a summer dies the swan.
Me only cruel immortality
Consumes . . .

Tithonus, ALFRED LORD TENNYSON

There was an awful rainbow once in heaven:
We knew her woof, her texture; she is given
In the dull catalogue of common things.

Lamia, JOHN KEATS

The Hunger

Prologue

JOHN BLAYLOCK CHECKED his watch again. It was exactly three A.M.—time to move. The small Long Island town was so quiet he could hear the light change at the end of the tree-lined street. John put his watch back in his pocket and stepped softly from his place of concealment in the shrubs. He paused a moment in the cool, private air of the empty street.

His target lived in the middle of the block. John's well-trained senses fixed on the black bulk of the house, testing for any flicker of life. As far as the Wagners were concerned, Kaye would just disappear. Within a month she would become another statistic, one of thousands of teenagers who walk out on their families every year. Kaye had good reason to run away. She was being expelled from Emerson High, and she and her boyfriend, Tommy, were facing a cocaine charge in JD court in a few days.

Both would disappear tonight. Miriam was taking care of the boyfriend.

As he walked, silent and invisible in his black jogging

1

outfit, he thought briefly of his partner. He wanted her as he always did at moments of tension. Theirs was an old love, familiar and comfortable.

At two minutes past three the moon set. Now, only the single street light at the end of the block provided illumination. That was as planned. John broke into a trot, passing the target house and pausing at the far end of the grounds. No light appeared from any angle. He went up the driveway.

To John, houses had an ambience, almost an emotional smell. As he drew closer to its looming silence he decided that he didn't much like this house. For all its carefully tended rose bushes, its beds of dahlias and pansies, it was an angry place.

This confirmation of the Wagners' misery strengthened his resolve. His mind focused with even greater clarity on the task at hand. Each phase had been timed to the last second. At this level of concentration he could hear the breathing of Mr. and Mrs. Wagner in their second-floor bedroom. He paused, focusing his attention with fierce effort. Now he could hear the rustle of sheets as a sleeper's arm stirred, the faint scratching of a roach moving up the wall of the bedroom. It was difficult for him to maintain such intense concentration for long. In this he and Miriam were very different. She lived often at such a level, John almost never.

He satisfied himself that the household was asleep, then began his penetration. Despite the dark, he quickly located the basement door. It led into a furnace room. Beyond it was a finished playroom and Kaye's bedroom. He withdrew a length of piano wire from a pouch concealed under his sweat shirt and picked the lock, then worked back the spring catch with the edge of a credit card.

A rush of warm, musty air came out when the door was opened. The night was only slightly chilly, and the furnace was running on low, its fire casting faint orange light. John crossed the room and went into the hallway beyond.

He froze. Ahead he heard rattling breath, not human. His mind analyzed the sound and concluded that a dog of about sixty pounds was sleeping at the end of the hall, approximately seven feet away.

Nothing could be done about it now. He was forced to use his chloroform. He removed a plastic bag from the pouch and took out a cloth. It was cold in his hand, dripping with the liquid. He was not as quick as Miriam, he needed chloroform to subdue his victims. The thought of the danger he would now face made his throat tighten.

His friend the darkness began to work against him; he stepped forward, calculating his distance as best he could. One step. The dog's breathing changed. Two steps. There was a shuffling sound, the beginning of a growl. Three steps. Like an explosion, the dog barked.

Then he had it, his fingers twining in the fur, his chloroformed rag going over the muzzle.

There was a furious struggle, not quite silent.

"Barney?"

Kaye's voice was bell-clear and edged with fear. John was aware of how much his odds were worsening. The girl was wide awake. He could sense her staring into the darkness. Normally, he would have retreated at this point but tonight he could not. Miriam was an absolutely intractable killer; she would not miss the boyfriend. The essence of the deception was that they would disappear together. Both gone and the police would figure it for a runaway and file the case somewhere below lost kittens. Only one gone and there would be much more suspicion.

As soon as the dog stopped struggling, John moved ahead. There would be perhaps ten safe minutes while the dog was unconscious. There must be no further delays; maximum efficiency was essential.

Kaye's bedroom was suddenly flooded with light. She

was beautiful, sitting on her bed in a nightshirt, her hand still touching the frilly lamp.

John felt the light like fire. He leaped on her, lunging to stifle the scream he knew was rising. Then his hand was over her lips, his arm pushing her onto the bed.

Kaye smelled faintly of cologne and cigarettes. John fought her, his body shaking above the dismal fury of her struggle. The intensity of her resistance conjured up anger in him. Both his hands covered her mouth and nose, his knees pinned her elbows.

The room was absolutely still, the only sound that of Kaye's legs thudding against the mattress. John looked at the pleading, terrified eyes, trying to gauge how much longer they would remain alive. He felt the girl's tongue darting against the palm of his hand. Careful, don't let her bite.

The five minutes it took to suffocate her stretched on and on. John fought to keep his attention on his work. If she got away from him . . . but he wouldn't allow that. He had, after all, years of practice. Just don't let the mind wander, the grip loosen—not for an instant. He was watching for the hemorrhage in the whites of the eyes that would be the sign of death. Kaye responded typically. She pleaded with her expression, looking desperately into his face.

Finally, her eyes screwed closed with the failure of consciousness. There came a series of frantic convulsions—the unconscious trying to escape what the conscious could not. After a moment of motionlessness the eyes opened again. The whites were the correct shade of pink now. The eyes slowly drifted to the right, as if trying to see the way. A deeper stillness fell.

At once John released his grip and leaned across to her chest, pressing his ear between the warm softness of her breasts, listening for the last thutter of the heart.

Perfection. She was just right, hanging at the edge of death.

All obstacles were removed. Steel discipline could give way now to his real feelings, to the raw truth of his hunger. He lunged at her, unhearing of his own excited cry. She exploded instantly into new life within him. His mind clarified as if he had plunged into deliciously cold water on a stuffy day. The achiness that had been threatening swept from his muscles. His hearing, his eyesight flooded him with impressions of almost supernatural intensity.

He soared from height to height. As always at such a moment, a vivid image of Miriam appeared in his mind's eye. He could taste her lips, feel her laughter in his heart. He longed for her cool flesh, the love within him growing rich with desire.

Then it was finished. He barely glanced at the remains of Kaye Wagner, a dark lumpy thing almost lost in the bedclothes. Time had to be addressed. He forced himself back to sordid necessity, slipping the frail husk of the girl into a black plastic bag. Briskly, he consulted his watch again. In exactly two minutes he must be at the pickup point.

Into the bag he also tossed the girl's wallet and hairbrush and some of the cosmetics scattered over her dresser. Then panties and bras and a stack of 45-rpm records from the floor. He stopped in the bathroom for toothbrush, hair spray, more cosmetics, shampoo and a somewhat clean blouse he found hanging on the shower-curtain rod.

In fifty seconds the car would come down the street. Miriam was always on schedule, so John hurried out the way he had come, pausing only to lock the cellar door behind him with his piano wire. He moved swiftly down the driveway and waited in a flowering dogwood.

His body tingled; his awareness seemed to extend into every detail of the world around him. No effort was needed to concentrate now. He could feel the peaceful presence of the dogwood, hear even the smallest sounds, the rustling of a beetle, the ping of a slowly cooling engine block in a car across the street. Above him the stars had resolved into myriad colors: green and yellow and blue and red. The breeze seemed to stir each leaf with a separate touch. John felt a sharp and poignant sense of the beauty around him. Life could not be sweeter.

The appearance of their car made him smile. Miriam drove with the caution of a blind octogenarian. Accident obsessed, she had chosen the Volvo because of its safety record and innocuous appearance. Despite its sturdiness, she had it equipped with a heavy-duty gas tank, truck brakes, an air-bag restraint system as well as seatbelts and a "sun roof" that was actually an extra means of escape.

Dutifully, he trotted over to the slowly moving vehicle, tossed his burdens into the back seat and slipped in beside her. There was no question of his driving, of course. She never relinquished the wheel unless absolutely necessary. It was comfortable to be with her again. Her lips felt cool and familiar on his cheek, her smile was bright with pleasure and success.

Saying nothing, she concentrated on the road. The entrance to the Long Island Expressway was two blocks away and John knew she would be worrying about the chance of being stopped by the local police before they reached it. They would have to answer embarrassing questions if that happened.

Until they reached the ramp neither spoke. As they pulled onto the freeway, however, he felt her relax. The last bit of tension broke.

"It was just *beautiful*," she said. "He was so strong."

John smiled. He husbanded his own exhilaration. Despite his years at it, the kill itself never pleased him. He was not excited by the actual act, as was Miriam.

"Yours went well, I hope." It was a question.

"The usual."

She was staring at him, her eyes twinkling like those of a pretty doll. "I had such a nice time. He thought he was being raped by a girl." She giggled. "I think he died in ecstasy." She stretched, luxurious with post-prandial ease. "How did Kaye die?"

He supposed the question was her way of giving him

support, to show interest, but he would rather forget the ugly little act and concentrate on the joy that was its reward.

"I had to use the chloroform on a dog."

Miriam reached over and kissed him on the cheek, then took his hand. She was so sensitive; she knew from that one remark all that had occurred, the difficulties he had endured.

"They all end up the same sooner or later. I'm sure you were very humane. She probably never really understood what was happening to her."

"I miscalculated. I should have anticipated the dog. That's all that's bothering me."

But it wasn't, not quite. There was also this feeling, strange and yet remembered. He was tired. It had been a very long time since he had felt so.

"You can never give a perfect death. There will always be suffering."

Yes, that was true. And even after all these years he did not like to inflict suffering. But it shouldn't weigh on him like this. Feeding was supposed to make you feed vital and alive.

This could only be a passing phase, the result of his having been thrown off-balance by the dog. He decided to dismiss it from his mind. He turned to the window, stared out.

The night was magnificent. He had always seen a great truth in the dark, a kind of joy, something forgiving of such violence as his. Thinking of it brought a welcome sense of justification.

The lights of towns came and went. John felt deeply in love with it all. He allowed himself a little of the pleasure of the kill, reflecting how he was fundamentally happy in his life.

Before he quite realized it his eyes had closed. The humming of the car began to mingle with voices of memory, distant memory.

His eyes snapped open. This was not normal. He opened the sun roof to let in some cool air. The pattern of their lives was extremely regular. You Slept six out of twenty-four hours, and it came upon you about four hours after you ate.

What, then, was this?

He was drifting, half-asleep, into a very pleasant sensation, his mind possessed by a soft sigh of remembrance, of dream . . .

For a flash it was as if he were in an enormous, cold room lit with candles, a fire crackling in the grate. He was surprised. He had not thought of the ancestral home of the Blaylocks since he had left England. And yet now he remembered his own bedroom so well, the incessant dampness, the grandeur, the familiarity.

Miriam was as beautiful now as she had been then. He would have touched her, held her, but she did not like to be disturbed while she was driving.

He remembered the tall windows of his room with their view of the North Yorks Moors, where gypsy fires flickered at night. The faces and voices of the past flooded into his consciousness. Drowsily, he watched the strange modern landscape pass the car, the endless lights, the cramped, scruffy little houses. How alone he was in this world.

He closed his eyes and was at once transported to a wet, gray afternoon at Hadley. It was a special afternoon—or would be within the hour. He remembered himself as he was then, a fashionable lordling just finished with two years at Balliol College. He had been dressing for dinner, his valet hovering about with stockings and cravat and shirt. His assumption was that the guest would be some ghastly political acquaintance of his father and the evening would consist of sanctimonious discussions about the mad old king and the profligate regent. John didn't give a damn about court. He was much more interested in bear-baiting and running his hounds on the moor.

As he was dressing, a carriage rattled up the drive. It was a magnificent equipage, drawn by six stallions, attended by two footmen. Their livery was unfamiliar.

When a lady in white silk emerged from the carriage John snapped his fingers impatiently for his wig. It had been too long since his father had brought a whore to Hadley. Despite all his infirmities and his frequent confusions, despite the goiter, the dim eyes, John's father retained a superb taste in females. When he sought a woman's company, he usually cast about among the shabbier edges of the aristocracy for some physically attractive, charming creature without sufficient property to interest his son.

Except they usually did.

"The master's away," he sang softly as Williams adjusted his cravat and sprinkled a bit of scent in his wig, "we shall have a merry day."

"The master is here, sir."

"I know that, Williams. Just wishful thinking."

"Yes, sir."

"The usual preparations, Williams, if she is appealing."

The man turned and went about his duty. He was a good valet and knew when not to respond. But John could be certain that the halls from the sitting room to this bedroom would be empty of servants at the appropriate time, and the lady's maid would not follow her mistress.

That is, if his father could be sotted with enough brandy to make him forget his plans, and enough bezique to bore him to sleep.

Yes, indeed, it promised to be an interesting evening. John went down the gallery that connected the two wings of the house, feeling the humid coolness of the evening beyond the windows, passing beneath the portrait of his mother that his father insisted remain outside her old room.

The stairway had been lit as if for a ball, as had the front hall and the large dining hall. Servants were setting three places at the massive table. Why his father had not chosen the more intimate yellow dining room John could not imagine. His father's voice could be heard beyond the great hall, in the formal parlor. John crossed the hall and paused as the door was opened before him.

Then he knew why the pomp. And he knew no amount of brandy would addle his father this night, nor bezique send him off to sleep.

There was no word to describe her.

Skin could not be so white or features so perfect, surely. Her eyes, as pale as delft, as pellucid as the sea, flickered to him. He fought for some appropriate word, could only smile and bow, then advance.

"This is my son, John."

His father's words were as distant as an echo. Only the woman mattered now. "I am charmed, ma'am," John said softly.

She extended her hand.

"The Lady Miriam," his father said, his tone revealing just a trace of irony.

John took the cool hand and pressed it to his lips, lingered just an instant too long, then raised his head.

She was looking at him, not smiling.

He was shocked by the power of that glance, so shocked he turned away in confusion.

His heart was pounding, his face was blazing hot. He covered his upset with a flourish of snuff. When he dared look, her eyes were merry and pleasant, as a woman's eyes should be.

Then, as if to tease him, she looked at him again in that shameless, wild way. Never before had he encountered such brazen effrontery, not even from the most primitive scullery or back-street whore.

To see it in such an extraordinary and obviously refined beauty made him shake with excitement. His eyes teared, involuntarily he extended his hands. She seemed about to speak but only ran her tongue along the edges of her teeth.

It was as if his father had ceased to exist. John's arms came around her, around Miriam, for the first time.

The embrace electrified him, inflamed him. His eyes closed, he sank into her softness, bent his head to her alabaster neck, touched her salt and milky flesh with his open lips.

Laughter sprang out of her like a hidden blade. He jerked his head up, dropped his arms. In her eyes there was something so lascivious, so mocking and triumphant, that his passion was at once replaced by fear. Such a look he had seen—

Yes, in a panther some East Indians had been displaying at Vauxhall Gardens.

The light, furious eyes of a panther.

How could such eyes be so very lovely?

All of this had happened in no more than a minute. During this time John's father had stood transfixed, his eyebrows raised, his face gradually registering more and more surprise. "Sir!" he burst out at last. "Please, sir!"

John had to recover himself. A gentleman could not so dishonor himself before his father.

"Do not be angry with him, Lord Hadley," Miriam said. "You cannot imagine what a flattery it is to be attended to so fervently."

Her voice was soft and yet it filled the room with vibrant intensity. The words may not have pleased John's father, but they foreclosed any further disapproval. The old lord bowed graciously and took the lady's hand. Together they strolled farther into the great room, pausing before the fireplace. John moved along behind them, his manner outwardly deferential. Within, his heart was seething. The woman's manner and appearance were the most wonderful he had ever known, a thousand times more wonderful than he had imagined possible. She trailed behind her an attar of roses. The firelight made her skin glow. Her beauty made the dank old room blaze with light.

At a signal from his father, a piper began to play on the balcony. The tones were stirring, some Scottish air at once beautiful and fierce. Miriam turned and looked upward. "What is that instrument?"

"A bagpipe," John said before his father's mouth could open. "It's a Scot's device."

"Also Breton," his father snapped. "That is a Breton piper. There are no Scotsmen in Hadley House."

John knew differently, but he did not contradict.

They ate a brace of grouse, high and sour, followed by lamb, pudding and trifle. John remembered that meal well because of how surprised he had been when Miriam did not partake of any of the food. Course after course went past untouched. It would not have been polite for them to inquire why their guest did not care for the food, but at the end of the meal John's father seemed sunken in dismay. When she at last took some port he brightened.

No doubt he had been afraid that his physical appearance was so unpleasant to her that she was not going to stay the night. John almost laughed aloud when he saw how his father grinned when she drank, his loose dental plates making it look as if he had a mouthful of stones.

During the course of the meal, Miriam had glanced twice at John and both times had communicated such warmth and invitation that he himself was greatly encouraged.

When the evening ended he went to his room full of eager anticipation. He dismissed Williams at once, dropping his clothes off, tossing his wig aside, standing at last naked. He went close to the grate, warming first one side of himself and then the other, and then jumped into bed. The sheets had been swept with a fire brick until they were warm and so the bed was quite comfortable. He lay sleepless, astonished that he had taken to his bed without his nightclothes, deliciously excited. On the nightstand he left three gold sovereigns gleaming in the candlelight.

He lay listening to the wind and the rain, warm and safe beneath his quilts, waiting. Hours passed. His body, fixed in the tension of extreme excitement, began to ache with need.

Without knowing it, he fell asleep. He awoke suddenly, dreaming of her. The room was no longer absolutely dark. Fumbling on the night table, he found his watch and opened it. Almost five A.M.

She wasn't going to come. He sat up. Surely any sensible whore would have understood the meaning of the glances that had passed between them. The three sovereigns lay untouched. The fool had not come to claim her own.

By now his father must long since have been done with her. Bracing himself for the cold, he swept his covers aside and rose from the bed. He could not find where Williams kept his nightclothes and so was forced to put on his pants and blouse of the night before. Grabbing up the gold coins, he hurried down the corridor.

A bright fire burned in the grate in the guest room. The bed was occupied. John went to it, placed his hand gently on her cheek.

He felt rather than saw her smile. There was no confusion, no befuddlement of awakening. "I wondered if you would come," she said.

"My God—you should have come to me!"

She laughed. "I could hardly do that. But now that you're here, don't catch cold." She let him into the bed. He tried to control his shaking but could not. This was like bedding the daughter of the greatest lord of the realm. There was nothing whorish about her now. Usually, they were at least a little coarse, their eyes hard with the truth of the world. But here all was innocence and fluttering purity—and the most blatant lust.

She allowed him to undress her. Naked, she drew him to her and deftly removed his own clothing. "Come," she said, rising from the bed.

"Come?"

"To the fireside." Their arms about each other's

waists, they walked to the fire. The room was warm because her maid had obviously laid this new fire within the hour. "Be truthful," she said. "Am I not the first?"

"In what sense?"

"The first you have really loved." She touched him most shamelessly, most wonderfully. He looked down at her hand, amazed that so simple a gesture could bring such pleasure. It was all he could do to keep his feet.

"Yes! I love you!"

Her body, perfect in shape, pert and yet voluptuous, overwhelmed him with its beauty. She lifted her face to his, brought her arms around his neck, parted her lips. He kissed her, kissed into her open mouth—and tasted sour, oddly cold breath.

"Come back to the bed," she said. She led him by the hand, paused, and held him at arm's length. "Let me have a good look at you first," she added. Her hands ran down along his chest, touched his hard-muscled belly lightly, and did not hesitate to examine his private parts. "Are you ever ill?" she asked.

"The whited sepulcher? Certainly not!" He was astonished by her impertinence. What business was it of hers if he had the infection?

"It is a disease communicated from body to body," she said absently. She was talking nonsense. "But it doesn't matter. I was curious about the general state of your health."

"I'm quite well, madam." He brushed past her, got into the bed. She looked down at him, laughed lightly, and twirled about the room, her body full of the grace and beauty of youth. John was entranced but he also was growing impatient.

Suddenly she leaped onto the bed. It was a tall four-poster and her jump was so high that it seemed almost uncanny. He tried to laugh, but something about her movements stopped him. She seemed almost angry as she came into the covers. "You know nothing of love," she said in a loud voice. Then she was beside him, squatting. A pixie smile came into her eyes. "Would you care to learn?"

"I should say so. You're already tardy with my lesson."

Without warning she grabbed his cheeks and kissed him fiercely. Her tongue pressed between his teeth. It felt as rough as a broom besom and he drew back in surprise. How could such a thing be in a human mouth? It was quite horrible. He looked at the door.

"Don't fear me," she said. Then she laughed, bright, ringing through the gray predawn.

John was not a superstitious man, but he wondered about the gypsy camps at this moment. Could this be a gypsy witch, come to claim Hadley for her own? She must have seen the expression in his face, because she all but flung herself onto him. Her hands moved across his body, her flesh touched his, her face presented itself for his kisses.

And he did kiss her. He kissed her as he had never kissed anybody before. He covered her lips, her cheeks, her neck with kisses. Then she took her breasts in her hands and offered them. Before this moment John had not known the pleasure of kissing a woman there. His heart welled up with happiness. Gypsies forgotten, he lost himself in the pleasures of the flesh. She pressed his head downward until he was kissing her most secret intimacy.

The pleasure of it amazed him. She moved with quick dexterity, and before he knew it he was also being kissed in this way.

In a few minutes she had awakened feelings in him he had known nothing of. Waves of exultant happiness swept over him. He could feel her excitement rise to match his own. Never had a woman made him feel so wonderfully competent, so *good*. Then her mood changed. Gently, insistently she moved beneath him until they were face to face. Her legs spread, her eyes

invited. A little sound, half joy, half fear, escaped her
lips when he slipped into her. Then her hands came up
and grasped his buttocks and they began.

John fought manfully, but his excitement was so
intense that it was only moments before he was pounding into her, pounding and shouting her beautiful
name, shouting without a care for the ears of servants,
shouting in great and glorious love.

He sank down on her. "Marry me, whore," he
breathed. Her fingers scraped slowly along his back,
the nails digging into his skin. Her face remained
impassive. Her nails hurt but he would not cry out. He
was too happy, too far transported. "Lady Miriam, you
must be my wife."

"I am not a real lady."

He laughed. "You *must* be!"

In that moment he had married her. Their spirits
would not again be parted.

He remembered those first wild years of love, the
wonder and the horror of it, the sheer blaze of lust. So
much had been gained and so much lost.

They raped the estate. The peasants ran away. The
gypsy fires died. The old lord withered and also died.
John was lost in her, lost and not yet found. Lost in love
of her.

Miriam was worried. John's head lolled, his mouth
hung open. He was obviously dozing. For them such a
thing was abnormal. Either they were awake or they
Slept, the deep and revitalizing trance peculiar to their
kind.

He shifted restlessly. There was only one thing that
could be wrong. She shook her head, refused to accept
it. Not so soon, surely not!

She slammed the car into fourth. Lights flashed by as
they hurtled toward New York.

"You're going too fast," he said over the roar of the
wind.

"We're the only car on the road." The speedometer

hovered near eighty. Miriam threw back her head and laughed, bitter and angry. He could not fail so soon. She loved him so—his youth, his freshness. She slipped her hand into his, felt him return the pressure.

"You were dozing, weren't you?"

She felt his eyes on her. "I had a dream."

"Like Sleep?"

"A sort of daydream. I was only half asleep. I was dreaming of when we met."

She could have shouted with relief. A daydream! Now the glorious feelings that followed feeding reasserted themselves in her. The bumpy old highway, the crumbling city, all revealed secret beauty. In her heart the sense of relief was followed by the familiar love, a sort of gratitude for the existence of humankind.

Her thoughts went to little Alice Cavender, whom she would soon transform. When John's winter actually came—many years from now—Alice would be rising to summer. As he withered she would flower, and Miriam's love would slip from one to the next with none of the agonizing sense of loss she had experienced in the past. To reassure herself she sought a *touch* with Alice. It came promptly—Alice's warmth, her smell, the fierceness of her heart. Then it was over, the bright little storm blowing away. A *touch* with Alice . . . how good. The girl was coming along well.

As they crossed Flushing Meadow Park with the enormous Mt. Hebron Cemetery on the left and the World's Fair Site on the right, Miriam watched John as closely as possible without ignoring the road.

"Remember the Terrace Club," he said.

"How could I forget?" That was in 1939; the Terrace Club had been at the old World's Fair. She could picture the cheerful beauty of its yellow and white walls and svelte stainless-steel furniture.

"We danced there."

"That's not all we did." She well remembered John's outrageous kidnapping of a girl from the powder room while she herself consumed the little creature's date.

Manhattan began to appear and disappear ahead as they rolled through Queens. How recent it all looked to Miriam. It seemed just a week ago the whole area had been swarming with builders. This had been a cobbled road; the air had been scented with the odor of tar and raw lumber. In those days the Long Island Expressway was not yet built and an electric tramway ran to Ozone Park. The bedroom suburbs beyond didn't exist then. They had ridden the tram often, sitting on the rattan seats as it clicked and sparked and shuddered along, a raft of light in a great dark ocean.

Soon the procession of cemeteries began: Mt. Zion, Calvary, Greenacres. A musty, cool odor filled the air.

John turned on the radio, and her mellow mood was interrupted by a long, sorrowful tale being told by an old voice from nowhere, some used-up insomniac pouring his losses out to a talk-show host.

"Please."

"I like it."

"Then your taste is more bizarre than I thought."

"I like to listen to the old. I gloat over their infirmities."

That she could understand. She could well imagine how it must feel to John to have defeated the curse of aging. What an absolutely perfect man he was. She also began to enjoy the presence of the old voice in the air. It became a kind of counterpoint to John's youth and vigor, making him seem more wonderful, a more inspired catch than ever before.

She drove swiftly through the Midtown Tunnel, up Third Avenue and across to Sutton Place. Their house was on the corner of a cul-de-sac, a small but elegant structure that revealed no sign that it was also a fortress. Miriam loved the sense of protection it gave her. She had lavished time and money on the security system. As technology advanced she had seized on every breakthrough and added it to the system. The window boxes full of petunias concealed a microwave perimeter alert. Each window and door was protected by an electrostatic barrier powerful enough to render an intruder unconscious. Even Miriam's bed was protected by a new system which would drop steel shutters around it if anyone approached. In the back garden, among the roses, were sensitive motion detectors that could pick up the step of man or animal, and tell the difference. Cameras with light-intensifying lenses watched the alley and the area near the garage, the computer that controlled them vigilant for human shapes moving within their range.

Once there had been a secret tunnel under the alley and garden, leading to a private dock on the East River, but the building of the East Side Drive had changed all that. Now protection was more important —and easier—than escape.

She stopped the car, turned out the lights, and pressed the dashboard button that closed the garage door behind them. John got out at once, heading for the furnace room to burn the bags containing the remnants of their victims. He was hurrying so that the smoke would be gone before dawn.

Miriam was embarrassed. She had allowed Alice to stay here alone this night, violating her own strict rules. Now John would have to know lest he make too much noise in the furnace room. "Don't wake Alice," she said.

"It doesn't matter, I'm up." Alice stood at the top of the stairs that led up from the basement. Her blue-gray eyes were directed at John and his two big plastic bags.

"Stay upstairs," Miriam said quickly. Alice ignored her, coming down the steps with feline grace.

"I dreamed about you," she said to Miriam. The eyes quested for more information. Alice had sensed something unusual about the dream. Miriam smiled at her. When Miriam *touched* Alice dreamed. On such beginnings great loves were founded.

"Since she's here she might as well help me," John

said acidly. "What does it matter, it's just garbage."
His anger was quite justified—and yet Miriam was so
glad that Alice was here, she found she didn't care.

"Fine," Alice said into the silence that followed
John's remark.

Miriam went upstairs. In spite of herself she felt a
pleasing thrill at the harshness in John's voice. He was
interesting when he was a little mean. Sometimes she
even evoked it deliberately. That, she supposed, was
part of the reason she had invited Alice over on a
forbidden night. That and the love she felt for the girl.

John watched Alice come down the steps. He disliked her seductiveness, her forceful personality, and
most of all the effect she had on Miriam. It was
infuriating to realize to what small degree Miriam
belonged to him. All of these feelings made him want
to consume Alice, to let his body do its will on her, and
not incidentally remove the threat, relieve the corrupt-
ing jealousy. At least it would be easier to bear tonight,
with the hunger in abeyance.

"Why don't you just leave your garbage in the alley
like everybody else?"

A typically bothersome question. Miriam certainly
couldn't claim that she needed the companionship of
this girl. John felt that he was more than enough
himself, and she had said he would be with her forever.
Accident was supposed to be all that could harm either
of them. He almost laughed at the thought that now
entered his mind. This sullen little creature was going
to be his backup, in case he got himself killed.

"Why don't you?" she repeated. Alice never let go of
a question.

"They don't pick it up often enough." He tossed her
the bags. "Hold these while I get the fire going." There
was little time left before dawn. They did not burn
evidence during daylight hours.

"They're so light."

"What can I tell you? We were hungry." He pulled

the lever that controlled the specially installed high-pressure gas line. There was a pop and a roar and the firebox was filled with blue flames.

"What is this stuff anyway, paper?"

He snatched the bags away from her and stuffed them into the furnace. "Count it as another of our mysteries."

"You bring garbage home in the car?"

John glared at her. "We had a picnic. How you managed to miss it I cannot imagine."

She smiled, too sweet. "You didn't invite me. I'm not the kind of person who tags along without an invitation."

"I hadn't noticed."

"I bet Miriam wanted me along. You probably wouldn't let her ask me."

"Sorry to disappoint, but your name never crossed her lips."

"She loves me."

It was said so simply and with such force that John could find no reply. Furiously, ignoring the girl, he tended his fire.

Miriam moved to the night table and began preparing for Sleep. She worked as quickly as she could, taking out the lenses that deepened the color of her eyes, washing off the makeup that concealed her pale white skin, finally stripping away the wig. She ran her fingers through her wispy dusting of hair, then stepped for a few minutes into the shower.

The voices of Sleep echoed more and more loudly.

John was sitting on the side of the bed when she came out. "Why did you let her stay here tonight?"

"Her parents are away."

"She saw me burning the remnants."

"She'll be helping you soon enough. Aren't you ready to Sleep?" She sank down on the bed.

"What you want with her I cannot imagine!"

"She keeps house. Aren't you going to Sleep?"

"I feel wide awake."

She concealed the thrill of fear that this statement evoked in her. He *must* Sleep! She raised her hand, touched him, tried to form a question. But her own Sleep would not be denied another moment. The last thing she was aware of as she sank away was his restless stirring. Then a dream captured her, as vivid as life, more a memory relived. She Slept.

1

ROME: 71 B.C.

SHE HATED THE CITY and hated it most in August. The streets burst with filthy life; rats and flies and the sneering, diseased poor of the Empire. Carts piled with everything from sausages to silks poured through the gates, choked the narrow alleyways, jammed into the forums. Exotic crowds from the edges of the world shoved and brawled and stole in every corner. Over it all a blue haze of smoke from countless sausage-stands and bakeries hung like dead fog. Rome was drowning in humanity: naked slaves, nobility preceded by lictors and followed by streams of clients, soldiers in creaking leather and clanging brass, aristocratic ladies held above the mass on litters, all surging around the gaudily painted temples of government, religion and wealth.

She drove her chariot like a centurion. Two slaves walked ahead of the horse and chariot with whips to force the crowd aside—she didn't give a damn how it made her look, she had no time for the effete ministrations of lictors with their delicate rods. She was in a hurry and Rome was just going to have to move.

As she proceeded along the Nova Via toward the Appian Way the crowds thinned somewhat; nobody was going out the Capenian Gate today.

The lush palaces on the Palatine Hill and the brightly painted Temple of Apollo disappeared behind her. Now her slaves were trotting. Soon she would flail her horse and burst past them. She was growing frantic, the heat made time short.

On this day she would find one of the strongest men on earth and make him her own. She passed under the Appian Aqueduct and through the Capenian Gate. Now that she was outside she thrashed the horse, rattling past the Temple of Honor and Virtue and over a little hill. With shocking suddenness the horror was before her.

Even in this age of cheap life it stunned her.

A dense, roaring mass of flies darkened the sun. Lining the Appian Way for miles, rising and falling over the gentle Campagnian Hills, were twin rows of crosses. The entire army of the slave rebel called Spartacus was being executed. They had been here for three days. The question was, could she find one still living?

Such a man would have to be incredibly strong. Miriam's father had theorized that selecting only the very strongest might be the solution to their problem. In the past they had too often chosen badly, and the transformed had always died.

Miriam needed this man. She longed for him, dreamed about him. And now she arranged her veils to keep out the flies and prodded her horse to find him. The shadows of morning stretched before the crosses. At least Miriam was alone on the road; travelers were detouring along the Ardenian Way as far as Capua in order to avoid this disgusting mess. Miriam's slaves came up behind her, gasping from their run out from the city, batting at the flies that settled around them. Her horse snorted nervously as flies alighted on its face.

"Groom," she said, motioning with her hand. Her slaves had wrapped themselves in cotton soaked with gall. The groom came forward. For an instant his costume reminded her of better times, when she had watched the people of the desert going forth in the sun with similar turbans on their heads. In those days her family had been nomadic, traveling up and down the desert, capturing strays on the fringes of Egypt's fertile plain.

She moved slowly ahead, enduring the sweet stench and the ceaseless energy of the flies, past corpse after corpse. A knot of loathing burned in her stomach. Rome was madness enthroned. And it would get worse. The city's rise to a world-empire was now inevitable. In time it would pass, but not soon. Many hard years lay ahead.

Every few minutes she stopped, lifted her veils, and stared long at one of the victims. With a flick of her wrist she would send a slave to test him by prodding him in the ribs with a stick. A feeble groan would be the only protest and she would continue on. Behind her one of her slaves had begun to play a flute to soften the ordeal. He played the plaintive music of Egypt, sad notes well suited to the situation.

She noticed one man from a long way off and stopped a moment to watch him. There was organization to his movements. Tied to a cross, a man must keep his legs straight or suffocate. To stay alive takes every human resource. Only sheer terror of death keeps a man struggling on a cross.

This man must have been at it steadily for nearly seventy-two hours. Yet he must realize that nobody was going to have mercy on him.

She clapped softly to signal the groom. It was all she could do not to whip the horse to a gallop, but then her slaves would have to run again. She was no Roman, she despised indifferent cruelty. So they walked to the prize. As they drew closer she saw that he was Greek or Middle Eastern, filthy and brutally wounded from whipping. His eyes were closed, his face almost peaceful in the extremity of his effort.

The next moment he straightened his legs and she heard an awful, ponderous intake of breath. Then the legs slacked again. One eye had opened a little, staring down at the approaching observers. But he was beyond caring about them, all his energy was devoted to his struggle.

He did it again without a cry or moan, and settled as quickly as he had risen. Then she noticed that his feet were moving back and forth beneath their seething mass of flies. He was actually trying to loosen his bonds!

And the flies were eating the blood on his ankles.

"Demetrius, Brusus, take him down!"

Two of her slaves ran to the cross and began shaking it, removing it from the ground. The man on the cross grimaced, showing his teeth.

"Be careful, you're hurting him."

They lowered the cross and she dismounted her chariot and ran to him. She ignored a distant noise, the clatter of hooves. There was no time to worry about soldiers now. She had gall and vinegar, and bathed his face with the liquids while the slaves untied him. The damage was appalling, there were even nests of maggots in his ears. His skin was cracked and black, his body bloated. Only the shallow rattling breath told her that he lived—that and the open eye.

He stared at her. She spoke as soothingly to him as she would to a son. The eye unsettled her. It was incredible that he could be so alert after such an ordeal.

"My Lady—" one of her slaves whispered.

She looked up. Standing like sentinels of death were three soldiers with drawn short swords. They were in the middle of the road, almost hidden by the clouds of flies. These soldiers guarded the crosses, their mission to see that nobody took down any of the condemned. Not a few might try. Motives were many—relatives, sympathizers, slavers after the quick profits of contraband.

"Get him to the chariot—be quick!"

He groaned when he was moved. Her slaves laid him with his knees to his chin on the floor of the chariot. There was no time to lose; even as she stepped up and grabbed the reins, the soldiers were coming forward. "Tell them I'm Crassus' wife," she said to her groom. The lie would make them hesitate. Roman soldiers would never impede the activities of the wife of Rome's current dictator. She snapped the reins and the horse broke into a gallop. She would allow it to gallop back to Rome; by now Victrix was desperate to return to her stall. As for the six slaves, they would make their way home more slowly. No doubt they would convince the soldiers of their innocence, they were sophisticated Egyptians and the troopers were only simple boys from Latium.

The man screamed when the chariot jerked and Miriam screamed with him. He was such an incredible find, it would be utterly desolating to kill him while trying to save him.

She had searched half the world for a man such as this, who clutched life with every whisper of strength.

They reached the Temple of Mars and she swung off the Appian Way. There was no sense in returning through the Capenian Gate; it would be certain to arouse the suspicion of the guard. She drove around the temple on a carter's track, moving close beneath the city wall. There were huts and holes in the shadow of the wall, and the track was stinking and awash in sewage. Floating in it were corpses in every stage of decomposition. Dozens of people of every race on earth huddled on both sides of the track, migrants who had come to Rome only to find that strict laws controlled their right to enter the city. If they were not citizens, enrolled freedmen or slaves they could not pass through the gates. A woman came forward brandishing a stick. Miriam showed the short sword that was scabbarded on the chariot. Most of these people were extremely weak and would be unable to subdue her, much less stop the horse.

There was a motionless mass of carts and wagons at the Naevian Gate. Miriam whipped the horse ahead. It was best to take advantage of any confusion.

She used her voice and her whip liberally, thrashing carters and their horses out of the way and making the soldiers guarding the gate roar with laughter. Nevertheless, her efforts got her through quickly, and the condition of her passenger made her desperate for haste. Nobody looked into the bundle on the floor of the chariot.

She passed the Circus Maximus and wheeled toward the Quadrata, an area of wealthy mansions and luxurious insulae. Miriam owned the Insula Ianiculensis and lived on the ground floor. Her upstairs rents paid her taxes and left her enough to maintain her apartments, a villa at Herculaneum and fifty slaves. Hers was a modestly well-to-do establishment, comfortable enough but unlikely to attract any notice.

She found her way through the labyrinth of side streets behind the Circus. Soon the Aemilian Bridge appeared and she crossed it into the stillness of the Quadrata. At this time of year the suburb was quiet, its inhabitants away at Capua or Pompeii for the summer.

At last she arrived at the Insula Ianiculensis. As soon as she came around the corner slaves rushed out, a stable boy taking the reins of the exhausted horse as the assistant master of conveyances stepped up to the chariot. Her Egyptian physicians came forward and took the crucified man into the house. She followed, not stopping even as the maid of the outer garments fumbled with her fibula and removed her fly-spotted cloak. They crossed the Atrium and went through the Peristyle with its flowers and lotus-filled pool and beyond into the suite of baths which had been converted into a hospital in anticipation of this arrival.

At her instructions the tepidarium had been salted and the frigidarium filled with equal parts water and vinegar. A bed had been installed in the solarium with a movable awning above it. Supplies of medicinals and such chemicals as saltpeter and alum had been brought in. Miriam would use all her medical knowledge—far more extensive than that of the idiotic Graeco-Roman "doctors"—in her effort to nurse the man back to health. She had learned medicine in Egypt, combining the ancient knowledge of her own people with that of the priestly cults.

She waved away the bath attendants, who were trying to wash her face and arms, and told the physicians to lay their burden on the bed. The three of them had worked for her long enough to follow her orders without argument; they considered themselves students in her service.

Only now, with the sunlight full on his naked body, did she really feel the presence of this man. Despite his wounds and sores he was magnificent, fully six feet tall with huge shoulders and arms, but surprisingly delicate hands. His face was covered with stubble; he was perhaps twenty years old.

The Romans had been as vicious as ever. Hardly any unmarked skin remained. Suddenly, he made a rasping sound and began to heave weakly on the bed. She lifted him by the shoulders, her fingers breaking through to the blood-wet skin beneath the scabs, and held his head between his legs. Great black masses came from his mouth.

"Gall him," she said. "He stopped breathing!"

With a funnel the physicians forced the sourest gall down his throat. He retched and gasped and vomited more, but when she lay him back down he was breathing again.

She had him soaked in the hot salt water and sat forcing cold fruit juice down his throat while the bath attendants scummed the water. Afterward her physicians rubbed into his wounds an ointment she had prepared from the fungus Aspergillus. Then they soaked him in the frigidarium and gave him hot Falernian wine.

He slept twenty hours.

For much of this time she sat at the head of his bed listening to his breathing. When he awoke he ate six dates and drank off a flagon of beer.

His second sleep lasted fifteen hours. He awoke at three in the morning, screaming.

She stroked his face, made soft sounds in her throat. "Am I dead?" he asked before lapsing once again into unconsciousness. His sleep, deeper than ever, continued until morning. Miriam saw that he had swollen to bursting. He looked like a wineskin. His flesh glowed red through the fissures opened up by the stretching skin.

He stank of death. His body grew hot and dry and she had him moved to the frigidarium. He became delirious, speaking elegant Greek, talking of the Attic Hills. She knew those hills, had watched evening purple them from the Acropolis of Athens. She knew also those breezes of which he spoke, fragrant with hymettus, bearing the music of shepherd's pipes.

A long time ago she had walked there, when Athens was the center of the world. In those days the huddled confusion of empire lay at Athens' gates, when her blue-sailed ships called at all the ports of the East. In such a place as that—or this—Miriam could most easily go about her business.

Against the expectations of her physicians the swelling subsided and the fever declined. Soon he could raise his head for wine or broth of Aspergillus, or the boiled blood of chickens and pigs. She knew his name from the ramblings of his delirium, and one day when she called "Eumenes," he smiled.

She spent hours gazing at him. As his wounds healed he became more and more beautiful. She taught her cosmetician to shave him and, when he was well enough to sit up, went out and bought him a body servant and a boy of his own.

Slowly a new feeling began to fill her. She ordered artisans in to mosaic the floors and paint the walls, just to give the house a fresh appearance, to fit the new mood. She clothed Eumenes in the finest silks, like a Babylonian prince. She dressed his hair with unguents and applied ocher to his eyes. When he was strong enough she converted the whole Peristyle into a gymnasium and hired professional trainers for him.

Her own beauty blossomed as never before. Her male slaves became awkward and silly in her presence, and if she kissed them they blushed.

No household in Rome could have been happier, no woman more gay. Soon Eumenes was strong enough to walk, and they began to venture from the Insula. Pompey filled the Flaminian Circus with water and ordered mock sea-battles for the entertainment of the public. They spent a day in a private box, drinking wine and eating cold meats: peacock and dove and pork seasoned in the Euboean manner. It was now September and ice had begun to appear for sale in Rome— at fifty sesterces a pound. She bought some and they took their wine cold, laughing at the mad luxury of it.

She watched Eumenes fall in love with her. It was, from beginning to end, a triumph. His ordeal proved his extraordinary strength, and his intelligence could not be questioned; he was the third son of an Athenian academician, sold into slavery to ransom his father's library after the Roman conquest.

"I've got to go to Babylon," she said one day to test him.

The announcement stunned him, but he recovered himself. "I'll accompany you," he said.

"I've got to go alone."

For a day her announcement hung heavily in the air

between them. Outwardly all was as before, but the strained moments, the increased silence of his contemplative nature, told her that he could not forget what she had said.

Finally, he entered the trap. In the small hours of a morning he came to her, moving softly through the sleeping house, his passage causing oil lamps to gutter in their pots, coming swiftly to her bedside. "I dream only of you," he said, hoarse with need. She received him with a cry of joy that echoed through all the years. It was a love that she remembered always, even after time proved her father's theory wrong.

That first extraordinary night, his passion, the intensity of his hunger, his pounding, relentless sexuality, that first night had been unforgettable.

She had searched eternity for a better moment.

She remembered the avid love in his eyes, the smell of his skin, sour and hinting of her own perfume, and his humid breath mingling with hers.

All of the tragedy and despair of subsequent years did not quell the remembrance of that moment, or of the joyous times they had shared then.

She remembered mostly the flowers and evenings, and the limpid beauty of the night sky in the imperial city.

Also, she remembered his initiation. She had imbued herself with an authority she did not feel, drawing him on. She invented a goddess, Thera, and called herself a priestess. She spun a web of faith and beguiling ritual. They slit the throat of a child and drank the salty wine of sacrifice. She showed him the priceless mosaic of her mother Lamia, and taught him the legends and truths of her people.

They lay together, mingling their blood. This was the hardest time; she was beginning to love him. In the past the mingling of blood had often killed. Only much later did she learn why this is so. She counted herself fortunate that it did not kill Eumenes.

Quite the contrary, he had thrived.

But in the end he also had been destroyed, as they all had been destroyed.

The Sleep lasted six hours. For most of that time John lay beside Miriam watching the shadows. Now sunlight was beginning to creep across the ceiling. It was as if the dozing in the car had been a herald of some change in him. He had dreamed vividly, as was characteristic of Sleep, but there had been no trance.

Beside him Miriam breathed more loudly, beginning to rise from her own trance. John grew afraid. He could not recall a time when the Sleep had not come to him when it was supposed to.

It was necessary to eat only once a week, but Sleep required six of every twenty-four hours. It was essential and it could not be delayed. Almost as absolute as death, it was the key to the renewal of life.

His arms and legs were tingling, his neck ached, his temples throbbed. He slipped out of bed and went into the bathroom, thinking only that he was thirsty for a glass of water. As he bent over the sink his reflection flashed in the mirror.

He stopped drinking, slowly put the glass down. The room was dark. Perhaps what the mirror had revealed was a trick of shadow. He flipped on the lights and looked again.

The tiny lines extending from the corners of his eyes were no illusion. He touched his cheek and felt a delicate dryness, a subtle stiffening. Weren't there also circles under his eyes, and even more lines around his mouth?

He took a shower. Perhaps the drive home with the roof open had chapped his skin. He let the stream of hot water sluice over his face, forced himself to spend fifteen minutes in the bath. He slid his hands up and down his torso and was reassured to find his body as lean and taut as ever. But he didn't feel lean and taut, he felt sapped.

After toweling himself he went back to the mirror. It

seemed that his youth had returned. He found himself almost laughing with relief. Having cheated time for so long, the idea that it might suddenly reassert itself had come like a freezing blast in midsummer.

Then he saw them again. They were visibly deepening. It was like some kind of hideous hallucination. He drew back from the mirror. The fear in his own eyes revolted him. In an instant his hand had smashed into the surface of the mirror and the glass was flying about his head.

The crash surprised him into stillness. Such anger! He looked at the shards of mirror strewn in the sink, each reflecting a tiny section of his face. There was a final crash as the mirror's metal backing came off the wall.

He tried to calm himself, closed his eyes, forced himself to rational thought. It was, after all, only the slightest of changes. Yes—but he couldn't Sleep. He couldn't *Sleep!* Miriam had always said that everything depended on that absolutely deep, absolutely perfect Sleep. Never mind that you dreamed. It was not like the dreaming of ordinary people; it cleaned the cellars of the mind. It was renewing, youth-giving, miraculous. When you awoke from it your whole life began again. You felt absolutely and completely perfect—and you were!

What was happening to him? Miriam had assured him that it would all last forever. Forever and ever.

He looked at her lying so still, the fluffy pillow framing her face. Only that bare motion of breathing said she was alive. Nothing could wake her. The beauty and peace of it fascinated him. The Sleep was so sweet. But it was also a state of complete vulnerability. John could not remember a time when Miriam had been like this while he himself was awake.

He went to her, kissed her. There was something pleasing about her helplessness, something that excited him. The pressure of his kiss parted her lips a little.

They stayed parted, the edges of her teeth just visible. He looked into her stillness, feeling rapacious. The thought that he could do his will on her—even murder her—made sweat pop out all over his body.

He took her pearl-white flesh in his hands and squeezed it. She was cold and dry. His lips dusted along her neck, tasting the bland flavor of the skin. She was so slick, like a plastic creature; as still as the dead. In a stately charade of anger he slowly shook her by the shoulders, watching her head bend back and her throat present itself to him.

He made a nervous decision. He was feeling powerful sexual needs, an urge almost to steal something from her. Thus, in guilty secrecy began a most awesome and terrible experience. He lay down on her and began to make love to her entranced body.

Physically, Miriam was perfect. She was firm and subtly muscled, always responsive. Yet when he took her in his arms now she was hideously pliant. He ran his fingers along her belly and down her thigh. Her absolute indifference only increased his urgency. Then he grabbed her face and forced his tongue into her mouth. Her own tongue was startlingly rough, like that of a cat.

He wanted to break her with love, to disembowel her with it. As he thrust into her he groaned aloud. His fingers were around her throat. Sweat ran down his body. His thighs pounded and he slid in wetness. He hardly noticed his thumbs pressing her throat, closing tighter and tighter as his body kept on, moving of its own accord through rising stages of pleasure. It crossed him in waves, almost rendering him unconscious. He strangled her harder and harder. His excitement rose. He gauged his motions carefully to prolong it. Her mouth opened, her bristled tongue crept between her teeth.

Then he exploded into her, pounding frantically, and was spent.

He sank down, burying his face in her breasts,

sobbing. Her body convulsed and he heard her draw a choking breath. Her throat was angry red, her face gray.

The voices of children echoed from the distant street, the hall clock softly chimed the hour. With her usual sense of the moment, Alice began running the vacuum cleaner downstairs. John hid his face in his pillow. Life was suddenly, absolutely empty.

He wanted to cling to somebody, to a living woman.

There was a gasp, then her hands came up to her throat. If only she had awakened a little earlier—or a little later.

She made an inarticulate noise. A prolonged silence followed. He opened his eyes. He was startled to see the rage that was in her face. As soon as their eyes met, the look disappeared. He tried to reject his impression of it, the inhumanity.

"I feel like hell, I haven't Slept," he said.

She got up, went to the bathroom, and turned on the light. Without commenting on the mess, she examined her neck in the full-length mirror on the door. She came back and sat on the edge of the bed, crossed her legs, and smiled.

"You bastard," she said.

It was chilling to hear those words through such a tender smile. He laughed nervously.

Then she turned to him and gathered him into her arms. Her fingers dug into his back, she made a sound like the rasp of a crow. He tried to twist his head but she was much more powerful than any human being. His only choice was to lie in her arms and wait. Suddenly, she withdrew and held his shoulders. Her face seemed to ask a question, almost to plead with him.

She dropped her hands to her sides and went back to the bathroom, shutting the door behind her. After a moment he heard the crunching of glass. Ever careful, she was cleaning up the wreckage of the mirror so she wouldn't get cut.

He found himself wanting something from her, a scream of anger, a threat, any sign of relationship. But he heard only the water being turned on. Now she was preparing for her day, keeping her feelings to herself. He got up, went shakily to the dresser and started putting on his own clothes. Still in his shorts, he was splashing cologne on his cheeks when he realized that his face was covered with heavy stubble. He didn't even know if there was a razor in the house. In a kind of wonderment his hands traveled over his cheeks, touching the hard little ends of hairs. From the bathroom he heard Miriam humming as she toweled herself dry, her familiar melody.

He dressed quickly and left, eager to get away from the pressure of the situation. There was a barber at Fifty-seventh Street and Second Avenue. He would walk up there and get himself shaved.

The shave was actually quite pleasant, the barber cheerful. In the pleasure of the moment he also got his hair trimmed and his shoes buffed.

He was feeling somewhat better when he left. The sun was shining, the streets were crowded with hurrying people, the air was almost sweet. For the first time in many years John enjoyed watching a woman other than Miriam. It was a relief after the fierce tensions of this morning. She was just one of the crowd, a girl in a cheap skirt and sweater hurrying to the bus stop with a paper cup of coffee from Nedick's in her hand. Her hair was dusty brown, her face too heavily made up. But there was such sensuality in her movements, in the way her breasts lay beneath her sweater and in the determination of her stride. Suddenly, he looked again at the face. He was horrified.

It might have been Kaye.

His heart thundered, he gasped for breath. Her eyes met his. They were deep with the mysterious sorrow of mortals, an expression he had been able to see in others only after it had disappeared from his own face.

"Was that a Number Two?"

She was speaking to him.

"Mister, was that a Number Two bus?"

She was smiling, her teeth yellow with neglect. Ignoring her, John hurried back to the security of the house.

As he approached he heard voices through the open window of the living room. At once he felt the hollow despair of jealousy—Alice and Miriam were chatting, no doubt waiting for him to appear so that they could begin practicing the Handel Trio.

He mounted the stairs, moved softly across the hallway, past the hall table with its spray of roses, and entered the living room. Miriam looked magnificently fresh and beautiful in a bright-blue dress. A blue ribbon was tied prettily about her neck. Alice lay on a settee nearby in her usual jeans and sweat shirt. He felt Miriam watching him as he went across to his place. Until he was settled, Miriam's body remained tense, as if ready to spring.

"John," Alice said, leaning her head back, "I didn't even hear you come in. You always sneak." Her thirteen-year-old smile made him catch his breath. She was indeed a marvelous toy, fragile and succulent.

Miriam crashed out an arpeggio on the harpsichord. "Let's get going," she said.

"I don't want to do that trio again. It's boring." Alice was in a typical sulky mood.

"How about the Scarlatti we were doing last week?"

Miriam went through some fingerings. "We could do it if John can keep up."

"All the music he knows is boring."

Miriam's fingers flew across the keys. "I know Corelli, Abaco, Bach—" She tossed a thick book of music at Alice. "Pick whatever you want."

There was a silence. "I barely know the Handel," John said. "It's hard for the cello."

Miriam and Alice glanced at each other. "We'll do the Handel," Alice said. "It's either that or finger and bow practice, right, John?" She picked up her violin and tucked it under her chin.

"I'm one of the few musicians who can do chopsticks on the cello, dear."

"As you always say."

Before he had even tuned they were starting. He entered raggedly, rushing after them, overtaking and then struggling to keep his place for the rest of the piece.

They played for an hour, repeating the trio three times. John eventually began to enjoy the way it became coherent, finally beautiful. He liked the music. It seemed to fit the moment, the rich quality of the sunlight, the beauty of the women.

"Well," Alice said when they were done, "that's that." She was flushed, which accentuated her incipient womanhood. A pang passed again through John's heart.

He knew all the things Miriam was able to do to people. It was impossible to tell exactly what treatment was intended for Alice. Miriam could bless or destroy. Sometimes she would compel them to violence as a cover for her own activities. Other times, there could be unimaginable bliss.

Miriam was practical; she did what was most useful. Alice, for example, would inherit a considerable fortune, as John had. That could well be the motive for Miriam's interest. She was always short of money, and those who loved her gave her everything.

"Let's have a drink," Miriam said. She picked up the Madeira from the bar. It was an 1838 Warre, bought from the old Berry Brothers Stores in London. As it had aged it had become first strong and sweet, then full of subtle overtones. Now it was almost light, but possessed of complex and ancient flavors. It was certainly the finest Madeira in the world, perhaps of all time.

"I'm not supposed to have liquor."

Miriam poured Alice some of the wine.

"It's very light. Only barbarians would refuse their children the right to a glass of wine."

Alice swallowed it at a gulp and held out her glass for more.

"That's a sacrilege," John said. "You're drinking it like tequila."

"I like the way it makes me feel, not the way it tastes."

Miriam poured her another glass. "Don't get drunk. John molests the helpless." The remark came unexpectedly and shocked John.

Alice laughed, her eyes regarding him with taunting appraisal. Rather than endure that, John retreated. He gazed out the window, forcing himself to concentrate on the view. Across the street was a block of cooperative apartments. It seemed such a short time ago that houses such as their own had lined both sides of the street, it was hard to believe that vines could already be growing up the front of one of those new buildings. The cries of children came as always from the street. John was touched by the eternal shrill excitement of those voices, a sound that belonged to all time. Maturing was the horrible process of losing immortality. John felt his face. Already the whiskers were coming back. He had inexplicably entered the deadly shadow; it could no longer be denied.

Alice came to his side, her shoulder just touching his elbow. No doubt she told herself that she ought to conquer him, to include him. But he suspected it was really a simpler and more morbid interest: she wanted to see him suffer. In that sense she was as natural a predator as Miriam herself—or as John.

"What are they playing, Alice? Ringolevio?"

"Ringo—what?"

"Ringolevio. The game."
"They're playing Alien."

Miriam watched her destroyed man. He could have killed her this morning. Killed. The thought of it made her feel cold toward him, but only for a moment. She had fought hard to make him perfect. It was so sad to see him disintegrating even more quickly than his predecessors. Eumenes had been with her more than 400 years, Lollia nearly as long. Until now not one of her transformations had failed to last 200 years. Was she getting worse at it, or was the strength of the human stock in decline?

She took another swallow of the Madeira, held it in her mouth. Time itself must taste so. In wine time could be captured and in life delayed, but not forever. In John's case not even for very long.

There was much to do and possibly only a few days of grace. She had been moving slowly, capturing Alice by careful degrees. Now it was an emergency. She had to prepare for the storm that was going to break when John discovered his predicament, and at the same time prevent Alice from knowing what was happening to him. As Alice was to be his replacement it would be most inconvenient if she learned the consequences of transformation.

Especially in view of the fact that, this time, there might be no consequences. Miriam would have to approach Sarah Roberts much more quickly now. The research she had done already into the woman's work and habits would have to suffice.

If anybody on this planet could discover what went wrong with the transformed it would be Dr. Roberts. In her book *Sleep and Age* Miriam had seen the beginnings of a deeper understanding than Roberts herself could possibly realize. The work that Roberts had done on primates was fascinating. She had achieved extraordinary increases in lifespan. Given the proper information, would she also be able to confer real immortality on the transformed?

Miriam put down her glass and left the room. She would have to risk being separated from Alice and John for a few minutes. His violence was still sporadic. And there was a task to be faced in the attic, a dreary task of preparation, amid the sad ruins of her past loves. Unlike the dusty and disused appearance of the rest of the attic, the door to this room was perfectly maintained. It opened soundlessly as Miriam unlocked it. She stepped into the tiny, hot space. Only when the heavy door was closed and she was safely hidden did she give voice to the turmoil of fears within her. Her fists went to her temples, her eyes screwed shut and she moaned aloud.

Silence followed, but not absolute silence. As if in answer, there came from the darkness around her the seething of slow and powerful movement.

Miriam hesitated a moment before beginning her task. "I love you," she said softly, remembering each person who rested here, each lost friend. Perhaps because in the end she had failed all of them she remained loyal to them. Some, like Eumenes and Lollia, she had carried across half the world. Their boxes were black with age, bound with leather and studded with iron. The more recent ones were as strong or stronger. Miriam pulled the newest box to the center of the little room. This one was about twenty years old, made of carbon fiber steel and locked by bolts, bought and stored on John's behalf. She lifted off the lid and examined the interior, then took the bag of bolts from inside. There were twelve of them, and she fitted them around the lid. Now it could be closed and locked in a matter of seconds.

She left it open, however, the lid gaping. When she brought him to this place, there might be very little time. With a last glance at the other boxes, pausing in the room's rustling silence, she whispered goodbye.

The door hissed shut on her tragedy. She secured the locks, which were there for two reasons: to keep danger out, and to keep it in. She went back downstairs, assured that she was well prepared for the worst, uneasy at leaving Alice unprotected any longer than necessary.

2

THE HOLLOW SHRIEKS of a terrified rhesus brought Sarah
Roberts to her feet. She ran down the hall to the cage
room, her shoes clattering on the linoleum.

What she saw when she peered into the cage of their
most important animals made her feel cold. Methuselah was brachiating madly through the cage screaming
as only a rhesus can scream. On the floor lay Betty's
head, its monkey face frozen in last agony. As he shot
around the cage Methuselah brandished Betty's arm,
the little hand open as if waving goodbye. The rest of
Betty lay scattered across the cage. As she rushed from
the room to get help Sarah almost slipped in the blood
that had run down to the floor.

Before she reached the door, it swung open. Methuselah's shrieks had brought the whole Gerontology
group.

"What the hell did you *do*, Methuselah?" Phyllis
Rockler shouted. She was the lab's animal keeper.

The monkey's face was as crazy as any Sarah had

ever seen, and a psychiatric internship at Bellevue had given her a look at a good number of crazy faces.

Charlie Humphries, their resident blood expert, pressed his face to the cage. "God, how ugly!" He stepped back, his sneakers squishing. "Monkeys are bastards."

"Get Tom down here," Sarah said. She needed him for her own sanity, forget the ape. Moments later he came rushing in, his face gray. "Nobody's hurt," she said, seeing the fear in his eyes. "No human body, that is."

"Is that Betty?"

"Methuselah tore her apart. He stopped sleeping two days ago and he's been getting increasingly irritable. But we had no reason to expect this." There was a flurry of activity behind them as Phyllis set up the videotape equipment. She would record Methuselah's further behavior for later analysis.

Sarah watched Tom react to the catastrophe. She could practically see him calculating how this affected his own career track. Number One was never far from mind with Tom Haver. Then he turned his eyes on her, full of wonderful, totally genuine concern. "Is this going to hurt you? What's the latest on the blood runs?"

"Still indexing to the same curve as before. No change."

"So there's no resolution. And Betty's dead. Oh, Christ, you're in trouble."

She almost wanted to laugh at the obviousness of his emphasis on the *you*. He didn't want to seem like what he was, to come right out and say it: my damn career rides on this too. She held out her hands, suddenly realizing that Tom was even more upset than she was. He took them, stepped toward her, seemed about to speak. She spoke first. "I guess I take my dead star performer to the Budget Committee tomorrow."

He looked sick. "Hutch was going to recommend against extension anyway. Now with Betty dead—"

"It means that we have to start all over again. She's still the only one that had actually stopped aging."

She stared at Methuselah, who stared back as if he were wishing he could repeat his little trick. He was a handsome ape, with his spread of gray hair and his powerful body.

Betty, who looked like an adolescent, had been his mate.

"Pardon me while I break down and cry," Sarah said in her most sardonic tone. But she meant it. She went gratefully into Tom's arms.

"Now, now, we're still on public property." That was old reticent Tom, embarrassed by any show of emotion.

"We're all family here. We're going on the unemployment line together."

"That'll never happen. Some other facility will pick you up."

"In a couple of years. Meanwhile, we lose all our apes, disrupt the experiments, and *waste time!*" It made Sarah crazy just thinking about it. Ever since she had accidentally discovered the blood factor that controlled aging while doing blood counts on sleep-disturbed rats, she had been a woman with a mission. In this laboratory they were seeking the cure for man's most universal disease—old age. And Betty had been proof that the cure existed. Somewhere in the rhesus' blood some hidden key had been turned by their application of drugs, temperature and diet. Whatever it was had deepened her sleep almost to the point of death. And as sleep had deepened, aging had slowed. The same set of conditions had worked for a while with Methuselah. Last week his sleep had abruptly stopped. He had dozed a little, then—a monster.

Betty might well have been immortal, if Methuselah hadn't killed her. Sarah would have shot him if she had a gun. She went to the gray-painted wall and hit it a couple of times. "We're dealing with a degenerating gene pool," she said softly.

"Not the apes," Phyllis answered.

"The human race! For God's sake, we're about to find the mechanism that controls aging and we're going to lose our budget! I'll tell you all something! I think Hutch and that whole crowd of senile appendix poppers on the board are jealous. Jealous as hell! They're already terminal geriatrics and they want to make sure the same thing happens to the rest of the world!"

The anger in Sarah's voice caused Tom to feel a familiar sense of frustration. She was and remained blind to the problems he experienced as an administrator. In part that was a proper professional attitude, but not the way she allowed it to sweep aside even the slim chance of survival that the politics of the situation might allow.

Yet he found himself seeking alternatives on her behalf. Her lust for success was contagious. There was something almost visceral in her belief, in her will. No doubt her faith in the value of her work mirrored that of others who had approached discoveries with great impact on humankind. But there was some deep thing in Sarah, a kind of cruel yearning, heedless of herself and others, that swept beyond the norms of duty or even scientific curiosity and colored her hope with the tint of obsession.

Tom looked at her, the brown hair, the frequently pretty face, her curiously flat pallor, and the rich, unquenchable sensuality of her compact body. He wanted to hold her again. After she had broken his last embrace she had hidden her feelings in gruffness.

He wished that she did not feel victimized by her femininity. To his way of thinking, her tough, brilliant mind should be satisfactory compensation for all that was wrong with what she referred to as her sexual conditioning. But it was not enough, not for her.

Tom was embarrassed for her. More, he felt sad. With the rhesus dead she was seriously set back. She couldn't possibly make a case for continued project funding before the budget committee. She was a small, fuming woman, her eyes flashing prettily as she faced the cancellation of an experiment to which she had given five years of her life.

Something ungenerous—a kind of glee—seemed to be hiding beneath Tom's genuine sorrow. He knew it was there; it had been a long time since he had taken his own surface feelings at face value. The destruction of her project would hurl Sarah back into the depths of her relationship with him, would make her seek the comfort of being a junior partner again—and a part of him welcomed the power her need would confer.

"I've got a meeting with Hutch now," he said. "We're reviewing the allocation requests." His mouth was dry. The stench of the apes was sickening. "Sarah," he said. He paused, surprised. Why had he used such a bedroom tone of voice? She whirled at him. Defeat had made her pugnacious. He wanted to comfort her, knew the condescension of it would outrage her. The touching a few minutes ago had been an unwilling concession.

"Well?"

For an instant the bluster in her eyes gave way. Then, with a tilt of her chin she was off, ordering a tranquilizer for Methuselah so they could get the cage open and pull out Betty's remains.

Tom left unnoticed, going slowly through the equipment-cluttered lab. Every item, every inch of space, had been pried out of Riverside Medical Research Center by the force of Sarah's determination. Her discovery had come as an accident, incidental to some conventional work on sleep deprivation. The fact that the inner rhythm of the sleeping process also contained the key to aging was a totally unexpected result. Her initial findings had been published in her book, *Sleep and Age*. It had caused certain stirrings; the rigor of her methods could not be questioned, nor could her skill in her experiments. The implications were so large, though, that they hadn't really been appreciated. Sarah's view that old age was nothing more than a disease, potentially curable, was just too enormous a change. Her book had brought her much congratulation, little support.

Tom exited into the wide tile hallway of the lab floor and took the staff elevator to the Sleep Therapy Clinic above. He occupied a small office beside Dr. Hutchinson's suite. The old man had founded the clinic ten years ago. After eight years the board had hired Tom Haver to step in "when the director elects to retire." It had been nothing more than sales talk; Hutch had not so elected. They had wanted a scientist-administrator with powerful credentials to draw more funding to the clinic.

Lately, Tom had begun to catch himself looking hopefully for some sign of senility in the old man.

Hutch sat in Tom's office, his angular form folded into one of the old chairs. It was an affectation of his to scorn his own sumptuous quarters. "Dimethylamino-ethanol," he said in a reedy, amused voice.

"She's far beyond DME research, you know that. Aging Factor is a transient cellular protein. DME is nothing more than the regulating agent."

"The philosopher's stone."

Tom went to his desk, forcing a thin smile. "More than that," he said quietly. He refused to acknowledge the sarcasm. Hutch tossed a typed budget survey sheet on his desk. It was hard not to resent the man's style. He picked up the summary. "What am I supposed to say, Doctor—'no gerontology appropriation' and fall to my knees?"

"You can if you want to but it won't work."

Tom disliked smugness; it was poison in a scientist. "If you cancel the project, she'll leave."

"Well, of course I'd hate to see that. But there just aren't any results. Five years and no progress."

Tom tried to contain himself. If only Methuselah had waited another twenty-four hours! "They've developed a damn good schematic of cellular aging. I'd call that progress."

"Yes, for a pure research facility. The Rockefeller

Institute would love them. But they don't belong in a place like Riverside. Tom, we've got to justify every penny to the City Health and Hospitals Corporation. How the hell does a hospital explain the purchase of thirty-five rhesus monkeys, even a research hospital? Seventy thousand dollars' worth of brachiating boobies. You tell me."

"Hutch, you weren't born yesterday. If we lose Gerontology, there goes ten percent of the clinic's overall budget. For that reason alone she should *not* be cut."

At once Tom regretted what he had just said. If Hutch was told to cut a budget he did it the hard way, by firing people and selling off equipment. He knew little of the reality of administration. To him the concept of maintaining functions while cutting dollars was a contradictory impossibility.

"You're going to tell me we ought to cut by charging for paper cups and installing pay toilets, I suppose." He tapped his worn class ring on the edge of Tom's desk. "I can't see it that way. They give me a dollar figure upstairs. I'm going to meet that figure and have done with it." Like an aging crane he rose out of the chair. "The committee convenes at ten A.M. in the board-room." He sighed, suddenly wistful, betraying his own losses.

Then he was gone, striding down the hall, a sad, fierce old warrior in the declining castle of his hopes. Tom ran his fingers through his hair. He knew how Sarah felt; he wouldn't have minded hitting a wall himself. The Health and Hospitals Corporation was so intractable, a bureaucracy of desperation. It worried about keeping emergency rooms in business, not obscure research projects. How ironic that man's fate, the very secret of death, would be almost found—and perhaps forever lost—in the rubble of a bureaucracy's dissolution.

Tom looked at his watch. Nine-thirty. It had been a

hell of a long day. Outside the sky was gray-black. There were no stars. It would rain soon, the promise of spring. Tom got his jacket and turned off the lights. Maybe he would beat Sarah home and fix her a nice dinner. It was the least he could do in view of the fact that he had lost her a career. It would be years while the bureaucrats at other institutions picked over the bones of her work and waffled about taking her on.

Meanwhile, Tom would have to watch her vegetate in the Sleep Clinic, back to her old job processing incoming patients for physical disorders before they entered the therapeutic track—if she could even be convinced to return to such work.

The sky was lowering as Tom walked down Second Avenue toward their apartment building. Gusts of wind lifted paper and dust around him and brought big, cold raindrops. Lightning flickered in the clouds. It was fourteen blocks from Riverside to the apartment building. Usually the walk was relaxing, but not tonight. He wished he had taken a cab but there were only a few blocks to go, no sense in getting one now. The rain came faster, and the brightly lit lobby of the building was a welcome sight when it appeared in the distance.

As he went through the door into the lobby Alex the doorman nodded greeting. Tom planned his dinner as the elevator took him to the twenty-fifth floor.

The apartment was freezing cold. This morning had been mild and they had left the windows open. Now the weather had changed and the wind was rising. It whipped through the living room dense with smells brought from far away, of darker country. Beyond the windows the lights of the city glittered, now obscured by a scudding tendril of cloud, now twinkling brightly.

Tom closed the windows and set the thermostat to 85° to warm the place up. Then he made the dinner. It turned out to be a lonely and unexpectedly tiresome job. He was a more than serviceable cook—his father had seen to that—but there was something about the lateness of the hour and the bitter disappointment; he just wanted to go to bed and forget the whole damn day.

By ten-thirty it was ready. It looked cheerful enough despite the way he felt. He finished tossing the salad and turned on the fire under the pasta. The only thing left to do when she came home would be the veal. That was a matter of the last moment. He went into the living room and had a drink.

At eleven he called the lab. It rang six times before there was an answer. "What're you doing?"

"Watching Methuselah not sleep. Even the tranks didn't put him down. We're trying to plug him in but he tears out the electrodes. So far we haven't got half an EEG." Her voice was leached of expression.

"Who's helping you?"

"Phyllis. Charlie's downstairs doing slides on Betty."

"Come home. I have something for you."

"Not tonight, darling." She was sad, of course. That was why her voice sounded so empty. There, he felt it again—that ugly little stab of glee. Soon enough her nights would belong only to him.

"I mean dinner. And it's raining, so take a cab."

"I can tell if it's raining, Tom."

"You might not notice. Look, you can always go back after we eat."

Coaxing Sarah out of her lab was never easy. He could only wait and hope tiredness and hunger would overcome her determination long enough to get her out the door. Salad, pasta, veal. Fruit and cheese afterward. Plenty of wine. By dinner's end she'd probably be so close to sleeping that she wouldn't try to go back. There has to be room for more in life than a laboratory, he thought.

Sooner than he expected, the familiar footsteps clicked down the hall, Sarah's usual quickstep. Then the door banged and she was home, hair wet from her walk in the rain, mascara running down her cheeks, and still wearing her lab coat. She looked lost and boyish. Her small mouth was set in a stern line, her eyes were startlingly alive. Tom went to her.

"Careful, I'm covered with monkey shit." She threw off the lab coat and only then let him hold her. It was so comfortable to feel her in his arms, even if it was only for an instant. "I've got to have a shower."

"Dinner'll be on the table when you come out."

"Thank God for administrative personnel who still have energy at the end of the day." She kissed him on the nose and broke away. "That damn rhesus is in bad shape," she said as she headed for the bathroom. "His hair's falling out and his bowels are loose. He's agitated and all of a sudden he *cannot* be made to sleep. Won't even doze. Poor thing." He heard the clothes hamper squeak. Then more words, drowned by the sound of running water. It was obvious that it didn't much matter to her whether he heard or not. The angry words themselves were all the comfort she demanded.

Tom felt isolated. People in love were supposed to be at the center of each other's lives. Sometimes it was hard to tell if she wanted to be in love, or simply to be loved.

As he cooked his veal scallopini he heard the roaring of the wind and thought how he loved her. It made him believe in her love also. And it made the fact that he was going to fail her, see her dropped from the budget, make him feel as caged as one of the experimental animals.

"Honey, thank you." She had come up behind him. She was wrapped in the blue silk robe he had given her for her birthday. Her skin was flushed from the shower, her eyes now shimmering gently in the candlelight. She looked altogether fetching. Sarah's miracle was the purity of her womanhood. She was not conventionally beautiful—eyes too big, chin too prominent—and yet men's eyes always followed her. One moment she would be aggressively neutral, and the next more a woman than any other he had known.

They ate quietly, relying on their eyes for communication, Tom and his magic lady. By the time the meal was over, Tom was ready to carry her into the bedroom, avid to possess her. He was delighted that nothing more had been said about Riverside. Let Sarah bank her fires for a few hours, let the problems wait.

When she stood up from the table he saw his chance. Tom was easily big enough to sweep Sarah off the floor. He knew it was an assault on her dignity, in a way a dismissal. But it was a loving dismissal. She made a little sound in her throat, drew her arms around his neck, fluttered her eyes at him. It was parody, but of the kindest sort, an affirmation of her love and respect for him. He would not have been surprised to be damned for what he had done. The fact that she had not done so was deeply pleasing, almost as if his physical strength and his need granted him rights with her that usually he did not have.

He put her down on the bed. She didn't speak. It was their customary way, honored from the beginning of their love.

He stripped in the dark, with only the glowing clouds outside to reveal him. Then he went to her, slipped the soft robe from her body, and climbed into bed beside her.

In their years together they had established few conventions; both were avid experimenters. But tonight imagination would rest. Tom sensed she also wanted the solace of simplicity, and they took one another's offering with the gentle acceptance of familiar lovers. She pressed herself close as he entered, and they sighed with the enjoyment of it. This was a lesser act of love, but it fulfilled its purpose and left them drifting to sleep in one another's arms. Tom's last conscious thought was of the wind, how it howled past the windows. A spring storm.

Francie Parker awoke suddenly. She was shocked motionless; she felt something crawling between her legs. Too late did she realize that she should have moved. The ropes tightened, she was tied to the bed.

An awful shudder coursed through her body. This was it, rape in the night. You heard about it on the news, talked about it in the office. She fought the wild terror, tried to keep her cool. The intruder turned on her bedside lamp and shined it in her face. He wasn't going to allow himself to be seen.

The blade of a surgical scalpel appeared in the light, hung there a moment, and was withdrawn. Francie felt tears pop into her eyes. A strange, low noise filled the room.

"Shut up!"

She hadn't realized she could make such a sound. Desolation filled her. Nevertheless, her mind kept working, trying to come up with some appeal that would save her.

It smelled as if there were something dead in here. She was aware of movement behind the light, then she could feel him at work on her nightgown. By looking down her front she could see his hands as he used the scalpel to cut away the cloth. That awful instrument could only be for one purpose; she just knew he was going to kill her. When she felt his hands pushing away the nightgown, exposing her nakedness, she moaned in misery—but also felt a horrible, unwanted tingle. This nightmare had another aspect. She began to anticipate seeing him, she visualized his sweating body plunging into the little pool of light. It made her angry. She had never imagined she could feel this debased, this betrayed.

As he bent toward her she caught a glimpse of him. At that moment Francie Parker, twenty-two years old, the frequent object of male desire, capable of eighty words a minute on an IBM Selectric, saw something that instantly and utterly shattered her.

The shock stopped her heart. All that escaped of the wild cry her mind had formed was a gurgling sigh.

When she died like that, before she should have, he growled his rage and stabbed wildly, hoping to get her before the last second.

He failed. Then he took her as best he could, keeping at it until she crackled like paper.

At four o'clock on a wet morning, Sutton Place was empty. Elegant windows were dark. Nothing moved except when an occasional gust of wind from the night's storm stirred some bit of paper or a broken leaf. Behind one window in one of the charming little houses that line the east side of the street a figure stood, absolutely motionless. Miriam was rigid with concentration, feeling the eerie echo of a distant *touch*. It was a facility she shared only with her own race, and some of the higher primates. Man, while capable of learning *touch* from an adept, was normally mute. But this *touch* was real, pulsating on the darkness.

One of her own kind?

Since the bloodbath of the Middle Ages the remaining members of her race lived solitary lives, each wrapped in his own longings and tragedies, an autumnal species too frightened of persecution to dare to foregather.

'We are not evil,' she thought as the strange *touch* rose higher and higher, 'we also are part of the justice of the earth.'

Fifty years ago she had seen one of her own kind, a tall figure alone at the railing of the liner *Berengaria*, looking toward her on the dock. For an instant they had *touched*, sharing their private hungers, and then it was lost, the ship's whistle sounding, the wake disappearing in the moonlight, journey without end.

Her tragic human companions were her only comfort. They could not conceive of the loneliness that drove her to transform them, to create her own image within them.

She loved them—and had destroyed each of them.

It could not continue, not any longer. She could not

stand to live with Alice, knowing all the while that she was going to end up like the others, like John.

The *touch* interrupted her thoughts again, running like thunder in the mountains, as huge and wild as night.

So it was an animal. And it was in agony. Absolute agony. The kind that would be felt by one deprived of Sleep. But there were no transformed animals.

Or were there?

Sarah Roberts, blindly experimenting, might have accomplished some rough approximation of transformation. So one of her beasts was meeting its end in a filthy cage. She felt the lost forests in its *touch,* the wide leafy spaces and the strength of the iron bars.

Her eyes widened, her hands snapped to the bars that protected her own window, closed around the cold iron. The window, its frame and the whole wall shook.

Soon after dawn Tom Haver opened his eyes. He had been trying not to wake up, but it was no use. The room was suffused with dull light. He looked at the clock. Seven-ten. Past time to get up. He swung out of bed and lurched in for his shower. The night had been spent sleeplessly in a fog of strategies, trying to find some way of extending Sarah's appropriation. Every road led back to the Budget Committee and Hutch.

He paused in the door to the bathroom and looked back at her. There came to him a feeling so strange and tender that it seemed as if it had entered from another personality, not his own. He found that he wanted very badly for her to succeed.

He went about his shower in a sort of fury, lathering himself, rinsing, drying, all the while wretched for her and angry that he must suffer on her behalf.

When he opened the door the smell of breakfast drifted faintly in. None of the usual singing, however, arrived with it. She was not such a cheerful riser today. He wished that he didn't feel so sorry for her; it reduced her, enlisted a kind of professional distance. A doctor's habit to withdraw one's emotions from the reality of pain.

"Happy meltdown," she said when he arrived in the kitchen.

"Meltdown?"

"What's happening to my lab is the equivalent of a reactor meltdown. Reaches critical mass and sinks to the center of the earth. Buried. Gone."

There were a hundred encouraging lies he could not tell. "I'll call you as soon as the meeting's over," was all that came out.

Once again he was cheating her. Why not simply let her know how he felt? Why was that such a frightening thought? Emotions confirm things, that was the trouble. Death, for example, always seems like a lie, a game of disappearance, until one's grief makes it true.

The phone rang. Tom blinked at the intrusion, snatched up the handset. A strange, whispering voice asked for Sarah. Her face puckered with details of concern; she was obviously hoping that some miracle had happened at the lab. "Luck," Tom said as he handed her the receiver.

She grabbed it, her expression now avid. After a long pause she murmured an assent and hung up. Swallowing the last of her coffee, she ran into the bedroom. "More trouble with Methuselah," she said as she pulled a raincoat from the closet. Her eyes were cold, bright.

"He's not dead?"

She glanced away. "No," she said with unnatural loudness, "something else."

"Who was that on the phone?"

"Phyllis."

"She sounded like a zombie."

"Thirty hours on the job. I don't have a very clear idea what's going on over there, but—"

"Maybe there's some hope. A last-minute breakthrough. Am I right?"

She laughed, a sniff, a toss of the head, and then

strode past him without a further word. The front door slammed. He located his own raincoat, crumpled amid jeans and coat hangers on the closet floor. By the time he reached the elevator bank she had gone.

Alice was listening less than carefully as Miriam read to her from *Sleep and Age*. That didn't matter, the girl's mind was wonderfully absorptive. Miriam glanced at her, full of the pleasure of being near her. Miriam loved her sullen intelligence, her youth and haunting beauty. " 'The key to the relationship between sleep and age appears to lie in the production of the transient protein group associated with inhibition of lipofuscins. At the molecular level the buildup of lipofuscin is responsible for the loss of internal circulation that leads to cellular morbidity. Thus, it is the prime factor in the overall process called "aging," being responsible for effects as subtle as the reduction in the responsiveness of organs to hormonal demands and as gross as senile dementia.'

"Why do you think I read you this material, Alice?"

"You want to test my boredom threshold?"

"What if I told you it might mean you would never get old. Never get gray hair. Stay young forever."

"Not thirteen!"

"No. It wouldn't interrupt the process of maturing, only getting old. Would you like that—staying twenty-five or so forever?"

"For my life? Sure."

"And your life would be forever. You should thank Doctor Sarah Roberts. She's discovered a great secret." It was extremely tempting to go on, to tell Alice the truth: that she could choose immortality right now, that Miriam could confer it.

If Dr. Roberts' data were correct, she might even be able to make it a lasting gift.

Alice sighed. "I'm not so sure I'd want to live forever. I mean, it's not all that great, is it?"

Miriam was surprised and a little sickened. Never for

a moment had she considered that Alice would hold such an opinion. The will to live was universal. Her own race, as ancient as it was, had fought valiantly through the persecutions of the Middle Ages, had fought despite their low birthrate and probable extinction. The very last of them willed only one thing: to continue. "You don't really mean that, do you, Alice?" There was anger in her voice, anger she had not intended.

The girl reacted. "You sound funny, Miriam. I wish you'd act normal."

Miriam did not reply directly. Instead she returned to the book. "'The mystery of how and why lipofuscin inhibition declines as a cellular system ages is the core of the problem. We have determined that the duration and depth of sleep are related to the amount of lipofuscin produced, with deeper sleep producing the greater level of inhibition.'"

"OK, I guess I'm supposed to ask a question. Why are you so strange?"

Miriam laughed at the audacity of it, felt herself flush. "You have a lot to learn. A lot. Just don't doubt me. You'll find everything I do is for a purpose." Alice smiled, her face suddenly filled with an innocence so beautiful that Miriam involuntarily *touched* her.

There was a moment's silence. Then Alice clasped her hands around her knees and giggled. "You and John really are strange. You make me feel weird."

John's name, intruding so suddenly, broke Miriam's mood. She got up and put the book away, then went to the bay window that overlooked the garden. These cool, wet springs favored the strains of roses she had developed in Northern Europe, but not the Roman and Byzantine ones. They would require careful attention if there wasn't some warmer weather soon.

She longed to be among them now, pruning them and forgetting her tragedies. If only John had lasted a few more years the discoveries suggested in *Sleep and Age* would have saved him. Miriam had hoped once to find an antidote for John and apply it before it was too late. She was convinced that some substance such as lipofuscin must be responsible. In her own body the immunity was permanent, but in a human being the Sleep only delayed it for a time. Then all the familiar symptoms appeared: Sleep ended, and with its termination came rapid aging, desperate hunger, destruction.

Her throat was tight, she could not help but sink into the grief of the situation. She forced her mind back to her roses; once she had created an arbor all the way to the river. They had had their own dock then and kept a pretty red-and-black steam launch with a furious little brass engine. What fun it had been pounding alone in that hilarious boat with its clattering steam valves and gushing torrent of black smoke. . . .

They had gone on fine afternoons to what used to be called Blackwell's Island. When evening fell they hunted couples in the woods.

Miriam heard Alice shift in her chair. Thank God for her, such an ideal replacement. She had a truly predatory psyche, something that was rare in humankind. John's unexpected decline greatly increased her significance. As had been the case with them all, it would be unwise to explain very much to Alice. A confrontation would eventually occur, but it must wait for the right context. The truth was somewhat horrible to them, of course, but that was only part of the problem. More than inducing them to accept its ugliness, she had to teach them to see its beauty.

They had to want what Miriam had to give, to want it as they had never wanted anything before, with their minds, their souls, every cell of their flesh.

Miriam was good at helping people discover their true lust for existence. Layers of inhibition had to be sloughed away until, unexpectedly, the subject found his deepest craving exposed to the raw light and air. Then the ancient instincts would come pouring forth. Beside them all aspirations, all experiences, would seem embedded in dark amber, utterly dead, not even worth the forgetting.

It was a beautiful and undeniable truth. If she wished to possess one of them, she had only to *touch*, to caress and cajole. Eventually, the savage inner being would rise to the stroking and Miriam would own somebody new. "It's a marvelous afternoon, isn't it?"

"It's OK."

The flat little reply ignored all the magics in which Miriam knew how to swim. It saw only passing time, the hours. The magnificent secret was context. Miriam perceived time as a vast caravan containing the richness of all moments, luxurious with the soft hours of the past and the fair future too.

It was tempting, very tempting, to take a first step with Alice this very moment. But prudence must reign, John came first. And the question of the science . . . Miriam must make her approach to Sarah Roberts, must find the link that would complete her chain. There was a matter of responsibility, after all. She drew them with a promise of immortality. The full truth was hidden until they could not turn back. For all these years the lie had been a clanging note. Now it might be changed, made harmonious with the whole. Alice would be the first one to join Miriam forever and fully.

The first one. She looked at the soft blond features in a rapture of the most poignant love. Alice came to her and they stood, arms entwined, at the window that overlooked the garden.

Miriam had been angered when Alice went earlier to the front window with John. The girl should not take such liberties. Miriam looked forward to the time when Alice would want only her, care only about her, live for their life together.

As she and Alice stood there, Miriam's eyes searched the garden. She was sure that she had seen movement. Had Alice noticed it? The girl was looking up at her, a question forming on her lips. "What's there?"

Miriam forced a smile. "Nothing." But that wasn't true, not at all. John was standing behind a hedge, his face turned toward this window. Miriam sensed menace. Her skin prickled beneath her clothes. "We ought to keep working on these ideas, Alice. Don't you agree?"

"I thought I saw someone out there. Where's John?"

"Not out there! You can see the garden's empty."

"Yeah."

"So don't change the subject. I asked you a question."

"And I ignored it. That was an answer."

Miriam turned from the window. "You'll find out soon enough how important these sessions are. You're learning a great deal. Later, it'll all be useful."

"You're the only person I know who cares about such weird stuff."

"You'll come back tomorrow, then?"

"Why are you acting so funny, Miriam? Course I'll come back tomorrow. I come every day. I don't even need to go now."

"You'd better. I'm expecting a guest." For the briefest of instants her fingers smoothed the girl's hair.

It was a mistake. Furious, she snatched her hand away, quelling the explosion of raw hunger that the contact produced. Then Alice was out the door, scampering down the steps, promising to return the next day. She would be such a good companion. For variety Miriam was in the habit of alternating men and women. Their sex was a matter of indifference to her. Miriam turned back into the house, to face John. This was going to be a painful confrontation. He would be returning once again from the hunt. His forays would be getting frequent now, and desperately less satisfying.

The garden appeared empty, but she knew he had not gone. She closed her eyes, hating so to fear her beloved. The fear, though, was appropriate. No longer the love. She moved swiftly through the rooms, striving to prepare herself for the return of her poor hunter, broken and furious, from his paths of hell.

The lab was dark, silent except for the soft *whoo-whoo* of the ape on the video monitor. Sarah had put it all aside—budget committees, allocation requests, threats—to concentrate on the spectacle being replayed on the videotape.

"Effective age thirty-five years at this point," Phyllis Rockler said. She was hoarse with exhaustion, she had been at work a long, long time.

"The curve starts accelerating now," Charlie Humphries added.

Charlie himself appeared on the tape and drew a sample of blood. The ape's protest was violent, but weak with age. "Effective forty," Phyllis said. "It's been seven minutes."

"That's a rate of one point four years a minute."

The ape's mouth began to work. First one, then another, then a cascade of teeth fell out. Its face was a study in black fury.

"Effective age fifty-five."

"What's the human equivalent of a fifty-five-year-old rhesus?" Sarah asked. They had logged the equivalences only as far as thirty years. Older apes of the species were unknown.

"I figured it at about ninety-two if the scale is a straight linear regression," Phyllis replied. "That would mean he gets to a hundred and thirty-seven equivalent age before death."

Long gray hairs were falling like rain around his head and off his shoulders. Slowly, a hand came up to touch the sinking lips. As the hand moved, the fingers grew disfiguring arthritic knobs. The monkey began to sway, and his body started curving to the right.

"That's scoliosis of aging," Phyllis said.

There came a heartrending, infuriated howl. All three of the viewers stirred. Sarah wondered if the feeling that they were intruding into something forbidden affected the others as well. The ape had been a good and loving friend to the whole lab. Had those he loved the right to bring him such suffering? And yet . . . and yet—Sarah wondered if death was such a certainty, if the gates of Eden were really locked forever. It was simple, wasn't it? A matter of finding the key. Once the gates swung open, man's ancient, lost war with death would be won. '*We need not die,*' Sarah thought. She folded her arms and looked with cold determination at Methuselah's remarkable destruction. His life was a fair price for such an enormous gain to humanity.

"Effective age seventy. Rate one point nine five years per minute. Equivalent age one hundred twenty-one." A last, despairing grimace of defiance crossed his face.

Then it happened on tape just as it had in reality two hours ago. Methuselah fell onto his side, a terrible look in his eyes. His mouth worked, his arms slashed the air.

Wrinkles and fissures raced through his skin. The face withered like a drying apple. The eyes glazed over with layers of cataracts and then closed to slits. Hands and feet balled to fists. The skin began slackening on the bones.

The whole skeleton, slowly moving, was visible beneath the loose skin.

"Effective age eighty-five. Rate two point four zero years per minute. Equivalent age one hundred twenty-nine."

There was a long, rattling sigh.

"Life signs terminate," Phyllis said.

Sarah was stunned yet again by the power of the unknown. The now-dead ape's skin cracked along the bones and began to fall like tissue to the floor of the cage. Soon the skeleton, still held together by tendons, lay amid a pile of rubble. Then it also collapsed, and what had been alive just minutes before was reduced to dust. "The process of postmortem decay accelerated approximately two years of dry-air degeneration into seventy-one point five six seconds." The dust in the bottom of the cage became finer and finer and at last was whisked away by an errant breeze.

At this point there was a sudden series of thuds on the audio track, then the brief clanging of an alarm. That had been Phyllis sealing the room to prevent spread of a possible disease vector.

"Methuselah remained awake one hundred nineteen hours," Phyllis said. "I noted the first overt degenerative changes after the seventieth hour."

"His lipofuscin accumulation rate started an exponential rise in sample two thousand one hundred forty-one, taken at the seventy-first hour," Charlie said. "Subsequently, his blood cells began to lose their ability to uptake oxygen."

There was a long silence. "I don't know what the hell to make of it," Sarah said at last.

"That's putting it mildly."

"Let's see. The time is now eleven-fifteen. My guess is that the board is just about to approve Hutch's budget appropriation. Us not included. What say we just crack the quarantine on the cages and go home."

"Don't get a heart attack," Charlie said softly, "they'll find the money for us now."

Sarah sniffed. She folded her arms. "As a matter of fact, I don't feel *one bit* like a heart attack. I'm enjoying thinking about the trouble this tape is going to cause him."

"The physical sciences are going to be in an uproar," Phyllis muttered. "There's something in the old body we don't know nothin' about."

"Hutch is going to be forced to go right back to the committee and ask for a review."

"Let's hope."

"Look, I'm director of this lab, so get ready for some directions. I want to get a thousand K of the computer *under key,* access limited to us three. We need a nice roomy memory bank to foodle our numbers in."

"How do we set it up for billing?" Charlie asked.

"Don't worry about it. The administrator will fix it up."

"You mean Hutch?"

Her voice gentled. "I mean Tom. Hutch might not survive this."

Charlie applauded expansively.

They laughed. Sarah looked at the glowing TV screen. The mystery represented by the empty cage was awesome. It meant that the body did indeed contain a secret clock, and the clock could be tampered with. If age could speed up it could also slow down. It could stop.

All three of them continued to watch the cage even though there was nothing more to see. Sarah found her mind racing from question to question. It was a high moment, the kind of discovery few scientists ever encounter. She was acutely aware that they had made history. Schoolchildren, if such would still be birthed after immortality, would read about this moment. Models of this very lab would stand in museums.

She stopped herself with a shudder. It was not healthy to think about such things. Her mind turned back to the more immediate questions but the chill remained, a feeling of disquiet that must mask, deep in her heart, the sick dread she suspected was there.

"The sleep deprivation was the triggering mechanism for the aging acceleration. But what caused him to stop sleeping in the first place?"

"His whole system collapsed."

"That's not an answer."

They lapsed into silence. Sarah suspected the others felt much as she did. She brushed aside her fear, told herself the situation wasn't threatening.

The cage on the TV screen had a dark and evil cast to it, almost as if some inhuman spirit now possessed it. Sarah did not believe in old-fashioned notions of good and evil; she told herself that she did not. But she wouldn't go near that cage unless absolutely necessary.

There was a noise and stab of light as the door to the hall was opened. Tom's angular form appeared, back-lighted by the cold fluorescent glow of the hallway. He came in quietly, a doctor among the sick, and put his hand on her shoulder. His stoop told her all that he planned to say. He did not yet know of the tape, and the triumph represented by Methuselah's destruction.

Miriam's worst fear surfaced when she realized that John had entered the house. In all time and in all the world, this was the most terrible thing. He would be fiercely angry in his aging, dangerous as he died. She breathed a charm against him, calling on the ancient gods of her species, seeking in her heart their embrace.

She hunted him through her cheerful rooms, happy places each. Warm memories of their long time here flooded her. She ran her hand lightly along the back of the rosewood love seat, touched the mahogany elegance of the side table. On it were gold candlesticks. They still enjoyed that courtly old light and often lit the house with it.

She heard, distinctly, the soft hiss of a door opening across a carpet.

The house was so still that she could sense the faint rustle of her own dress as she breathed. She stood in a corner of the room. To her right was the hallway and the front door. Ahead the arched doorway into the dining room. She knew now that he had come up the basement stairs and must be at this moment standing between the pantry and the dining room. Then she heard a sound, a much aged voice, singing. "Sweetest songs of saddest thoughts, of times we've lost and loves forgot." The voice sank to a mutter and stopped. That song had been a popular tune of his youth. She remembered well singing it with him.

Then he came into the light. She concealed her surprise; he was naked. "Please," he said softly. "Please, Miriam, help me."

The firm, young body that had so delighted her was

gone. In its place was this thinned form, with liqueous pouches where muscle had been.

"Look at me, Miriam!" He sounded so pitiful, she hated to hear him.

"Put your clothes on."

"They don't fit!" Now he spat his words. Sudden rage was one of the most common characteristics of the disease. This time it declined as quickly as it had risen, leaving him only his despair. Before the reality of his suffering, Miriam's thoughts seemed to move slowly, her body to be stilled. Hesitant, not sure he would be tolerated, he came to her. His breath was so foul that she turned her head aside. Her mind, revolted by the ugliness, used as an antidote an image of Alice's bright face, of her creamy young skin. As his lips touched hers she took solace in this image.

"Don't you enjoy me? Please try." His face, spotted, sunken, bearded with hard white stubble, bobbed before her like the glowing image of death itself. He squeezed her shoulders, his hands sliding up to the base of her neck. "*You're* just as young as ever. *You* look marvelous." Suddenly he stepped back, blocking the door to the hallway. "Don't leave me," he said. His eyes were wide. "Don't leave me!"

She stood, head bowed, wishing that—just once— she dared surrender herself to another being. But she remained wary. The rage may come upon him again at any moment. Her throat was still a little raw from yesterday's episode. She looked up, met his eyes. "I won't ever leave you, John, not ever."

"Miriam—" He sobbed, wretched, obviously furious with himself for being so blatantly emotional. She could no longer ignore the plea in his voice. Against her own best judgment she went to him, put her arm around him, and guided him to the leather library sofa.

He leaned his head against her shoulder. "I'm so old. How did I get so old?"

"Time—"

"*What* time? It's been two days!"

"A great deal of time concentrated in a small space."

He looked at her, eyes stricken. "Where does it end?"

This was the hardest part. How do you face it, the fact that the seed of death, hidden deep in the body, has started to grow? She could not speak. Overcoming her revulsion, she stroked his head, held his hand. There was a low, awful sound from his throat. "I loved you," he whispered. "I trusted you so."

It hurt most terribly.

3

JOHN RUSHED BLINDLY down Eighth Avenue, heading toward Forty-second Street. It was four the next morning. He wore an overcoat, a wide-brimmed hat to shadow his face and carried a Samsonite briefcase. Energy was leaving him like light from the sky. He kept the hatbrim snapped low over his face. Occasionally, he attracted some interest from a dark doorway. A boy woke up long enough to make a few disinterested sucking noises, a thin girl muttered again and again, "wanna bj, wanna bj," like a grotesque machine, stopping the instant he had passed her doorway.

He was here because he was desperate and this was fast. The people on the streets now were more ruined than he was, too damaged to compete with the dirty glittering mob of the early night—or, perhaps, with him.

Then he saw what he was looking for, sitting in the window of the Mayfair Pancake House. The Mayfair was the hub of the neighborhood and John knew it well.

In times past it had been a nickelodeon. A man would buy a paper flower and hold it in his lap while the latest epics from Union City jittered across the screen. When a girl took the flower he had a date.

His victim came out, having been summoned by his tap on the glass. She sidled to him like a dog, her face looking upward and to the right. "Ain't I great?" she said. "Twenty bucks. You don't see the bad side." Her good profile was pure Cincinnati. But she had only half a dream—acid had melted the rest of her face into a glaring scar.

"Five bucks all the way," John said.

"Hand job money if you come fast."

"Ten bucks, that's my offer."

"Mister, you don't look at the goddamn scar. I got my moves down. You never see it."

"Ten." They had to be bargained with; he would end up getting attacked in a dark hall if he bore the scent of the victim.

She grabbed his groin. "Fifteen."

He pulled away.

"Anything for fifteen," she hissed. "You can do anything."

He hesitated. They stood as still as cats.

"SM," she said, "beat shit outa me."

"I don't like that."

"Man, you don't want extras?" She came close again, her half-face smiling. "I thought you wanted extras. I'll go ten, just a fuck."

They went through a doorway on Forty-third Street, down a gray-painted hall disfigured with graffiti, up some low stairs to a damp-smelling lobby. A black man slumped in a broken chair. John put the ten dollars in his open hand.

They went up a steeper staircase. She stopped before a tall wooden door. The room was tiny: a dresser, a folding chair and a lamp with a melted plastic shade. The bed was a mattress on the floor with a wadded yellow sheet on it. "The laundry ain't been in this early," the girl muttered. "Get your clothes off, we got ten minutes for ten bucks, that's house."

Blaylock took off his hat. Even though the room was deep in shadow, its window overlooking an airshaft, the girl could see enough of him to be startled.

"You got somethin', man?"

"I'm well. Just thin."

She moved slowly away. "What's the matter with you?"

He took his scalpel out of his pocket. The girl was grimacing as if in pain, backing toward the window. "Come on, honey," John said. "You belong to me."

Her good eye widened, the good side of her mouth twisted. Her hands came fluttering up to her neck. From her mouth there was a sort of barking sound, midway between terror and madness. When her back touched the wall she crouched down, bark bark bark, like a whispering dog. The eye kept looking around and around, unable to focus on the face before her.

John raised his scalpel with swift expertise and plunged it in behind her collarbone. It popped through the viscera and just touched the artery. In an instant he was upon her.

At last. This.

He felt life filling him again, purple and rich. He knew he could now walk the streets without attracting attention, no more decayed than any other old man. In the past he had felt the hunger perhaps once a week. Since this—whatever it was—degenerative disease started, his need had risen and risen. When would he be hunting again? Six hours? One?

Now the Samsonite briefcase came into use. Inside was half a gallon of naphtha and some simple incendiary materials. He laid the girl—so light—on the bed and soaked her with naphtha. Then he put an ashtray full of butts beside her. Carefully, he poured potassium permanganate crystals into a matchbox and soaked them in glycerine. In three or four minutes spontaneous combustion would cause the potassium to catch fire and explode the naphtha.

After placing the matchbox in the ashtray, he left.

The fire would be a furious one. Ten minutes from now only bones would be left. If the fire went much beyond that everything would be destroyed.

When John reached the street dawn was already beginning. A few day people were about, a girl in a white leatherette car coat clopping toward the W. T. Grant Building, a young man with a shade of moustache getting out of a cab. The second edition of the *Times* was being tossed off a ' truck at the corner newsstand.

Nobody noticed him. For now. His whole body was relieved as if of gravity itself. Later would come desolation as the new blood died, but for the moment he felt as if he could leap up into the spreading sunlight. As he proceeded along Forty-third Street the last of the night people crept away. There sighed from them all a weariness completely at odds with the spring dawn slipping down the office towers. They dragged themselves away while pink clouds glided westward in a luminous sky.

A fire engine blared past, the firemen clinging to it. Their faces were bored and determined, frozen with the expression common to men who are intimate with death.

Manhattan began to come alive more rapidly. People were pouring out of the Seventh Avenue Subway, coffee shops were getting crowded, buses were swinging past with windows darkened by the crush of passengers.

John could feel her in him. Her past seemed to whisper in his veins, her voice to jabber in his ears. In a sense, she haunted him; they all did. Was the hunger satisfied by their being or just their blood? John had often wondered if they knew, if they felt themselves in him. From the way he could hear them in his mind, he suspected that they did. Miriam angrily dismissed the notion. She would toss her head and refuse to listen when he brought it up. She would not accept that you could *touch* the dead.

As he walked he counted the hours since last he had closed his eyes. Thirty-six at least. And during that short time he had needed three victims. Their energy was some compensation for the lack of Sleep, but it couldn't go on forever. Each one had less impact than the last.

He found that he could almost hate Miriam if he wished, she who had made him. It was not so much the fact that she had lied to him about his life-span as that she had trapped him in an isolation even more awful than her own. He had come to terms with his cannibal life, accepting it as the price of immortality. Even for that the price was high. But for this? His hunger had cheated him. For this he had paid too much.

He went on foot to Sutton Place; there was no percentage in risking a cab. When he turned onto the street there were shafts of sunlight between the buildings, well-dressed people hurrying to work, cars pulling up before elegant foyers, doormen whistling down cabs. The innocent brightness of this world assaulted his conscience, made him feel the blackest shame. Their own little house with its green shutters and marble sills, with its red-brick façade and window boxes full of petunias, contrived an atmosphere of warmth and joy. A repulsive falseness. It seemed to John like a newly cut tree, its leaves still robust, the message of death not yet risen up the trunk.

"Morning," Bob Cavender said. He was a naturally ebullient man, the Blaylocks' neighbor, Alice's father.

"Morning," John said, affecting a slight accent.

"New on the block?" Cavender did not recognize this suddenly aged version of his neighbor.

"Houseguest. Staying with the Blaylocks."

"Oh, yes? Good people. Music lovers."

John smiled. "I am a musician. With the Vienna Philharmonic."

"My daughter's going to love you. She spends half her life at the Blaylocks'. She's a musician too."

John smiled again and delivered a courtly Viennese bow. "We will meet again, I presume," he said.

Cavender passed on down the street, trailing a hearty goodbye. How normal men could maintain their confidence and good cheer amid the chaos of life was one of the most fascinating mysteries that John had encountered. The Cavenders of the world never realized the truth of generations, how short was their time and brief their ways.

There was a hush inside the house. Miriam had opened a pomander jar and the front hall was full of its rich scent. John went upstairs. He was eager to examine his face in a mirror. But when he got to the bedroom he hesitated. A deep, dead cold spread through him. He stood in the sunlight beside the pink-curtained window, terrified of the mirror on the back of the bathroom door, afraid to take another step.

For so long he had been balanced at the age of thirty-two. Along with the sudden aging of his body there had come a black flood of confusion as his brain atrophied. The assurance of youth was rapidly evaporating, and in its place was this preoccupied stranger, rapt only to the betrayal of the flesh. He found himself unable to remember dates, names, events. Things were colored by an unsettling newness, even things he must have seen many times before.

A tiny sound broke the stillness, the drip of a tear on the floor. "Coffin," he said. His voice had changed so, deepening into age. All the years he had cheated were taking their revenge on him at once.

At the end of the last century he had visited a medium, planning to take her when the lights were out. But just as her fingers twisted down the gaslight something awful happened. With a sound like a tearing curtain dozens and dozens of different faces appeared in her face, like a crowd at the window of a burning house. All were known to him—his victims. The medium screamed, her eyes rolling, head lolling.

He had run from that horrible place, literally staggering with fear. A day later the *New York Evening Mail* published an item to the effect that the body of Mrs. Rennie Hooper had been found in her parlor. Her fingers were still on the key of the gas lamp. They assumed it was heart failure. Miriam insisted there was no *touch* with the dead. But she wasn't human, she didn't know anything about the relationship between a man and his dead.

The dead world glowered forth at him. Suddenly, an image of the whore exploded into his mind's eye, her flesh blackening in the flames.

His stomach twisted until it felt as if it were ripping out of his body and he clamped his fists to his eyes, willing with all his strength that the vision of death before him, of deliverance into the hands of his victims, would dissolve. But it did not, rather it focused and confirmed. He realized that the demons of hell were not demons at all but the men of earth without their costumes.

To Sleep in safety, Miriam had gone to her attic room. John might well be able to penetrate the security system around the bed. She huddled on the hard floor fighting a nightmare. But it came relentlessly on, bursting through the Sleep like fire through straw, grasping her mind, forcing it to see:

A foggy morning near Ravenna. She had come here with the other citizens of property, when the Emperor fled Rome fifty years ago. Dew lies on the marble sill of her bedroom window. From deep in the fog comes the singing of rough-voiced Vandals on their way to raid the Imperial Palace. They move slowly through the mist, marching along just beyond the herb garden, their horned helmets making them look enormous. They will not pass this great house without plundering it, not even on their way to the palace of Petronius Maximus.

Keeping her voice steady, she calls Lollia. The girl comes swiftly across the marble floor, her slippers hissing on the stones. Miriam does not need to speak. "It is finished," Lollia says. "He hasn't made a sound in hours." Miriam takes Lollia's white face in her hands and kisses her full on the mouth, feeling the trembling fervor of a kiss returned. "My love," Lollia says softly, "the barbarians—"

"I know."

Miriam drops her nightclothes on the floor and strides naked across the room. The smell of the oil lamp guttering on her night table mingles with the sharp scent of the leather cloak she removes from her chest. She dresses in traveling clothes, aided by her lover, who has kindly taken the place of the dead servants.

Then Lollia goes off to her own room to change. They have hidden the horses and carriage in the Peristyle. Distantly, there is a crash, the sound of merry laughter: the Vandals are at the stables. Miriam races across silk carpets, her cloak swelling behind her, and goes down the stone stairs to the basement where in olden times slaves attended an elaborate furnace. With the coming of inflation those slaves were sold, and the dying convulsions of the Empire diminished the amount of coal available. As for the slaves who remained—Eumenes saw to them.

Miriam had stationed Lollia beside the great oak door all night. Only an hour ago had she reported silence. Now Miriam feels safe in opening the door. She throws back three bolts and pulls with all her strength. Slowly it swings wide.

She screams.

The shriveled *thing* attached to the door by its finger and toe nails is unrecognizable as Eumenes. The room reeks of new blood. On the floor are the husks of his last five victims. Around him is a puddle of blood, having run out through his dead digestive system. His skeletal form is gouged; at the end he was terribly weak, his victims were almost too much for him.

Miriam swallows, forces self-control. She grasps the thing by its shoulders and peels it off the door.

Her ancient and beloved companion, her Eumenes. Odysseus returned at last, neither dead nor alive, somehow still attached to this ruined corpse—a spirit perhaps unwanted among spirits and forced to remain in the dead house of its body.

She pulls his knees to his chin and forces him into a box of the hardest wood, feeling the quivering pulsations of his body. The box is fastened by brass and reinforced with iron. Hefting the precious burden on her shoulders, she mounts the stairs. She will never abandon him, she murmurs, never, never. In the hallway Lollia is dancing with agitation. She is a simple girl, accepting without question Eumenes' "sickness," never imagining that she must one day follow. The elegant rooms are filling with smoke. The girl's eyes dart toward the rising Gothic shouts. Despite her terror she helps Miriam; together they take the chest to the carriage. They throw open the gate and Miriam snaps the reins.

Behind them the ancient villa fades gracefully into mist and past times.

It is slow going along the unrepaired roads. They must not approach Ravenna, not at any cost. Two women in a carriage loaded with baggage and gold coins are as vulnerable as it is possible to be.

"Constantinople," Miriam says, thinking of the boat waiting at Rimini and the terrors of the sea. Lollia huddles against her.

Before her she saw a dark wooden wall. She was in the ship, hearing the wind shrieking in the rigging, hearing—

A pigeon coo.

Her eyes opened. She did not move at first. Then she remembered, she was in the attic. Her mouth was dry, the dream clinging like a rotten flavor. She sat up. Close beside her was the new steel chest.

She hated these dreams. They did not interfere with renewal; indeed, they might be part of it. But they hurt so very much.

Well, she'd have to put it out of her mind. She had a great deal to do. She had been methodically preparing for Alice's transformation. It had taken all last year to sift through the literature of sleep disturbance and aging research until she had pinpointed the most knowledgeable person in the field.

Her approach to Sarah Roberts was to have been subtle and slow. Over time she would have befriended her, made Sarah's knowledge her own, then slipped out of her life as easily as she had entered.

She had never expected John to die so soon. Even after transformation Alice would have grown to maturity. The three of them were to have shared those years.

But no more. Alice *had* to last, Miriam could bear nothing less. She ran her fingers through her hair. With the coming of the sun this little room under the eaves turned into an oven.

Miriam left, taking care to cross the attic on the beams so that the ceilings under her feet would not creak. While John was still strong she could not afford to let him know where she Slept. He felt cheated and betrayed; they always did. The next time his fingers might well close around her throat for good.

As soon as she opened the door to the attic she knew that he was home from another hunt. From their bedroom came a rasping sound that tore at her heart. He was crying. His intelligence, his sweetness, his exuberance—and above all the truth of his love—remained as alive as if the old John still existed. As she entered the room he fell heavily, thudding against the wall.

He began to pull himself up on the dressing-table chair. She watched the wheezing struggle appalled—he had weakened badly in these past hours. The gray skin was cracked, the hands reminded her of the claws of an animal.

His eyes, yellow and watery, sought her. He looked at her. She could hardly bear his face. "I'm hungry," said a screeching, unfamiliar voice.

She could not reply.

He managed to pull himself to his full height and stood swaying like a hobbled buzzard. His mouth opened and closed with a crackling sound. "Please," he said, "I've got to eat!"

Without the Sleep their hunger became unendurable. The flawless pattern of life was broken, and the delicate balance crumbled.

"John, I don't understand this, I never have."

He leaned toward her, gripping the chair tightly. She was relieved to see that he dared not launch himself in her direction. It was unlikely that he could hurt her, but not completely impossible. She preferred distance between them. Her control of any situation had to be flawless. "But you *knew!* You knew it would happen!"

There was no point in lying, the truth was obvious. "You must help me. You must!"

She was unable to look at the accusation in those eyes. Before the truth of what she had done she could not find words, either of comfort or denial. She was lonely and human beings gave her the love that pets give. She sought companionship, some warmth, the appearance of home. She rejected her tears, her shame at what she had done to him. After all, did she not also deserve some love?

John had heard her from the first moment she had moved. The fact that she had been Sleeping in the attic locked away from him decided it. For him it was a surprisingly cool decision and it admitted no room for reconsideration. He was going to hurt her. He was going to take her throat in his hands and crush it until she admitted the evil of what she had done.

He watched her come warily into the room and feigned weakness, pretending to fall against a table. It was clear that she wouldn't come near him if she thought that there was the least danger. Miriam was obsessively cautious.

He was agonizingly hungry. Miriam was so healthy and beautiful, literally ablaze with life—what would happen if he took her? Would it be enough to cure him? Her odor was dry and lifeless, like a starched dress. She did not have that wonderful, rich smell that John had come to identify with food.

Maybe she was poison.

His anger poured out in everything he said to her, he could not prevent it. She told him she did not understand what was happening to him. He wanted to believe that she was a passionless monster. He tried not to think of her as human. But he loved her, and now he needed her. Why wouldn't she understand that?

He stretched out his arms, pleading for help.

She moved back toward the door, the silken gesture of a cat. Her eyes regarded him as if there was something she was about to say. He realized how great the gulf between them had really been all these years.

"I'm dying, Miriam. *Dying!* Yet you go gliding along, perfect and untouched. I know you're much older than me. Why are you different?"

Now her face clouded, she seemed about to cry. "John, you *invited* me into your life. Don't you remember?"

This was too much. He launched himself toward her, growling his rage, his arms extended toward her neck. Miriam had always been able to move fast, and she slipped away easily, retreating to the hallway. On her lips was a sad half-smile. The one thing that gave him hope was her eyes. They were glazed with fear, swimming with what could only be sorrow. As he approached her she turned, quick as a bird.

He heard her feet drumming down the stairs, then the front door slammed.

He was desolated. She had left him. Now he regretted his attack. Yet he hadn't been able to stop himself, the urge was so sudden. Sooner or later she was bound to come back, though. She couldn't bear to Sleep in hotel rooms for fear of an intruder or a fire. This place was so thoroughly equipped that a match couldn't smoulder without being noticed, nor a burglar touch a window. No, this was her haven and she would return.

John would be waiting.

For fifteen minutes he lay on the bedroom floor trying to reach Sleep. But the hunger was there, insinuating itself into his veins, making him tremble with need.

He pulled himself to his feet and went downstairs, paused at the door to the library. Books and papers were strewn about. Miriam was normally obsessed with order. He slumped down behind her desk, thinking that he might prolong his strength if he didn't move so much. It was going to be damned difficult if he had to eat in broad daylight, and in this condition.

There was a magazine lying open on the desk. *The Journal of Sleep Disorders.* Some project of Miriam's. It was laughable, Miriam's silly faith in science. The magazine was opened to an article with the wildly exciting title of "Psychomotor Dysfunction in Abnormal Dreaming Response: The Etiology of 'Night Terrors of Adulthood,'" by S. Roberts, MD, Ph.D. The article was an utterly meaningless mass of statistics and charts, interspersed with sentences in the incomprehensible language of technology. How Miriam managed to make anything of such material was a mystery to John, and what she expected to do with it was just as obscure. Science, which so involved and excited her, seemed fearful to him, the work of the mad.

John pushed the magazine aside, staring blankly. He had begun to hear a sound, a sort of high-pitched noise like a siren. It was a moment before he realized that it was coming from inside his right ear. It peaked and then died. In its wake was nothing: the ear had become deaf. He had to act, the deterioration was now very rapid.

He went to the daybed, a place where he had Slept many times, and lay down. He closed his eyes. At first there was bone-tired relief. Again he did not Sleep. Instead, bright geometrical shapes began to appear before his eyes. These resolved into burning images of Miriam's face, of Miriam standing over him during the agonizing time of his transformation.

His eyes opened almost of their own accord. Other faces had been about to replace Miriam's.

The sound of a raging crowd evaporated into the soft morning air. Where, after all, do the dead go? Nowhere, as Miriam said—or is there a world beyond life, a world of retribution?

"You can't blame me," he growled.

He was surprised to hear a voice answer. "I'm not! You can't help it if they forgot!" Alice.

John turned his head. She stood frowning, her violin case in her hand. She was here for her music lesson. Her odor, rich beyond description, poured into the room. "Good morning," John said as he clambered to a sitting position on the side of the daybed.

"I do music with the Blaylocks at ten. But they're gone."

She did not recognize him.

"Yes, yes—they had some kind of a bank meeting. They told me—told me to tell you."

"You must be the Vienna Philharmonic musician. My dad told me about you."

He got to his feet, went to her, bowed. He dared not touch her, dared not even brush his hand against her. The hunger had become an inferno the instant he had caught scent of her. He had never experienced so much concentrated need, had never wanted anything so badly.

"Are you a regular with the Vienna Philharmonic?"

"Yes." His hands shook, he clutched them together to keep from grabbing her.

"What's your instrument?"

Careful here. He couldn't say cello because she might ask him to play. It was completely beyond his capacity in this condition. "I play—french horn." There, that was good.

"Heck, I was hoping you were strings." She looked at him with her soft, intense eyes. "Strings are a lot of fun. They're hard, though. Do you have your horn?"

"No—no, I prefer it does not travel. The tone, you know."

She glanced away. "Are you all right?" she asked in a small voice.

"Of course," he said. But he did not feel all right, he felt like splitting her in two.

"You look so old." Her voice was low and hesitant. The knuckles of the hand gripping the violin case were white.

John tried to lick his lips, realized that they were stretched dry. The faces of other children swam into his memory. Miriam had insisted he take them when he was a beginner because they were easier. In those days homeless, unknown children were commonplace.

Taking human life had slowly lost its significance for him. He no longer remembered the number of murders he had committed. She had sucked every cell of humanity out of him and left him as he was today, at the end of his life with this to face.

"Have a seat," he heard his voice say, "we'll talk music until they get back."

His hand touched the scalpel in his pocket the instant she accepted his invitation and came through the door.

That was all he needed, he was on her. Screams exploded from her, echoing flatly through the house. Her lithe body writhed, her hands tore at him, she slapped at the cracked skin of his face.

He pulled at the scalpel, twisting her hair in one hand, yanking her along the floor. Her arms windmilled, her feet scraped and banged. Her screams were high pitched, frantic, incredibly loud.

The damn scalpel wouldn't come out of his pocket.

She managed to bite his arm, her teeth crunching out a half-moon-shaped hole in the loose skin.

Her eyes rolled when she saw the damage she had done. A column of black vomit shot from her mouth, splattering on the floor. She threw herself back and skittered along, trying to reach the door. He leaped at her, finally ripping the scalpel from his pocket. Everything except the hunger disappeared from his consciousness. His mouth opened, he could already taste her. It took all of his strength not to gnash his teeth like a famished dog. She was on her back, pushing herself away with her feet. He grabbed her ankle, held it with all the strength he could find. She sat forward and began batting at his hand.

He drove the scalpel down behind her collarbone. The pain threw her head back and made her shriek wildly. Then he was lying on top of her. Her breath rushed out of her lungs with a *whoosh*. She lay jerking in shock, her tongue lolling, eyes growing filmy.

With his mouth wide he covered the wound. He probed with his tongue. It hurt, it always did. Unlike Miriam's, his soft human tongue was not adapted to this.

After what seemed an endless amount of probing, the blood burst from the vein, filling him at last. He sucked hard, lingering until the last drop. Only when there was nothing left but a dry rattling did he stop. His body felt loose and easy now, his mind was clearing. It was like waking up from a nightmare, or like the time as a boy when lost on the dark North Yorks Moors he had finally discovered a familiar path. He sighed deeply, then washed out his mouth with a glass of Madeira from the library stock. The wine seemed to contain a million delicious flavors, and he sensed each one individually. It was so beautiful he wept. His hands went to his face, feeling the softening skin and the warmth. He lay back on the daybed again and shut his eyes. The wine had been a fitting complement. Unlike other food, alcohol remained delicious to him. He tried to relax, savoring the immense relief.

Alice, as serene as a goddess, appeared behind his closed eyes.

It was so real that he shouted. He jumped up from the daybed. A sweet scent filled the room. It was every beautiful memory he had ever known, every kind voice, every loving touch.

He remembered when he was fourteen, waking on a summer's morning at Hadley House, knowing that he would meet Priscilla on the other side of the lake as soon as she had served morning tea to himself and his parents.

He remembered the humid woods, the swans in the lake and the wildflowers. There was a hurting, queasy tickle when she touched him. By now she was dust beyond dust.

He sat down beside the rumpled clothes that hid the remains of Alice Cavender. The perfume was strongest here, it must have been something she was wearing. Gently, he touched the red T-shirt with its decal of Beethoven.

The perfume faded as quickly as a departed mood of love. It left him feeling as if he were already dead. He sighed. There was an ugly chore just ahead that wouldn't wait. If Miriam found any evidence of whom he had taken—he couldn't allow that.

He forced himself to pick up the little bundle and carry it down to the basement.

Miriam had walked the streets, sorrowing at the ugliness of what John had become. Despite her caution he had nearly . . . she couldn't even think about it. She was going to have to capture him soon. As soon as she dared. Even with his present weakness he was still too strong.

She returned home after an hour, unwilling to expose herself more than necessary to the random accidents of the city streets. When she turned the corner onto

Sutton Place she stopped in surprise and stared. There was smoke rising in a thin trail from her chimney. John was burning evidence, and in broad daylight. The fool must have hunted right in this neighborhood, he hadn't had time to go farther away. No doubt he had taken some local child.

Toward the end they always lost all caution. She wanted to be angry at him, but she pitied his desperation too much. She ought to count herself lucky that he bothered to destroy his evidence at all.

Although she did not relish the prospect of confronting him, she was going to have to re-enter the house. It was hers, after all. And it was a safe place to Sleep. Somehow, John would have to be restrained. She could not allow him the freedom of house and streets much longer.

She marched up the front steps and went in. The rumble of the furnace was audible. The poor man. At least it told her his whereabouts. The high-pressure gas lines that fed the thing couldn't be left unattended.

She paused in the hall, savoring for a moment the peace and life of her house. To her it was like a well-rooted rose bush, lively and enduring. Soon it would contain a new voice, that of Alice, light and golden. Miriam's tiny infirmary was prepared for the transfusions. The approach to Dr. Roberts had begun. The good doctor herself would in the end be Miriam's assistant. For an instant her mind remembered John as he had been and she experienced a quick sinking of the heart. But she pushed it aside.

She began to move toward the library. That pomander was too sweet, it was getting rotten. And the ceiling needed some plaster work; the house had settled a little recently. She had to prune her roses. It would soon be a necessity as well as a pleasure. And she was crying all over the hall rug. There was no use trying to stifle her feelings. Her despair broke through in a torrent.

John, you loved me.

You loved even the sound of my name.

He had been so happy with her, always laughing, always full of delight. She sank into a side chair and rested her chin in her hands, shut her eyes tight against the tears. She wanted so for him to hold her once again. She had been his prize, his adored one. In the end that was all that mattered, that was life itself, to be needed.

His aging was so ugly, she couldn't remember that the others had been that ugly.

There had been such good times.

The night she first met him, for example. She had only recently returned to England. She hadn't seen one of her own kind in twenty-five years. In those days she still hoped that they had migrated to America, seeking a less organized community. She was miserable with loneliness, an unwanted creature in a world she could not love.

That night it had been cold, the rain pounding and the wind blowing. She was toying with Lord Hadley, a foolish old man. His estates were vast and full of itinerant workers and others of the dispossessed. She longed for the freedom to roam unhindered in such lands. She had accepted his invitation gladly. And this glorious young man had appeared at dinner. He had about him all the important signs: the arrogance, the determination, the intelligence. A predator.

She had drawn him to her that very night, to teach the poor inexperienced thing a few secrets. The rich hunting of the estate could wait now that she had the opportunity to possess its heir.

She had taken rooms in the town of Hadley and visited him each night. Two weeks later she had started his infusions. If only she had known then how weak he really was; he had been intended to last the longest. Look at him now.

In those days she used india-rubber tubing and the hollow needles made for glassblowers. It was a great advance over the past method, in which she simply used her mouth and hoped for the best. Although she knew nothing of immunology then and would never have thought to test him for tissue rejection, John had not died. His wound had become infected, but that always happened. He had gone pale, but they did that too. Unlike so many, he survived. Together they had depopulated Hadley. The old Lord had hung himself. The estate had reverted to the wild.

He was a delighted child in those days. They went to London to join the bright social whirl of the declining Regency. God, how times had changed.

John. She remembered the time he had burst in on her disguised as a policeman. And the time he had chosen their victims in Glasgow and the next morning she discovered it was the Lord Mayor and his wife.

They used to ride to hounds. He had taught her that there was a thrill in challenging fear. She had accepted a little bit of the lesson to please him. How fine he had looked mounted, his boots gleaming in the morning sun. She remembered the mad dash of the horses, the smells and the noise and even the unaccustomed sweetness of danger. He had once leaped onto her horse at full gallop and tumbled them both off into a ditch—and made love to her with the bracken bobbing about their thighs and the huntsman's horn echoing in the distance.

She sighed and tried again to forget. Nostalgia was useless—she had to get down to that basement and deal with the poor man.

4

TOM SAT IN HIS OFFICE in the gathering dark. Although it was late he was crackling with energy. Hutch had just turned down Sarah's application for a funding review. Even better, he had ordered the project closed down, its records sealed.

Battle was joined. Tom could now challenge Hutch directly by demanding a Board of Directors' meeting himself. If Hutch was reversed it would break the old man's authority. Tom could then move in on him, shoulder him aside. Welcome to the next Director of Sleep Research.

He took out a cigar and held it between his lips, then put it away. One a day was his limit. If he smoked this one he would break that limit and force himself to confront his own iron rule: smoke two and go without any for a week.

He saw a shadow appear on the frosted glass of his door. The knob rattled. "When's the review?" Sarah asked as she entered. "We're ready to go."

"Not tonight. The board goes home early."

"Board? You mean the Board of Directors—of the Center? I thought we were dealing with the Budget Committee."

"We're not. Hutch blocked a committee review. I'm left with no alternative but to go to the board itself."

"I'm not prepared for that."

"Don't quaver so when you talk, my dear. You're prepared—brilliantly so, knowing you. And you can prepare me."

"I've never even *see* the board."

"I have. They're formidable as hell. Exactly what you'd expect of three world-class tycoons, a retired governor and two Nobel prize winners." He smiled. "Pardon my intimidation. I'm just challenging you to do better than your best. Give me what I need to impress the hell out of them."

"Yes, sir." She snapped off a ragged salute. "Shall I get a new dress? A permanent?"

"You just get the data. I'll confront them alone."

"Thank God!"

"Confidence." He leaned back, being careful not to allow the old chair to fall off its base. It was going to be quite a pleasure, and a deserved one, to allocate himself some decent furniture. Part of Hutch's psychology was to make sure he had the worst office, the most decrepit furniture in the whole clinic. Transient interns rated better space.

"You seem curiously happy."

"I should be. I think this might get me the directorship. If the board starts dictating policy to Hutch, he'll have to go. There's already board sentiment to that effect, I suspect."

"Tom, you're using me again."

"You're useful, lover."

She laughed, shook her head. Tom disliked the moral tone of her position. Operating to mutual benefit wasn't using somebody, not in the way she meant. "I'm saving your career."

"To further your own."

That was unfair. He felt wronged. "I'm getting what we both want, Sarah. That's all that's important."

Her eyes were closed, she looked pained. "It's just that I don't like this side of you. It scares me. I don't like to think you walk over people."

"Then delude yourself. I don't mind."

"Tom, I guess what scares me is that I love you so much. I feel so vulnerable."

He wanted to hold her, to somehow reassure her. They sat silently, the space between them making movement seem impossible.

"What if you fail?" she asked in a flat voice.

"Now who's the betrayer?"

Her hand went to the desk between them. She must want him to hold it, he could see the sparkle of tears in her eyes. "We both have a lot to lose," she said. "You're making this thing into a life-or-death crisis."

"It's been that all along. I'm just trying to use it to our advantage."

"That's what I hate about you! You use everything. Me. Even yourself. Sometimes I see you as so—so dark and frightening. You're somebody I don't know, somebody who would do anything—too much—to get what he wanted."

They had often had versions of this conversation. Originally, Tom had dismissed it as the histrionics of an insecure woman but recently had begun to suspect that it was more deeply felt than that. Sarah's insecurities did not extend to her career, despite its precariousness. Tom wondered how long they would last as a couple. Would she leave him over such an issue? He reached out and took the hand. He knew that she was waiting, but for what he was not quite certain. Probably she wanted him to protest, to deny the truth of what she had said. It was like Sarah to see a truth and try to enforce a more palatable illusion in its stead.

"It's the way I am," Tom said. "I won't deny it. I want his job. It's that simple. I'm better qualified. And I'll get it too. He won't be able to stop me." Saying the words offered him a satisfactory illusion of confidence. Actually, what he was conscious of was fear. He might get himself fired or, worse, might end up stripped of all power, condemned to be Hutch's batboy until the old man died.

"Let's go someplace and drink. It's that time."

"This is you talking? Leaving the lab at seven P.M.? Maybe you *have* given up."

"They're running statistics on the changes in Methuselah's blood composition. There's nothing for me to do."

"You have computer access? I thought that'd be cut off by now."

"Charlie broke the codes. We're patched in through his home computer."

Tom smiled. You couldn't help but be proud to work with people such as Sarah and her group. She wasn't one to be stopped by something as minor as having her budget cut and the door slammed in her face. "How can you get the memory space? Won't the computer alert the Programming Group?"

"It's an assembly from dozens of different files. A little here, a little there. Not enough to notice—from any one file."

"How much space do you have?"

"Ten thousand K."

He burst out laughing. It took a supplementary request to the Programming Group, six weeks' wait and a special budget allocation to exceed 500 K. So much for bureaucracy! "How is this getting billed, for the love of God?"

"It's going on Hutch's personal account. The effective cost is eighteen hundred dollars an hour."

"I hope that's not true. He'll end up going to jail for stealing computer time."

"That would be delicious. Unfortunately, the truth is more prosaic."

"May I know?"

"Nope."

He could respect that. She was into a substantial bank of Riverside's enormous computing power. The fewer who knew, the better. Not to mention the safety there was in ignorance.

They didn't talk on the way down in the elevator. The lobby was quiet as they crossed to the door. He hailed a cab on York Avenue. "How about making this a catered affair?"

"Chinese food?"

"It's a deal." He couldn't face some depressing bar right now. He wanted Sarah very badly. The thought of losing her came cold into his mind. He loved her so much. Right now he wanted to slide across the seat, to put his arm around her, to melt the barrier between them. During the day she was so crisp and professional and cool. At night he wanted another Sarah, one who would shelter him. He watched her gentle, tense face, the soft curve of her bosom, smelled her faint perfume and longed for her.

The harsh words she had spoken in his office returned to mind now. 'You use everything. Me. Yourself.' Was it really true? Did he have to think that about himself? If it was true, it was not something he could help.

"I love you," he said softly so the cabdriver wouldn't hear. Public intimacies annoyed Sarah.

She smiled briefly, allowed him to cover her hand with his.

"Love solves problems," he said.

She was silent a long moment. "It survives them."

He wished so very much for her happiness and success. She had made an extraordinary discovery, he was sure of it. He wanted her to taste the sweetness of recognition, to receive all the benefits such a thing could bring. "I want to help you, Sarah," he said, "I want to so badly!"

She smiled broadly. "I wish Hutch could hear you. He'd be terrified."

"Left side or right side?" the cabdriver asked.

"Building on the left. The high-rise."

The big blue "Excelsior Towers" sign glowed in the deepening night. An elderly woman with a dog came out, the spiderlike creature trotting along beside her. Alex seasoned a cigar at his post by the door. He lit it, took a deep puff. Tom watched with the avidity of the denied, envied the man his indifference to his health. They got out of the cab.

"Good evening, Doctors," Alex said around the cigar. Tom couldn't bear to smell the billow of smoke that came toward him. At least it was a cheap one, it lacked the fetching aroma of a good Montecristo. Thank God.

"A habit is an agonizing thing," Tom said as the elevator doors closed behind them.

"I wondered how you were taking that."

"Badly."

"How many have you had so far today?"

He raised one finger. She reached up, took his hand and shook it. "It's surprisingly hard to do," he said. "The body demands its fix."

"I know. It took me two years to give up cigarettes. That and my father."

Tom had never met Samuel Roberts. His death had occurred before he and Sarah really knew each other. Lung cancer, she had said.

Sarah followed him into the apartment, pausing to put her rain coat in the closet. He turned on the lights in the living room. She came up beside him. "I like our place," he said. She nodded. "Sarah, can I kiss you?" She turned to him, put her hands on his shoulders. He bent to her, looked for a long few seconds into her eyes, then sought her lips. The warm sweetness of her kisses always renewed him. It was as if his body wanted to do what his heart could not, and once and for all seal their love.

"Do you really believe I love you?" he suddenly asked. The question had popped out before he had even thought about it. He wished that he didn't do things like that. It was a question he might not want answered.

"I know you do."

He tried to kiss her again but she turned away. His impulse was to force her. Angry with himself, he quelled it. She had sensed his anger, though, and stood still and small, her chin jutting out, her hands twisted together. "Not now," she said.

"I won't hurt you."

She laughed as if to reassure him that she trusted him. "Tom, if our careers didn't mesh the way they do—if mine was in the way—what would you do?"

He reached out, took her hand. "They do mesh, so why worry about it? We're in a perfect position. By saving your career I'm going to make my own."

"But what if it was the opposite? That's the question you won't answer."

"I'm jeopardizing myself as it is."

She shook her head. "I love you, Tom. God help me but I do." She came to him, her forehead was at eye level. He kissed it, then drew her to him, feeling the smallness of her body, disturbed by her vulnerability, obscurely pleased.

She let him lift her off her feet, bend to her upraised face. He kissed her long and hard, as if to kiss away the space between them, wishing he could, wanting his love to sweep her doubts aside and draw her to him forever.

"Oh, Sarah. You're so beautiful. I can't believe a woman so beautiful would be interested in me."

"Put me down, and don't sell yourself short. You aren't exactly ugly."

He smiled. "Not exactly." Gently, she brushed his cheek with her hand, an admonitory gesture. "I wasn't referring to my physical appearance. I can't quite—" He stopped, found he didn't want to say that he could not command her love.

"I do love you. That isn't something I say lightly."

He nodded, kissed her briefly. "Let's go to bed," he murmured into the warmth of her hair.

"I want to order up Chinese food. Then we can do it."

"Now."

Laughing, she pushed him away. "Prolong our pleasure. Let's anticipate a little."

He felt subtly rejected. "I'll go take my shower," he said, covering his hurt. If she really wanted him, she would not have been able to resist his invitation. Leaving her to work out the menu for their Chinese meal, he went into the bedroom and stripped off his clothes.

He felt better when he was standing in the warm shower, clouds of steam coming up around him, making his skin tingle. In the shower he could forget his disappointments, his problems, his fears. His mind went back to the clinic, however. Was her discovery going to grow and grow until it consumed her and eclipsed him? Their love had never seemed so frail, or so terribly important.

A shadow moved on the other side of the shower curtain. Then she was there, happiness again, slipping in naked, the water bouncing against her marvelously beautiful body, running down its curves, flowing between her breasts, bouncing off her nipples. "I thought you might need a little help," she said, taking the soap from the dish and picking up the washcloth.

She had come to him. He almost laughed aloud. But he didn't, instead he let himself fall into the familiar little game they played in the shower. "Only one part of me is dirty."

"What part?" Prim, eyebrows raised, face glowing.

He had been hiding himself behind his hands. Now he removed them.

"Oh! It looks like a bratwurst."

"Then eat it."

"And get my hair wet? Not on your life. I'll clean it up, though, since you say it's dirty."

He enjoyed these showers enormously. She washed

him slowly, sensuously, concentrating on the most sensitive parts, on her face the gentlest, sweetest expression imaginable. And when he washed her, touching her whole body, feeling the life of her flesh beneath his hands, it was like a miracle.

Afterward she was flushed, her eyes sparkling. He knew that she was terribly excited and he teased her. "Did you order the Chinese food?"

"Sure. Oh, *damn*. I guess we'll have to wait."

"Really?" He went to her, lifted her up and leaned back.

"Tom, don't," she said. He noticed that she didn't struggle. Doubtless she was afraid he'd lose his balance if she did. "To-o-m." He entered her standing, his legs spread, his arms around her waist. Her feet dangled inches from the floor. "Tom, you madman, let me down!"

"The Chinese food's going to come."

"Oh, *Tom.*"

He couldn't stand it anymore. He put her down, but only because it was impossible to remain standing together as they were long enough to consummate the act. "Get in that bed," he said gruffly. She ran to the bedside.

"Tom—" She put her hands on his cheeks. "Never think I don't love you." She kissed him hungrily, drew him down on her. They made love slowly for a few moments, then became more intense. The act grew more fierce by stages. Sarah sweated, screwed her eyes closed, cried, and dug her fingers into his back. He went on, driving, relentless, pacing a steady rhythm. At last she shouted aloud, stared wildly, her legs pumping furiously, cried out again, and was quiet. He followed her in this surging, innocent act, sinking down into her hot, sweaty flesh, calling her name in an ecstasy of completion and . . . longing.

The barrier remained.

He looked at her, now lying by his side. "Sarah—"

"Sh!" She giggled a little, kissed the tip of his nose. She also must feel the barrier; there were tears in her eyes that proved it. "Tom, I love you."

It could be repeated forever, this invocation of a false magic. He wanted to ask, to demand she tell him, what was missing. It hurt like hell to think how very much of himself he had given, how very much of herself she had given—and this was what resulted. A good time in bed, a lot of fun together. Fine, but if they loved each other, why didn't either of them really believe it?

Tom was grateful when the buzzer rang. "We just made it," he said. "Here comes the food."

"We should have waited."

"We couldn't."

She laughed, got up, and threw on a robe. "Where's your wallet? I haven't got a penny."

"In my pants." He watched her rummage on the floor, take out the money. She got the food and laid it out on the table in their small dining room. He followed her in, still naked. They were hungry and they ate all of it even though she had as usual ordered too much.

Tom got cold and put on his robe. They sat a while after dinner trying without success to watch TV. "You're very quiet," he said at last. He was obscurely afraid, almost unwilling to break the silence. Yet he was more afraid to let it go on.

"I'm thinking about the lab," she said, drawing her knees up to her chin and clasping her hands around them. "Thinking about what in the name of God happened to that rhesus."

"Even now?"

She looked at him, her face wide with curiosity. "Why not now? We're finished making love, aren't we?"

"If you say so."

"Tom, I'm always ready for you. Don't you ever think I'm not."

"I know I'm more physical."

"Yes, but that doesn't mean I don't welcome your love. It's just that we were finished. Naturally, I want to talk about the lab. It's the rest of my life. And if Hutch—"

"I've got him beat. This thing is so big they're going to roll right over him. You'll get your appropriation."

"I hope."

"Trust me. I'll put it all back together again."

"I trust you." She slid along the couch, snuggled into the crook of his arm. "I trust you implicitly."

There was such sincerity in her tone that his fears were almost defeated. "You have every reason to," he said. "I'd rather die than let you down."

She kissed his hand. "That's what's so beautiful about you. That's really true, every word of it."

At that moment, at least, he did not doubt it. "It is true," he said.

They sat in silence, close together. The only sounds came from outside, sirens in the distance, an occasional horn, the sighing of the wind. "I think we've sort of been avoiding talking about the lab," Sarah said at last. "I know I have."

Tom knew exactly what she meant. The lab was a place of death. He nodded, remaining silent.

"I still can't believe it. As a phenomenon, I mean. What agent could have caused such profound decay? And it was so fast! It was a horrible thing to see."

"It's going to be a great breakthrough, Sarah. A great advance."

"Yes, but toward what? At the end—before he died, I mean—that ape was the most totally brutal thing I have ever seen. I saw the look on his face. I looked right into those eyes. Tom, the hatred I saw there wasn't an animal hatred—not a human hatred either. It was something alien, something beyond all that we know or have ever experienced. It was the hatred of the monster for the normal."

"Aren't you imagining just a little?"

She shook her head vehemently. "I turned that rhesus monkey into something savage. I'd hardly call that imagining."

It was three A.M. when the Sleep released Miriam. Once again she was in the attic room, its door locked. She opened her eyes. The room was thick with darkness. Absolute blackness, but not quite absolute silence. There was creaking movement all around her, whispering, shifting sound, the noise of ceaseless tiny motions. It was horrible to think of them in their chests, of how close to them she had Slept. She turned on the light.

Despite the bright light and the obvious tightness of the chests, claustrophobic fear overcame her. She clambered out of the tiny room, crossed the attic, and hurried downstairs. Now she paused to listen. Before she continued farther she had to locate John.

Miriam's hearing was acute. She had no doubt that he was gone. The firebox in the basement was not yet cool, and he was off hunting again. She glanced at her watch. It had been less than eighteen hours since he had taken the neighborhood child. Soon he would be as frail as paper, and easily confined in his chest.

She hoped that he would be more responsible on this hunt. The first rule of survival was to take only the unwanted. Otherwise the police just never let go. It was especially foolish to take young children of this era.

She went down to the library and opened the wall panel that gave her access to the security system. The perimeter alarms were on but the electrostatic shields were not. She activated them. If he slipped up and tried to come through the door they would stun him long enough for her to do what had to be done.

Now she pulled out some information about Excelsior Towers she had obtained from the renting agent. She looked carefully at the floor plan of an apartment identical to Sarah Roberts', memorizing the layout.

The next step in the infiltration of Sarah's life was to

touch her. The human sense of *touch* had atrophied. They called it extra-sensory perception, wrongly assuming it to be a means of reading thoughts. It was rather a means of sharing emotions. *Touch* could be a beautiful communion of hearts, or if the controlling partner wished it, the meeting of nightmares.

To awaken Sarah's sensitivity to *touch,* close physical contact, the kind that aroused passion, would be necessary. Miriam folded up the floor plan and mentally reviewed her intended access to the building itself. Except for the extraordinarily difficult few minutes in the apartment, the whole entry and exit would be routine.

Miriam walked to avoid the exposure that a taxi or bus would entail. At this hour the risk of accidents in the streets was low, the risk of being remembered by a driver high. As for muggers, she was indifferent to them. Occasionally, she had consumed them while they tried to rob her. Man was rarely a threat to her, at least not on a simple physical level.

Dawn would come in two hours and fourteen minutes, first light about twenty minutes earlier. She walked briskly, keeping to a schedule that would get her back home just before sunrise. Her black hat and raincoat gleamed with mist, her boots splashed in the dark puddles. The walk would take half an hour. Fifteen minutes would be spent getting into the building. She would have another fifteen minutes in the apartment itself. It was going to be just a little close; she might have some light on the way back. She went under the Queensborough Bridge, leaving Sutton Place and going north on York Avenue. The sound of a lone truck crossing the bridge echoed in the street. The blocks swept past; she kept up a quick pace. Once a figure appeared far ahead, but aside from him the street remained empty. She passed dark stores, locked doorways, parked cars. Overhead the moon had given way to heavy clouds. Although the air was motionless, the clouds raced northward, their bottoms sweeping the pinnacles of the city. Another storm was coming, this one from the south.

It was easy to break into these "secure" luxury buildings, and she quickly established a good method of penetrating this one. There was a maintenance door at the end of a narrow alley. It was locked, of course, but Miriam would have no trouble with the familiar Loktite spring-loaded bolt.

She slipped into the pool of light before the door, working swiftly until she heard the click of the lock. She entered the building's machine room. It was dim, almost dark. Holding her hands out at eye level to ward off low-hanging pipes, she moved carefully until she was across the room, then let herself into the basement proper. Here the light was bright and harsh. She climbed the stairs for a few floors—calling an elevator to a basement at this hour would certainly alert building security. She felt the fourth floor was high enough not to cause suspicion and took an elevator from there.

When she got to Sarah's floor she opened the door to the fire stairs so that there wouldn't be a click if she had to use it. The hallway was silent. Her feet whispered on the brown carpet, her shadow preceded and then followed her as she passed under the lights.

She leaned close to the door of the apartment and took out her cylinder pick, a three-inch length of Number Two piano wire. With her eyes closed she worked the wire into the lock, lifting the tamper shields and rolling the cylinders. A lock such as this was somewhat more delicate than the crude mechanism on the back door. She could picture the structure of any model of any brand of lock used in the United States. Some of them might slow her down and a few would even stop her. But most yielded soon enough, as this one did.

Next, she slipped a credit card into the crack between the door and the jamb and used it to press back the tongue of the lock. The door swung partway open and she replaced the credit card with duct tape. Now for the night latch. Another length of piano wire, this the heavier Number Six, was used to work around the end of the latch and move it along its track. As it slid she pulled the door closed. After a moment there was another click and a rattle. The night latch had fallen out.

At once she got out of the hall, remembering to remove the duct tape so that nobody passing would see the edge of it. She followed her long-established procedure on entering an occupied dwelling. First, she shut her eyes tight and listened. She heard breathing off to the left. That would be Sarah and Tom in the bedroom, and in stage three sleep judging from the rhythm of their breath. Sarah's own book had taught her that. Next, she looked around. In the time her eyes had been closed they had adjusted to the darkness. She made a note of a chair in the way of a fast escape via the living room, noted the lab coat on the hall floor. This was a simple one-bedroom apartment with a separate dining room. Sarah and Tom were alone in it, as she had already ascertained they would be.

She carried out the last test of her surroundings: smell. She inhaled deeply, identifying the faint odors of Chinese food and wine and sweaty bodies. They had banqueted and made love.

She moved toward the bedroom, pausing every few steps. Absolute care was necessary. Mistakes could not be covered up by killing the victims of this intrusion. She knew a good deal about Sarah Roberts, right down to her height and body weight. But there had been no time to study her personal habits. About Tom Haver she was even more vague. Hopefully, she had enough information to serve her purposes. He was not useful to her because he lacked the deep bloody instincts of the true predator, but he would have to be dealt with. Like many of his nature, he covered his inner softness with a cloak of aggressive bluff. As she reached the bedroom door she could smell the powerful musks of human sex. Their lovemaking had been intense, full of passion.

She cursed it. Sarah was needed for other loves; the presence of Haver was a distinct inconvenience.

Miriam went to the bed, sat down beside it, and contemplated her victim. She was like a ripe little apple, this one. Very carefully, Miriam slipped back the bedclothes and revealed the woman's neatly curved body. She longed to draw the life out of it but rather she hovered close, inhaling its sharp, humid aroma, listening to its little sounds: the breath soughing in and out, the heart beating slowly, the slight shifting of the torso on the sheets. Beside Sarah, Tom Haver stirred, but it meant nothing. His sleep remained undisturbed.

To begin the *touch* that would enter Sarah's dreams, she took her hand, which dangled off the edge of the bed, and ran her lips across the back of it, kissing lightly, brushing it with her tongue. Sarah inhaled a long breath. Miriam stopped a while, then leaned close to Sarah and breathed her breath, smelling its sharp warmth, mingling it with her own. Sarah's head moved and she moaned. Her right breast was exposed and Miriam held it briefly in her hand, then slid her palm back and forth across the nipple until it became erect. She took the nipple between two of her long fingernails and squeezed until Sarah tossed her head. The girl's mouth hung slackly opened. Miriam covered it with her own, pressing her tongue against Sarah's with the utmost care. She remained like that for fully half a minute, feeling the faint movements of Sarah's tongue that indicated her unconscious excitement. She drew back and listened once again. Tom was still in stage three sleep. Sarah was nearly awake, making little noises as she dreamed. Miriam now felt powerfully drawn to her, could almost see her glowing dreams in her own mind's eye.

Soon Sarah's sleep deepened again. Slowly, gently, Miriam slipped her hands between Sarah's thighs and parted her legs. Moving quickly, ready for an immediate departure, she bent her head and kissed the hot, odorous flesh, pressing her tongue once hard where

Sarah would feel the most intense pleasure. Sarah arched her back and cried out, and at once Miriam retreated to the living room.

Her heart was pounding. She glanced quickly toward the front door. In a few moments, after they settled down, she could escape. But not now. The least sound would alert them both.

"Tom? Oh . . ."

"Yeah?"

"Oh, I love you—"

"*Mmm.*"

There was a creak, the sound of one of them shifting position. Miriam's mind now *touched* Sarah's, sensitive to the recent contact of their bodies. She could feel the blazing intensity of the passion she had awakened in her and could also feel the confused question that surrounded it.

"Tom? Are you awake?"

"If you say so."

At that moment a shaft of light burst across the room, hitting Miriam in the face like a blow. Instantly she stepped into shadow. The little fool had turned on her bedside lamp. She could have slapped her.

"I feel odd. I had a funny dream."

"It's four A.M."

"I feel kind of sick."

Sarah got up and came down the hall, throwing another light on in the bathroom. She was a handsome creature naked. Miriam liked her a good deal more than she had thought she would. There was a certain quality about her—an obvious hunger for pleasure that Miriam found very appealing. She felt more comfortable around people who could not control their lusts, because they could most easily be brought within her power.

She watched Sarah sitting on the toilet, her chin cradled in her hands, staring with a frown at the wall before her. In the fluorescent light Miriam could clearly see the blush of excitement in her face.

After a moment Sarah spread her legs and laid her hand over her vagina. Sensuously, rubbing her legs back and forth, moving one hand over her vagina and with the other stroking her breasts, she masturbated.

From the darkness six feet away Miriam *touched* and *touched*, forcing images of soft female flesh, smooth flesh, into Sarah's mind, making her writhe with longing even as she satisfied herself. At the end Sarah threw back her head and whispered, "Kiss me." Then, hunched, her robe clutched at her neck, she hurried back to bed with Tom.

So that was what lay beneath the brilliance and the independence. Hunger, raw and unfulfilled, for a truly passionate lover. Miriam was proud of herself. This had been a most successful beginning. Now that her inner self had been aroused, Sarah's hunger would grow and expand, as beautiful in her heart as a flower, as relentless as a cancer, until her present life would seem like a desert.

Then Miriam would come to her and Sarah would feel as they always felt, that she had met the most wonderful, the best friend of her life. John had said it many long years ago, standing in the abandoned ballroom at his ancestral mansion, naked amid the rotting silks, shivering as the evening wind came down the moor and through the gaping windows: "Miriam, you make me feel as if I've come home."

Sarah awoke just before the alarm buzzed. Knowing Tom as she did, she let it ring. He fortified his head with pillows. Throwing the covers off them both, she got up and began to get dressed, leaving him to cope with the clock.

After about thirty seconds he groped out and turned it off, then sat up in bed. He emitted a groan, complex with woes. They had had wine with the spicy Chinese food and then spent a restless night.

More or less dressed, Sarah went to the kitchen and put on some coffee. She stood amid the details of their

world: hissing old percolator with charred handle,
Chinese food cartons tumbled in the sink, the refrigera-
tor humming, the wind rattling the kitchen window.
Her mind slipped suddenly to a chilling memory, the
intense residue of a dream.

It was disquieting to have dreamed with such lust of a
woman. All that remained was an image of bright flesh,
sultry eyes and wet lips, and the sweet smell of her.
Sarah shuddered. She poured an experimental half-cup
of coffee. Still weak, but she wasn't willing to wait. Cup
in hand, she went back to the bedroom to busy herself
with preparations for the day. At least the dream had
given her an urge to plunge with even more than usual
energy into her work, if only to forget the damn thing.

"Hurry up, Doctor," she yelled at the closed bathroom door.

"I need a cigar," he said coming out.

"So eat one."

He took her in his arms. She was not sure of him; his
eyes seemed angry and loving at the same time. With
elaborate nonchalance she drew away from him, went
to brush her hair and put on some makeup.

"I really would like a cigar."

"You're on your way to a neoplasm of the mouth.
Anyway, a cigar will make you sick on four hours of
sleep."

"I love you, damn you."

He would say it at such a moment, as a means of
walling off the anger beneath the banter. Love seemed
to Sarah more and more an urge to containment, a
hunger to fill oneself with another. As she pulled her
brush through her hair she wondered if there could
ever be anything more than the desire to fill the
hollowness inside. She winced; she had brushed too
hard, pulled out some hair. "I love you too," she said.
Her voice was quick with duty. She remembered how
she had recited in school the responses to prayers in
which she had no faith. He came, trying to seem gently
forceful, sexy. He appeared behind her in the mirror,

lifted her hair, and kissed the back of her neck. How wooden could a man get? He needed her, though, which was fascinating. They kissed, his lips crushing hers. She felt deep twinges of response, the secret pleasure of the thief. He was trembling, his hands feverishly caressing her back. Then he lifted her off the floor and she felt a wild thrill of helplessness, a powerful urgency to let someone do his will with her. Someone . . . beautiful.

By abandoning herself to him she closed herself off. He carried her, as easily as he might a child, to their rumpled bed. When he put her down she slipped dutifully out of her clothes. "I'll be quick," he said with the assurance of the beloved.

As they swung together in their groaning bed she allowed her mind to drift, and it inevitably drifted to that glowing dream-body. When her imagination was at last possessed by those smooth and exotic images, when she could taste the taste of that dream-skin and smell the dream-being's musty secrets, she experienced a moment of pleasure, rare and stunning. He kissed her afterward, assuming that her wide look of surprise belonged to him.

Tom's heart continued to swell with love as they dressed and went to the kitchen. It seemed so simple and so right. Last night and now this morning had banished all his doubts and angers; he was in a kind of ecstasy. If *she* needed, then *he* would offer. He felt that they belonged to each other. It was incredibly good to think, 'I belong to her.' He watched her pour him coffee, butter some toast for him. He almost hoped that he would have to give everything up for her. The nobility of it fascinated him. An awesome proof of love. This thought led him to the problems he was going to face at the clinic. It was time to discuss the board meeting. Almost past time, as a matter of fact. "It occurs to me," he said, "that you ought to give me something to work with at the meeting. Some kind of definite statement about what you think happened to Methuselah."

"You don't need it. Just show them the tape."

"Give me something—even the raw computer print-outs. Show them you're on to something."

"You know what's available."

"Sarah, your work is precious. Let's not allow any chance of failure. None."

"In other words, you're getting cold feet. If the board turns you down, if it doesn't reverse Hutch, you can't bear the humiliation. You'd have to resign and you're afraid. I thought you were so sure you'd win."

"I'm doing this for you," he said miserably. He couldn't explain it better than that.

"Finish your toast, we've gotta get moving. Who knows, maybe a miracle occurred and the statistics prove something. Best thing to do is get down to the lab and find out."

The tonelessness in her voice was almost cruel. She was still punishing him for his ambition. The growth of love he had felt apparently meant little to her. She didn't really understand the situation. Perhaps it was beyond her understanding. Her every gesture, every look and movement, radiated betrayal. The jeopardy that he had accepted in going over Hutch's head to the board was a matter of indifference to her.

He ran his hand along the table, closed it into a fist. "I should have squeezed Hutch out a long time ago. Before I met you."

She nodded, barely glancing at him. "You've got to be careful, darling." There was something obviously false in her tone. He was seized with a desire to explain.

"If Hutch wins, I'm out. I don't see any other alternative."

"You wouldn't." She pecked him on the cheek, smiling too brilliantly. It seemed at least possible that she was not indifferent to his sacrifice at all, but rather so guilty about it that she couldn't bear to acknowledge it. Perhaps he was fooling himself, but it felt better to believe this than the other, cold thing.

"Let's get going," he said. "We've got a lot to do." An image from the past floated into his mind: school play, eighth-grade year. Before them all he had forgotten his lines. He remembered his silence, and the way the faces of his jealous and resentful audience lit up when it was realized that the faculty's darling was failing, and the roar of delighted laughter when his silence did not end.

Miriam's visit to Sarah Roberts had worked well. A vestige of what Sarah had experienced remained in Miriam's own heart. It had been a strong *touch*. The next phase of the plan was very much more problematic.

She would have to "meet" Sarah, and the only fast way she could do it would be to become a patient at the Sleep Research Clinic. It would be the most dangerous thing she had done in a very long time. For the first time in history human scientists were going to get a chance to study a member of her species. They didn't exist in human scientific literature, only in mythology. What would the scientists do when they tried to take the measure of her mystery?

Most of all, she dreaded captivity.

She was terrified by bars, such as the ones that surrounded Sarah's ape, the one that had *touched* so powerfully as it died.

Miriam did not like the feeling of being menaced by humankind. And the thought of being studied by them was even more disquieting. They might consider her to be without human rights and cage her just like an ape.

The risks were frightening.

But Sarah could solve the problem of transformation, could make it permanent. That made all the risks seem trivial. If Miriam could only have known what was going to happen to John, she would have captured the doctor earlier. There might have been some small chance. . . .

At the thought, her mood shifted to gray sorrow. But she refused to live in grief. Her life must be rebuilt. She would comfort John and protect him if she could, but she would not obsess herself with his suffering. Life was full of tragedies. You buried the dead.

The *touch* that had been broadcast through the vast emotional babble of the city by Sarah's experimental ape was like a beacon to Miriam. It told her how very close Sarah had come to inducing transformation, and therefore to understanding it.

Miriam's next move had been carefully planned. As soon as she successfully *touched* Sarah she went home and made an appointment for an interview at the Sleep Research Clinic. Now that Miriam had hidden a part of herself in Sarah's heart the next step was to engage her mind.

A part of Miriam might have enjoyed the danger of all this, just as she might have enjoyed fox hunting with John. There was something exhilarating about jeopardy. Safe air was stale, but dangerous air was silver clear. Love your enemy, her father used to say, for without him you would never taste the flavor of victory.

Yes, the noble sentiment of the past.

Forget the past. Go upstairs, change clothes; you'll be late for your ten o'clock appointment. She had made it of necessity at the last minute. "We'll fit you in, but please expect a delay."

She wore her blue silk Lanvin suit for the occasion. As she dressed she reviewed all she had rehearsed for the sleep clinic interview. She would enter as a patient suffering from night terrors of adulthood. Before branching off into gerontology, Sarah had specialized in this rare disease. Even yet she was the clinic's only expert. The three or four cases they got in a year didn't justify a full-time staff position. Sarah would certainly be called in.

Sarah. Miriam thought of her, huddled in her robe,

shaking with passion that she could not possibly have understood. It was going to be most interesting to contend with somebody as intelligent and spirited as Sarah.

Miriam did not scorn human intellectual achievement. She had developed a keen interest in science. She had identified her own animal ancestors. She belonged to mankind and mankind to her, just as the saber-toothed tiger and the buffalo had once belonged to each other.

She put the finishing touches on her outfit. It would do: she looked beautiful, just a bit tired, eyes rather sad.

Eyes rather sad.

Time was passing, time could not be stopped. If only . . . but it was no use thinking about it. John was a dead man. "Dead." What mockery there was in that word.

The doorbell rang. Miriam looked through the peephole, observed a man in uniform. Her chauffeur, appearing at nine thirty-five as requested. When she had to do any driving in the city she used a limousine. Her own car would be an inconvenience and taxis were too unsafe; she used them only when necessary.

As she walked out the front door, she noted with approval that the car provided was a dark-blue Oldsmobile. It was foolishly risky to use the more pretentious cars; they only attracted unwelcome attention. The driver, who was young, clear-eyed and sober, opened the car door for her. She fastened the seatbelt and settled back, locking her door but leaving her hand near the catch in case it was necessary to exit quickly. Her analysis of automotive design led her to conclude that this make was safer than most, and less prone to explode if hit from the rear. The driver started the engine. She sat well back, relaxed and yet attentive, ready if her luck ran out and there was an accident. Her ride was so pleasant that she found herself envious of those who could afford such transportation full time.

The medical center was swarming with people. Miriam rode to the twelfth floor in a jammed elevator, trying not to inhale their scent. Unfortunately, the waiting room of the Sleep Research Center was also crowded. The smell and feel of so much human flesh was unnerving.

Nevertheless, she waited with the others, thumbing through a well-worn copy of *Book Digest*. Ten became eleven, then eleven-thirty.

"Blaylock," intoned the receptionist, at last. "Desk three, please." This was the only facility of its kind in the city. The crowding and impersonality of it indicated that there ought to be more. Miriam was interviewed by a pleasant young man in shirtsleeves who took her name and asked her to describe her problem.

She knew what the effect would be when she mentioned the intensity of her "nightmares." He looked at her with renewed interest. Most of their cases must be common insomnia, cured by teaching the patient how to cope with stress.

Medicine knows night terrors of adulthood as one of mankind's most frightening problems. Miriam could have quoted Sarah Roberts: "These terrors arise from the primordial depths and induce in the sufferer perhaps the most intense fear that a human being can know. In quality and intensity they are to nightmares as a typhoon might be to a spring shower."

"How often have you been having these . . . troubles, Mrs. Blaylock?" The interviewer's voice was calm but his eyes regarded her sharply.

"All my life." How pitiful that every word was true. The vividness of the experiences she had during Sleep were probably even worse than night terrors. But she had long ago learned to endure them. They went with Sleep and therefore must cleanse the soul.

"When was the last one?"

"Last night." She watched his face flicker at that. This was working well. Mrs. Night Terrors Blaylock was going to become a priority case, she suspected.

Now his voice dropped and he leaned closer to her. "Can you describe it?"

"The ocean was chasing me." It had just popped into her head, but she thought it a lovely night terror for the spur of the moment. Much nicer than the one she had planned, about hands choking her.

"The ocean?"

"Huge, towering black waves that stretch up forever. Roaring and crashing over me and I'm in the sand, I'm running, I can hear it over my shoulder, it comes right up the dunes, nothing's going to stop it. You can see a shark cruising in the waves. Everything smells horrible, like it had all gone rotten." Gooseflesh had broken out all over her body as she talked. Her hands were grasping the edge of the table. She was surprised at the intensity of her feeling. It ceased to be an act. Had she ever experienced such a dream? Perhaps it was *behind* the dreams she remembered, perhaps there was something in her, coiled like a snake, spitting out recollections so monstrous that her mind dared not touch them directly.

The worst of it was something she didn't tell the shiny young doctor: she was indeed the woman running from the ocean. But she was also the shark.

5

JOHN WAS RUNNING through the early morning, running like a slowed-down movie past the blooming flowers, the tulip trees with their buds, and the new-sprouted grass of Central Park. His hunger made him feel as if a living thing were moving in his stomach. His eyes bulged, his mouth opened wide as he ran. He must be hideous in his flapping raincoat and dirty blue suit, with the fingernails of a demon and the face of a corpse. People shrank from him, children shouted alarm. He felt like a hermit who had been knocked out of his hiding place by a wrecker's ball.

His heart skipped and thuttered. Pain shot down his shoulder. He staggered. Then the beat started again: food, foodfood, food, FOODFOODFOOD! He coughed, running along the Bridle Path, lurching past Cleopatra's Needle, finally plunging into the shrubbery beside the path.

He could go no farther, his breath was fire, his heartbeat a confused rattle. This place was redolent of hot, strong flesh. Every few minutes another jogger

117

passed. He listened to one, a big man breathing easily.
Too strong. Then another—lighter but still not tired
enough. His victim would have to be practically exhausted, just at the end of a long hard run. Yesterday
little Alice had nearly gotten the better of him. Today
he was even weaker. In his extremity he began to
recollect an almost forgotten time of his life, which he
now saw as the best time—before he met Miriam. He
remembered the grassy slope at Hadley where he and
Priscilla lay intoxicated with the smell of the heather on
windy spring days. The clouds rolled madly down the
sky. God, what wonderful times! He was ceasing to
love the drama and speed of this age, and to cherish the
quieter time before. Even old Hadley was gone now,
the ruined house rebuilt and turned into an orphanage
by the strange populist state that had followed the
Empire.

Without warning, a cough burst out of him. He found
himself pitching backward, almost losing consciousness. Above him he saw the sky through a tulip tree.
And the clouds in it were the same! The same as that
day at Hadley! "Oh, Johnny, my pladies awa'," Priscilla had cried, "awa' with the win'!" And there
bouncing across the heather went her fluffy plaid skirt.
How he had run! Run in the wind and the kind land,
run for that plaid with all the might of his young years.

Another cough, not his own. He struggled up, heard
it again. Thud-thud on the gravel, thud-thud, thud-
thud. Here came a girl who had put on a little extra
during the winter, jiggling along in a purple sweat suit,
gasping like a tophorse at a coach stop.

He connected with her right side as she jogged past.
She let out a surprisingly shrill scream for one so heavy.

A pack of crows took flight, their voices echoing in
the sky. The wind tossed the trees and the clouds
scudded past. John grabbed her hair and pulled her
head back, jammed his scalpel in until he felt the "pop"
as it penetrated the pectoral muscle. He fell on her,
clasping his hands behind her neck, adhering to her

with desperate energy. She staggered and flounced and shrieked for help. Pain flashed through his joints as she struggled, but he had a good hold. He placed his mouth over the wound and sucked with every last whisper of energy. Slowly the life oozed into him. As her movements weakened, his became stronger and more assured. She grew lighter and he expanded in size, filling his slack clothes, gaining pinkness in his cheeks and sharpness in his eyes. Her screaming lowered to a hoarse rumble, then a growl, finally a rasp across a dry and withering tongue, past lips become strips of leather. The skin sank to the bones and the lips cracked away from the teeth. After a moment the girl's jaw snapped open, her gums contracting. Her hands had become black claws, the flesh tight and splitting on the bones. The eyeballs sank into their sockets, collapsing in on themselves.

John jumped away from her. Stiff and light, she toppled to the ground like a papier-mâché toy. He was bloated and flushed, his eyes ablaze. He pounded his temples in an ecstasy of relief. Snarling with his victory, he snatched the remnant up and threw it high into a tree where it caught and fluttered in the wind.

He gnashed his teeth, he was far from satiated. Without the Sleep, his body demanded ever more energy. The longer he remained awake the more he needed.

"I'll never need more than I can get," he said aloud, testing to see if the softness of youth had returned to his voice.

What a delightful surprise *that* was! He hadn't sounded like that in days. "O mistress mine," he sang, listening to the sweet smooth tones. "O mistress mine, where are you roaming? O stay and hear, your true love's coming!" And then he laughed, rich and deep and full, and ran with a firm step down the path after stronger, better, even more enriching prey.

Behind him shouts were rising, feet thundering past Cleopatra's Needle. (Miriam always laughed to see that thing here, occupying such a place of honor. She said that the Egyptians had considered it the worst obelisk in Heliopolis.) Young men were bearing down on him. On the roadway to his right a scooter cop stopped and got off his machine, looking with a frown in the direction of the shouts. He began to trot up a low hill to the scene of the crime. John moved toward him, down the same hill.

With the strength he had gained it was just possible to take the strapping young policeman. As they were passing each other he slammed his fist into the side of the man's head, sending him reeling, his cigarette flying from his mouth and his cap sailing into a bed of begonias. He made quick work of the struggling, cursing man. In another twenty seconds he was fitting the remnant back onto the scooter. The devil take caution, let them figure this one out. He could see the headlines: COP TURNS TO MUMMY; RADIUM DIAL WATCH TO BLAME?

Now he felt really wonderful. He might as well be flying above the roadway, above the lawns, above the trees—flying and free.

Others only thought they were alive. They never knew *this!* His heart was beating perfectly. If he looked at a building he could hear the sounds behind the windows. People talking, TVs going, vacuum cleaners roaring. And he could hear the clouds like a great song, not meant for the ears of man.

Sirens were rising to the north and the south. A patrol car came blazing up the roadway.

John spent the rest of the morning in the Metropolitan Museum, lingering for hours in the costume exhibit, looking at the bustled dresses and frock coats, remembering his own time, so utterly lost and far away.

It was a relief when the interview was completed. Miriam was beginning to feel a need for Sleep. She returned to the house in her rented limousine. A test—called a polysomnogram—was scheduled for tonight. And Sarah Roberts would surely be there. *Must* be there. Night terrors indeed. If they knew the real depths of fear they would not be able to live. Mankind was in the bland middle of the emotional spectrum. Miriam lived at the extremes.

She was let out of the car. "I'll need you again at six-thirty," she said as she went up the front steps. The Sleep was coming upon her, right on schedule. She heard a faint tinkling from inside the house. The telephone. She fumbled with her keys and rushed in. A bad moment to take a call. Her time awake was now limited.

"Miriam?"

"Yes. Who is this?"

"Bob."

For a moment she was blank. Then it came back. They hadn't seen the Cavenders for months. "Oh, hi! It's been a long time. I hardly recognized you."

"Miriam, we've lost Alice."

She doubled up as if she had been hit in the stomach. Then she straightened and took a deep breath. "How long?"

"Since yesterday when she left for your place."

"She never came here, so far as I know."

"Amy saw her go in."

"She came in here?" Miriam's mind turned to John, to the—no. No matter what state he was in, he would never do that.

"She usually comes home for lunch after she sees you. Yesterday she didn't."

A trembling shock coursed through her. "She's not here."

Not in the hallway, not in the music room. Oh, don't let it be, not in the furnace.

Don't hurt me this much, John, please!

"I know that. I just wanted you to be on the alert." He paused. There were a series of stifled grunts, the sobs of a man who doesn't know how to cry. "On the alert," he said again. "I'll call you with any news." The line clicked, the cutting of the wire of life. The phone slipped from Miriam's hand, banged on the oak floor. She closed her eyes. Snarling pain gripped her temples. Ice-cold air seemed to enclose her. She craned her neck like a woman seeking to rise from the bottom of the sea.

She ran her hands along the fabric of her suit, bowed her head. When her clock tolled one, she looked, startled, at its ancient face.

Impulses raced through her mind: kill John, kill herself. She rejected them both as beneath her. He was helpless in his actions, driven by forces beyond his control. And she had no intention of voluntarily giving up life.

Bit by bit she regained her composure. There came into her heart a new feeling toward John. His suffering mattered less to her, his potential for destruction more.

How dare he take Alice. She belonged to Miriam, not to him. Rage blazed up in her. It was lucky for him that he was not home. At this moment she would have faced knives, guns, tearing claws to get at him.

Yet he had given her all of himself that he could give. For love of her he was paying an exorbitant price. He was losing much more than life, facing an end more terrible than even the worst death. She could not let herself hate the damnable creature.

She was alone again.

In all the world there was not one friendly soul, not one being with whom she could share anything.

She ran into the library, the place where she habitually did her planning and thinking. "ALICE!" With a moan she yanked the heavy drapes closed and sank into her desk chair. The only sound in the room was the steady tinkle of the old Roman water clock.

Her whole future had been planted in Alice. The possibility of losing the girl had simply never occurred to her. Oh, what plans she had made!

She had always loved her life with joyous intensity. Over the years she had ruthlessly blotted out every memory of her family, had shaken off all the tragedies, and pressed ahead. She had seen humanity rising out of the muck, had learned to respect it as the rest of her species never could, had come to anticipate the future with zest, especially now that overtones of barbarism were re-entering human culture.

In one mad instant John had taken the future away.

Tears she would not allow, even for an extinguished love. She and Alice were made to be together. And now instead there was this pit. A black pit. The room around her was cold. The paneling, grown rich with years, frowned ominously, making the dark even blacker.

She opened the curtains. It was such a bright day, the storms of dawn blown on their way. Her petunias were thriving, choking the window box with at least a hundred blossoms.

She found that she could not bear to look at the street, it could not seem more empty. She shook herself—the Sleep demanded her.

She didn't want it now, not after this. It doomed her to terrible dreams, she was sure of it. How could she bear this! She groaned and ran out of the room. Her body was slowing down, her eyes growing heavy. Where could she go? Not the attic, not enough time to get all the way to the top of the house.

The floor waved beneath her feet. She couldn't Sleep here! But it was intractable, nothing would stop her. In moments she wouldn't be able to lift her arms. She thought of the basement. It might still be possible to make it down.

With long, shaking steps she went to the door. There was a place, uncomfortable but safe, that John had hopefully forgotten that led to the secret tunnel they had built to the East River. Years ago it had been destroyed by the FDR Drive but the basement entrance and the section under the garden still remained. She hoped she could find the right stone in the basement floor.

By the time she got there the world around her had receded as if to the end of a long corridor. She knew that she was still moving but she was absolutely out of contact with her body. Her hands felt the slate floor of the basement, pushing for the slight looseness that would tell her she had found the place.

Looseness—somewhere . . . she felt something hard and cold hit her. Hard and cold and wet . . . she had fallen to the floor. Sleep came, and dream . . .

The lamp was bobbing, flashing in her eyes with the roll of the ship. As it creaked, water spurted in between the planks. "Father?" The lamp shook wildly and then fell to the floor, plunging the little cabin into green half-darkness. What was happening? When she had gone to bed the sky had been clear, the wind just strong enough to snap the sail.

What was that horrible shrieking?

She got up and wrapped a cloak around her silk tunic. "Fa-a-ther!" The ship began shaking from side to side as if it were being worried by a sea monster. Miriam staggered to the cabin door, pushed it open.

Wake up! You're in danger!

The door . . . was so hard, so hard—but she pushed it open and struggled out into the raging green hell of the storm.

The voice of the wind mixed with the deep thunder of the waves. Perhaps twenty feet overhead great clouds seethed. There was no mast, no sail, only a deck strewn with tangles of rigging and bits of red sailcloth. Sailors, naked, lashed together, staggered here and there on what task she did not know. "FAAATHER!"

Powerful arms grabbed her from behind. He took her to his bosom, pressed his mouth against her ear. "This ship is doomed," he said, "we've got to save ourselves, my daughter."

"The others—"

"The other ships made landfall in Crete. A great disaster has occurred. I did not foresee it. An island has exploded. I think it must have been Thera. You must go to Rome now, leave the east alone. Greece will be in ruins—"

"Father, please help me, save me!" She clung to him with her legs and arms and sobbed into the wrenching wind.

His head turned. "It's coming," he said. She felt it rather than heard it, a deep pulsing throb like the heart of a giant. At first there was nothing to see in the black mist, then, far up in the sky, a white line appeared. Her father's arms clutched her until she could hardly breathe. His face terrified her, it was wretched with anger, his lips twisted into a grimace, his eyes glaring horribly.

"Father, is that a *wave?*"

He only clutched her more tightly.

The ship began to rise, its prow lifting higher and higher. There commenced a great fusillade of explosions as the hemp lashings that held it together snapped and the boards sprung straight. The hiss of water rose from the hold, and with it the hideous screaming of the oar-slaves. Sailors threw themselves to the deck. Behind them, on the low forecastle, the captain was staggering about trying to organize another sacrifice to Nereus, god of storms.

The ship rose higher. It felt as if it had taken wing. Behind them the surface of the sea shook and boiled. Before them the great black leviathan bore on.

"We must jump! We'll have to swim."

He dragged her to the side. She had swum only in the Nile, never in an ocean. And this—it would swallow them!

Her father ignored her frantic protests.

John will come! Wake up!

The dream held her as surely as if she were bound to a rack.

The bubbling, inky water closed over their heads. Even beneath it there were noises, a deep boo-o-om bo-o-om. Was there really a sea god down there bellowing his anger?

Her head popped to the surface. She felt her father's arms come around her again. Not ten feet away the ship slowly upended and fell backward with a tremendous explosion of foam. It wallowed, its black bottom exposed briefly to the air, and was gone.

They were swimming on the side of an enormous wall of water. And they were being swept higher. The white line at the top had grown to a maelstrom of roaring breakers.

They came rapidly closer. In them she could see fish and branches of trees and bits of wood. Her legs drove like pistons but the current grabbed at her, pulling her down and down. Her head was in a vise, her hands grasping water. She was ripped from her father's arms. It got cold and dark. Great creatures were moving in the deep, their cold flesh sliding against her. Her arms and legs thrashed but still the powerful flow dragged her down. She was being crushed, like the death of stones inflicted on her kind by the Phoenicians.

Something had grabbed her hair. It yanked her so hard she saw flashes. The current lost its hold on her. Even though she knew she was rising—it was getting warmer and lighter—her mouth was going to open in a moment and she was going to breathe water. She would die.

She clamped her jaws shut, finally clapped her hands over her mouth and nose. Perhaps the sea-thing that was dragging her upward would break the surface.

And then she was tumbling in the white water, gasping gulps of wet air, swimming like a demon. She heard her father's own ragged breath in her ear.

He was the thing that had saved her.

Then she was through the breakers. Before her was a limitless plain of water, rolling gently. She understood that she was now on the back of the enormous wave that had destroyed the ship. On the horizon there stood a vast black pillar of cloud full of red cracks. Enormous tendrils of lightning coursed ceaselessly through it. It grew steadily, a great dark finger poking into the sky.

"Father," she gasped, trying to point.

She swam in a circle.

The empty waters did not look back.

"Father! Father!"

Please, gods, please, we need him. We have a whole family! Please, gods, we cannot survive without him.

You cannot kill him!

She pounded with her legs and slapped the water with her hands and spun around and around. She screamed for him.

A shadow rolled in a low wave not far away. She dove after the snatch of blue, beside herself with terror and grief.

Then she saw it, the vision that would never leave her again: his face, mouth distended, eyes bulging, disappearing into the abyss.

"Please! Ple-e-ase!"

A wind like a Titan's breath burst from heaven and the waves came on.

The salt water made her throw up again and again. Her father, her beautiful father—the family's wisdom and strength—was dying. She dove beneath the waves seeking him as he had sought her, swam deeper and deeper until she felt that ice-cold current—into which *he* had plunged without regard for his own life, to save his daughter.

She was the oldest, the others needed her now. Alone in Crete, their Akkadian barely passable, they would certainly be destroyed. Her life was precious. She must choose to preserve it. Her father would certainly have demanded it. As hard as it was she closed her mind to him.

She turned toward the dim gray light of the surface and swam. Once there she began to plan her own salvation. The very morning they left she had taken food and Sleep, so she knew that she could go on for at least three or four days.

She opened her eyes in a chilly dungeon smelling of damp stone. Her mouth tasted awful, she had vomited in her Sleep.

The dream had left her sullen with grief, remembering her father's face in the waves. "I could have saved him," she said into the darkness.

"But it's too late now, isn't it?" screeched an answering voice.

John!

Something gleamed before her eyes, then she felt the cool pressure of a blade against her throat.

"I've been waiting for you, my dear. I wanted you to be awake for this."

Tom glanced at the admission recommendation on top of the pile. Dr. Edwards had quite properly marked it for special handling. Procedure required Tom to initial any priority admissions. The clinic had a waiting list three months long.

He called Sarah. "How would you like a case? There's a lady with night terrors of adulthood waiting for admission."

"Are you nuts?" she roared into the phone.

"Just do an evaluation and workup. It'll take a couple of hours. Think how it'll look with the board. Brilliant researcher, and so dedicated she keeps her finger in the clinical pie as well. That's heroine stuff."

"Oh, for God's sake!"

"If you will be true to this your oath, may prosperity and good repute—"

"Hippocrates doesn't enter into this. Night terrors, you say?"

"That's what I like about you. You're so damn curious. I like that in a scientist."

There was a moment's silence. "When's she due to start?"

"Seven-thirty tonight. She's on priority."

"I should hope so."

They rang off. Tom had almost laughed aloud. Sarah

was so predictable. Her willingness to pitch in tonight was typical. Complaining and protesting all the way, she went through life doing the work of three people. It would be good for her to have contact with a patient again—a real, hurting human being. She needed the perspective.

He snorted at that thought. How the hell did he know what Sarah needed? She was so complex and mercurial, with a dark depth to match every bright height. All he could really do was offer her what he thought might be appropriate. But to assume that he could ever really know her heart, even as her lover, would be very foolish.

It took him another hour to go through all the admission recommendations, initialing some, sending others back for follow-up evaluations, noting a few of special interest for routing to Hutch. But not the Blaylock case, not that one. He had a strong feeling that it would be useful to Sarah. In any case, it was hers by rights. She had written brilliantly on night terrors of adulthood and had achieved a couple of cures that lasted beyond the imposition of sedatives and tranquilizers. The case belonged to her. There was no sense in letting Hutch in on it, he would just assign it to somebody else to prevent her getting points with the board.

When Sarah appeared at seven her mood had lifted considerably. She came around his desk and kissed him on the forehead. "Methuselah's beta-prodorphin levels were dropping like crazy at the end," she said in a voice rich with excitement. "We are on our way."

He gave her a hard kiss. It felt good to do it, all through his body. "You're wonderful," he said.

"I might have that breakthrough you've been looking for," she said, obviously not even aware of the kiss. "I think we just might be able to establish a viable level of control over beta-prodorphin production. We won't be able to stop the aging process, but it'll give us the ability to slow it down, or even turn it back."

He looked at her, right into the directness of her eyes. He was absolutely stunned. "What are you saying?"

"I'm on the threshold. I'm going to get the key." She tossed her head, went on. "It isn't a matter of a drug at all. We can achieve our results by controlling the depth of sleep and the temperature of the sleeping body. Just with what we know now we could probably add ten or fifteen percent to the life-span of the average individual. With no pharmacologic side effects."

"My God."

"The data is falling together, I guarantee it. You were worried about the board. Don't be. You'll win in a walk."

Tom was too relieved to be elated. He took her cheeks in his hands and kissed her again. This time she responded, making a pleased sound in her throat, drawing a leg up behind his, slipping her arms around him. Behind it all was this simple love, the cherishing of each other's dreams. She was so close!

He remembered the case he had imposed on her. "I really am sorry about this patient," he said. "If I had known what was going on I never—" She touched his lips, smiling.

"The patient needs me. I'm the best choice in a case of night terrors." It was his turn to smile. At least she wasn't holding it against him as she had so many other things recently, in that stubborn way he found so hard to accept.

Wordlessly, he handed her the computer printout on the night terrors victim.

Miriam's arm flashed up with stunning speed and knocked the cleaver from John's hand. Instantly, he realized what a mistake it had been to wait for her to wake up. He had stood here, stupidly exulting as she Slept, her body glowing softly in her silk suit. The cleaver had felt good in his hand, the blade was honed to slice deep with the lightest stroke. He could almost hear it singing through the air, almost feel the soft *chuck* of it connecting with her neck, almost see the awful awareness flashing and then fading in her eyes.

The hand closed around his wrist like a manacle. He tried to pull away, to pry back the fingers. Miriam rose to her feet, snatched his other arm and held them both out before him. He twisted away but she raised him off the floor. He could see her face inches away from his, her teeth gleaming, her eyes darting like a crow's eyes.

He threw his head back and pushed against her belly with his feet. It was useless, she might as well be a stone statue. His heart bumped in his chest and pain radiated down his arms. "You're killing me!"

Then she said something that astonished him, especially after what he had seen in the attic. He was certain he had heard the words correctly: "I love you." She asked his forgiveness and hissed out a prayer. Whenever she was about to enter danger, she called on the gods of her species.

She dragged him to a far corner of the cellar. There came a grating sound: she had lifted with one hand a slate block right out of the floor.

He was still trying to understand what she was doing when he was tossed like a rag into the space beneath the block. He fell hard, landing in six inches of freezing water. With a crash that made his ears ring the slate block was dropped into place above him.

Absolute dark. Dripping water.

John now felt a sweeping wave of despair. He wasn't going to be escaping from this place. She had buried him alive!

He screamed, he hammered on the slate, he cried out her name again and again. His hands clawed the cool stones until his fingers tore. Death was going to catch him here, jammed into a space barely as large as a coffin!

"Please!"

Dripping water.

Panic. Images of home. Clear sky. Spring meadows. Off to westward, the huntsman's horn.

Hands clutching him, tearing at him, pressing his face into the muddy, stinking water. Crushing, agonizing weight. Stones. Stones and utter helplessness.

Consciousness left him. But it was not replaced by oblivion. Instead, he was back in the attic, where he had been earlier, searching for Miriam.

The terror of what he had seen there now exploded out of his unconscious into a madness of clutching, leathery fingers and ivory nails, and the foetor of dead breath. The sound that issued from him, reedy and mad, did not bring him back to consciousness.

He remained still, knees jammed against mouth, nose touching the surface of the water, back screaming with the pressure of the stones, mind dancing through the peering dark of hell.

Sarah met Mrs. Blaylock in the receiving lobby. Until recently, it had been a dreary institutional waiting room with brown walls and plastic chairs. But Tom had insisted that it be redecorated to offer the patients the kind of supportive atmosphere they needed. Now it looked at least livable with wallpaper of pastel green, easy chairs, even a big couch.

Sarah picked Miriam Blaylock out instantly. She was easily six feet tall, blond, with eyes so gray they looked white. There was a sort of fierce inquisitiveness about her face, something that made you want to look away. She sat on one of the more rigid chairs. The other patients being admitted tonight stood in a little knot near the door, like nervous mice.

"Mrs. Blaylock," Sarah said in a loud voice.

The woman fixed her with that stare and moved toward her. Their eyes met, and Sarah found herself in the presence of something much more profound than physical beauty, and yet the sheer magnificence of the woman's body and the serenity of her expression were remarkable. There was also a sort of wary grace about her, a way of moving that wasn't quite right, an atmosphere of absolute—and therefore strange—self-assurance.

"I'm Doctor Roberts," Sarah said, hoping that her expression hadn't betrayed her surprise. "I'm going to be managing your case."

Now Miriam Blaylock smiled. Sarah almost laughed, the fierceness of it seemed so misplaced. It was not the smile of a stranger at all, but something else, almost of triumph. Sarah was tempted to make a professional judgment about such inappropriate behavior, but she felt she needed more data. Carefully, she infused professional neutrality into her voice. "First, we'll go on a short tour of the facility and I'll explain our procedures. Follow me, please." She led her into the observation room. For companionship's sake, Tom intended to stay and operate the equipment. He slumped in a chair before one of the computer consoles. "This is Doctor Haver," Sarah said.

Tom turned, his face registering obvious surprise when he first saw Mrs. Blaylock. "Hello," he said. Sarah found herself obscurely annoyed at him. He didn't have to look so appreciative.

"Doctor Haver will explain our monitoring system."

"Will it hurt?"

"Hurt?" Sarah asked.

"Any part of it."

Her voice seemed to fill the room with its rich, sultry timbre. Yet there was an uncanny intonation, almost childlike. "No, Mrs. Blaylock, it won't," Tom said. "You'll find that nothing we do will be in the least uncomfortable. The facility is designed to insure you a good night's sleep." Tom cleared his throat, whipped his fingers through his hair. "This system will read and analyze the electrical impulses that your brain makes when you sleep. It's called Omnex and it's the most advanced computer system of its kind in the world. As your sleep progresses to deeper and deeper stages, we'll be watching and we'll know not only where you stand but how your sleep compares to the various models we've developed here at Riverside."

"He's telling you it's very advanced and wonderful," Sarah said through a smile.

"If the computer analyzes the polysomnogram, what do you two do?"

Quite a well-informed question coming from a patient. Sarah was tempted to answer with the truth—they sat around and drank coffee. "We watch the graphs and try to form an overall picture of your personal sleeping pattern. And of course we watch for signs of your problem."

"I'm not afraid to refer to it, Doctor Roberts. It's called night terrors. Will you wake me up when they come?"

There was a plaintive note in her voice now that made Sarah want to comfort her. "I can't promise you that, but we'll be here if you do awaken. Let's go down to the examining room, then you can use the patient's living room for the evening or go to your cubicle, whichever you prefer."

A glance inside the examining room told Sarah that it was properly prepared for the job she had to do. "Please take off your blouse, Mrs. Blaylock. This will take only a few minutes." Sarah put on her stethoscope. It was to be a cursory examination, over in a few minutes, intended to uncover only the most gross disease process.

Sarah was astonished to find Mrs. Blaylock naked when she turned around. "Oh, I'm sorry, I didn't make myself clear. I just wanted you to take off your blouse."

Miriam Blaylock looked directly into her eyes. The moment was filled with tension. Mrs. Blaylock opened her mouth, seemed about to speak. The room was incredibly claustrophobic.

Before she realized she would do so, Sarah had herself spoken. "What do you want?"

"Want?" Miriam Blaylock parted her lips. "To be

cured, Doctor." There was something mean, almost a sneer, in her tone.

Sarah was embarrassed. "Just sit up on this table." She gestured toward the examining table. Miriam slipped onto it, leaning back against her hands. Her legs were spread wide. It would have been obscene if the woman hadn't seemed so utterly oblivious.

As Sarah prepared her test tubes for the blood work, she realized that she could actually smell the faint musky scent of the woman's vagina. She turned around, syringe in hand. Miriam made a sound in her throat and moved one of her legs. The whisper of flesh against the examining table sheet was disturbing. "I'm going to be taking some blood, Mrs. Blaylock," Sarah said in what she hoped was a thoroughly professional tone. Miriam extended her right arm.

The arm was beautifully shaped, the hand delicate and yet strong. A frightful and sensual image flickered in Sarah's mind, so disturbing that she shook her head to suppress it.

Something made her own flesh crawl when she began stroking Miriam's skin. "I'm trying to raise a vein," she said. "Make a fist, please." She inserted the needle. Miriam made another noise, one that was familiar to Sarah. It was her own little chortle, the one she always made when she was penetrated. To hear it under these circumstances, in the throat of another woman, was faintly revolting. Sarah had to concentrate every ounce of attention on what she was doing just to avoid tearing a hole in the woman's arm. Mrs. Blaylock's hand lay palm up in hers. Perspiration blurred Sarah's vision as the syringe filled. She longed to be free of Mrs. Blaylock's touch. It was undeniably pleasurable and the very delight of it was what was so awful. She looked down at the palm, noticing its bizarre preponderance of vertical lines.

At last the syringe was filled and Sarah could withdraw it. "Don't drop it," Mrs. Blaylock said.

Her tone was so light, so kind, but so chilling. With

as much calmness as she could muster, Sarah set about filling six test tubes with the woman's blood.

"I've got to examine you," she said in what seemed a silly little voice. "Please lie on the table." She fingered her stethoscope.

Mrs. Blaylock lay with her legs bent at the knee, hands folded across her abdomen. Her nipples were erect.

Sarah was transfixed, she had never seen such supple perfection. The woman's flesh was as fair as gold. She turned her face to Sarah and with the gentlest, the sweetest of smiles, murmured that she was ready.

Sarah applied the stethoscope to the center of the chest. "Breathe deeply, please." The lungs sounded as clear as a child's. "You don't smoke?"

"No."

"Good for you."

She continued the stethoscopic exam, exploring the heart sounds from the front, then asking Mrs. Blaylock to turn over and completing the procedure for both heart and lungs on the back. As she worked she regained some of her composure. She was a doctor after all, and this was a patient. Women held no sexual attraction for her. "Turn back over, please." She placed her hands around the crown of the woman's left breast and gently felt downward to the base. "Any pain or discharge from your nipples at any time in the past three months?"

Mrs. Blaylock's tongue glistened behind her teeth. Sarah saw Miriam's hands come up, felt them cradle her face. She did not move, more from amazement than anything else. Her stunned mind thought only that she had never seen such pale eyes before. The hands guided her head downward and her lips touched the nipple.

The shock of pleasure was so great that she nearly collapsed across Mrs. Blaylock's chest. Something within her, which she had been utterly unaware of, awakened in joy and gratitude. Her mind screamed at her—Doctor, Doctor, DOCTOR! For the love of God, this is not *you!*

But she had kissed the breast, she could taste its salt-sweetness, remember the tickle of the nipple against her lips. Mrs. Blaylock's fingers brushed against her cheek.

Sarah's heart sank. This was awful. Mrs. Blaylock lay almost indifferently on the examining table. "You'd better dry your face," she said. "You're sweating." And she gave her a mischievous look.

As Sarah splashed water on her face and toweled herself dry, Mrs. Blaylock dressed. "Are breast exams part of the procedure?"

Sarah was startled. Until this moment the thought hadn't even crossed her mind. Of course they weren't part of the procedure. It was strictly blood, lungs and heart. Her cheeks grew hot, she could sense the woman staring at her back.

"I thought not," Mrs. Blaylock said. Sarah hadn't needed to speak, her silence was sufficiently eloquent. Mrs. Blaylock's hands touched her shoulders, turned her around. She pulled Sarah to her and hugged her closely. Sarah had never felt quite this way before. The power in Mrs. Blaylock's arms sent shuddering waves through her whole body. She was unable to move, she lay like a rag in them. The woman was strong, she easily lifted Sarah off the floor, then lowered her until she rode her knee. Intense little shivers coursed through her as Miriam moved her back and forth. "Open your eyes," she said.

Sarah was ashamed, she could not look at Mrs. Blaylock. "We have to stop," the woman said, "you'll get my dress wet." She slid Sarah down her leg a couple of inches, until her feet reached the floor.

Her heart was soaring, yet her mind was filled with shame.

"You've got to show me where I'm supposed to go, Doctor Roberts."

If only there had been some scorn in that voice. But

it was neutral and pleasant. There wasn't a whisper of response to the emotional explosion that had occurred in Sarah.

"You're going to five B," Tom called from down the hall as they appeared in the corridor. "New room assignment."

"Now I'm beginning to feel like this is a hotel," Mrs. Blaylock laughed. When they reached the cubicle she was amused again. "Talk about small! It's more like a Pullman berth."

"You can spend the evening in the patient's lounge," Tom said.

Sarah was utterly miserable.

6

Miriam sat in the grimly cheerful patient's lounge with the other patients. She faced the television screen but her thoughts were elsewhere. This visitation had changed drastically in significance since Alice's death.

She felt so wronged, so betrayed. Not since she had crawled exhausted up a beach in Ilium had she been this lost in the world. Even after her father's death, wandering in strange lands, she had reconstructed her life. She intended to do it again. The little doctor was her new object. Before, Sarah Roberts would have been used and discarded. Now she would be kept.

In a way it was good; it would have been a pity to destroy such a person. Sarah was bright, full of kindness, and possessed of the rare avidity for life that was so basic to the development of hunger.

Miriam would think more on this during the next few days and weeks, but she was resolved to transform Sarah. If the choice had imperfections, they would have to be faced later. At least Sarah's motive to solve the problem of transformation could not be better. Her own life would be at stake.

A sound behind her made her start. Miriam felt like an animal in an open cage in this place, waiting to hear the clang of the shutting bars. By revealing herself to them she would certainly draw Sarah's total and absolute interest—but it was a dangerous technique. She could imagine herself strapped to some table, the victim of rampant scientific curiosity and the fact that human laws would not protect her once they discovered that she was not one of them. Sarah's was a ruthlessly predatory personality. She, the one who had so indifferently destroyed Methuselah and no doubt dozens of other primates, would capture Miriam. Intelligence might or might not convey rights in the mind of such a person. If their curiosity was intense enough, their ambition sufficiently excited, Miriam had no doubt that Sarah and her colleagues would not hesitate to commit her, or simply confine her as an experimental animal "for the good of humanity and the furtherance of science."

The thought that she might be confined, unable to serve her hunger was terrifying. She had seen up close what extremes of suffering that involved. Such anguish lived in her own attic, stirring restlessly in the boxes.

The more she considered Sarah, the more certain she became that she had a companion—or a jailer. The trick would be to excite hunger in Sarah before she could fully understand what was happening to her. Hunger would ride like the red moon over her psychic landscape. Sarah would be ripe then for whatever harvest might suit Miriam's needs.

It would be a matter of exploiting Sarah's need for love. Each age and each human being betrayed itself with a characteristic falseness. The Romans had their decadence, the Middle Ages its religion, the Victorian Era its morality. This age, so full of equivocation and guilt, was much more complex than the others. It was the age of the lie. Its nations were built on lies, and so were the hearts of its people. Miriam could fill the hollow that a lie leaves in a human being. She could fill the hollow in Sarah.

She remembered the trembling shoulders, the humid touch of her lips on her breast . . . she breathed deeply, closed her eyes, tried to *touch* Sarah's heart.

There was an impression of an empty forest. Here was Sarah, desperately lonely, rushing into the details of her outer life to avoid the secret emptiness within.

Miriam could bring Sarah the gift she most craved: the opportunity to fill that void, absent as it was of real purpose, bounded by the terror of a pointless death. The forest could be peopled with meaning and love and direction. Miriam sat, her eyes narrowed, looking inward. Sarah had despaired of ever really being loved. She wanted Tom, enjoyed him sexually, but the old hollowness asserted itself, the reality once again emerging. Miriam could work in the forest of Sarah's emotions. She knew well her role in this age: the bringer of truth.

Tom scraped his mug as he stirred his coffee. To Sarah the small sound was like screeching chalk. The horrible, unbelievable pleasure of the thing that had happened in the examining room made her want to retreat from any sort of intimacy. Tom turned toward her, kissed her cheek. To escape she shuffled the Blaylock computer printout. "Let's check out the cubicle again." She couldn't endure kissing him right now, facing his love of her.

"You enjoy that? We've already done it twice."

"So let's do it again. I don't want any problems. I can't afford to spend another night up here."

"You were invited, Sarah, not commanded."

"I had to come. The woman's got night terrors."

"You aren't the only doctor who can treat night terrors."

"I'm the only one—" She broke off. She had been about to say, the only one who can treat *her*. But why?

What was so special about her? What made Sarah react
to her like a confused adolescent? She jabbed the
checklist code into the computer console. Instantly,
the screen printed a list of functions: electroencephalogram, electrocardiogram, galvanic skin response,
electro-oculogram, respiration monitor. Each was confirmed functional. Next, she opened up the intercom
and turned on the TV monitor.

"It's all perfect," Tom said, "just like it was ten
minutes ago." There was an edge of humor in his voice,
as if he was amused by what he assumed was her
oversolicitousness. He laid his big hand on hers, his
familiar gesture. She looked down at it, felt its weight.
It might as well be the hand of a statue. Earlier Sarah
had wanted him here tonight to keep her company.
Now she wished that she had let one of the regular
console operators do the job.

"I really want to get this over with," she said.

"I hope she has a night terror, then. For your sake."

"Tom, will you do me a favor?"

"Sure."

"Please don't touch me."

He snapped his hand away, glaring needles of hurt
anger. "OK, what did I do?"

Instantly she felt a wave of regret. Why do that, why
be nasty to him? The devil of it was, she felt under such
a compulsion to do it. The thought of Miriam Blaylock
burned in her mind. She told herself that what had
happened between them was a sort of accident. She
was under pressure; she was exhausted. And yet if she
had observed such behavior in another she would have
considered it an intolerable professional lapse. She
tried to be as hard on herself, but explanations kept
demanding attention. She hated herself for it, perfectly
well aware of what she was doing. "Honey? What did I
do?" He was pressing for an answer, his face full of
wounded decency.

She clung to him, to the faint smell of Old Spice on
the stubbly face, to the scratched-up glasses nobody

could possibly see through, and most of all to the patent honesty of his attempt at love, his flawed attempt.

He hugged back, no doubt not understanding at all what was happening, but willing to accept whatever part in it she might choose for him. Her own disdain for him, her angry rejection of the way the various parts of him used one another with ugly facility, now seemed extremely ungenerous. The man was trying to love. He wasn't good at it, never would be. He was not free enough for it; the goodness of his heart was corrupted by his overweaning ambition. So be it. He was no girlish dream, though, he was real. If you kicked him he hurt. If you felt sorry for him he was diminished. If you loved him something might—or might not—come of it.

"Ten-thirty and I'm tired," she said at last. She wanted to close the curtain, go on to another act. The situation obliged her: a chime rang in the patient's lounge. Time for the sleepless to seek their rest. People began filing past the open door of control room three. The other staff members followed them, intent on their charges. "I'd better go tape her up," Sarah said. "I'll be right back." She glanced away from him as she left, unwilling to meet the eyes that sought hers.

Miriam Blaylock lay in her cubicle in a magnificent and wildly inappropriate silk dressing gown. It was pink and white, embroidered with the flowers of some past and distant place. In this austere little room it looked like a museum piece. So did Miriam Blaylock, for that matter. Her face had the closed, secret look you see in old photographs. It was a face from another time, when people hid out of social necessity all that was in their hearts.

"Do I get undressed for you again?" There was just the edge of a smirk in her tone.

"That won't be necessary, Mrs. Blaylock."

She sat up in the bed, her eyes wide. Incongruously, Sarah recalled the black Statue of Isis in the Egyptian Section of the Met. "You needn't sound like ice," Mrs. Blaylock said. Sarah felt herself flush. The professional distance of her tone had been used by Miriam to do exactly what Sarah didn't want, to create intimacy. She was suddenly aware of the smell in the room, heavy and sharp but with an underlying vulgar sweetness.

"I'm going to apply a group of connectors to your forehead, the sides of your face and around your heart. They don't hurt and they won't give you an electric shock." She used the litany remembered from her clinical days, even took a certain pleasure in it. To begin she applied conductive gel for the facial group and then taped down the electrodes one by one. "I'll have to ask you to open your clothes." Miriam removed her robe.

"The nightgown goes over my head."

"Raise it, please."

Mrs. Blaylock laughed, touched Sarah's wrist. "You really mustn't be so afraid, dear. It was just an accident. We don't ever need to think of it again." Her eyes twinkled. "It doesn't mean a thing."

Sarah was absurdly, ridiculously grateful, but she controlled the hot embarrassment. "Let me apply these connectors, and then you can try to get to sleep."

Mrs. Blaylock took off the nightgown. The electrodes went on quickly. Sarah told herself that this was just another female body, no different from all the others she had seen and touched in her career. As soon as she was finished she turned to leave. Mrs. Blaylock's hand came up, took her wrist. Sarah stopped, did not move.

"Wait." It was a command, beyond resistance, delivered as softly as a plea. Sarah turned and stood before her. Despite the forest of electrodes and her nakedness Mrs. Blaylock seemed no less imperial. "Your generation has no respect for what is sacred." Sarah glanced at her. Whose generation? Miriam Blaylock was easily five years younger than Sarah herself. "Love matters, Doctor. It cannot be imprisoned."

"Of course not."

Very slowly, with the exaggerated humility of a bad actress, Mrs. Blaylock inclined her head. It should have been laughable, the set piece of some dreary melodrama, but instead it moved Sarah deeply, making her feel brutal and indifferent to the delicacy of the human heart.

What gave this woman the right to make her feel so awful about herself!

Sarah snatched her hands away and went back to the control room. The moment she entered it she realized how very alien Miriam Blaylock really was. This seemed such a welcoming, familiar place, cozy with a purpose she appreciated. There had been something in that cubicle, some indefinable thing, that reminded her in an odd way of the evil in Methuselah's cage. As in the cage, there was a dirty scent in the cubicle, but sweet rather than sour—and the raw seductiveness beneath the cloak, almost of majesty, as wild as Methuselah's rage. . . . A demon—if such a thing existed—would, like Miriam, be too beautiful. Methuselah had been another manifestation of a demon's evil: naked and real, screaming hate even as he died. But Sarah didn't believe in evil. Rather she believed in the shadowed inner world of man, where to lose is to win and to win is to fail to see the truth. "She'll have a night terror, all right," Sarah said. She was absolutely certain of it. No one like Miriam Blaylock could pass a night without one.

Tom was amazed at what he had seen on the monitor. There was something between Sarah and Miriam. His own reaction to Miriam Blaylock was now established: she was not the kind of patient he liked to treat. And he wished he hadn't gotten Sarah involved. She didn't need the kind of psychological warfare that the Miriams of the world indulged in. "That's a rich little bitch in there. I don't like her."

Sarah nodded. Tom could see how upset and distraught she was. She had been ever since she had first seen Mrs. Blaylock. The poor girl was terribly insecure as it was. Put on the pressure and she lost all perspective.

"Let's get this show on the road," he said. Tom had decided to let the coolness Sarah had shown him earlier dissolve of its own accord. The mature thing would be to make himself accept it. He knew that he wasn't more than average as a lover, not good at all as a friend, but he wanted to give Sarah what he had. To keep the interest of one such as she, Tom had accepted that he would have to concede many things.

Sarah leaned her head against his shoulder. "You've gotten awfully laconic." It was an opening, and Tom almost threw his arms around her with gratitude.

"I'm worried about you, darling. You seem upset."

Sarah nodded at the monitor. Miriam lay reading a magazine. "I am."

"What don't you like about her?" He thought of the murmured conversation between them, the strange gesture of the holding of hands.

"She's—I don't quite know how to express it. Perhaps the old definition of a monster, the Latin one."

Tom smiled. "I have no idea what it is. To me a monster is a monster."

"A divine creature. A *thing* of the gods. Irresistible and fatal."

Tom looked again at the monitor. It seemed a great distance between the gods and the woman with *McCalls* in her hands. "I just don't like her," he said. "Bored, selfish, rich, a little on the compulsive side, judging from the fastidiousness of her clothes. Probably collects dicks like shrunken heads."

He was delighted to make Sarah laugh. It always relieved him, like discovering that a gift has been appreciated beyond one's expectations. "Sometimes," she said, "you have a way of cutting through that's just priceless."

"Thank you, ma'am. Now I hope you won't worry instead of kiss me." Her eyes at last seemed happy. He kissed her lips, puckering them with the heels of his hands.

With an annoyed little jolt he realized that she was staring past him, at the damn monitor. "My God, Tom, what did she just pick up?"

It was a book. Tom knew it perfectly well. "Was there a copy in the patient's lounge?"

"Of my book? *My* book? Certainly not, it's not for patients." She looked wildly around the room. "This is crazy! What kind of game is she playing?"

Miriam lay reading, her bottom lip caught prettily between her teeth, her eyes avid with concentration. Sarah put her head down on the desk and let out a long, racking sigh, almost a sob. Tom leaned close to her. "I'm too tired for games," she said. "A stupid woman and her stupid games."

"Honey, why don't you just knock off. Go home or go back to the lab. Let me deal with Mrs. Blaylock alone."

"I ought to be here. I'm the expert."

"This place is loaded with good doctors. Me, for example."

Sarah sat up, shook her head. "I accepted the case," she said, "I can't think of one valid reason to abandon it."

Miriam closed her copy of *Sleep and Age* and lay back. The bed was tolerable, but best of all was this wonderful feeling of safety. Her own house was a superbly designed refuge, but a hospital with its large staff and twenty-four-hour operation was almost as good. No night clerks drowsing while fire spread up the stairwells as in a hotel. No robbers prowling the halls or defective wiring electrocuting the unwary bather. Hospitals were safe enough for a Sleeper. Even after burying John in the tunnel, she did not feel completely comfortable at home. He must yet die more completely, he knew the house's security system too well. She relaxed into welcome peace. Maybe this time she would dream as she once had, of the sylvan blessings of long ago, or of the endless promise of the future. The unquiet dreams were most frequent during bad times. Her Sleep was more persistent when she was tense. She might need it as often as every twelve hours at the height of a crisis instead of every twenty-four. The harder things got, the more it interrupted.

She snuggled down into the bed, smelling the starched sheets, quivering with delight at the safety and thinking of Sarah, poor girl, who was about to walk through the fire.

The patient interrupted their conversation; professionalism demanded that personal matters now be put aside. The electroencephalograph, monitoring brain waves, was showing a pattern characteristic of drowsiness.

"There goes a roll," Sarah said as the electro-oculograph jiggled. Mrs. Blaylock's eyes were rolling into her head, an indication of stage one sleep. Sarah cleared her throat and swigged some coffee. Tom had to admire her. She was bursting apart inside and he damn well knew it. But you couldn't tell it now. That was a pro. The alpha-wave arrhythmias that indicated dozing sleep appeared. Then the skin galvanometer jumped and the heart rate increased.

"Oops. Must have gotten stuck with a pin. She wearing any pins?"

"The electrodes must be bothering her."

After a moment the electro-oculograph indicated left-to-right motion. "She's reading again."

Sarah shook her head. Tom wished he could find some way to lighten Sarah's mood. "At least she respects your work. She's reading it."

"I wish I knew more about her, Tom."

Behind them Geoff Williams from the blood analysis lab cleared his throat. "I hope I'm not disturbing any lovey-lovey, dears, but I have a problem for you. You got the wrong blood."

"What wrong blood? What're you talking about?"

"The blood you gave me marked 00265 A-Blaylock M.? It isn't human blood."

"Of course it is. I took it out of that patient right there." Sarah pointed at the monitor.

Geoff pulled out his computer printout. "You'll note from the machine's attempt to analyze it that something is amiss." The sheet showed the blood's ID and then a list of zeros where the component values should have been.

"Machine's on the fritz," Tom said, turning back to the monitors. "Another roll," he said. "She's trying again. Sweet dreams, dearie."

"No computer problem, Doctor. I ran the test program and then ran other bloods back to back with yours. You did not give me human blood. Whatever this is, the machine cannot analyze it."

Sarah looked up at him. "You know, I seem to remember a time when blood analysis was done by hand, when it was between a man and his centrifuge."

"I did it by hand too. Here's what I found." He thrust a sheet of numbers at them. "It isn't a human type as far as I'm concerned. It has a whole extra component of leukocytes, for one thing."

"Could a human being survive with it?"

"It's a better blood than ours. Very similar, but more disease resistant. The cellular material is more dense, the plasma less. It would take a strong heart to pump the stuff and there might be some minor capillary clogging, but whoever had it in their veins could forget about sickness if their heart was strong enough to pump the stuff."

Tom gestured to the screen. "We have a patient right before our eyes who is clearly thriving with it in her veins. Before we draw any further conclusions I think we'd better retest."

"Of course."

"It's her blood," Sarah snapped. "I didn't make a

mistake." Tom blinked—he was surprised at the ferocity in her voice.

Geoff must have heard it too, because he paused a moment before speaking again, and then went on very gently. "This cannot have come from that patient, Sarah. If it did then she isn't a human being. And I can't believe that."

"It could be a congenital defect, or a hybrid."

Geoff shook his head. "First off, we're dealing with a very dense blood. A human heart could pump it, but just barely. The component mix is all off. The counts don't make sense. Sarah, it cannot be human blood. The closest would be one of the great apes—"

"It's not from one of my monkeys," she said woodenly. "I don't make mistakes that simple." Her voice lowered. "I wish I did."

She took Geoff with her and got another sample. Mrs. Blaylock had fallen asleep only a few minutes before. When the needle entered her arm her lips parted but her eyelids never flickered. Tom watched the graphs for some sign of disturbed sleep. After taking samples from rhesus monkeys Sarah must be a true expert. Certainly it wasn't waking up Mrs. Blaylock.

Tom was about to turn away from the graphs when he paused. A thrill, as if of danger, had coursed through him. He found himself wishing that Sarah would hurry up and get out of there. When she did return he nodded toward the readout.

"There's nothing right about her pattern, is there?" she said promptly.

"I'd say she was in coma except for those voltage bursts in the delta wave." Delta was the indicator of conscious mental activity. "It's like a dead brain that's somehow retaining consciousness."

"Isn't that a very muted sleep spindle in alpha?"

"It could be background noise. A passing radio cab, for example. We've had that problem before. It's too low-level."

"Respiration's almost nil. Tom, it's quiet in that room. So very quiet. It's rather horrible."

"Don't go in there again."

He felt her eyes on him. "OK," she said softly. This time she put her hand in his and they looked steadily at each other. There was no need to speak.

LONDON: 1430

Yellow light filters through the curtains. She had drawn them against the noise and stench of the street. Although it is May, sullen, cold rain sweeps from the sky. Across Lombard Street the bells of St. Edmund the King ring the changes. Miriam has been almost mad with the damp, the filth and the endless ringing bells— and the fact that Lollia has been taken to the torturer.

She rushes out into the garden behind the house to escape the ringing. But here resound the bells of St. Swithin's across the reeking waters of the Lang Bourne. Rats slither away as she moves among her beloved roses. Six of the plants are already aboard ship, these others must be left behind. She sobs as she paces, horrible images of that poor, wonderful girl lying in a rack, her hands bulging purple in iron pilliwinks.

They have overstayed here; long ago they should have left London, left England. There are places in the wild east of Europe where it is still possible for Miriam's kind to thrive. They had been planning, considering and suddenly here was Lollia, captured as a witch.

A witch, of all the superstitious blather!

"Lady, farthing, please farthing."

She tosses some copper to the ratcatchers who have begun to creep up from the Bourne. Swarms of them live off the rats of the open sewer. She has seen them devour rats raw. She has seen them drain the blood of rats down the throats of their children.

She has heard their songs: "He that will an alehouse keep, sing hey nonny nonny . . ."

Occasionally, the king's men come and kill some of them. But they multiply in the benighted ruin that is fifteenth-century London. Everything is wrong here. Death and disease stride through the populace. Houses burn nightly and the rains bring the roar of buildings collapsing. The mud is always ankle deep and full of rotting garbage. The streets are sewers. Wild pigs, pickpockets and cutpurses seethe in the markets. At night come the cutthroats and the shrieking mad. Over it all there hangs an endless brown pall of peat smoke. The city does not rumble as Rome did or clatter as did the marble streets of Constantinople, but rather it breathes a great moan, as winter wind coming down a moor. Occasionally, amid a flash of silk and the rick-rack of a gaily painted coach an aristocrat passes by.

The sundial tells her that four hours have passed since Lollia was taken away. The bailiffs will be heard in Lombard Street soon, bearing their burden in its black muslin shroud. Then Miriam must be ready, for Lollia will have "confessed." Oh yes, Miriam has seen them at their art of torture. Beside it the other arts of this age are but pale shadows. Men are skinned amid jovial crowds, their parts tossed as souvenirs to putrid children. The victims howl out any calumny or sorcery, whatever is wanted of them.

Miriam cannot find the depth of her contempt. She goes through the night streets with real pleasure, a thousand times more dangerous than the quickest knifeman, stronger, faster and more intelligent.

Her belly is always full. Or was, until the soldiers of King Henry began to organize a competent night watch.

Lollia was netted like a plunging doe in the Crutched Friars by St. Olave and dragged off to the gaols. She had been a child of the streets, a Byzantine Greek whom Miriam discovered in Ravenna in the Clothmakers Market near the Palace of the Emperor, working as a weaver of linen. How long ago that was! Nearly a millennium. Miriam had been staggered by her beauty, uplifted from her despondence at the loss of Eumenes. As Rome died they went to Constantinople but left when the old, familiar signs of imperial decline began to appear there as well: whole quarters deserted, palaces left to ruin, arson and corruption and wildly escalating prices.

London had been a good choice—populated, chaotic, growing. They had come with nothing but a single Venetian gold ducat and six Burgundian pennies.

The ducat bought them a year's lodging. To obtain more money they scavenged the palaces of the aristocrats.

A hundred years of love and prosperity passed like a winking dream.

Then Lollia changed. Her youth evaporated. She ate weekly, then daily and of late every few hours. Recently, she has been going on night-long frenzies, giving herself up to the hunger until she becomes bloated. And her beauty, once so great that it made men bow their heads, has dissolved into memory. She has grown horrible, her voice shrilling through the house, her eyes agleam for blood. And now she has been captured, dragged gnashing and growling to the Assizes. Miriam raced down Eastcheap to Tower Street—just too late.

She waits for whatever they are going to bring home. She cannot look at the gowns, the street-worn slippers, the brown ringlets Lollia had bought for her hair. They lie now in a little paper box beside her wig fork. Miriam gathers handfuls of coins from their cache, pouring them into a leather pouch and lashing it under her breasts. She will take a boat from Ebgate down to the docks. Because of Lollia's certain confession, all of this is lost, and Miriam also will be seized if she waits too long. Three days ago she placed her chests aboard a Genoese galley, all except Lollia's. The ship sails tomorrow or the next day and she will be on it. But she will not leave without Lollia. To keep them safe has been her promise to all, and to herself.

The girl's resting place is ready, a squat box of oak and iron sitting in the middle of the room, its newly rubbed wood smelling faintly of fish oil.

If Miriam cannot escape, she will be burned at the stake.

Now she counts her coins—fifty gold ducats, three gold pounds, eleven ecus d'or. It is enough to keep all of Cheapside for a year or support Cardinal Beaufort for a week.

They come.

She bites her tongue when she hears the blaring crumhorns of the Waits that precede the cortege. This must work, it *must!*

If only she could leave Lollia—but she would never forgive herself. There is a powerful morality in her relationship to her lovers. By vowing never to abandon them, she gives herself the right to deceive them. She rushes into Lombard Street, pushes wildly through the crowd toward the squat figures with the black-shrouded body on their shoulders.

She has a fistful of silver. It will take at least two silver pence to get Lollia's body and another one to save herself. In one man's hand she sees a flutter of seals—the writ ordering that the body of one woman called Miriam, accused of being a witch, be brought with all haste—

"I have silver," she says over the roar of the Waits, "silver pennies for my poor mother!"

"Oho, pretty, we've got to take thee too!"

"I have silver!"

The big man with the writ comes up and jolts his hand down on her shoulder. "The King cannot be bought with a scrap of money."

The Waits have stopped. All is silence. The crowd is fascinated as Miriam pleads for her life. She displays two silver pennies on the palm of her hand.

"That's what you have?"

"It is, all in the world."

"Then three it must be!" And he laughs, the whispering cackle of a man with diseased lungs.

"All my monies in the world," Miriam wails. She takes out another little coin and holds the three in cupped, trembling hands.

They are snatched up and Lollia is dropped onto the stone stoop of the house. The Waits melt into the throng, the bailiffs march away, the writ is lost in the mud of the street.

Miriam can hardly bear to unwrap the shroud. Lollia is bright red, tongue like a purple, blistered flower, eyes popping half out of her head.

They have boiled her in oil. Some of the stinking stuff still clings to her distended flesh.

And there is a tiny noise, the sound of skin breaking as her hands slowly unclench.

"It's a nightmare," Tom murmured.

Sarah was mesmerized by the racing graphs. "I know," she said distantly. The blood had astonished her. Tom was no doubt waiting for some error to emerge, but Sarah knew that the sample Geoff was testing now would only confirm the unbelievable. Her mind rang with the question, what is she, *what is she!* It made her almost dizzy, her own voice shouting in her head, confusion threatening to become panic.

"I'm going to wake her." Tom started to get up.

"Don't! You—you'll disturb the record."

His eyes searched her face. "She's obviously suffering—"

"Look at the graphs! You don't want to disturb a unique record. We don't even know if it's a nightmare. It might be a dream of paradise."

"The REM readings are consistent with a high-intensity nightmare."

"But look at respiration and skin conductivity. She's practically comatose."

Sarah was relieved when Tom's eyes returned to the monitors. Their place right now was here, recording phenomena. Mrs. Blaylock's extraordinary sleep pattern continued to flicker across the displays. Sarah tried to add it up—low-intensity delta waves, alpha waves curving as in a trance state. This was the intercranial activity pattern of an injury victim or perhaps some kind of meditation master. "Let's do a zone scan," Sarah said slowly.

"You think there's something we're not picking up?"

"We're getting too many nil readings. Yet her eyes are moving as if she was in an intense dream."

"Maybe it's the hippocampus. You can get intensive hallucinatory effects when it's stimulated. They'd cause REM."

"That's a good idea, Doctor. But to pick up electrical activity from that deep we're gonna have to move our electrodes."

"So let's do it."

"You're elected, Thomas. You told me not to go back in there alone, remember?"

"OK." He started for the door, then paused. "You're better at placement than me, darling."

"One on each temporal bone and two side by side just above the lambdoid suture. If we can't read the hippocampus from there we need a probe."

"How the hell can I get to the lambdoid suture? I'll have to lift her head."

"Tom, the woman is immobilized with some incredibly powerful equivalent of dreaming sleep. She's not going to know if you lift her head." Sarah felt her stomach turn. The very idea of being near that creature again made her feel queasy. This brain acitvity was no more human than the blood.

Tom left, but there was a long pause before he appeared on the video monitor. He wasn't hurrying. She watched him move the electrodes. At first the graphs went absolutely straight. No pickup. Sarah was adjusting electrode sensitivity when all hell broke loose. The four electrodes were switched into two different needles in case pickup was better from one region than the other. But it didn't matter, the voltage surges were tremendous.

"God damn," Tom said as he returned.

"It's brain damage," Sarah said. "Has to be."

"If it is, then there aren't any gross effects."

A hand dropped to her shoulder. Leaning her head back, she saw Geoff standing over her, the rims of his glasses glittering in the fluorescent light. "You were right," he said, "she's a freak."

Sarah looked at the woman on the video monitor. She was a stirring beauty, there was no doubt of it. But she was also this other thing, what Geoff called a freak.

The needles swung wildly across the graph paper. Sarah remembered the hippocampus from her studies. It is one of the deepest brain areas. When it is stimulated electrically, patients sometimes relive their past in every detail, as if it were happening again. It is the seat of ancient senses, the most hidden country of the mind. It is perhaps the place where the unconscious stores the remembrances by which we are ruled. Certainly dragons march there, and deep creatures crawl. When it is destroyed by injury or disease, the victim's past disappears and he lives forever in that disoriented state that is felt upon waking from a particularly terrible nightmare.

The graphs hissed in the silent room. Geoff dropped a yellow sheet of paper on the desk space before the computer console, his new workup on the blood.

"The woman must literally be reliving her life," Tom said. "It must be a thousand times more vivid than a normal dream."

"I hope it's been a nice life." Geoff was fingering his workup sheet.

"It hasn't," Sarah said. She knew that it was true.

7

JOHN SAW DIM PATTERNS against his closed eyelids. He could not tell exactly when he had become conscious, but he knew that he had ceased to dream in the past few minutes and returned to the agony of his body.

What a fool he had been to stand over her like that, savoring his victory, waiting for her to awaken. But he had wanted her to *know*.

He could still hear the carbon steel blade of the cleaver ringing on the slates.

He had to move! He longed to stretch out, to feel fresh movement in his joints. Panic started again, but he quelled it. He felt his tomb's walls and low ceiling, touched the mud beneath the puddle of water he was in. And he heard that dripping, steady, echoing, as if it were in a larger space.

He shouted. Also an echo. He took a deep breath. The air was fresh and cool. In such a small space as this even a few minutes would have made the air heavy.

Unless there was an opening.

He couldn't turn around, there wasn't enough room. His feet rubbed along solid stone, however. Plunging his fingers as deep into the mud as they would go also brought no results—until he clawed at the place where the wall before his face met the water. Here there was no mud.

A current went under the stone, through an opening about eight inches deep. Perhaps he could push himself under. He leaned down as far as he could without immersing his face in the water and waved his hand in the opening. He could not feel a surface to the water, but he could feel a distinct flow. If he stretched his arms full length and pushed with his feet he could get his head and shoulders through the opening. There was no guarantee that he would reach an air pocket, but even drowning seemed like a relief compared to this.

He plunged his face into the water, pressing himself as far into the mud as he could, found purchase with his feet and shoved. In order to get through he had to turn his head to one side. Water poured in his nose, seared his throat and lungs. He screwed his eyes shut, fighting the impulse to gag, and shoved and kicked and twisted. Pressed tightly between the mud bottom and the stone, his head pounded. The ear that was scraping against the stone felt as if it were on fire. He realized that it was being torn off, so tight was the space.

The mud seeped between his lips, poured into his mouth. He began to need air. Helpless, he convulsed, felt a rush of bubbles pour from nose and mouth, gagged. Somewhere far behind him his feet were kicking, drumming impotently in the shallow water. His hands, stretched before him, clutched water.

Then his ear stopped hurting. He could lift his head! More frantic jerking and his eyes were out of the water. He pushed against the mud, heard bones crack as he pulled his legs up under him, heaved again and again.

Bright red flashes filled his eyes, his mind began to wander. The withering sensation of air hunger coursed through his body. He felt himself urinating, a hot stream in the freezing water.

His struggles were becoming more sporadic. The

pain was giving way to a kind of release, a relaxed drifting. He hungered for the peace that seemed to lie just beyond the last of his struggles.

He remembered Miriam, saw her face glowing before him, her lips parted, teasing him to passion.

Mocking his love.

He couldn't let her win! She had lied to him from the beginning. For weeks after their first encounter she had come to him nightly with her evil little kit and sat stroking his head as her blood ran into his veins and the fever raged. It nearly killed him, but he recovered. And when he did he was a new man, impervious to sickness, ageless, with new needs and an extraordinary new lover to fulfill them.

He also had a new hunger. It had taken him years to get used to it, to reach a point where his moral revulsion was at least equaled by his sense of acceptance. At first the hunger had propelled him, wild with need, through the streets of London.

She had caused that.

Finally he had learned, bitter and desperate and trapped, to satisfy the demands of this hunger.

She had taught him how.

He had to reach her!

A last frantic heave brought him clear of the water and he sucked in air at last. He could hear his heart clattering, feel exhaustion in every muscle and bone. For how long he did not know, he lay where he had fallen, his head and arms entangled in a thick mass of roots, his legs still in the muddy water.

But he was free of Miriam's tomb.

Free. An image of the steel box waiting for him in the attic flashed in his mind. He gasped air, coughed, spat froth from his lungs. A cold steel box in a stack of such boxes.

And in each—one of his predecessors.

She had always said that he was her only one.

Now that he saw the truth, he was horrified by the sheer coldness of the creature, the depths of its indiffer-

ence, the extent of its power. Some of those boxes were
old! The thing itself must be ancient, some dreadful
exponent of Satan himself. He no longer thought of it
as male or female. It chose to call itself "Miriam" but
that was doubtless only a matter of convenience.

John's hands clutched up among the roots, seeking
some further passage out of the prison. Everything that
he believed about Miriam had proved to be false. All
that she had told him was a monstrous lie.

One among many. Miriam had been doing this since
the beginning of time.

He had to break the chain of destruction in some
way. His revenge was due him a thousand times over.
The very earth around him seemed to seethe with the
restless souls of those he had killed in service to his own
immortality.

Indeed. The 180-odd years he had lived seemed only
a moment now that the end was near. Certainly they
were no eternity. If he had known that he was only
delaying the inevitable he would never have wasted the
lives of others. "Or so I tell myself," he said aloud.

Something brushed past him. He remembered the
awful sense of movement in the attic. Clawing frantically at the roots that surrounded him, he screamed.
This was a wet, stinking grave if ever there was one. It
wasn't quite as confining as the stone chamber, but it
was just as deadly in the long run. He pushed at the
roots, trying to progress toward the surface. His mind
contracted to a single thought: hurt Miriam. If possible,
destroy Miriam. If not, then die trying.

In his final effort, at least, there would be some small
nobility. He was the last of a great line, after all, who
had fought in many a noble war. There had been brave
men among his forefathers. He would remember them
now. His hand reached ancient, sodden brick, the
vaulting of their old tunnel to the East River. So that's
where it had put him. He pulled the bricks down easily.
The mortar was rotten, the bricks themselves crumbling.

Suddenly, he found that he could stand to full height, even raise his arms above his head.

It took him a few seconds to realize that he had broken through into the old tunnel, not out of it. The echoing water was much louder, so loud that he could hear it even with his injured ear. His hands clutched mud, flailed, found a curved brick ceiling a few feet above. It was rank, the great roots twining everywhere. Waving his hands ahead of him in the total blackness, he began to move forward.

After ten steps the tunnel ended in a jumble of bricks and concrete chunks. Roots formed a slick forest. Above the dripping there rose another sound.

Was it the tide, perhaps? Their house was not far from the East River. Then it hit him all at once—he was hearing traffic on the FDR Drive.

This old escape tunnel was built back when the recently formed New York City Police Department seemed a threat. It had been covered over with the construction of the highway thirty years ago. That slate she had lifted was the door to the tunnel.

He began to claw at the dirt. Not so far above must lie the garden. Maybe it wasn't over yet, maybe he would get another chance after all. Roots tore at his fingers, scraping them raw. Only by digging around them and pressing himself up between their strands could he make progress. He worked with the furious strength of rage. He must not fail now. When he felt this same strength surge in the bodies of his victims he knew they were at wit's end.

There came a blaze of light. John recoiled—had he shorted some kind of buried electrical cable? As his eyes grew used to the brilliance he also found that he was covered with flat flakes of a pink material. For a moment he was utterly confused, then he smelled the flowers.

He lifted his head into Miriam's garden, right into the midst of her treasured roses. They were her own special hybrids, created over God knew how many years of patient grafting. Some blossoms were enormous, others tiny. Some plants bore thorns, others none. And they ranged in shade from delicate pink to deep red. Most of the thorns were strictly ornamental, soft to the touch. Five of the larger blossoms at high summer would fill a substantial vase, and the fragrance would cover a dozen rooms.

Only his face and one arm were worked out of the earth. The house was invisible behind him, but he could feel its menacing presence. He hoped she wouldn't so much as glance out a window—Miriam had the eyes of a falcon.

The roots clutched at him, impeding every movement. He was tiring quickly now that the rush of panic had ended. His heart bounded raggedly along and his lungs bubbled.

It was a triumph when both arms lay among the rose bushes and he could press against the ground. Inch by inch he freed himself. At last his hips jerked through the final impediment and he pulled himself out. He lay beneath the sky of morning, feeling the hunger rising yet again, barely able to move, save only to tear blossoms from their branches. When he was done he rested, then pulled himself to his feet. The house stood in its garden, somber to John's eyes. He looked high to its roof, to the tiny window of the room where Miriam kept her dead.

There was something he could do there, if he dared, if he could bear it. The house was silent. Taunting. Daring him to enter. He would, when the moment was right. If she captured him first he would lose his revenge forever. And if she did not? Then it would not matter.

The whole clinic was electrified with the news of Miriam Blaylock. By six-thirty A.M. a stunned, hollow-eyed crowd was huddled around Tom and Sarah, watching the monitors. At seven Sarah pressed a button that sounded chimes in the sleep cubicle. Miriam had been awake but motionless for two hours; her sleep had lasted exactly six. She stirred, stretched luxuriously, and opened her eyes. She looked directly into the monitor. Sarah was surprised; it was one of the gentlest, most beautiful expressions she had ever seen. "I'm awake," said the rich voice.

The whole group stirred. Sarah knew that the others felt as she did. "I'm gonna get on the horn," Tom said. "I'd better get things moving." He headed toward his office to call specialists—geneticist, physiological biologist, cellular biologist, psychiatrist, and half a dozen others.

It hadn't taken long for them to realize that they were in the presence of a potentially marvelous discovery. The gross abnormalities of the blood and the completely alien brain function left no room for doubt: Miriam Blaylock was not a member of the species *Homo sapiens.*

Sarah's intense reaction to her was partly explained. There must have been some awareness on an unconscious level and a corresponding attempt to compensate. The unconscious reaction to a living, intelligent being of an unknown species was itself unknown. Now that the alienness lay uncovered, the woman—female creature—seemed subtly less threatening. Unknowns were the familiar ground of Sarah's work, and Miriam was a confluence of unknowns. Although an extraterrestrial origin could not be ruled out, it seemed unlikely in view of the physical similarity between Miriam and a human being.

In spite of her position as a scientist, Sarah could not shake the feeling that she was in the grip of some enormous mechanism of fate, something pulling her toward some destiny, and that it was not blind at all, but rather entirely aware of her smallest response.

"Good morning, Mrs. Blaylock," she said into the intercom. "Would you care for some breakfast?"

"No, thank you. I'll eat later."

"Coffee, then?"

She sat fully up in bed, shook her head no. "Come tell me, Doctor, what you've learned. Can you help me?" Suddenly even through the filter of the TV monitor, the eyes were fierce.

Sarah felt no further reticence. She marched right to the cubicle. It was warm and smelled of Miriam's sweetness. "May I call you Miriam?" Sarah sat on the edge of the bed trying to feel neatly enclosed in herself. "We learned a great deal. You're a unique person."

Miriam said nothing. A tiny doubt crossed Sarah's mind. Of course Miriam herself knew what she was. She must. So they had assumed.

"Did you sleep well?"

She looked surprised. "Don't you know?"

They both laughed. "I'm sorry. I'm sure you remember a dream. A particularly vivid one."

Miriam's face grew solemn. She drew herself up, dangling her legs over the side of the bed. They were beautiful, outlined under her nightgown. "Yes, I had a vivid dream."

"I'd like to know about it. The information will be very helpful."

Miriam glanced at her, said nothing. That look stabbed Sarah deeply. She felt in her own heart a glint of Miriam's pain. The thought came that someone ought to take Miriam in her arms and hug away that loneliness. It would be a noble thing to do, a bridge across worlds.

Sarah opened her arms, turning toward Miriam with invitation, oblivious to the gleaming lens of the video camera attached to a corner of the ceiling. Miriam clung, it struck her, as a child. "There, there," Sarah said through feelings of awkwardness. She wasn't really very *good* at this sort of thing.

Miriam sobbed, quickly cut it off. Sarah stroked her soft blond hair, made soothing sounds in her ear.

The loneliness was palpable, as real as an odor. When Sarah felt her stir she released her grip. Miriam sat back against the wall, took Sarah's hand in hers, and kissed her fingers.

Now Sarah did think of the monitor. Embarrassed, she withdrew her hand. "Perhaps we'll talk again after you're dressed," she said as calmly as she could. "I'll beep you when I've turned off the video." She tried to smile. "You're allowed to get dressed in private."

Miriam seemed about to say something but Sarah did not wait to hear it. She was not at all sure why the creature seemed to compel such intimacy, but this was not the time to probe further. She retreated to the observation room, determined to be more careful in the future. Other patients were being awakened and the group around Miriam's monitor was smaller. Phyllis Rockler and Charlie Humphries had arrived, however. They were talking heatedly with Geoff Williams, who waved his now-wrinkled sheet of blood component statistics as he spoke. When Sarah reappeared Geoff called out that Tom had gotten his core group together and a meeting was scheduled in the conference room.

Sarah followed standard procedure in killing Miriam Blaylock's monitor during her dressing period. Mrs. Blaylock would have to be processed further by a resident. Sarah and Tom both had to attend the core conference. "Just don't let her get out of here," Sarah said to the eager kid who was assigned to the job. "She's precious. *Precious.* I want the standard post-observation interview right off the form. Then stall her. Say we need her here for another twenty-four hours." When she left for the conference the resident was scribbling on a clipboard. For an instant she allowed herself a privilege reserved for the successful, delighting in the fact that he was obviously a couple of years older than she. Life on a fast track had its compensations.

Sarah walked into a packed room. People looked disheveled, bleary-eyed. She wondered what Tom had said to pour so many senior men out of bed so early.

Tom sat playing with an unlit cigar, which disappeared as she entered. She took the chair that Charlie and Phyllis had saved for her. Around the table were twelve people, ranging in age from thirty to seventy. Hutch sat straight, his lips a thin line, his face frozen in a manufactured expression of curiosity. Underneath it Sarah sensed something else. Their eyes met and his sadness surprised her. So Tom's assault was progressing. Hutch had not called this meeting, he was here by invitation only.

"OK," Tom said, "thank you very much for your time, Doctors. I'm sorry to get you out of bed so early in the morning. I must say, however, I think you'll be glad I did once we review the record. Just briefly, the subject in question is named Miriam Blaylock. She appears in excellent physical condition, aged thirty years, and she has received a working diagnosis of night terrors. That diagnosis has been revised to include grossly anomalous brain function."

"Doctor—" It was Hutch.

Tom held up his hand. "Doctor Hutchinson hasn't been briefed because of the need for haste," he said. Sarah blinked. The riposte was deadly. Now Hutch must remain silent. He had been neatly exposed as being among the uninformed. A figurehead of the department. Tom took his blood in drops, but each one counted. "We'll get our first report from Doctor Geoffrey Williams, who did the blood grouping and analysis on the patient."

Geoff rattled papers, pushed his glasses up on his nose. "Put simply, the woman's blood is completely mutated, to the extent that she might well be a varietal species and not a member of *genus homo* at all." The few preoccupied faces came to attention.

"It could be a genetic defect," Hutch said. He had leaned forward in his chair, his face full of interest and concern. Sarah realized a truth—he did not view the clinic as a possession, but himself as the property of the

clinic. Of course he would continue to talk, he saw no
humiliation in being relieved of the captaincy as long as
he remained in the group.

"It isn't a defect, the blood—"

"You don't have a chromosomal yet, you couldn't. I
think you're being quite hasty—"

"Hush up, Walter," a deep voice said from the back
of the room. All eyes turned. Sam Rush, Riverside
Medical Center's Chief of Research Staffs, leaned
against the door, his arms folded before him. Sarah
raised her eyebrows. He counted for more than the
entire board. Considerably more.

Geoff cleared his throat. "Mutation, even parallel
evolution, are the appropriate concepts. The kicker is
in cellular detail. First, the erythrocytes are off color,
practically purple. Yet there is no indication that the
patient is suffering from any oxygen-uptake problems.
The cells are also less than half-normal size. Second
and perhaps most important, we observe seven varieties of leukocytes instead of five as in a human body.
The two new ones are among the most extraordinary
cellular structures I've had the pleasure of observing.
As a first guess, I'd say that the purpose of number six
is heightened control of invasive organisms. It is active
against all test cultures so far, including _E. Coli_ and
salmonella. And it shares a totally unexpected property
with number seven in that it resists death even in a
saline solution.

"Now, the number seven. This is the reason I
mentioned the possibility of parallel evolution. It is
literally a factory, consuming dead blood cells of all
kinds and birthing new ones, including its own type."

The room was silent for some time. Finally, Dr.
Weintraub, the cellular biologist, spoke. "Doctor, what
kind of breakdown process occurs?"

"This blood sample is exceptionally resistant to morbidity. I suspect it would even cause such diseases as
virally induced cancer to be self-limiting and transient
events in the life of the organism. If this blood wasn't

flowing in the veins of a mortal being, subject to time and accident, it might itself be immortal."

"Structural detail of the seventh leukocyte?" Weintraub's eyes were tightly closed, he was deep in concentration.

"Complex tripartite nuclei. The structure appears to change according to the type of cell being consumed and reproduced. They birth living versions of the other types as fast as the originals die. The blood is in the lab now, six hours old, still as fresh as the moment it was taken."

"Doctor, surely that's a side effect of preservation—"

"Doctor Hutchinson, the sample I am referring to is being held at a temperature of fifteen degrees Celsius. It ought to be dead and decaying by now. But in fact we could reintroduce it into the donor's veins if we wanted to. It's quite self-maintaining."

Sarah could hear the rustle of suppressed movements. She looked around the table and was at first perplexed by the uniform woodenness of the faces. Then she understood that they were all holding themselves in, restraining every outward manifestation of their excitement. All except Hutch, who was beginning to look like a little boy attending a carnival. Tom's power play seemed more and more superfluous. Sarah suspected that Hutch's type was that most dangerous of opponents for the Tom Havers of the world: a truly committed man—or truly clever—or both.

A face appeared in the doorway behind Dr. Rush. Sarah excused herself; the resident she had detailed to hold Mrs. Blaylock looked upset.

"She left," he said with a squeak. "I waited a few minutes for her to dress and when I went to the cubicle she was gone."

Sarah restrained her first impulse, which was to shake him. "Did reception see her go? Try to stop her?"

"She never went through the reception area."

"Then how did she leave?" He said nothing. River-side was a labyrinth of nineteenth- and twentieth-century buildings all thrown together, she could have gone in any number of directions. Sarah clutched at a possibility. "Maybe she's gotten herself lost."

"Her stuff is gone. She intended to leave."

Sarah closed her eyes. This was going to embarrass Tom. She thought of Hutch and found she wasn't exactly displeased by that. "Call me out of here if there are any developments." The resident turned and hurried away. As Sarah went back to her seat she contemplated whether or not to interrupt the proceedings with the bad news.

"To my way of thinking, the first order of business is tissue sampling," Weintraub was saying. "I really can't go very far without some cellular material, and I don't think genetics can either." Suddenly he opened his eyes wide. "Between us I think we'll be able to examine the larger questions pretty thoroughly."

Bob Hodder, geneticist and one of Riverside's young Turks, spoke up. "Obviously, a chromosomal analysis will give us a definitive answer as to whether or not this is a human organism we're dealing with." He was almost handsome, Bob was. Sarah could remember his big tan body, his rippling muscles . . . he had been one of her more miserable affairs, prior to Tom. A good lay and a good date, but a man barricaded in a fortress of unfeeling. He knew genetics and sex and could order well at a restaurant. But he was as cold as death itself. Not nearly the breadth of old Tom, who sat leaning tautly into the conference, his glasses down his nose, his cigar now clamped between his teeth but unlit.

She took a deep breath and delivered her news. "The patient left."

Hutch reared back, seizing his opportunity with an almost audible *chomp*. "That was stupid."

"It's nobody's fault," Tom yammered. "We're not equipped to hold people. This isn't a secure facility."

"Who the hell was in charge?" Hutch's voice was

strident. He intended to use the mistake to embarrass Tom in front of Rush. He knew how to score when he had the opportunity. Neither he nor Tom so much as glanced at the impassive face of Sam Rush. If he hadn't been there, however, Sarah doubted there would have been more between Hutch and Tom than a mutual glare.

"That's not the point! They followed procedures—did more than that, as a matter of fact. But she slipped out. You know what this place is like. You can exit Sleep Research in a dozen different directions. Anybody who wants to can get out no matter how careful we are."

Sam Rush spoke. "Doctor Haver, you'll have to locate your patient at once. I really do think it's essential that we get her into confinement." Tom's eyes sought Sarah. The message was clear: '*You* let her go, *you* get her back.'

Sarah shook her head. She wouldn't take the responsibility. Her own attitude toward Miriam Blaylock was now quite clear to her: the woman—thing—was frightening and dangerously seductive. She had the power to call up desires best left sleeping. Sarah wanted no part of her.

"I've got to ask you, Sarah. You know her best."

She looked down at the table. There was no way to refuse such an open request.

"I don't know how to go about it."

"Call her," Tom said.

"Visit her. Don't risk a call. Bring her back." Hutch's voice was full of sincerity and concern.

"Your director is right," Sam Rush said. Tom looked down at his papers.

"I don't know where she lives," Sarah muttered desperately.

"We have her address—don't we, Tom?" Hutch sounded almost as if he hoped "we" didn't.

"Of course," Tom snapped.

Sarah fought to control herself. Her hands twined

and twined together, until she snatched them from the table. All eyes were now on her. "Yes," she heard a small, unfamiliar version of herself say, "we've got to get her back. I'll go at once."

Miriam Blaylock's home was unexpectedly charming. Sarah got out of the cab before the compact red-brick row house with its white marble trim and window boxes full of flowers. It was all so fresh and light. The windows were open and cheerful rooms could be seen beyond them. Private house on Sutton Place, Lanvin suits—Miriam Blaylock's *genus* certainly had no difficulty coping with the human milieu.

Sarah mounted the steps and pressed the doorbell. From within she heard a chime. A policeman strolled past whistling. Across the street a group of children huddled together talking quietly.

The door swung open on Miriam Blaylock. She wore a pink-and-white dress. When she smiled, any thought other than that of being welcomed into a lovely home by its charming owner instantly left Sarah's mind.

"May I come in?"

Miriam stepped aside.

"Oh, I love pomander," Sarah found herself saying. "It reminds me of my childhood." The richly antique scent evoked an image of her grandmother's front hall, of sun slanting in the windows on just such a day as this. She inhaled. "That really does take me back."

"Would you like to sit down?"

Sarah followed her into a marvelous living room. Morning light poured in the windows, which overlooked a garden. The room was furnished with Regency antiques, lightly graceful chairs and couches. On the floor was a silk carpet from China, depicting many of the very flowers that bloomed in the garden. Blue silk curtains hung at the windows and the ceiling was a trompe l'oeil rendering of a summer's sky. It was the kind of room that almost made you laugh with delight. Sarah stood in the doorway, her hands folded under her chin. She knew she was smiling like a little girl. Miriam turned, met her eyes and burst out laughing. Her eyes sparkled with true and unrestrained warmth.

Sarah came into the room and sat on one of the two facing love seats.

"May I give you a cup of coffee? I've just made some."

"That would be lovely."

Miriam's voice floated back as she went to the kitchen. "I'll bet you didn't get a wink of sleep. It's lucky I just happened to be making some coffee."

She handed Sarah a cup. It was rich and smooth, altogether extraordinary. Its taste was all the aroma promised. "This is nice," Sarah said.

Miriam sat beside Sarah, placing her own cup on the mosaic-covered coffee table. Sarah's eyes were attracted to the mosaic's delicate beauty. It portrayed a goddess standing on a rainbow with a sickle moon above her head. "Lamia," Miriam said as Sarah's fingers caressed the tiny stones. "Her food is youth. Her symbol is the rainbow because of her beauty and elusiveness. She is one of the immortals. The mosaic is from the lost city of Palmyra."

"What happened to it?"

"Greed. Like the rest of the Empire. It was a Roman city."

"This must be worth—" She stopped, embarrassed. How crass to gush about the value of somebody's art objects.

"I'll never sell it. Can you see why?" With loving grace Miriam ran her finger along the outline of the face.

The resemblance was amazing. "I certainly can! It could be your twin."

Miriam looked suddenly toward the windows, her mind seemingly drawn to something outside. Dropping the conversation, she got up and went over to them. Sarah had conflicting impressions: Miriam had seemed delighted to see her at first, but all at once had apparently lost interest. Sarah began to want to get it over with. It was as if Miriam were waiting for somebody else. This place, so ruthlessly pleasant, began to contain the suggestion of nasty shadows.

"Your coffee's getting cold," Sarah announced in her most cheerful tone.

"You drink it. I had a cup before you came."

"I won't turn you down on that. It's so incredibly good. I mean, I know it's just coffee, but—" She was gushing again. Calm down, girl. Bring up Riverside and get thyself gone. "Listen, if you're busy I'll get right to the point. Obviously, I came here for a reason. Riverside—"

"It's such a beautiful day. We get the nicest breeze when the wind is off the river."

"Your garden is wonderful. We at Riverside—"

"I have over ten thousand plants. The roses are my real prize."

Sarah went over and stood beside her. There wasn't a rose to be seen. "Where are they?" Obviously, Riverside would have to wait until the damnable garden was praised.

"Behind the stand of snapdragons." She became very still. "Good gods, why can't we see them?" Sarah noticed that she was glaring like the rhesus did when you surprised them. Miriam went out the French doors and across the brick porch. Sarah walked behind her. The whole garden was redolent of flowers. The invisible roses could certainly be smelled. Beyond the garden could be seen the glimmering water of the East River. A sailboat passed, its white canvas flapping in the sun. The dull roar of the FDR Drive rose as an undertone. Miriam swept down a winding garden path and past the stand of snapdragons. When Sarah caught up with her she was squatting on the ground, her fingers clutching torn flowers. "My ROSES!" she shrieked. Sarah was amazed. Before her was a horrible sight, a vandalized flowerbed. Even the petals of the destroyed plants had been ground into the earth. The leaves had been stripped off and the stems split. Some of the smaller plants were uprooted. There was a powerful attar, the blood of the flowers.

Miriam stiffened, slowly standing up, facing Sarah. It was somehow a terrifying gesture, one that made her step back. Then Miriam was past her, crouching down again, her hands flitting over a hole in the earth. When she shouted down it Sarah heard a deep echo. Slowly Miriam got to her feet. Her lips were moving and Sarah strained to hear.

She said, *"He's out!"* and whirled like a tiger in a cage.

Her head snapped toward the house. With a sharp intake of breath she was off, racing up the garden path, toward the open French doors. "Come on," she shouted, *"hurry!"*

Her obvious fear infected Sarah. She began running as in a nightmare toward the door. It seemed more and more distant, the flowers spreading for acres and miles.

Miriam's eyes were bulging with fear more raw than anything one saw in a human face. Her arms stretched out, the hands clutching and opening like those of an infant seeking help. *"Sarah, hurry!"*

Sarah's progress was dreamlike. She felt heavy, she thought of sleep. Every detail of the flowerbeds she was passing stood out. There were daisies bobbing, zinnias spreading to the sun, snapdragons and many more exotic varieties. She saw a bee standing on the stipule of a pansy, its pollen sacs dusted gold. Behind her there arose a great crackling, like a bear coming forth.

Miriam's arms twined around her, the French doors closed with a bang. With a snap of her wrist Miriam locked them, then pulled the curtains. She opened a box on the coffee table and began to press buttons inside it. The row of red lights that winked on suggested it was a burglar alarm.

Of all things, Sarah found herself getting woozy. The lack of sleep was really hitting hard, despite the coffee. She let Miriam hold her, watched fascinated as the

woman's expression shifted to absolute calm. That was
iron control, considering the fear. "Did you see him?"

"Who?"

Miriam looked away as if struck by some new
realization. "Mine were the best roses in all the world.
Did you know that? Do you know roses?"

"I'm sorry, Miriam. They must have been beautiful."
Sarah wanted to calm the woman, wanted also to sit
down. She was really quite tired.

"There is no word in this language to describe them.
They were—*amoenum*. It's Latin, it refers to the
heartbreaking beauty of nature. Vergilius Maro used it
to describe Aeneas' last vision of Ilium. Such flowers
are like that. A last vision, the hurting beauty of a
rainbow."

"I see." Sarah knew some Latin, mostly as a professional language. "Why don't we sit down? I feel a little
off." She smiled. "The excitement." Nervously, she
touched Miriam's shoulder—and snapped her hand
back in surprise. The skin was as hard as stone, for
God's sake. Was it an artificial limb?

"Get some more coffee," Miriam said. "It's in the
kitchen." Wishing Miriam would get it for her, but
wanting it badly, Sarah found her way through a dining
room that had been made over into a den. The kitchen
told why; it was completely empty. Nobody ate in this
house, not ever. Sarah checked a couple of cabinets.
Absolutely pristine. Stove, ancient but perfectly clean.
The only litter was on the counter—an open half-pound
bag of coffee beans, a grinder and a Melitta pot
containing the cooling coffee.

This wasn't a home.

She didn't have a chance to think about it, she had
noticed a shadow on the curtains of the kitchen window. It moved away, then appeared again before the
door, sharply outlined against the white chintz that
covered the glass. There was a whisper, but Sarah was
too startled to reply. When the doorknob began to
rattle she found her voice and called out.

Instantly Miriam was beside her. She stepped right up to the door. "It's locked," she shouted, "locked and set!"

The shadow disappeared.

Sarah began to want very badly to get out of here. But she couldn't just leave the woman, not like this. "Call the police," she said. Her speech was actually slurred. Despite the obvious danger she felt curiously calm.

"No!" Miriam grabbed her shoulders and shook them. It rattled her teeth in her head, it was like being gripped by a powerful machine.

Remember, she is not human. *Not human!* Whatever might be going on here, it could be very different from appearance. Sarah must not allow herself to forget that. And for the love of heaven she must not fall asleep! What was the matter with her?

"I—I'm sorry," Miriam said. She found some Kleenex in a drawer and took a couple of sheets, blew her nose. "Let's go to the front of the house. He won't bother us there."

Sarah was led into a library, somewhat darker than the other rooms. "History," Miriam said, waving her arms at shelves and shelves of books, "do you believe in history?"

Sarah was beyond answering complex questions. With the clarity of exhaustion she heard a horn honk outside. The shadows were deeper here. There were ancient-looking volumes, and glass-fronted boxes containing stacks of scrolls. It was not a pleasant room. In a way, with its musty smell and black old books, it was quite horrible. Sarah wished Miriam would just get out of this place with her. "We would like you to return to the clinic."

Miriam's look was almost coy. "Why should I? So you can put me in a freak show?"

"So we can relieve your suffering."

Miriam came over to her, took her hands. This close the woman seemed almost larger than she should be.

Sarah wanted desperately to take a step back. But she couldn't move, she was just too tired.

Miriam's speech was measured, her eyes watching Sarah closely.

"Sarah, we have a great deal to learn from one another, but I've just sustained a shock and I need some time to pull myself together. Please forgive me if my behavior seems strange."

"I still don't understand why you don't call the police. They would give you some protection—"

"For a time. But what happens when they go away? And they will, sooner or later."

"OK, it's your decision. I'd do it, though. You're being menaced. Whoever it is could get in here at any moment."

Her words made Miriam flash a glance toward the hallway that led to the back of the house. "An alarm will go off if he comes in. I'll have plenty of warning."

"But what if he does something else—sets the place on fire while you're asleep, you never know what such a person might do."

"He won't—surely!" She looked around as if in a cell. "No—" She seemed very much afraid.

Summoning up her last reserve of unclouded consciousness, Sarah tried to press the advantage. "I'm sorry to keep returning to the other subject, but I suspect it fits in."

"I'm not going back to Riverside now, Sarah. You and I have a great deal to discuss and we can do it right here."

"The equipment and the people are at Riverside, and at the moment it's a little early for discussion. That'll come later when your therapy gets under way."

"And who will be my therapist? You?" Miriam took a step toward Sarah and this time the menace did not come from outside. "We have a great deal to discuss."

"Please, Miriam." Now *that* sounded downright pitiful. Pull it together, girl! She closed her eyes, opened them with surprise. For an instant she had been asleep on her feet.

Miriam snatched her wrist. "Surely you're willing to give me some of your time."

Sarah couldn't stand it, all of her carefully contained emotions were exposed by the steely power of that grip. "You let me go," she mumbled, twisting weakly, feeling sharp pain in her wrist.

Miriam laughed, a brittle tinkling. For an instant the truth flashed in her eyes. Sarah saw abject, heartrending terror there, the awesome fear of a cornered animal.

Miriam enfolded her in strong arms, pressed her against the pretty pink-and-white dress. Sarah's sheer exhaustion overcame the panic that wanted her to kick and scream. She was vaguely aware that Miriam had lifted her off her feet.

Only the rocking, pleasant motion of it reached her consciousness as Miriam carried her out of the room and swiftly up the stairs.

8

THERE WAS SINGING somewhere far away. Its purity drew Sarah from the comfortable warm place where she had been hiding. She rose swiftly into red fog. Beyond the fog was the source of the song. Sarah almost wept, she had not seen her mother since she was fifteen.

—her mother, who sang as she braided Sarah's hair.

—singing on the car trip to Yellowstone.

—the voices of the church choir, her mother's rising clear.

—her mother dying, the memory of her voice fading. "Open your eyes, Sarah."

The booming resolved into a headache, the red fog dissipated. Sarah was in a high old bed with satin sheets. A canopy of blue lace hung between her and the ceiling.

There came the hiss of a faucet. Then Miriam was handing her a glass of water. "It'll make you feel better."

Sarah took it. The liquid would certainly be welcome. When the coolness touched her lips she was brushed by a small memory. "I ought to go," she said.

"Yes. It's nearly noon."

Sarah looked at her watch, hesitating an instant because of a dull pain in her right arm. "Why am I in bed?" she asked.

Miriam threw back her head and laughed. It was reassuring, so open and innocent that it made Sarah want to laugh too. Miriam slid close to her and put her arms around her shoulders, looking into her face with a chummy smile. "You fell asleep, Doctor. You're not good at staying up all night."

Sarah couldn't find a thing in her memory to contradict this. "Fell asleep?"

"You wanted to try the bed. What can I say? You've been there an hour and a half."

A breeze billowed the curtains, bringing with it the scent of the garden. "It's so hot," Sarah said. Her skin was warm and dry.

"Take a shower before you go."

As she started to dismiss the idea, Sarah thought of the long day ahead at Riverside, the turmoil of work awaiting in her lab, all the other tensions and problems. She probably wouldn't get another chance until midnight. Miriam went toward the bathroom.

"I'll turn it on. You can leave your clothes in there."

Sarah got up, grabbed the bedstead as mild vertigo passed through her system, then unhitched her skirt and tossed it on the bed. In a few moments she was naked, walking toward the roaring of the shower. Miriam looked pleased. Her sleeves were rolled up, an old-fashioned bath brush dangling from her hand. The room was filling with a marvelous rough-sweet scent. Sarah hesitated, suddenly aware of what she was doing, astonished at her own nakedness. But the scent was so appealing, it seemed to draw her on. "Is that your soap? I love it."

"Brehmer and Cross make it up for me. I send them my own flowers to mix the perfume."

Sarah stepped into the tub, moving the showerhead so that her hair wouldn't get wet.

"Is the temperature right?"

"Maybe a touch warm."

Miriam turned back the hot water handle.

"Perfect."

"Open the window, you can look out on the garden while I do your back." When Sarah hesitated Miriam laughed. "It's OK, it's perfectly private." Sarah raised the sash. The breeze was delicious coming into the shower, and the only way she could be seen would be with a telescope from a boat on the East River. She leaned against the sill and looked down into the flowers as Miriam first massaged her neck and shoulders and then washed her back and buttocks with mountains of heady lather. The delicately bristled brush tickled delightfully. It was most relaxing. She didn't stir as Miriam did her thighs and calves, then sluiced her with water. There came a gentle tug at her shoulder and Sarah turned around. She let Miriam bathe her, feeling a little embarrassed and more than a little touched. It was very, very pleasant to feel the brush on her abdomen, then sweeping down her legs amid all that wonderful yellow-green soap. "Close your eyes." Miriam did her face with a lighter brush and with brief flutters of a cloth, her breasts. Sarah did not move until she heard Miriam's voice and realized that the shower was over, it was time to dry off.

Miriam rubbed her down with a coarse towel, then followed it with a very soft one, moving it smoothly against her skin. "You can use some of my powder if you like."

"I already smell like your flowers."

"So does my powder."

"I'm going to have to go to Brehmer and Cross. Where is it?"

"They don't have a retail store, unfortunately. But if

you'd like to order something I'll give you their address."

"It's probably horribly expensive." Sarah had fluffed some of the powder on and was redoing her mascara and lipstick.

"You use makeup? I don't think you need it."

Sarah smiled. "It's just a habit. I don't use a lot."

"People used to paint their faces with lead pigment. The women looked like Chinese porcelain. Can you imagine?"

"That must have been before my time. Lead is poisonous."

Miriam smiled. "How Tom must love you." She said it with such feeling that Sarah turned in surprise. The kiss that came was small, little more than a peck, but it was on the lips. Sarah chose to take it as a gesture of friendship and smiled into it. "You're just trying to smear my lipstick."

She sat watching as Sarah dressed. To be admired so openly was pleasing to Sarah and she found herself adding a touch of grace to every movement. Miriam made her feel beautiful, and as she regarded herself in the dim mirror that hung above the vanity, a little proud. Her mother kept coming to mind. She had not felt this sense of intimate female friendship since she was a child.

Miriam walked her down the stairs. "When you get back to Riverside, they're going to want to know what you accomplished. Tell them I'm still trying to make up my mind."

"You?" For a moment Sarah was utterly confused, then she remembered the purpose of her visit. "Oh! Yes. I'll tell them that."

Miriam took both of Sarah's hands in hers. "I called a cab. It'll be here any minute."

How considerate, Sarah thought.

Miriam leaned toward her, smiling. "You smell like a—"

"A rose?" Sarah offered.

A dark look crossed Miriam's face. "I never use them in fragrances." Her voice was harsher, almost strident. Then it all evaporated into another of those wonderful, warm smiles.

On the way to Riverside as Sarah lay back in the cab, she thought of how long it had been since she had enjoyed the special friendship of another woman, how very long.

Tom looked up as Sarah came slowly into his office. He had been developing a table of organization for the Blaylock project—if only he could find a way to split it off from Hutch's control. He had been about to greet Sarah, but her condition silenced him. Her clothes weren't on straight, her hair was tangled, and she smelled like a cathouse. When she saw his expression she returned a guilty look.

"I took a bath," she said. He heard a lot of strain in that voice.

"You sick?"

She shook her head, then dropped to the couch. "I feel hot. Is it hot in here?"

Maybe it was, a little. He pushed the window open the inch it would go. "Did you see Mrs. Blaylock at all, or just go home?"

He was stunned to hear her laugh, bitter and raucous. "I took the shower at her house."

He was at a loss for words. Her house? "You mean—Miriam Blaylock's house."

Sarah smiled mirthlessly. Her face dissolved by anguished degrees. He knew how she hated to cry. To see her try not to was more painful than if she had done it. Tom went to her, sat down beside her. The smell was quite sickening this close. It was one of those foul covering perfumes that must have been popular in the days before people bathed.

"I'm sorry. Very unprofessional of me." Now she broke down, grabbed his shoulders, and buried her face in his chest. Twisting as far as he could, he managed to kick the door closed. He wasn't entirely sure why she was so agitated, but he didn't try to find out more details. That could come later. Right now she needed reassurance and a little tender care. He held her, stroking her hair. He would have kissed her but for the repellent odor. Despite himself he just could not get that close to it.

The funny thing was, he had smelled it before. Somewhere, in the mists of the past. Perhaps it was the perfume one of Granny Haver's friends had favored.

Despite the smell it still felt good to have Sarah in his arms. "I'm so glad you're back," he said softly. She only clutched him tighter. The bitterness of her tears made him wish that he had not made her go to Miriam Blaylock. Obviously, she was way out of her range of skills. But who wouldn't be, given the circumstances. "Will you take a Valium?"

"I don't want a Valium."

"Sarah, this is clearly a stress syndrome." He held her by the shoulders. Her face was red and swept with tears. She refused to be held away from him and took him around the neck, hugging him so tight that it hurt. "I love you," he said.

"Oh, Tom, I'm so glad."

He squeezed back, wishing that she had repeated his words, wondering why she hadn't. "I'm going to go get that Valium. You put your feet up here, darling." He had no trouble getting her to lie back on the couch, then hurried down the hall to the dispensary to sign out the pill. Never, ever should he have sent her on such a dangerous mission. He could be so damn ruthless when he felt threatened, and Hutch had really been putting him on the spot. Now Sarah was hurt, hurt bad. He had a mental image of Miriam Blaylock, strange, sexless creature, beautiful without being the least bit attractive.

Did Sarah feel the same way? Hadn't Tom seen a

curious moment of intimacy between them on the sleep cubicle monitor? Certainly, it wasn't sexual, not in the usual sense of the word. But there must be something between them, some attraction. Tom shuddered, thinking of being touched by that . . . thing.

Sarah's clothes, though—had she only taken a shower? What if Miriam had come to her, run those beautiful hands down her thighs, touched Sarah where she so enjoyed being touched. Yes, what if she had done that?

Poor Sarah! Above all, she treasured her professionalism. If she and Miriam had gone to bed together it meant that Sarah had violated every professional standard in the book—and right at the start of the most important case she or anybody else had ever had.

No wonder she was distraught. She might well have good reason to be.

He returned to his office to find her lying in a more relaxed pose, with eyes closed, one arm loosely across her face.

"I have the Valium."

"No."

"Why?"

"I dislike weakness, you know that." She sat up, a rush of motion. "Tom, she's very beautiful. Almost magical. A magical being." She smiled. "Can you *believe* this?" The tears of a few minutes before still shone on her face. But now she smiled.

"No. But I have no choice. The data is there." Tom could hardly believe it was the same Sarah. Were the contradictory emotions she was displaying even real? Was this how Sarah broke down—swinging between extremes?

"It's been quite a week," she said with enthusiasm. "First Methuselah, then this. I keep thinking there must be a connection."

He had wondered that himself, refused to entertain such a seductive and unscientific notion. "No, Sarah. Don't start thinking like that."

"Perhaps there's something about what happened to Methuselah that . . . attracted her."

"Moth to flame. What was the mode of attraction? Scent?"

"A mode we know nothing about. She is an unknown, after all."

She was being cryptic. Tom wished that he didn't always have this sense of sparring with her. "Telepathy, then. But why? Methuselah was maybe a relative of hers?" Sarcasm. Did she deserve it? Possibly.

"Come on, be serious. Help me."

"You won't accept my help." He held out the Valium. She was under extreme stress. This latest mood swing proved it, or so he willed himself to believe.

"I don't like palliatives. I'd rather face myself."

"Noble. Just don't go bathing around. It doesn't help your reputation. Not to mention the fact that you seem to have gotten perfumed in the basement of Kleins."

"Kleins is out of business."

"My point exactly."

She grasped his hands, intense, an undertone of fear in her face. "Tom, am I in danger?"

The question had a nasty impact. He wanted to push it away but it remained there, demanding an answer. "Of course not," he said and instantly cursed his own guilty lie. How could he be so sure? Paradoxically, he was angry with her. She had confused and upset him. He wanted his hard-driving professional back again, not this vague, dreamy creature off taking baths in the homes of her patients and failing to serve the vital interests of Riverside. Especially with Sam Rush peering over their collective shoulder.

"I *feel* like I'm in danger. I feel manaced. That incident at Miriam's was very odd, Tom. I haven't told you the half of it."

"Is that an opening?"

She told him all that had happened, her voice curiously absent of emotion. "I think your own supposition was right," Tom said when she was finished. "We're dealing with an unknown. There isn't yet any way to evaluate Miriam Blaylock or her behavior."

"But it's directed at me."

"You don't know that." Why did he lie so? To make her feel better, or perhaps to delude her into staying with it? Yes, that was it. He needed Sarah to keep after Miriam—she was their only established link. That, beneath it all, was his true motive. He felt dirty and crass, seeing such a thing in himself. But he didn't try to change it.

She grew silent. He waited through a minute for her to respond to him but she only sat there, hunched, almost contemplative. He wanted to press her for more information, but hesitated to do so. There was very little to be gained by cross-examining Sarah, he had long since learned that.

"I *do* know it," she said at last. "Miriam Blaylock's actions *are* directed at me."

"Yes," he said, hoping to draw a little more out of her. He became aware of a tension in the room, almost a charge, as thick as the air before a storm. In his mind's eye he saw sick green clouds shot through with lightning. Sweat tickled his eyebrows and he wiped it impatiently away. She sat forward on the couch, grasped her hands around her knees.

"I feel like a kind of tentacle just reached out and touched me. I hate to say it, Tom, it's so subjective that it's embarrassing. But I do feel it."

"Miriam Blaylock is hostile to you?"

Her eyes widened, all innocent surprise. "No, not at all. She's part of it, but so is Methuselah. It's not a coincidence. I feel almost as if Miriam—I know that this is a subjective way of putting it—Miriam in some way sought me out after Methuselah. As if it's some-how very important to her."

"I thought we discounted telepathy a second ago. As of this moment only a few people know about Methuselah, and Miriam Blaylock isn't one of them."

"Tom, what is she?"

Now he smiled. "You're the genius in the family. You tell me."

"Not from another planet. She's too close to human. Another species, living right here all along. An identical twin."

"Does that wash? Five thousand years of civilization and nobody's noticed?"

"Maybe and maybe not. What about the Amazons? What were they?"

He raised his eyebrows, thinking of large, domineering blondes. "Maybe she ought to run for office. Keep the mobs in line."

"You're a master of the extraneous comment, you know that. It's perfectly possible that a twin species would go unnoticed. Maybe they don't want to be noticed. If I was hiding and you didn't even know to look for me, you'd never find me—unless I wanted you to."

He kissed the top of her head, knelt down beside the couch. The odor was less strong, or perhaps he wanted her more. "I love you," he said again. The intensity of the past few days was still very much with him. The sense of devotion he was beginning to feel was a very new thing for him. Almost absently she stroked his head, pulling it down into her lap. He crouched there, afire with this terrible need for her that left him feeling utterly alone.

"Tom, I'm frightened."

"It's a frightening situation."

"Something brought her out of hiding. Something about me." The hand stopped stroking his head. He reached up and grasped it, then raised himself and slipped onto the couch beside her. She snuggled into his shoulder.

"I won't let it happen."

"What?"

"Whatever it is you feel might happen. I'm slow but I feel it too."

"Don't let's both panic!"

"I'm not scared. Concerned and protective. You've got my primitive male juices flowing."

"Not here in the office." She arched her back, ran her hand along his thigh. He kissed her. The office was quiet, the hubbub outside far away. Beyond the windows small white clouds sailed through the sky. Tom extended the kiss, finding an urgency in himself that he had not expected. There came a sweeping, aggressive wave and he took her in his arms and laid her on the couch. There was barely room enough for the two of them. Her face, framed by brown curly hair, caught in the crook of his arm, looked up at him happily. "Not here," she said again. "Anybody could walk in."

"Don't you like danger?"

"I'm not the type."

"I find it exciting." He opened his trousers, let her see his eagerness.

"Tom, really, this is crazy!"

"We need it."

"What if Hutch comes in? You'll look like a fool."

Her resistance drove him on, created in him a compulsion to the act. "Let him come. Exposure to a little human love would do him good." He slipped his hands under her skirt and rolled her panties down.

"Tom, this is *crazy!*"

"You sound like a broken record."

"Well, it is—oh—"

The relentlessness of his thrust excited him more. Her face flushed, she shook her head from side to side. "I love you," he breathed, and whispered her name with the rhythm of their bodies. Voices rose outside the door but he chose to ignore them. When her eyes flickered concern he smothered her with kisses. Then he pressed his lips close to her ear and whispered the sort of things she liked to hear, the words that excited her. It was silly, perhaps, certainly childish, but Tom knew that there had to be a certain dirtiness, a sense of evil, for Sarah to really enjoy herself.

He brought her to a climax, her thighs pumping, her face sweaty and surprised. He lost himself in the quivering pleasure of his own love, barely aware that the voices in the hall had not gone away. "For God's sake, it's Charlie and Phyllis out there! Hurry!" He pumped frantically. There came a tapping at the door. Sarah cleared her throat, changed her tone to one of businesslike precision. "One moment, please," she sang out, "he's on the phone."

"You're not a phone."

"Hurry up! You're a man, you're supposed to be fast!"

"Don't whisper so loud, they'll hear you."

Never before had he made love under such circumstances. Every movement, no matter how small, bore with it a sense of stolen delight. Taking Sarah here on the couch, with the door about to be opened on them, was delicious beyond belief. 'A little of the exhibitionist in you,' he thought.

They knocked again. "Who's he talking to, God? We've got important business."

"I know that, Phyllis," Sarah said, her voice wobbling with his thrusts. She was now rubbing against him with all her might, trying to speed things up. The couch, the whole office was shaking. "Hurry dear, hurry dear," she breathed in rhythm to their movements, "let it go, let it go—"

And he did, like stars exploding, huge and rich with a thousand wild tickling joys. They lay still an instant, both breathing hard, a moment's deference. He rose off her, closed his pants over his still-enormous organ. "I'd better hide behind the desk, my love," he said as she smoothed her skirt and went to the door.

"Sorry," she said, swinging it wide, "come on in."

Charlie and Phyllis glanced at each other. Tom controlled himself carefully. Sarah was sweating and flushed, obviously trying to conceal her ragged breathing. "Some phone call," Charlie said in a nervous voice.

"Let's get on with it," Tom growled. "I haven't got all day."

"No," Phyllis murmured, "obviously not."

"Come on, come on." He was pleased to see Sarah blow a kiss at him, roll her eyes in an exaggerated pantomime of ecstasy. He began to feel rather proud of himself.

"Briefly," Charlie said, "we've been doing a little comparative analysis between Methuselah and Miriam Blaylock."

"Why?" Sarah's voice was sharp. She stood up and came to the desk where Charlie had laid out some glossy color photographs of various blood cells.

"We noticed that Mrs. Blaylock's erythrocytes were the same color as Methuselah's, when he was in his terminal phase."

"Which means?"

"The color of his deepened right before the end. His need for oxygen seemed to be declining at that time."

Sarah was literally sparkling. Maybe Tom ought to hit her under a restaurant table next time. She appeared to like the threat of exposure very well. "What are you driving at? Was the same pigmentation factor present in both bloods?" There was the brilliant scientist Tom knew and loved.

"It sure as hell looks like it. But that isn't the whole story." Charlie pulled out some more glossies. "Here you see Methuselah's erythrocytes in a time series. They get darker and darker." In the final photograph they were deep purple and misshapen. "Remember that Geoff took another blood sample after Mrs. Blaylock had been asleep a couple of hours? Well, look." The purple pigmentation of her blood cells had faded to a healthy pink-white.

"Conclusion," Phyllis added, "Mrs. Blaylock slept off something similar to what destroyed Methuselah."

Tom spoke quickly, trying to cut the edge of panic that had flickered in Sarah's eyes. "At least this means that there is no further question of the Gerontology budget being cut. I doubt if we'll even need a meeting of the board now." Nobody smiled. "Clap clap clap. I thought you'd be delighted."

"We're not surprised," Charlie said. "It was obvious as soon as we compared the bloods."

"Tell me, what does it all imply?"

"How should we know, Tom?" Sarah's voice was high, nervous. "It suggests a lot of things."

"Some of them downright strange," Phyllis added. "Like why Mrs. Blaylock came here."

"Smart girl," Tom said. "That is indeed what Sarah and I have been trying to understand. It seems as if she somehow discovered Sarah's work and was drawn to her—for some reason we do not know."

Sarah's face had become waxlike. Concealing. Sarah hid her feelings. "Your thoughts, Doctor Roberts?"

"That's an unfair question, Tom."

"You thrive on unfair questions."

She tossed her head, her chin jutting up. Her lips were set in a line, her eyes glaring defiantly at him. It was pitiful to see how hard she had to work to hide fear.

"I think we'll all have to pull together," Tom said. "I'm going to declare Miriam Blaylock a special project and get myself appointed director. We'll budget it from the general fund, go around Hutch."

"Why is that necessary? Hutch'll cooperate completely. He might not agree with everything we say and do, but he's a scientist, he sees the importance of this work."

"Thank you, Sarah. May I remind you who it was just about destroyed your Gerontology lab? I can settle it all with a single telephone call to Sam Rush. He'll confirm our request before he even thinks of Hutch."

"Hutch founded this lab!"

"He's as good as dead. I'm very sorry, but it happens."

"I'm going to tell him—"

"No, ma'am. You have your job and I have mine. Let's not let our differences come between us." He held out his hand. "You don't know a thing about front-office politics."

There was a silence. "I get the impression that this meeting is concluded," Charlie said into it. He gave a nervous laugh. "You can count on me, boss."

"I won't talk to Hutch," Sarah murmured. "I don't have time."

Charlie and Phyllis gathered up their materials and left. Tom sat, trying to feel the impassivity of a Buddha. He expected to get a real chewing-out from Sarah, but instead she went over to the couch and flopped down with her arm once again over her eyes.

Tom seasoned and lit a cigar. Now was a good time for his one shot of the day. He reached up and opened the window so that Sarah wouldn't complain too much.

But she didn't complain at all. Tom was surprised to see that she was asleep. So suddenly, poor, tired Sarah. He got his raincoat from the hook on the door and covered her with it. He would let her sleep, call Rush in an hour or so. There was no need to hurry. This latest discovery propelled him into a very strong position. Obviously the Blaylock project should be under a special administrator. He had no illusions about getting Hutch to resign, but he was sure that he could capture for himself management of the project, and take Gerontology along with it. That would leave Hutch on the trailing edge, administering the conventional parts of the clinic, the parts that were of absolutely no interest to the Dr. Rushes of this world.

Tom sucked his cigar, inhaling deeply, feeling the warmth of the smoke in his lungs. He exhaled. All forbidden, all dangerous. It was so typical of the human predicament that something as pleasurable as a cigar would have to be so damn unhealthy.

Largely to stop feeling guilty about the cigar he turned his mind to the more puzzling apsects of Miriam Blaylock. She had certainly had a hell of an effect on Sarah.

There was something about Miriam that recalled Granny Haver after her husband and all of her friends were dead. Granny had seemed as bright and spry as ever, laughing all the time, raising her flowers, baking pie after pie. And yet, if you really looked at Gran Haver—looked beyond the tantalizing hints of former beauty and the present ruins—you got a hell of a chill.

Late one winter night she screamed horribly. Tom's first waking thought was fire. By the time they had gotten upstairs she was dead, not of fire but of something else. Her eyes were wide, her hands like claws. Had she had a nightmare, died of fright?

Tom had helped his father carry her to the parlor. The wind had howled and he had felt presences. A nightmare—or a night visit?

Afterward he had always assumed that Gran Haver had died with some hidden thing on her conscience. That scream had been her last utterance on earth, her first in hell.

"Who are you, Miriam?" he asked softly, chuckling to himself. 'OK, scientist,' he thought, 'here you are ready to believe that she can hear you, read your mind.'

Well, why not?

What was "this world"? The hospital? This office? The warm taste of the cigar? What, really?

Tom reassured himself that he was grounded in the practical. It was possible that this planet did indeed hold two species who were superficially similar. The perfect predator would be indistinguishable from his prey. That would be beautiful. Once in college someone had asked the question, what if the essence of reality is belief? That which is believed is real. What if real witches flew on wings of belief through the nights of fourteenth-century Europe and consorted with demons in a real hell? Or if the gods really walked among the Greeks?

Or Miriam Blaylock among us?

Sarah believed in Miriam, that was the source of her

fear. Perhaps Miriam was what you wanted her to be—*whatever* you wanted. Perhaps that was the definition of a monster.

SWABIA: 1724

It is freezing cold in the carriage. A candle guttering in a socket is the only light. Thick fog chokes the way. Trees pass like shadowy towers, their branches swishing down the sides of the coach.

Across from Miriam sit her three sisters. Her brother is in her arms. She found them in Paris, half-starved, subsisting on the flesh of diseased beggars, constantly on the run. The girls huddle in their broadcloth cloaks, their faces the color of stone. Her brother leans stiffly against her. She touches his cheek, wiping away the dew that has settled there.

Her hand snaps back, she comes fully aware. Trembling, she touches him again.

The skin is like a mask stretched on a skull. And the mouth is opening.

She screams, but the sound is choked by a violent lurch of the carriage. The driver has whipped the horses up. Wolves stand beside the road, dozens and dozens of them. The horses bolt, the carriage careens.

Without a word, their faces fixed in grief, Miriam's sisters open the door and throw out their brother's body.

Miriam protests. They are not yet animals! She unlatches her own door and jumps from the carriage. Her silks splash in the muddy road. The carriage sways off.

Suddenly, quiet. Ten feet away lie his huddled ruins. She can see the blowing breath of the wolves. There is such serenity in their faces. That, and death. She can smell it in the wet air, an exhalation of demons. One of them dashes up and worries her brother's filthy gabardine cloak.

She drives it off, drags her brother from the sucking mud. Bearing him in her arms, she begins to plod down the road. Her heart is dull with hopeless sorrow. Ahead the carriage has stopped, rising enormous in the fog. She can hear the driver singing some lament of his wild Carpathian people.

Without a word she returns to her place, hugging the withered remains close to her. Her sisters sit bowed, their shame too great for them to bear looking at her.

A little before noon they arrive in a village. The driver climbs down and doffs his filthy cap. "Zarnesti," he says. Miriam hands out a silver florin, holding it between her fingers so that he can take it without touching her.

Zarnesti is a poor place deep in Swabia. They have come here following rumors that their kindred have found a measure of safety in these wild regions. The village reeks, it is sick and starving. There are wattled houses here and there and in the center a church made of logs. Behind the church is a long building, an inn. On all sides the forest threatens. In the shadows of the closer trees there are ruined cottages. Miriam's sisters cross the clearing, their cloaks trailing in the muck. They are followed by hungry pigs.

Miriam leaves her brother in the carriage and hurries to catch up with his sisters. They are so desperate that she is afraid they will ignore her careful plan of attack.

They are negotiating with the innkeeper, their high voices mingling with the screams of birds in the forest. The innkeeper grovels when he is given a gold penny. He pulls back a greased cloth that covers the doorway, and the four of them stoop to enter. The odor forces Miriam to breathe in gasps. She sees that her sisters' nostrils are dilating toward a young woman who is stirring a stewpot. Wicks gutter on the two tables in the room; the walls are slick with grease. When she notices them the young woman drops her spoon and comes over. She is covered with boils. Her mouth hanging open, she kneels before them and stretches out her arms like a supplicant. She is asking to take their cloaks.

One of her sisters inclines her head, her eyes avid. Miriam frowns furiously. Would she really take this vile thing?

Her sisters ignore her. They move like shadows in the smoky darkness. Silently she pleads with them. Their hearts do not feel her *touch*. They continue searching the darkness for hidden treasure. Knives and eyes and teeth gleam in the flickering light.

It is a dance, Miriam moving from one to the other. Both turn away.

A shout of furious pain is suddenly stifled. The innkeeper has been taken. Then the coachman, too late in rushing for the door. Then, in a filthy corner, they descend on the girl. But something is wrong. A struggle starts, the girl squeals and skitters, knocking one of the wicks to the floor, spreading coals across the dirt to roll under her attackers' dresses.

While they are jumping away from this danger she tears a hole in the wattled wall. Her gray form bobs among the ferns as she disappears into the forest behind the inn.

Now they must hurry, before she raises the alarm. All of this country lives in terror of their kind. Packs of them have been ranging through Swabia, Transylvania, Hungary, Slovakia, falling on villages and taking whole populations. They Sleep in graves to deter the superstitious, who will not approach a graveyard at night without much priestly preparation. When a village is depopulated they pull it down and throw the remains into the river, going on to the next town up the road.

Rumor has spread through the mountains. The whole region is obsessed with them.

It is a bad time for their kind. They had grown used to anarchy in the centuries that followed the fall of Rome. Now that government is returning to Western Europe they have been forced to the hinterlands.

Not a day passes that they do not have news of disaster. Ancient names are dying, names taught Miriam by her father: Ranftius, Harenberg, Tullius. All Europe is inflamed against them. Idiots creep about with crosses and garlic, spouting bad Latin.

Idiots though they be, the Inquisition is winning. Not a town west of the Oder has not burned at least a few.

The church bell begins to peal.

There is a horrible shriek at the door. Miriam's sisters, now wild to escape, throw back the greasy cloth. A crowd of thirty or forty people is outside, standing around the overturned brougham. Her brother is being handed among them, his clothes being ripped from his body.

Suddenly, there is a shaft of light—other villagers have broken into the rear wall of the inn. Miriam moves quickly. She digs herself into a pile of hay in a corner. The roar of excited voices fills the room.

Heartsick and terrified, Miriam huddles in absolute stillness. The voices drown the frantic shrieking of her sisters.

Protect them, her father had said.

How can she face his memory now? And what of her mother, who died during the birth of the triplets? Was her death pointless?

Miriam is stronger than the three of them together because she has for a long time been better fed. But is she strong enough to free them from these maddened villagers?

The voices have become joyous as the villagers loot the carriage and rob the captured sisters. They are finding a few pitiful gold pennies, to them the treasure of kingdoms.

Suddenly men and women bustle over and pull away some of Miriam's cover. She prepares herself to face them, but they rush off. The straw is to start a fire. They have not noticed her.

Against one wall of the inn stands a great iron spit,

used no doubt when this village had porkers large enough to roast. There is crackling as the straw blazes up around logs.

Realizing what is going to happen, Miriam's sisters begin to bellow her name. "MIRIAM! MIRIAM!" A part of her is secretly glad that they do not know where she is hiding. She tells herself over and over that she cannot save them, she cannot prevail against fifty people. She lies amid the fleas and lice, feeling rats run over her from time to time, listening as her siblings bawl their pleas for help.

She has never been so needed. Again she remembers her father. He was a hero.

She begins to remove the straw, starts to sit up. But she freezes, the spectacle before her is so awful. Her youngest sister is naked. They lash her to the spit. Then she is laid across the flames.

A great sizzling starts, like parchment burning. She shrieks and shrieks, her urine steaming into the flames, her head shaking, her hair smoking and red with fire.

They damp the fire and slowly begin to turn the spit.

Her screams continue a long, long time. After an hour her voice breaks and all that issues are hisses.

Miriam's other two sisters slump in a corner, tied as tightly together as two geese on market day.

It is night before all three are roasted.

Miriam has bitten her lips raw to keep from screaming. Her whole body buzzes with the pain of a thousand flea bites. Until late at night the room is filled with the sharp odor of cooking flesh and the gay shouts of the crowd. Of course they are gay, they have captured gold and been sated with her sisters, more meat than they have eaten in years. As dawn threatens, the villagers drink their foul black beer and have their couplings. Then they sleep.

Miriam bursts from her hiding place and runs. She lifts her brother's body from the mud where it has been thrown and carries him into the forest, rushing as fast as possible through the trees, wild to escape this horrible place. Her heart aches for her lost sisters, but she dares not even approach their bones.

Soon she is in a dawn-filled glade. Flowers bob at her feet, the Carpathian massif rises in the clear sky. Before that majesty she shouts her grief. The sound is absorbed.

She is flooded with an agony of loneliness. Perhaps she should deliver herself to the villagers. But she cannot go back, cannot give herself to the flames. The beauty of life remains. Let the dead be their own heroes.

With her brother in her arms she sets out to cross the mountains, intending to seek a better land beyond.

9

JOHN HAD WAITED to return until Miriam was gone. It was the safest way. It was easy to defeat the electrostatic barrier. He came in through the disused tunnel he had used for his escape. He had a mission here. He went through the silent rooms. Scattered around the library were newspapers, all containing sensational stories about his crimes. He sneered at her caution. This was a big city. The police had a long way to go before they brought him to ground.

He paused, shut his eyes. Another hallucination was beginning. This time a healthy girl of about fourteen swam into view before him. John ignored the delicious figment, impatient with this latest side effect of his desperate hunger. She stepped forward, her smell filling his nostrils. It was maddening; he swiped angrily at the empty air. The hunger cloyed and strained within him. Soon he must take to the streets again.

He went upstairs, paused in the door of their bedroom. Although he was on his way to the attic he wasn't in any hurry. There was something to be savored in how he intended to harm her.

Tom had coaxed Sarah out to a celebration after his conversation with Sam Rush. She had wanted to stay with her lab group, but he had managed to convince her that the project could go through its next phase without her in attendance. Her failure to get Miriam Blaylock to return to Riverside had stopped much of the work anyway. Without a subject, they couldn't very well make observations.

"You're celebrating a man's destruction," Sarah said as they sat down to a Mexican dinner at Las Palmas on Eighty-sixth Street.

"I'm celebrating nothing of the kind. Hutch still has his job."

"The biggest discovery in history, and you took it right out of his lap. You."

He winced. "OK, I'm an ogre."

"Ambitious bastard." She smiled. "I wish I could punish you, Tom. God knows you need it. But the truth is I'm so damn relieved, I can't see straight. Knowing that we're out from under Hutch is—well, it does deserve a celebration."

"I'm only an ogre when it comes to protecting your work."

"Wipe that sincere smirk off your face, my love. It makes you look like a card sharp."

"I think I resent that."

"You love it." She lifted her glass of beer. "Here's to you, you bastard."

"And to you, bitch."

"Don't call me names. *I* don't deserve it."

He could see a real argument developing out of this, so he said no more. The waiter returned and they gave their orders. Tom was surprised to hear Sarah order the biggest dinner on the menu; she normally subsisted on nibbles and snacks. Sometimes he thought a handful of

birdseed a day was all she really needed. "At least
you're really hungry for once. That's a good sign."

"Developing neurosis. I'll be as plump as a pigeon in
a few years."

"You don't care?"

Her eyes flashed. "Tonight I want to eat. There's
nothing the matter with that." She paused. "I'm raven-
ous, as a matter of fact. A second ago I felt like taking a
salad right off that tray." She gestured toward a waiter
wheeling among the tables.

Their food was served promptly. For five minutes
Sarah was silent, digging at her enchiladas and tamales.
"Care for more?" Tom asked.

"Yeah!" He signaled the waiter and she ordered
another round. An appetite was fine, but she was going
to turn into a sausage if this kept up. "Got a pencil and
paper?" she asked. "I've had some insights."

"I'll memorize them. Tell me."

"One. We're correct to assume that Miriam is
evolved from a primate ancestor. She's too close to us
not to be. Two. We therefore need skeletal X rays so
that we can determine which primate line is involved.
Three. One thing is certain, she and her kind are in
some sort of symbiosis with us, otherwise why would
they keep themselves hidden? They take something
from us we wouldn't otherwise give."

"Why does that follow?"

"What else would be their motive for secrecy? And
it's not a matter of being overlooked. It is deliberate. It
must also be hard to do. It can't have been easy to
remain undetected for so long." She paused, ate a
couple of bites with birdlike speed. "I wonder what
they take from us. I wonder if we'll find out."

Tom envied her the clarity of her mind. She had
reduced the whole affair to two important questions.

Suddenly she stopped eating. She dropped her fork
on the plate and looked up at him, her face pallid.
"Let's get out of here." Tom obediently paid the bill
and they went out into the crowds thronging Eighty-

sixth Street. Smoke billowed from chestnut stands, radios under the arms of geeks blared disco music. They passed a Chinese restaurant, a German restaurant, a Greek restaurant. Only when they had rounded the corner onto Second Avenue did the crowds thin.

"I'm going to lose my lunch, I'm afraid."

"OK, honey." He wasn't surprised, the way she had eaten so much spicy food. "Can you make it—"

She let go in the gutter. Fortunately, their building was just at the other end of the block and Herb, the late-shift doorman, had seen it happen. He trotted up with a towel in his hand. "Doctor Roberts," he said in a gruff, surprised voice. "Jeez, you must have got the stomach flu, ma'am."

Tom was holding her head. He brushed her sweating face with the towel. Cars rushed by three feet away. Pedestrians passed up and down the sidewalk. A fire truck, complete with balancing Dalmatian, roared by. Sarah coughed mightily.

"Oh, I feel *awful*," she moaned. "Tom, I'm so cold!"

"Come on, let's get you to bed!"

"Can you make it, Doc? You want I should carry her?"

Sarah staggered to her feet. "No thanks, Herb." She tottered into the lobby on Tom's arm. His mind inventoried the various types of food poisoning it could be. The onset was too sudden for botulism. They hadn't had mushrooms, so it couldn't be that. Probably old friend salmonella, or just plain overeating. He'd keep her quiet and warm, she'd be on her feet in no time.

"Gonzalo," Herb said into the housephone, "come watch the door. I'm goin' upstairs with the Docs."

They rode up quietly, the only sound in the elevator Sarah's breathing. "Tom, it's going to happen!" Her voice quavered.

They were at nineteen and rising. "Just another second, honey."

Herb looked miserable, he was about to get one messed-up elevator. But he didn't, she made it as far as their foyer. Tom was half angry with her, half pitying. She didn't have to eat like a hippo, after all. But she was suffering for it, and he suffered with her. "C'mon, honey," he said, "it's bed and bucket time." All he got was a moan.

He left her sprawled on the bed with their mop bucket on the floor beside her and strict instructions to use it. Then he went about cleaning up the mess in the foyer without getting sick himself. Herb had slipped away while he was bedding her down. The man couldn't be blamed.

When he returned to the bedroom he was surprised to find her sitting up. "I'm better," she said. She glared, as if daring him to contradict her.

At that moment the doorbell rang. "God damn, they never leave you alone—who is it!"

"Herb again. You got a package."

Tom pulled the door open. "A Fleet Messenger come up and delivered it while Gonzalo was workin' the door, Doctor Haver." It was a compact box wrapped in beautiful blue paper and tied with a ribbon. It was addressed to Sarah. With a shrug Tom took it to her.

"Who could have sent me a present?"

"Open it, maybe there's a card inside."

She shook it and listened.

"Expecting a bomb, sweetheart?"

With a slight smile playing across her face she tore it open. At once powerful perfume filled the room. There were six cakes of yellow-green soap.

"Good God, throw it out, throw it out!"

"Miriam sent it."

"Don't you think it's a little sweet? As a matter of fact—"

"Come on, honey, it's nice." She held a bar to her nose and inhaled. "Wonderful. I told her how much I liked it while I was at her house. She's just being considerate."

"All right already, seal it up in something for now. Let me get used to the idea." Then a thought struck him. "Good God, I *know* that soap!" He took a bar in his hand. Sure enough, a label was imprinted on it, *Brehmer and Cross, to the Trade.* Tom burst out laughing, tossed the soap on the bed.

"What the hell's so funny? She has it made up specially."

"Oh, yeah! Sure she does! You know what that stuff is? Mortician's soap. They use it on corpses. That's where in hell I've smelled the damn stuff and why it makes me sick. They used it on Gran Haver when I was a kid. Kept her from stinking up the living room."

Sarah touched the bar of soap, withdrew her hand. Tom came close to her. "Her thought processes are different from ours."

"But she said—"

"Who knows what she said? You shouldn't assume you understand her motives. Maybe it's some kind of joke."

After a long silence Sarah said that she supposed it must be. There weren't any arguments when Tom threw the soap away. Her nausea appeared to have stopped and she didn't have any significant fever so they contented themselves with doing nothing for now about her sickness.

"You probably don't even need electrolyte replacement," Tom commented.

"Good. I really don't even want water right now."

"Wait till you feel thirsty. Hey, look at this." He was glancing through *TV Guide.* " 'Great Performances' is on thirteen at nine. It's nine now."

While they were watching, Tom noticed Sarah rubbing her right arm. "You OK?"

"Yeah."

"Maybe you sprained it in the street."

"It's hurt all afternoon."

Midway through the show she turned on her bedside lamp. "Tom, look at this." There was a pinhole lesion on her forearm.

"Did you give blood?"

"When would I give blood? Maybe something stung me. I'll bet that's what made me sick."

Tom examined the wound. The bruise running along the vein, the redness of the wound itself—it looked for all the world as if Sarah had been given a transfusion.

"A spider bite," she said.

Tom noticed a rasping undertone. Sarah was scared. He touched her shoulder. "If that's what it is, not to worry, it's a mild one."

"Yeah. Mild."

"That's right, darling. No myalgia, no cramps. Those are both present when you have a serious spider bite."

She sighed. "It's disgusting, but I'm incredibly hungry again."

Tom didn't know what to say. His mind moved through the catalogue of her symptoms. He thought of suggesting that Sarah check into the hospital but immediately dismissed the idea. The symptoms were too minor. Thousands of people suffered slight cases of food poisoning or insect bite and never went to a hospital. Yet Tom worried. He looked at her face. Its color was poor, and its unusual roundness indicated slight edema. Her skin felt cool and rather dry. "Hungry or not," he said at last, "I think you ought to try to get some sleep. We'll eat a big breakfast in the morning."

She didn't argue but her eyes were pained. They took off their clothes, settled into bed. After five minutes with *Time,* Tom turned out the light. He patted Sarah's bottom, then listened to her tossing and turning for what seemed a long time. Only when her breath became regular and deep did he begin to relax. A last touch told him she had no fever. Finally, sleep took him as well.

Thunder rolled and blue lightning flashed against the ceiling. Sarah stared into the darkness that followed the flash. Hadn't that been a silhouette in the hall? Sheets of rain fell. The wind moaned past the building. She lay absolutely still, barely breathing, waiting for more lightning so she could see.

When it came the hall was empty. Her heart began to beat more slowly. She had been about to wake Tom. Now she withdrew her hand and threw her forearm across her eyes. Her skin crawled, she ached, she was freezing. A vision came to her, of a Big Mac and double fries and a huge, cold Coke. Disgusting, she hardly ever ate that sort of stuff. Yet it remained there, a powerful temptation. Her eyes went to the clock on the dresser. It was hard to read the dial from here but it appeared to be about two-thirty.

A bad time to go outside in New York City. She visualized the McDonald's on Eighty-sixth Street: a few people huddled over coffee, maybe a couple of cops taking a break. She could almost smell the place, a scent of heaven.

She slipped out of bed slowly and very carefully. If she woke Tom she sure as hell wouldn't be able to do what she intended. The McDonald's wasn't far. She would probably be fine. She pulled on jeans and a sweat shirt and laced up her jogging shoes. As she left the apartment she noticed that Tom—typically—had forgotten to lock up. She paused to lock both the dead bolt and the mortise lock with her key and then went to the elevator. For a supposedly ruthless type Tom was surprisingly absentminded.

The elevator doors opened onto an empty lobby. There was a stentorian rattling sound—Herb asleep at his post. The lobby doors were locked to the street so Sarah would have to let herself in when she got back.

Outside the air was storm-fresh, smelling wet and green. But for the soughing of the wind the street was quiet. Sarah found the emptiness of it all quite wonderful. She strode along feeling as if she had acquired a sort of secret power just by coming out at this hour. She went two blocks down and turned east on Eighty-sixth.

The McDonald's was open, as she had known it would be. There were many more people inside than she had visualized. In fact the place was humming. She had to spend five minutes in line, finally all but hopping from foot to foot with hunger.

She ordered two Big Macs, double fries, a pie and a jumbo Coke. Cradling her food, she found a seat across from a hulking young man who ignored her. After a couple of annoyed tongue-clicks he got up and pranced off to another table. For the first time Sarah really looked around. She almost laughed, everybody in the place was gay except her. There were transvestites huddled over milkshakes, leather boys devouring Steakburgers, men in all variations of straight and drag dress, all engaged in a slow dance among the tables.

Sarah was left alone, which was fine with her. The hamburgers seemed unusually good, rich with flavor, aromatic, cooked just right. Better than Big Macs usually were, far better. Even the Coke and fries were wonderful. What did this place do—serve gourmet junk food after the moon went down?

The only thing that prevented her from getting another couple of hamburgers was the memory of what had happened earlier. She didn't feel full but good sense told her not to overeat. At least Tom had promised a big breakfast. She pictured eggs and hot, spicy sausages and a mountain of buttered toast, and maybe pancakes on the side. Her mouth watered. The big clock above the take-out counter read 3:00. It was at least four hours until she could taste that breakfast. She got up, forced herself to leave the restaurant. She'd pass the hours walking, she had no intention of cooping herself up in their bedroom until dawn.

Her earlier indisposition seemed to be gone. There was more rain threatening, but she didn't care. She would welcome the bracing cold of it. Her hunger was still with her, but it only added intensity to the glorious way she was beginning to feel. She found herself walking east past empty shops and dark apartment houses, and with a more rapid step into the quiet stretch between York and East End avenues. Here the buildings are older, the lights dimmer. Across East End lay the darkness of Carl Shurz Park. With its few old streetlamps lighting the paths, and the mist that hung beneath the tall trees, the park reminded her of a scene from childhood, from her teenage years in Savannah. She had a vivid memory of Bobby Dewart, the sour smell of his skin and the lovely, adolescent hours they had spent touching one another among the headstones in the old Savannah City Graveyard. They had walked along the docks afterward, smelling the salt breeze that came up the Savannah River at night, watching the last tourists leave the Pirate House Restaurant, and declaring the eternity of their love.

Being fourteen, she had known nothing of the ways of time. Soon her father had been transferred by International Paper, next stop Des Moines. And Bobby Dewart? She had no idea.

At this moment, as she crossed East End, drawn by the sensuality of the night park, she remembered that love in all its timid eagerness. It had been young and doomed—and yet hadn't it also in a sense been eternal?

There came into her heart a painful longing for all her lost secret places: night and empty benches and abandoned paths. She went slowly down the tarmac sidewalk, recalling with this same delectable pain her great loves, Bobby and the others, and yes, Tom too. He ranked as a great love, she could not deny it. She went through the park until she came to the esplanade that stretches beyond it, bordered on one side by buildings and on the other by the East River. The current, always swift, hissed in the darkness below. Far out in the river a small boat was defined by its bobbing lights. Along the esplanade the benches gleamed, still wet with rain. Immediately behind the benches rose the apartment buildings. The terraces of the lower floors jutted out perhaps ten feet above the walk. In their darkness these buildings acquired something that they did not possess during daylight hours. Sarah could not define it exactly. Certainly it wasn't menace. More a sense of mystery.

Their blank windows were . . . interesting. It didn't seem impossible, the way she had begun to feel, that she could climb to one of those terraces.

Then what would she do?

She could taste a peach breaking in her mouth, its juicy sweetness filling her with delight.

People lay sleeping in those buildings, thousands of them, each locked in his own dreams, vulnerable and quiet.

Sarah walked softly along, full of an obscure and subtle longing. She felt a lust for all things beautiful, reflected that there was no such thing as an ugly human being.

She wanted to get into one of their apartments, to touch their belongings, to listen to their soft breathing.

She found herself standing on one of the benches. With her arms raised to their full length the lowest balcony was three feet above her. She crouched down on the bench. By springing straight up she might just be able to catch the edge of the balcony.

Do *what?* This was absurd. Aberrant behavior. Psychopathic. Still, her muscles were tensing, her hands stretching to grasp, her eyes measuring the distance. There wasn't a trace of psychopathic behavior in her personality. If anything, she was too civilized.

Then she was hanging on the edge of the terrace, her fingers grasping, her legs swinging. It was impossible and yet she had done it.

Her arms and fingers did not ache as they should. Rather they felt like steel. She raised herself to the edge and looked onto the terrace itself. There was a bar-beque, a couple of canvas chairs, a tricycle. Her right hand grasped one of the iron bars that formed the railing of the terrace.

She was beginning to feel a strange aggressive anger, an eagerness to get in there and—

She dropped to the ground, the thud echoing up and down the esplanade. The image that had made her release her grip now made her hunch her shoulders and clasp her arms around herself, hugging herself against its ugliness.

She didn't feel things like that! She loved mankind, that was the foundation of her life. How could she possibly, even for an instant, have wanted to kill innocent human beings, to crack them open like—like she had imagined.

It was as if somebody else was living in her body, some wild being, driven by needs of which she herself was ignorant.

'Has this always been in me, deep back behind the me I know?'

Yes. Hidden, but there.

Now given life. Something enormous was stirring and waking in her, she felt. It was as old as life, perhaps, but also new. It was what had driven her out here in the middle of the night, had converted a simple thing such as hunger into a gluttonous lust, had made her so abnormally interested in the people in the apartments.

She began to walk quickly along the esplanade, seeking a more open area, a place where she would be less tempted to this behavior.

As she moved she had the uncanny sensation that somebody or something was moving with her, walking as she walked, breathing as she breathed.

Something not quite of this world.

It was tall and pale and as quick as a hawk.

She started to run. Her footsteps whispered on the pavement; the sneakers deadened the sound. But not the fear: she grasped her hands over her head and crouched low.

Great wings seemed to rise into the sky.

Hallucination.

Abruptly, the needle mark came to mind. That was,

of course, what it was. Not an insect bite or some other innocent wound. Miriam had given her something with a needle.

The pale thing moving, rubber tubing, blood packs, red blood—

Dark-red blood, like that of a reptile.

Sarah ran wildly through the park, passing the motionless swings, the places where children played ball, the slides, the sandbox, the tall dripping trees.

'I've been infused. She gave me blood. Her blood.' Memory: Miriam drawing blood from her own vein with a primitive catheter.

Sarah unable to move. A voice, Miriam's voice, saying again and again, you cannot move, you will not remember, you cannot, will not.

But the voice did not come from Miriam. It came from that strange unhuman creature, the statue with the catheter in its arm, the catheter that led to a blood pack.

When it was bulging with black blood it had been applied to Sarah's arm. She had watched it go in, the warmest, most delicious feeling making it impossible for her to stop it, impossible to pull out the needle.

Help!

She was in the streets now, running through familiar intersections, past stores she knew well, but also through a strange and unfamiliar world, a planet of the dead that was also this planet.

She stopped, suddenly winded. Her heart was knocking, her breath was coming in gasps. 'I'm not meant to know this,' she thought. 'This is unbelievable. But it's true, it must be true.' She felt her arm, could feel the hard knot of tissue where the needle had entered. When she pressed, it hurt.

It was real.

Right now, this moment, Miriam's blood was in her veins, mixing with her own.

Black blood? A hideous thing with Miriam's voice? A nightmare? Some kind of trick?

There were a hundred desperate questions, and at the moment not a single clear answer.

For example, it could be that her mind had broken through a hypnotic block, but it could also be that the block was meant to come down.

She tried to calm herself. Breathe deeply, remember your own strengths. She could think, she could apply reason and science to the situation. She could save herself with her knowledge.

Her first impulse was to get home as quickly as possible, get Tom, and go over to Riverside for some tests. But instead she sat down on the curb. To do this right she was going to have to collect her thoughts, organize her mind. If she wasn't careful it was all going to come across to others as some kind of irrational aberration.

There was peace here in the empty street. A nearby building had planted tulips and they glowed in the light from the streetlamps. Trees spread new leaves overhead. This little corner of New York could have been a small town, so quietly did it sleep, so sweet did it smell.

Sarah looked up. Clouds moved past, glowing yellow-red with the lights of the city. Here and there a star shone through. To the west the moon rode in the rushing sky.

There was a stirring in the air all around her, like the sound of enormous wings.

Hallucinatory phenomena again.

It recurred, as if a large bird were flying restlessly back and forth just overhead. Suddenly, Sarah had a vivid impression of Miriam, her face utterly serene—

She jumped up, stifling a cry. That face had been *real*. But it wasn't here. Sarah was alone. It was only another symptom and would have to be accepted as such.

Methuselah's dying howl filled the air.

Sarah clapped her hands over her ears, feeling in her right arm a sharp stab of pain from the needle mark. Another symptom. In fact all of the night's experiences were nothing more than symptoms, from the vomiting to the hallucinations to the cloying hunger. And all could be dealt with once the parameters of the problem were known.

She set off, this time walking with resolute intention. She would not fall victim to transient psychosis. She would approach this as a professional and overcome it with the assistance of one of the best research institutes in the world.

Miriam's motives, whatever in heaven's name they might be, could wait until later.

They would have to take that one well in hand. She was dangerous, she needed careful observation. Fine, there were involuntary commitment procedures for just such situations.

When she reached the Excelsior Tower, she had more or less regained her composure. She fumbled for her keys rather than wake poor Herb at such an hour. He was huddled, a snoring bundle, on one of the lobby couches. Poor guy probably held down two or three jobs.

Despite the urgency she felt, she found Herb curiously interesting. He looked so helpless. But when she drew near she found his smell overpowering, like rotting meat. She went on to the elevator bank and rode to her floor.

The apartment was silent. From the bedroom came the faint sound of breathing. Obviously Tom hadn't missed her. Sarah went into the bathroom and turned on the light.

It was definitely a needle mark, and slightly infected. The first problem must be to test for type-incompatibility. If Miriam's blood did not interact normally with her own she could easily lapse into irreversible shock.

They would have to act fast. The fact that nothing had happened during the past eight or ten hours was cause for hope but it proved nothing. Shock could set in at any moment.

"Tom!"

He shifted in the bed, groaned. She put her hand on his shoulder to shake him.

It was like an electric shock. Lights flashed before her eyes, an agonizing thrill ran through her body. She staggered back, astonished by the furious clash of sensations.

His skin was so good to touch. A strange, evil tickling made her break out in gooseflesh. Her nipples swelled against her sweater. There came a feeling not unlike the one she had experienced hanging on the terrace, a sort of aggressive longing, something related to her new lusty appetite.

She noticed a strong—quite wonderful—smell. It wasn't food but at the same time it was. Had he gotten up and taken some food to the bed? That would be just like him, to get up for a snack and never even notice that she was gone.

Tom woke to the sound of excited breathing. Startled, he sat up. At first he was afraid. His eyes could not penetrate the darkness.

"Sarah?"

"Yes."

What the hell was going on? "Are you up?"

She turned on the bathroom light. Not only was she up, she was fully dressed. He couldn't see her face with the light behind her, but her hair looked wild.

"Sarah, are you OK?"

When she didn't answer he got out of bed and grabbed for her. She moved, it seemed very quickly, back into the bathroom. "Give me a second," she said in a hoarse voice.

"You sound funny." He didn't add that she also looked very strange now that she was under the light: eyes wide and glistening, face smeared, sweat shirt smeared, muddy sneakers. "What the hell have you been doing?"

She seemed about to run as he moved toward her.

He went into the bathroom, held his hands out to her, stood over her reasserting himself if only by their difference in size.

Suddenly, she sank to the floor, clapped her face into her hands and twisted back. A choked sob. He went down beside her.

"Darling, are you in pain?"

"My arm!" The sob became a moan, warbling and crazy. Tom touched the proffered arm, looked at the ugly mark just below the crook of the elbow. A needle track. Sarah's eyes searched him. "She infused me with her blood. Now I'm hallucinating."

"Fever. Transfusion reaction."

She nodded, tears popping out from behind her tightly closed eyes. He took her by the shoulders, his own heart pounding. A transfusion reaction, caused by blood of an incompatible type, could range from nothing more than mild discomfort to vascular collapse and death. "Let's get over to Riverside." He went to the phone, called Geoff's home number. They would need the best blood man available. Geoff's voice, sleepy and a little confused, sharpened when Tom told him what had happened. They agreed to meet at the blood analysis lab in ten minutes.

Tom phoned ahead to send Herb scurrying out after a cab. By the time he had gotten some clothes on and Sarah in a coat, a Checker was waiting at the door.

They hurried through Riverside's main lobby, at this hour empty and quiet. With a wave to the night guard, Tom propelled Sarah to the elevators, jabbed at the eleventh-floor button.

Geoff was waiting, his face sallow and tired. As they entered the lab Phyllis Rockler rose from behind a workbench where she had been preparing the necessary glassware. She took Sarah by the hands. "Let's get you in a pressure cuff," she said, her voice urgent.

"Do you live here?" Sarah asked. Tom was reassured to hear strength, even a touch of acerbic humor.

"Geoff and I—"

Sarah smiled softly, looked a moment at Tom. Phyllis pushed up the sleeve of Sarah's sweater and applied the blood pressure indicator as Geoff examined the other arm. The four of them waited while Phyllis took her reading. "One hundred and twenty over eighty. We should all be so lucky."

"My pressure's always been good."

Tom closed his eyes, felt some of the tension creep out of his neck. The blood pressure would have been abnormal if vascular collapse had been imminent. Phyllis then counted Sarah's pulse and read her temperature with a digital thermometer. "Here's something. One hundred and one degrees."

"There's a slight subcutaneous infection connected with the lesion," Geoff remarked. "The fever could be from that."

Sarah closed her eyes. "Aside from the fever and the lesion, my gross symptoms are psychological. Extreme restlessness. Odd hallucinations."

"Orientation problems?"

She shook her head. "Consistent with fever and loss of sleep. I've been up all night."

Tom asked a question that had been much on his mind. "How did she do it?" He couldn't imagine Sarah sitting still for such a thing.

"When I went to her house we had coffee, then I woke up in her bed in a . . . state of confusion. I took a shower and left. But tonight I remembered more—a—a—sort of thing standing over me with a blood pack—quite strange."

"Hypnosis and drugs."

"I agree. The combination fits my symptomology."

"Phyllis, why don't you draw a couple of hundred ccs and we can get to work." Phyllis prepared a syringe and withdrew the blood from Sarah's unwounded arm.

"It looks good." In gross blood disease there is sometimes a change of color or consistency. Sarah's blood was a rich purple-red, completely normal. Tom found himself hoping for the first time that nothing was *really* wrong. So far the symptomology was reassuring, except for those hallucinations. But there was something about Sarah's tone of voice he didn't like. He couldn't get rid of the feeling that she was holding something back. "What kind of hallucinations?"

"Visual, mostly. I went out, I was terribly hungry. If you can believe it I went up to McDonald's on Eighty-sixth at three." She sighed. "I'm hungry now, as a matter of fact."

"What kind of hallucinations?"

She flared at him. "I told you! That creature with the blood pack! God, Tom, you can be persistent. Let's talk about it later, I really can't deal with it right now."

Phyllis had transferred Sarah's blood to ten test tubes. "One through eight are treated with anti-coagulant," she said. "Nine and ten are clear."

"I'd like to pitch in. I can't just sit here waiting, it's making my flesh crawl. Let me do the centrifuging." Phyllis handed Sarah two tubes of blood. She placed them in the centrifuge, adjusted the rpm gauge, closed it, and flipped the switch.

"Listen," Geoff said, "it's harmonizing with Mozart." He had turned on his radio a few moments before. Tom almost screamed at him to get on with it, then forced self-control. Geoff was right to treat the situation lightly. Panic and professional standards of practice don't mix. He looked at his Sarah, bending over the centrifuge, still a bit pallid, perhaps slightly swollen, her face sharply intent on her work.

Phyllis prepared slides, placing a drop of blood on each and smearing it to a thin film. Each slide was numbered and slipped into a rack beside Geoff's microscope. "I'll do a reticulocyte count first," he said. That made sense to Tom, it would tell them at once if any internal bleeding was taking place. If the blood was type-incompatible, hemorrhage was certainly a possibility.

"Set up a Westergren tube," Sarah said. "We'll want the sedimentation rate."

As Phyllis prepared the tube, Tom mentally ran down the list of reasons for doing a sedimentation study. He couldn't understand why Sarah would feel a need to know about possible infection and inflammation. "It takes an hour," he said, "and it'll mean two hundred ccs just on that. I think we'll have apparent pathological signs if the infection proceeds out of the arm." The beautiful arm.

"Methuselah showed an elevated sedimentation rate before the end."

So that was it. She hadn't forgotten about the connection between Miriam Blaylock and the dead ape. She must be thinking that she was about to go the way of Methuselah, poor woman. He wished to God that he could somehow reassure her. But it would be a waste of effort with Sarah. Once she got an idea it took a lot more than reassurance to convince her she was wrong. The worst of it was, he didn't feel so certain himself. The physicists had long since dispensed with commonly held notions of coincidence, replacing them with more elegant and truer ideas of space-time as a whole event, a woven continuum. In the light of such concepts the relationship between Miriam's appearance and Methuselah's death was not only not accidental, it wasn't even coincidental. It followed as certainly as one brick after another in a wall, or the spewing of radiant poisons beyond the horizon of critical mass.

The centrifuge wound down and Sarah removed the now-separated tubes of blood. "Is there somewhere she can lie down?" Tom asked. She was rapidly losing all color.

"I'll tell you if I need to be admitted," she snapped. "I know this place has hospital facilities." She put the tubes in a rack and started drawing out the various blood components with a pipette.

"Let me see a slide of whites," Geoff said without moving from his microscope. Sarah quickly prepared one, placed it in the scope's receiving tray. Tom admired the superb laboratory technique being displayed by the three of them. By Sarah in particular. All of his caring and love was surfacing. What bravado she had. "I want another slide," Geoff murmured. "Wright's stain, please."

There was a silence while he examined it. "I observe foreign leukocytes." Tom felt a wave of new anxiety: this was confirmation, ugly and real. Miriam's blood was actually running in Sarah's veins. "The eosinophilelike cell is present at a concentration of about three percent. Pseudopodial activity is high. The cell is thriving."

"What is the concentration in Miriam's own blood?" Sarah asked. Her tone was clipped. She was forcing calm.

"Eighteen percent."

"You mentioned pseudopodial activity. What's taking place?"

Geoff leaned back from his microscope. The fluorescent lighting overhead threw his face into shadow. His forehead glistened. "It appears to be consuming your blood," he said carefully, "and reproducing cells of its own kind."

10

MIRIAM AWOKE FROM THE first peaceful Sleep she had experienced in days. It was nine A.M. At once she *touched*, sensing for John's presence. Her whole body jerked with the intensity of the feeling. He was here, and in a highly charged emotional state.

He was exultant.

She frowned, confused. The clarity of the *touch* told her that he was nearby, probably inside the house. She shrank against the head of the bed, looking desperately around the room. But it was empty. His happiness apparently wasn't because he had managed to defeat her defenses and get into the house. She checked the control panel in the footboard of the bed. All the alarm indicator lights were green. He hadn't used any conventional mode of entry. And the electrostatic barrier hadn't been activated. The motion sensors told a different story. There were indications of movement in the basement at 3:52 A.M., in the front hall two minutes later, in the attic at 4:00. They revealed a slow progress from the bottom to the top of the house. And from 3:59

to 5:59 the steel shutters that protected her bed had been closed, responding automatically to the unexplained motion in the house.

So he was in the attic. As well that she had abandoned Sleeping there. When the time came she wouldn't have the difficulty of hunting him down. But why did he exult so?

She decided to *touch* again, hoping to catch some emotional clue to what he was doing. Of course, care would have to be taken. John was sensitive to *touch*. She didn't want to alert him to the fact that she was awake.

She cleared her mind, closed her eyes, opened her inner eye wide. Then she sought John's place in her heart. The *touch* sprang out of her, connecting with powerful and complex emotions. John was overwhelmingly sad, angry, but most of all he was filled with wild glee.

He was savoring the fruits of victory.

Why?

She inventoried the possible reasons for his happiness. He had successfully entered the house against her will. Not sufficient cause. He had gotten to the attic, perhaps to the room where the chests were kept.

She almost laughed aloud when she realized what he must be planning. Let him do his worst. How ironic that what he must perceive as a great threat was actually going to be helpful to her. John, waiting for his big moment in the attic, could safely be forgotten. And that was well. She had much more pressing matters to attend to.

It was going to be a difficult day.

She set about turning off the various devices that protected her during Sleep. In the past, finding safe places to Sleep had been an obsession with all of her race. During the greatest period of persecution, when they were being hunted down by experts, burnt, garrotted, walled up in tombs, they took to hiding in graves, lying among corpses to avoid detection. As often as not, they were followed even there, dragged from their hiding places, and destroyed by having wooden stakes hammered into their hearts.

Miriam turned off the electrostatic barrier and the alarms, then deactivated the steel shutters that surrounded the bed itself if danger threatened. Her theory was that hiding was a far less effective deterrent than fortification. Before electronics Miriam had kept a kennel of killer dogs.

She dressed quickly, unlocked the bedroom door, and looked out. Dawn filled the upper parts of the house with golden light. She was beginning to feel the hunger again, but she had no time for it now. She wished that she was already with Sarah. Without Miriam's help the woman would go mad, unable to satisfy her own hunger, unable to stand the agony.

Once the transfusion was completed the body reacted in a predictable way. Before the advent of modern medical techniques the transfusion was a slow process, subject to the collapse of veins and infection from the crude apparatus available. Now it could all be done at once.

The physical effects would devastate Sarah's body, but the psychological impact, as a new set of needs and instincts replaced her established human ways, would be catastrophic.

Miriam had nursed many of them through the agony of it and she intended to do the same for Sarah.

It would mean returning to their hospital, possibly to danger. They might try to capture her, even to kill her. If she was not very careful indeed she was likely to become their prisoner once she went back to Riverside. They would have ample justification to commit her, and the legal machinery was certainly available.

She could picture herself starving in agony as they prodded and sampled and tested. The trouble was, you didn't die. You just got weaker and weaker until you ended up like the ones in the chests.

It took months to starve. King Charles IV of France

had walled up twenty of her kind in a sewer where they were hiding in May of 1325. It was November before the last muffled wail was heard in the streets above. And even after that, they suffered.

She was clammy, trembling. For the first time in many years she was genuinely terrified. It had always been hard to do this, and Sarah Roberts was proving to be especially difficult.

But worth it. Well worth it.

She descended the steps. There was no time to call a limousine. She would have to break one of her rules of safety and take a taxi. Moving through her house, she checked the rooms for damaged belongings. John had left things alone, it seemed.

She examined the mosaic portrait of Lamia carefully. Miriam kept it with her always, to look into those resolute eyes and remember. Her mother had been strong. She devoted herself to the incredibly dangerous process of childbearing, for the good of the race. Miriam could still remember the last pregnancy, her mother gushing blood, her father trying to cauterize the wound, the puddles horrible on the floor. Her mother had died in a hide tent on a desert night when Egypt was still young.

Miriam opened the front door onto a luscious spring morning. She hurried up to Fifty-seventh Street. The first two cabs she saw she rejected. Too many rattles, drivers too tired. A third one was acceptable. She got in, sat well back, felt compulsively for seatbelts she knew would not be there.

Sitting in the cab, she considered what must be done. In her previous *touches* Miriam had experienced Sarah's fierce will directly. The woman would not cease making efforts to save herself until she was beyond rational thought.

And yet it was that fine will that could blossom into a true hunger. Nothing less would suffice. Of course, it was going to be a struggle. Miriam consoled herself that she had never yet failed. True, some had died during the transfusion process, but not one who lived through the kiss of blood had long resisted her. And yet . . . she had never taken one with so much will or quite so good a mind.

Would she succeed this time?

Sarah must be made to realize that she could not save herself. When they were together Miriam could *touch* her deepest being, guide her, comfort her. It was not hard to transform a body, but the matter of capturing a heart was much more difficult.

Even with *touch* it was going to take time. She shifted uneasily in her seat, watching nervously as the cab went straight through a changing light, thinking of all the different kinds of danger she was being exposed to today.

For a long time she had known that her own mind was delicately balanced. She was so profoundly alone. She believed in her vulnerability to accident, but she had constantly to remind herself that humankind was also a threat. She had once seen a film of a tiger being captured in a net, and it had made a profound impression on her. Despite the gravity of its situation, the beast had remained calm and confident until the ropes actually sprang up around it. The men laying out the net seemed of little danger to the tiger, it having eaten one of their number the night before. That they might actually capture it was so far beyond its belief that they were able to do so.

The tiger spent its remaining years in a six-by-ten cage, the property of a circus.

What would she do if they brought out guards with guns to capture her?

Her heart began thundering as she considered the choices she would have. Die before the bullets or accept imprisonment.

She longed to abandon this whole endeavor, but she could not risk it. Sarah already knew far too much to be allowed to remain free.

She was fighting a wave of raw fear when the cab

pulled up in front of Riverside. She paid her $3.50 fare and got out. The entrance that yawned before her was so prosaic, so human, it could not possibly be a portal of death.

No?

She pushed through the revolving doors into a crowded lobby and was immediately assailed with the odor of human flesh in great quantity. Automatically, she evaluated the members of the hurrying throng: this one too strong, this one too small, another too sick. It was hard to bring herself into such a crowd with even the slightest hunger. The passing of perfect specimens kept distracting her.

She crossed to the elevators, pressed the button for the twelfth floor. As soon as the doors were closed she began to experience an agony of unease. She stood near the control panel, pressed by a solid mass of humanity, waiting through anguished moments as the thing stopped at every floor.

When the doors at last opened on twelve she popped out with a gasp of relief. But the doors closed behind her like the entrance to a tomb. And she was on the inside. A bell rang somewhere, a doctor was paged, two interns strolled past without glancing at her. To the right was the waiting room with its inevitable crowd and questioning receptionist. A black door to the left led back into the suite of offices for executives and medical personnel. During her night here Miriam had been careful to memorize the layout of the clinic, and she took this door rather than face the receptionist.

Before her was a gray institutional hallway lined with more doors. Each practitioner working at the clinic had a small office. At the end of the hallway were the offices of the executive staff. Miriam went to Sarah's door, third down on the right. She placed her hand on the knob, paused to prepare herself for the confrontation, then went in.

But the office was empty. There was, however, a

powerful feeling of Sarah in the room. The desk was piled high with file folders and rolls of graphs. On the floor was a two-foot-high stack of computer printouts. Three soiled lab coats hung on the door. A poster of a grinning rhesus monkey was the only decoration. A stupid choice no doubt to many eyes, but to Sarah it must be a symbol of her triumphant research.

Just being in the room, Miriam realized that she was already beginning to love the woman. She didn't want Sarah to suffer unnecessarily. Miriam was giving her a gift, after all, of something humanity had been trying to attain through all of its history. The great human religions all involved an assault on death. Man thought of death as a helpless concession to evil, and universally feared it.

Miriam must not forget the impact this gift had had on Sarah's predecessors. In his heart each man feared and loved death. The release from such a contradiction was in itself an offering of great value.

She felt Sarah's chair, her desk, fingered her nibbled pencils, stroked her lab coats, all the while trying to get a sense of her emotional state.

It came, thin and distant, a vapor of fear, hardly a *touch* at all.

One could tell very little from such a weak *touch*. There was nothing else for it. She would have to confront her directly.

'If they try to keep me here I'll need her loyalty,' she thought as she went down the hall to the secretarial pool to locate Sarah. Physically, she was much more powerful than they. She could outrun, outclimb and outmaneuver them. She also had her intelligence, which was greater than theirs, especially in the speed with which it could assess rapidly changing situations.

"I'm trying to locate Doctor Roberts," she said to the secretary, who looked up, cracking gum.

"You a patient?"

"I'm expected." Miriam smiled. "I'm not a patient."

"They're down on the lab floor," she said. "I think they're probably in Gerontology by now. You know the facility?"

"Oh sure. I've been up here a number of times."

"Want me to say who's coming down?"

"Don't bother, I'm already late. Let's not call too much attention to that!" She smiled again, backing away, turning to go to the elevators.

"I understand," the girl said, laughing, "just want to edge in."

Miriam took the stairs beside the elevator bank to save time and ascertain if there were any inner doors that might impede escape. Large signs indicated that all floors below ten were locked for security reasons. Useful if not helpful information.

Contrary to what she had said to the girl, Miriam did not know the plan of the lab floor. When she emerged she found the whole layout was different from the floor above. Riverside was a hodgepodge of old buildings connected by unlikely passages and confusing hallways. This floor had halls going in three directions from the elevator bank. The lighting was poor and the large gray doors were unmarked. Each door opened on a separate laboratory. To find the one you wanted you simply had to know where it was.

With no choice, Miriam opened the first door she came to. Before her was a vast array of electronic equipment. The air was crackling with ozone, and motors hummed through the silence. "Excuse me."

"Hey?" A voice from within the forest of equipment.

"I'm looking for Gerontology."

"You're at the opposite end of the wrong hallway, if that helps. This is Gas Chromatography."

A face appeared behind a virtual wall of wires leading from a lab bench to a shelf of equipment above. "I'm trying to locate Sarah Roberts," Miriam said.

Excitement registered in the face, which was concealed by welder's goggles. A hand pushed the goggles up. "Welding a feeder line. No assistant. So you're looking for Sarah. You involved in the project?"

"Which one?"

"There's only one project around here at the moment. A hell of a project. Incredible. You a reporter?"

"No."

"Well, I don't think I'd better go shooting my mouth off anyway."

"I'm from the Rockefeller Institute. Doctor Martin. Are you involved in the Blaylock project?"

"Look, I really can't talk about it. If you want info go to Sarah or Tom Haver. Gerontology's to the left past the elevator bank and four doors down. You'll be able to locate it by the smell of the rhesus colony."

He returned to his welding and Miriam left the lab. Too bad he hadn't been more forthcoming. At least it was reassuring to know that they were keeping the details secret. No doubt they didn't want information leaked until she was thoroughly measured.

She went down the hallway counting doors. 'Very well,' she thought, 'measure me. The more you poke and prod, the more time I'll have with Sarah.'

The technician had been right, you could certainly smell the Gerontology lab. Miriam opened the door, fully expecting the confrontation.

Instead, she found herself in a small outer office not unlike the one Sarah kept upstairs, but even more crowded with records. A computer terminal, glowing with numbers, stood on an old desk. Miriam spent a moment watching the display but it was useless. She couldn't understand.

Miriam passed through the room to an inner office which contained rolled-up cables, television equipment and stacks of empty cages. There were two exits beyond. Miriam chose one and went through.

There was a thunderous uproar. She was in the rhesus colony. Monkeys leaped about their cages, gesticulating, posturing at her. Many of them had sockets embedded in their skulls so that electrodes could be plugged in at the researcher's convenience.

How would it be to wear such a socket in her own head? Would they go that far if they had the chance?

The monkeys were made frantic by her presence; the odor of a strange animal disturbed them. She backed out of the room. The other door would certainly lead to Sarah. Once again she prepared herself, blanking her mind, opening the inner eyes to receive and evaluate Sarah's emotional state. Even now she could feel it fairly well, but not well enough to understand it. Years of training were necessary before a human being's emotional field extended much beyond his own body, years of loving someone with *touch* and wanting desperately to please him or her.

She turned the knob and swept the door open. Marshaling all of her confidence and power, forcing back the hunger their scent evoked, she strode into the room.

The warm emotional flow that emanated from Sarah Roberts was not what she had anticipated. It was the most delicious *touch* that she had experienced since her own family was alive. Sarah's heart was full of eager curiosity and love for her co-workers. The edge of fear was still there, but in her laboratory, among friends, Sarah obviously felt secure despite the blood running in her veins.

Miriam had hoped that Sarah would be a good choice, had come to be sure of it, but had not dared hope for anything like this. If only these emotions could be redirected toward herself!

But not at this moment. As Sarah looked up from her work and saw Miriam the emotional atmosphere changed to anger and wary fear. The face was haggard too. Sarah would have had periods of great difficulty by now. She had the sunken cheeks of one who was ignoring the hunger. From now on, each time it came back it would be stronger.

"Hey," Sarah said into the hum of voices, "a problem just arrived." Miriam noticed that they were working with another computer terminal.

"Let's see what happens if we standardize the baselines," Tom Haver said to a woman, who punched the keyboard. The graphs glowing on the screen jiggled and changed shape.

Sarah grabbed his shoulder, turned him around. "Hey, folks," he said in a quavering voice, "we have a visitor."

A small, fat man, bald and sweating, said in an undertone to the one Miriam assumed was the computer operator, "Match the curves to standard deviations—"

"Charlie, Phyllis—heads up."

"Oh."

Miriam moved toward them. They drew together, four frightened people. "Sarah said yesterday that I was supposed to come back."

The computer warbled and the woman Tom had called Phyllis turned it off. As did all moments of great importance in her life, this one brought Miriam a flash of understanding. If things had been just a little different, she realized that she would have been able to simply tell Sarah to come along and that would have been that. Sarah thought her beautiful. Her mind was full of avid fascination, guilty passion. Fear must be an aphrodisiac for Sarah.

Fear, then, would be the key.

Tom Haver went to a telephone. Miriam spoke, trying for every bit of authority she could muster. "Stop. I have a proposition. You may study me if you promise to let me go free at the end of the day."

Haver responded smoothly. "We have no intention of keeping you against your will. For that matter, we haven't got the right."

Miriam ignored that issue. If it was obvious to her that they could commit her it must be obvious to them too. Human courts were not set up in the expectation that situations such as this might arise. Miriam felt safest assuming that they would grant her no rights at all.

"Why did you do it, Miriam?" Sarah's eyes were steady, cool. Behind them Miriam could sense the conflict and the turmoil, but the surface was admirably unruffled.

"Do what?"

In answer Sarah extended her left arm, the one Miriam had chosen for the transfusion. A purple blotch disfigured the white skin. Because of the need to create a maximum effect fast, the transfusion had been very large. Seeing its result, however, made Miriam want to help Sarah, to save her. Unbidden, a *touch* rose out of her heart. Sarah blinked and averted her eyes, her face flushing red. This *touch* was like a kiss, the kind that follows a first admission of love. Tom Haver's arm came around Sarah, and she huddled against him. Miriam's extended hand was not taken.

"Mrs. Blaylock, she asked you a question. I think you'd better answer it." There was real menace in Haver's voice. It told Miriam that he was very much in love with Sarah. Would he die for his love? Did he understand that it might well come to that?

"I came here to help you," Miriam said gently. "I think you know why."

Sarah shook her head. "We do not know why. We'd like very much to know."

Miriam didn't like that "we." It was a wall between her and Sarah. "I want to share myself with you. I have read your work. I have reason to believe that my physical makeup may be of interest to you."

"Is that your motive?" Haver asked. "Is that why you contaminated her with your blood? Don't you realize how dangerous that is?"

"You could have killed me, Miriam!"

They were like two shrieking crows.

"I am the last of my kind," Miriam said grandly. "What I gave you was a great gift. You should take it in that light."

"The last?"

Miriam nodded. It perhaps wasn't true, but it fit her needs at the moment. "I knew you would never take it voluntarily and I may have very little time. At the least, Sarah, it will double your life-span."

Haver was becoming less menacing. There was also a slight reduction of tension in Sarah's face.

"We have a battery of tests," the fat man blurted. "We'd very much like to run them."

"I'm ready." There it was; the price and the payment. Now she must enter their dull catalogues, be weighed and analyzed. She, who soared so far above them, must submit to their machines. But what would they learn? Machines only gather facts and must therefore lie.

"I'd better get the bureaucracy rolling," Tom said. "What shall we start with, Sarah?"

"X ray."

"I'll set up the appointment."

Sarah nodded. She spoke gently to Miriam, a tone she might use with a frightened child. "We'd like to do an epidermal biopsy, which just involves scraping off some surface tissue, take some more blood, and run electrograms of various types. Would that be acceptable to you?"

Miriam nodded.

Sarah came to her, seemed about to touch her. "Why are you the last?"

Miriam hesitated. As an individual, she was so powerful that it was hard to think of herself as a member of a failed species. And yet, if she was not the last, she was certainly one of a very few. "I don't know," she said. The sorrow and the truth in her own voice surprised her.

"We have half an hour in X ray," Tom said, putting down the telephone. "Let's get going."

Miriam followed them down the hallway feeling somewhat more confident. They hadn't done anything violent to her yet. And Sarah was not in a state of panic. In fact, there was even some warmth there. A crack such as that in somebody's resistance was to Miriam the same as a chasm. If she was bold and careful she had a very good chance with Sarah. She watched Sarah walking along, her gait a little heavy, her hair gleaming softly in the corridor's shadows.

It would feel so good to take Sarah in her arms, to comfort her as a lover, to teach her as she might teach a daughter.

Perhaps the secret of why her species had dwindled was hidden in emotions such as these. If one loved human beings, how could one also kill them and still be happy enough with oneself to love one's own kind, and bear young?

Sarah dropped back until she was walking beside Miriam. They did not speak. Miriam *touched* and found friendly interest.

Her face revealed nothing of her triumph. She knew now that the two of them were going to walk many paths together, and serve the hunger well.

Sarah's earlier symptoms had disappeared during the course of the morning. Despite not having slept all night she was beginning to feel extraordinarily alert. They had left Geoff an hour ago working on a method of removing Miriam's blood from Sarah's body, but as time passed it was beginning to seem less necessary. If there was going to be any damage, it would surely be happening by now.

She walked along beside Miriam, her mind full of the test protocols that had been developed yesterday afternoon. This was an extremely excited place. Sam Rush had called Miriam history's most important experimental animal. That reflected the thinking of the whole institution. And Sarah's as well.

Obviously, they wouldn't be keeping her in any cages, but the paperwork had been started for an involuntary commitment to Riverside's Psychiatric Center. The board wasn't too worried about the details. Legal didn't feel that Miriam Blaylock could successfully press a suit to win her freedom.

They had a nice room all ready. Sturdy, well locked. On the violent ward. Sarah felt like ordering flowers for it, she was so delighted that Miriam had returned.

Only God knew what this was going to mean. Prizes, grants, extraordinary breakthroughs. The kind of incredible chance that scientists don't even dream about.

As they passed people in the halls eyebrows were raised, smiles opened up, Sarah got a few quick arm squeezes. As soon as Tom had called Marty Rifkind in X ray word must have spread through the institution. People thought of Miriam as the find of the century, perhaps of all time. And rightly so.

Rifkind bustled around his equipment making fussy, excited preparations. The receptionist had directed them to his best suite. When they came in he was all but dancing with anticipation. Sarah watched his reaction when he first saw Miriam. He suddenly became very serious, almost wary.

It reminded her of the way fodder mice acted when placed in a snake's terrarium.

"Miriam," Sarah said, "we're going to want you to lie on this table."

"It's quite comfortable, really," Marty blurted.

"It'll be moving around a lot, but you won't fall off," Sarah continued. Was she the only one here capable of dealing with Miriam? Rifkind was scurrying around all over the place, completely forgetting the requirements of the profession. Miriam got up on the table. "I'm sorry," Sarah said, "but you'll have to take off your clothes." Miriam began to comply. "Not everything," Sarah added hastily. "Just your outer garments and any metal objects." Miriam's eyes met hers, gay, laughing. It was an awful moment.

Rifkind controlled himself enough to affix the straps that would restrain Miriam as the table moved from position to position. She allowed herself to be strapped down, but Sarah noticed the rigidity of her face, the watery stare. Miriam was frightened. Somehow it touched Sarah. "You can unbuckle those yourself if you want to," she said. Miriam looked at her, the relief obvious.

Rifkind plastered on his most ingratiating smile. "We're going to do a full-body scan. One picture for each quadrant of the body, one for each skull view and two for the legs. That way we'll have a full record of your skeleton."

"Minimal dosage. I don't like X ray."

Rifkind grinned, his face popping sweat. "Minimal dosage it is. That's a promise." He beckoned the group into the control room. With the X ray head on a tracked grid and the table fully mobilized, all of the pictures could be aimed from the control panel. Once the patient was positioned there was no need for the radiologist to enter the room until the session was over. Thus, staff dosage was kept to a minimum and sessions were greatly speeded up.

"She wants minimal dosage," Rifkind said when the control room door was closed. "Too bad we've got to fry her."

"Don't you dare hurt her, Marty!" Sarah wanted to hit him, pulp his fat face.

"What?"

"I'm sorry. I mean, let's keep the dosage to the minimum necessary. She's valuable, remember. No risks, however remote."

Without replying, Rifkind flipped the switches that controlled the table and started aiming the X ray head. Sarah was surprised at the intensity of her own feelings. Was it really appropriate for her to want to protect Miriam? She did not know the answer to that question.

The woman remained absolutely motionless, her lips parted, eyes staring straight at the window into the control room. Those eyes seemed to seek Sarah's and she allowed them to meet. All through the skull series Sarah let Miriam stare into her eyes. It was a wonder-

ful, mesmerizing experience, like being naked before
one you truly loved.

Tom was watching Sarah carefully. "I'm not so sure
that Miriam isn't dangerous," he said. He was beginning to think that Sarah hadn't heard, when she swung
around, her face flushed, her eyes blazing.

"That's an unprofessional statement!"

"She drugs you, transfuses you with foreign blood,
and you defend her. I'm afraid I can't understand
that."

"She's precious. I admit that her behavior is highly
unpredictable. But there's so much knowledge to be
gained! Think of the recognition, Tom."

"Thank you. I'm just glad Miriam Blaylock has a
nice secure place to spend the night."

"Look at it from my standpoint. I want you to
understand what I feel about her—"

"Do you?"

"I almost halted the aging process with Methuselah.
And now what drops into my lap but this . . . female
being with blood characteristics similar to his right
before he died. The only difference is she's perfectly
healthy."

Sam Rush had come into the room behind them. His
voice startled Tom. "Just don't let her get away from us
again. Consider her continued presence your most
critical responsibility."

"Very good, Doctor." Tom thought of the Psychiatric wing with its burly guards—carrying only night-
sticks. He made a mental note to post an armed guard
as well on Miriam's cell.

"Doctors, please, let's keep it down so I can concentrate. I'm going to make a fluoroscope run of the skull,
if anybody's interested." Rifkind spoke into the intercom. "Mrs. Blaylock, turn your head to the right,
please." He adjusted some knobs, then turned on the
fluoroscope. "Abnormal," he said in a tight voice.

"Wonderfully abnormal!" Into the intercom: "Open your mouth, please. Thank you. Close it. Swallow." He was almost jumping with excitement. "Look at that inferior maxillary! Jack, give us the lowdown," he said to the osteologist Tom had called earlier. He turned off the fluoroscope. "Don't want her to glow in the dark."

"There are a number of gross variances," Jack Gibson said. He was a resident in osteology, attached to the hospital, and obviously pleased to be invited to a project in the elite research section. "The angle of the inferior maxillary is significantly more pronounced than normal, and the symphysis is more apparent. The whole structure is developed to a more powerful jaw. You could see the compensation in the heavier malar bone and much more developed zygoma. I also noticed more curvature to the cranium. We'd have to measure, but I'd say the brain case was larger than normal by a good twenty percent."

"So you'd say it's definitely not a human skull." Tom knew the answer, but he had to ask the question just in case. If his Christmas candy was going to be taken away, he wanted to know it now.

"Humanoid, certainly. I'm sure it's a derivation of the primate line. But human, in the strict sense of the word? No. It's a completely valid structure, though, not the result of some deforming process."

That was the kind of supporting observation that would eventually wind up in the paper Sarah would already be planning on Miriam, a paper that would stun the scientific community, not to mention the outside world.

Miriam's voice crackled through the intercom. She wanted out. Rifkind took a final series of the skull and neck. They would have to pursue more detailed work later. But this had been an excellent start. "She sounds angry," Tom said. "Sarah, you try to pacify her. We don't want her walking out of here again." She went into the X-ray room. "We're finished, Miriam," she said in what Tom hoped was a calming tone, "you can get up now." The Velcro straps could easily be removed by the patient, but Miriam seemed to be having trouble. Tom watched Sarah help her. As she drew near he saw Miriam gaze fiercely at her. The look was deep and personal. Intimate. Much too intimate. Sarah assumed a posture Tom was familiar with. She put her hands behind her back and bowed her head, almost as if to say, "do with me as you will." Tom had seen it in their bedroom.

Miriam's lips moved. Tom turned up the intercom, hearing only the last words, ". . . need help."

"What was that?" Charlie Humphries said. Tom shook his head. Had Miriam been reassuring Sarah?

Tom resolved not to allow the two of them to be alone for even ten seconds. There was something hypnotic about Miriam Blaylock and it was his Sarah who was the victim. Already Miriam had induced enough bizarre behavior in her to last the rest of her life. There was no way to tell what more might happen.

He saw that Sarah was still fumbling with the damn Velcro straps. He followed her into the X-ray room.

Miriam had done nothing more than stroke Sarah's arm. But it was nevertheless the warmest, most reassuring thing Sarah had ever felt in her life. She was so close that she could smell the pungent sweetness of Miriam's breath. "I transfused you for both of our sakes," Miriam said very softly, her lips barely moving. "But you're going to need help." Then she smiled and Sarah wanted to laugh with delight at the radiance of it. Her whole being seemed to rise to higher and higher levels as Miriam continued to look into her eyes. It was as if she could feel Miriam's feelings inside of herself, and those feelings were pure and loving and good. She became acutely conscious of her body and almost laughed aloud when she noticed how she was standing. She folded her arms and tossed her head, breaking the gaze. Miriam rose from the X-ray table and at the same moment Tom appeared.

Sarah felt like an angel who had just fallen from some high grace. She could have choked Tom!

"Your Doctor Rifkind broke a promise," Miriam said to Tom. It was a timely interruption. Tom's interest was deflected from Sarah. She was grateful for Miriam's perceptiveness.

"Broke what promise?"

"He said he was going to 'fry' me, I think. It wasn't exactly a minimal dosage."

"I don't recall—"

"I read his lips, Doctor Haver." She smiled again, nastily. And strode into the control room. Tom followed her and Sarah followed him. There was something extraordinary about the way Miriam dominated situations. Sarah envied her that skill.

When they reached the control room Marty Rifkind was looking quite chastened. Sam Rush was speaking, his voice as smooth as a mirror. "There won't be any dangerous tests, Mrs. Blaylock. You're not an experimental animal. Nobody at this institution would want to cause you the least harm. I'm sure I speak for the whole staff when I say that."

Sarah thought again of the room that awaited Miriam in the Psychiatric Clinic. She thought of the commitment papers in process right now. She found that she could not think of Miriam as a prisoner. And there was no other way to think of her, or wouldn't be when the commitment was approved.

They ought to let Miriam go home. The more Sarah thought of it, the more outrageous and high-handed this whole thing began to seem. Miriam had come back voluntarily, after all. That fact ought to be respected.

"We've got to get moving," Tom said. "There are four more labs to go." He glanced at Miriam. "If you're agreeable, Mrs. Blaylock."

All through the morning and into the afternoon they worked on the tests. Sarah moved in a sort of dream of fascination. Miriam was so very beguiling, as mysterious and beautiful as a jewel.

As they left the Brain Studies Lab Sarah noticed a security guard in the hall. Two more guards were in the elevator. Everybody except her and Tom and Miriam dropped back as they entered the elevator. When the doors closed, the three of them were alone with the guards. Tom punched the sixteenth floor. There was a key in the manual override control and one of the guards reached forward and turned it.

So it was to be now. Miriam had just been netted.

She saw the guards, she saw their guns. With a supreme effort of will she did not bolt as they passed the fire stairs. She was confident of her ability to go to the top of the building and escape across the roofs, or break down one of the lower doors if necessary.

But it wasn't going to be necessary.

"Where are you taking me?" she asked, playing out her role. "I thought we were finished." She imagined how it would be to satisfy her hunger with Haver.

"We'd like you to stay the night," he said. If all went as she hoped, there was going to be an interesting fate reserved for him. Miriam disliked him intensely.

The elevator doors opened. Miriam knew at once that they must be on the psychiatric floor. The walls were white and there were heavy screens on the windows. She felt quite sick at the sight of it all. Everything on this floor would be locked. Her last chance of escaping was now gone. It all depended on Sarah. Such a thin cord bound them. Was it strong enough?

"I want to leave," she said. The guards came closer. Other men appeared from behind a door with a tiny window in it. One of them took her firmly by the arm. "I've decided to go home." She put all the frantic terror into her voice that she could. Sarah's instincts had to be mobilized. "Let me go! I want to go home!" She sought Sarah's eyes, capturing them, *touched* with as desperate a plea as she could feel.

Sarah clapped her hands over her face. Tom Haver's

arm came around her. Miriam was pulled forward. She moaned, sank in the arms of her captors, and allowed herself to be dragged sobbing through the ugly little door and down the hallway beyond.

The cell was not padded, but it was no hotel room. It stank of despair and madness. There was no further need to act. Miriam sat down on the miserable little bed. She closed her eyes, *touching* for any faint contact with Sarah that she might pick up.

She thought of the French king and his dungeon, and the sounds of the starving.

Sarah was upset. Tom had become virtually monosyllabic. Now he was forcing her back to Geoff's lab just as certainly as he had forced Miriam to the Psychiatric Clinic. "I'm fine, Tom. I feel marvelous, as a matter of fact."

"You look rotten. You're gray. There must be some sort of cyanosis setting in."

"Maybe I'm a little shocked! This place is turning into the Third Reich. You just threw that woman in a cell without so much as a trial!"

"We need her. Anyway, the commitment is perfectly in order."

"She's sane!"

"Define your terms! I don't think so. Sam doesn't think so. In view of the fact that she's not even a human being—and we have proof that she carried out a totally irrational assault against you—I think we're doing the right thing. Now come on."

When he tugged at her arm, anger flared in her. Before she could think, she had slapped him so hard she all but lost her balance. He gasped, shook his head. For a long moment he was absolutely still. She thought he was going to hit her, then he seemed to shake it off.

"If you're up to it, darling, I think you'd better come." She didn't argue further. She was too astonished with herself.

Geoff hardly greeted them. He simply started talking, bringing them up to date.

His eyes were red from the hours he had been spending at the microscope. He extracted a smeared yellow sheet from a pile of papers on his lab bench. "I'm calling this the curve of transference. It shows the amount of time by blood volume that it will take for the native blood to be completely replaced."

"What's that supposed to mean?" Tom's voice was sharp. Sarah tried to take his hand but he moved away.

"The transfused material will replace the natural blood. No question about it. The native blood is now nothing more than a nutrient bath for the new tissue."

"The body produces blood. Replaces the whole volume eventually."

"New blood is the stuff's food supply. It's a parasite except that it carries nutrients and performs gas transference."

"Poorly. She looks gray."

"It isn't very efficient yet. But the receptivity is changing. A gas chromatograph shows oxygen uptake subnormal but improving."

This was bizarre. Sarah rubbed her fingers against her face. Her skin was slick and cool, like Miriam's. "What color are the leukocytes?"

"Purple. Deep, as if they were oxygen gorged."

"Miriam's leukocytes were deep purple before she slept. Methuselah's were before—" She stopped. Methuselah had torn his cagemate to pieces.

"I think we've got to deal with it as an invasive organism. Parasite. I can't see how we can avoid the conclusion that it's going to come to dominate your system."

"Get it out of her!"

"We might try a blood replacement. If we do it right away it just might work."

"So do it!"

"I intend to, Tom! But I've got to get more blood.

It'll be a few more hours. That's the best I can do. I hope we'll be in time. I think we will."

Silence fell. A few more hours. Tom's arms came around her. She felt his trembling body, saw the fear in his eyes. "I feel just fine," she said. "I'm sure it'll all work out perfectly well."

But when he clutched her more tightly, she let him.

11

Miriam stood at the barred window of the dingy little room. Evening was becoming night. She was growing more and more hungry. Her fingers touched the bars once lightly, then ran along the sill. If only Sarah would come!

Miriam had allowed them to lock her up to give Sarah the chance to come and free her. Sarah's loyalty was the issue. Miriam wanted it, and the best way to win it would be to get her to volunteer herself on Miriam's behalf.

Miriam was relying on the strongest aspect of Sarah's personality, her sense of independence. Surely Sarah would not be able to countenance the idea of someone being unjustly imprisoned.

Miriam shook the bars. The more hungry she got, the more the minutes counted. She imagined the hunt, the kill. Her head throbbed, her body began to feel heavy. Without quite realizing it she had examined the whole window frame. The bars were bolted into the brickwork on the outside. The frame itself was hard-wood.

As she was now, Miriam could probably bend back the bars. But in another two hours she would be too weak. Is that how the victims of Charles IV had died, by waiting too long for deliverance from outside? Miriam threw herself onto the bed, then jumped up and went to the door. All she could see through the barred peephole was an expanse of white wall on the opposite side of the hallway.

A powerful, delicious scent was entering the room through the tiny cracks around the door. There must be a guard posted just out of sight, probably sitting in a chair beside the door. That would be another of Haver's precautions.

At first she had discounted Haver as a threat to her relationship with Sarah, but the more she understood about him the more formidable he became. Deep inside that man there was something strong. That was the part of him Sarah loved.

Such a love was powerful. Miriam could see why Sarah endured the outer man with his arrogance and his manipulative nature, as long as there was hope that the inner man would eventually emerge and sweep the rest aside.

She wished that the guard would leave his post and give her some peace! She dreamed of the hunt—where she would go and whom she would take. There was a couple living in the top floor of a house on West Seventy-sixth Street, in an apartment Miriam had entered a few years ago. By now the last disappearance from the place was forgotten. It was time for another couple of tenants to jump their lease. No advance planning would be necessary. Miriam already knew her route and the locks she would encounter.

"Please, Sarah," she moaned. She *touched*.

In the emotional silence, there was an angry stirring. Somewhere in the building, Sarah was upset.

The attic grew darker as evening took the last glow from the westward-facing dormer windows. John had been lying on the floor of the tiny room that contained the remains of his predecessors, listening for Miriam to return to the house. He was almost too weak to stand. For hours he had been motionless.

This was going to be his last act. The steel box that would contain him stood bulky and black in the center of the room. Slowly John's hand rose until he could grasp the edge of that box. Then he pulled himself up to full height, tottering, fighting to keep his balance.

Dizziness washed over him. The room retreated farther and farther away. Only his burning hunger remained, like a fire in the center of his body.

By slow degrees the room swam back into focus. He felt like stone. His head lolled as if his neck were broken. His knees wobbled, forcing him to lean heavily against the wall of sealed boxes.

It took him an hour of agonizing effort to break the locks on five of them. The others were too strong. Those he had been able to break were at the bottom of the stack, the most ancient ones. He threw his weight against the ones on top, sliding them to the floor, allowing the ones below to open.

The room was now pitch dark and choking with dust. But it was not quiet. Everywhere there was seething, hissing motion. John threw himself out the door and closed it. He leaned back against it and turned the lock. After a few minutes the door began to creak, then to groan and rattle, finally to shake.

Sarah stared sightlessly at the electroencephalogram. The mass of complex lines would not become clear. She was so tired. But she was also terribly angry. Her mind was in turmoil. Time after time she had looked up from her work startled, thinking that Miriam was coming into the office.

They had wronged Miriam. The trumped-up commitment was an evil thing. It made Sarah question the real value of her own work, but more the truth of what she loved about Tom. He had conceived of the idea, managed its realization, and executed it with the dispassionate precision of a police officer.

Through it all he had been as cold as death. And now that poor creature sat up there, her dignity—her very rights as an intelligent being—stripped away.

Sarah glanced up at the clock. Nearly eight and time for the so-called Blaylock Group to meet and share findings. The Cytogenics Lab was preparing a chromosome analysis. Osteology was working on bone structures, Cardiology on heart and circulatory systems.

Sarah tried again. She had to have something to show at the meeting. The EEG was radically disturbed. It offered few real comparisons to a human encephalogram.

Sarah could not stop thinking of Miriam, nor could she stop wanting food. It was absurd, but her hunger was really getting obscene.

When Miriam had been near her, she had felt greatly comforted. There was something kind about that woman. Of course, it had been stupid for her to carry out the transfusion, but one should not forget that Miriam's thought processes were not human. In her mind it was probably a perfectly logical act.

Until now Sarah had not allowed herself to consider whether or not she would really stop aging. Was that the effect of Miriam's blood?

If so, it was a gift not only to Sarah Roberts but also to all mankind. Miriam had said that she was the last of her species. The more Sarah thought of it the more the nobility of the act became clear.

Noble captive. What suffering Miriam must be enduring right now, four floors above.

Ten minutes to the meeting.

Her mind had to come back to the problem at hand. The EEG was a mess, she realized, because Miriam's brain had more than one voltage level where a human brain displayed only one. The needles of the EEG machine had each been picking up at least two signals; thus, the hodgepodge.

Sarah swept the graphs off her desk. She had her damn conclusion. Most of a human brain was inactive, mysteriously turned off, apparently unneeded. Not so with Miriam. This was a picture of a fully functioning brain, so active it was beyond the capacity of the instrument to record.

What an extraordinary mind must be there. The commitment was more than a moral lapse, it was the blackest of sins, an obscenity. Sarah was ashamed for them all.

The Hutch that now sat across from Tom was a changed man. Miriam Blaylock had been severed from his control and there wasn't a thing he could do about it. Too late he had realized the importance of the case. Not only had he lost status at Riverside, he had lost something else—something Tom himself couldn't have borne to lose—his authority.

"I want to help," he said.

Tom was shocked. In Hutch's position he himself would have resigned on the spot. "OK," he said, "be my guest."

"We'll pretend to be teammates for a little while longer, if it's all right by you."

What was he implying? "Of course," Tom said with an assurance he no longer felt. He never underestimated the enemy. That was his cardinal rule.

"I worry about Sarah," Hutch said.

"So do we all."

"Why doesn't she check in for observation? Let's not forget that we have a top-flight hospital attached to this place."

"I've discussed that with Geoff and we both feel it

would be better not to alarm her. Anyway, she'd never go."

"Intervene. You can convince her."

"Short of an armed guard—"

"Then get one! She's in trouble. I'd expect that you of all people would want to help her!"

"What's that supposed to mean?"

"Don't you realize what's happening to Sarah?"

"Sarah's busy with her work. And she's not reporting any symptoms. Geoff's going to do a blood exchange within the hour."

"Didn't you see the effect that . . . thing had on her when they were together?"

"She was awed. I think that's a very appropriate reaction. Miriam Blaylock *is* awesome."

"She was seduced! It wants her, Tom. Surely you can see that!"

"*Wants?*"

"Didn't you feel it? Sarah was being hypnotized or some such thing. I'd put Sarah in the hospital for observation and I'd post guards—"

"Commit them both? Come on, that's absurd."

Hutch leaned forward, gripped the edges of the desk. Tom had never seen him so agitated. "I would post guards to keep that creature away from her. At all costs!"

Tom could only shake his head. He had always suspected Hutch of a paranoid streak. Now, under pressure, the weakness was surfacing. That was always the way when people faced pressure. Some of them caved in, others did their best work.

"Look, I'll take all this under advisement. But the project group is due to meet at eight and I want to make sure everybody's on schedule."

That was enough of a dismissal to make Hutch stalk out. Fine. Calling the labs could wait five minutes. Tom needed some time alone. So many contradictory thoughts were pouring through his mind. It had been a matter of pride to reveal nothing of his feelings to

Hutch, but in truth he also was frightened. Sarah had a much more serious problem than she would admit, that was obvious from the tests. Geoff's analogy comparing Miriam's blood to a parasitic organism was proving to be correct. Soon Sarah would be suffering from all of the effects of massive parasitization. Terminally, if it came to that, she would starve, her body overwhelmed by the nutritional needs of the parasite.

That possibility, however, was not what most bothered him. He had almost unlimited confidence in Riverside. If all else failed, they would save Sarah. The thing he could not understand was why Miriam had done it. He remembered that she had been reading Sarah's book in the sleep cubicle two nights ago. Numerous times she had made reference to doing "research" on them all.

The more he considered the situation, the more obvious it became that Miriam's appearance here was planned right down to the claim of night terrors, which had been used to draw Sarah's interest.

The approach was subtle, to be sure. But Tom was himself quite good at designing plans that bore a superficial appearance of accident. Such was the nature of the political mind. He had to admire Miriam's expertise.

It had all led up to the transfusion. Surely it was not simply a crazy attempt to kill. Why go to such pains? There were a thousand easier, less detectable ways of killing a person. That blood running in Sarah's veins was far more identifying than a fingerprint. No, there had to be another reason.

As to what it might be, Tom simply could not imagine. Possibly it was too alien even to make sense to a human being. They had only just begun to study Miriam. The more distant reaches of her mind might elude them for years—or forever. Yet they had to try to understand. He could see a situation in the near future—if Sarah became seriously ill—in which her very life might depend on their insights.

He pressed his intercom, hoping that his secretary hadn't left for the day. There was no response. It was his own fault, he hadn't asked her to stay. With a tired sigh he returned to the schedule and began to call the various labs.

Phones were answered by bright, excited voices. What irony. Here he was in the center of one of the most extraordinary discoveries ever made, right at the core of the event, and all he could feel was foreboding.

He called Sarah last. She pleaded for more time. He had to tell her that the others would all be ready at eight.

"No doubt you're saying that to everybody."

He supposed that he deserved such suspicions. "I'm not, it happens to be true."

"I'll just have to be there, then. These EEG's are an unholy mess. Not only are the alpha and lambda waves close to unreadable, nothing else follows any established patterns. I suspect that we'll have to relearn brain function before we can figure out what's going on here."

"You feeling all right?"

"I'll tell you when and if my symptoms require more attention. I don't want to hurt your feelings, Tom—"

"You're sure? Wouldn't it be just a little fun?"

"Feeling sorry for yourself? I was trying to be kind. Just let me do my work. If I have any more problems, believe me I'll tell you."

Sarah was in agony. She forced herself to appear interested in the meeting, but all she could think of was eating. Soon there would have to be some kind of reckoning.

They all looked so evil—or so blind. "We have a most interesting picture," the geneticist droned. Sarah couldn't even remember his name. He fumbled with the overhead projector, finally casting a karyotype of Miriam's chromosomes on the meeting room's whiteboard.

Poor Miriam, she was becoming a bunch of charts and graphs. But what could they tell of her beauty? She was the most free spirit Sarah had ever known. Free, and also brave. Sarah had decided that the transfusion had really been an act of courage and love. Miriam wanted to transmit her gift to mankind.

She had chosen Sarah as the recipient because Sarah knew so much about aging. There was brilliance in such a choice. They were all making a great mistake about Miriam. In a sense they had not the right to disturb the experiment any more than they had the right to imprison Miriam. She was a genius, perhaps even beyond that. They owed her trust, not suspicion and the violence of involuntary commitment.

The transfusion was an act of courage. As the recipient, was she not also called to courage?

How dare they consider a blood wash.

A wave of hunger made Sarah gasp. Tom and Hutch were both looking at her. She managed a smile. 'Miriam will know how to take care of me,' she thought. 'She would never have done such a thing in ignorance.'

The geneticist's drone reached her ears again. "To complete the cytogenic analysis, we stained for G-banding and Q-banding. The specimen presents the longest chromosomal chain yet observed in a higher animal: sixty-eight chromosomes. No trisomes or other identifiable translocations or breaks are observed."

Sarah could hardly sit still. If they had been more cooperative Miriam would probably already have helped her with this terrible feeling. It was greater than a simple appetite. Sarah didn't want food. This felt like some kind of addiction. Hunger. God help her.

"Both 'p' and 'q' arms are of equal length, an unusual finding. There is superficial resemblance to a human chromosome, but only in the most general terms. The broad primate characteristics can be observed, however."

Shut up, you long-winded bastard.

"The sexual component presents another sort of problem. I would doubt that the sexual functioning of this species parallels our own, or the rest of the primates, for that matter. The ambiguity of the sixty-six, XXY tripartite structure certainly implies both male and female components in the same personality. I would recommend a thorough examination of the sexual organs as the next step in this study."

That did it. She could not abide the idea of Miriam strapped to some table with this bastard examining her sexual organs. She found herself on her feet. Tom started to rise as well. For an instant she was desperate, cornered. She had to get upstairs! "Relax," she said as calmly as possible. "Does it have to cause a panic when I go to the bathroom?"

Only Hutch followed her out of the meeting. They walked down the hall side by side. It seemed that he had to go to the bathroom too. Sarah waited for him to disappear into the men's room and then headed for the stairs. She paused on the landing. Sure enough, Hutch appeared a few moments later in the doorway. She realized that he would have to be dealt with. They were standing face to face. He held out his hand. She wasn't really sure if it would work, but she had read somewhere that a blow to the side of the head could stun.

She hit him above the temple with her closed fist. His eyes rolled and he sank to the floor. "I'm sorry," she said. She hated violence. Always, she had been a person of the deepest humanitarian ethic.

She took the stairs three at a time.

Tom could not contain his own excitement as finding piled on finding. These results were marvelous. There was going to be recognition for everybody. Extraordinary discoveries. Fame. It was like the best of Christmases. No, better.

All it would take would be a few more weeks of intensive testing of Miriam and they would be ready to make everything public. The discovery of the new species could be announced at the same time they announced the antidote for aging. During her deep sleep, it seemed, Miriam's body generated the same lipofuscin inhibitor that had been briefly present in Methuselah's blood before he broke down. The difference was that for Miriam there were no breakdowns. It was only a matter of time before they understood why.

He thought of that cell on the Psychiatric Ward. Involuntary commitment. Unpleasant, but unavoidable.

Hutch reeled into the room, shattering Tom's thoughts and the whole meeting with the sound of the door crashing back against the wall. Hutch didn't have to speak, they all knew that something had gone wrong with Sarah.

"Which way did she go?" Tom heard Charlie Humphries ask.

Tom waited until he heard Hutch breathe the word "stairs" before he was off.

He headed for the sixteenth floor. Bursting into the reception area, Tom caused the attendant to vault his desk, his nightstick in his hand.

"Is Doctor Roberts up here?"

"Jesus! You goin' to a fire?"

"IS SHE!"

"Lessee. She signed into room fourteen ten minutes ago. Signed out three minutes later."

"Goddamnit!" He signed himself in, waited for the attendant to buzz him through the door to the ward, rushed down to Miriam's room. The special guard sat with his chair tilted against the wall. "Open it."

The man looked up, recognized Tom. "Hasn't been a sound since Doctor Roberts left." He unlocked the door, swung it wide.

The room was cold with the night wind. The window, its bars gone, gaped darkly. "Sarah left here alone?"

"Yeah! Not five minutes ago. She didn't say a damn thing about this."

Tom went over to the window. He couldn't have

climbed up or down from here. But Miriam evidently
could, because she was gone.

Miriam went swiftly through Central Park, heading
for the West Side. She was literally wild with hunger.
By the time Sarah had come she had already pushed the
bars off the window. It was just as well. Sarah had
wanted to be held. Miriam did not trust herself so far,
not in this state. She reassured the suffering woman
that there would be relief, and told her to meet her at
her house in half an hour. Then she had climbed down
to the sidewalk, with Sarah leaning far out the window,
watching her progress.

She ran across the Sheep Meadow with the soaring
cliffs of buildings sparkling beyond the dark trees. She
had much to do in half an hour.

Only when she emerged onto Central Park West did
she break her run. Now she walked swiftly, crossing to
Seventy-sixth Street and counting the houses to the one
she would enter.

She chose a house four doors down from the target in
case she was seen on the stairway. Taking the steps
four at a time, she passed the doors of apartments,
the sounds of television, the smell of frying steak.
When she got to the top of the house, she climbed
the ladder to the roof and let herself out. New York
building codes require that tenants have free access to the roof. This made things much more con-
venient.

These old row houses were connected by shared
walls. Miriam passed silently across the tar-paper roofs
until she reached her objective. The landlord of the
target house had been clever. He had gained an extra
apartment by building a bedroom on the roof. The
apartment was a duplex, fashionably provided with a
spiral staircase to connect sleeping and living quarters.
Miriam considered it an ideal early evening choice
because you could get into the upstairs bedroom and
await your chance at the top of the spiral stairs. From

there you had a view of the whole living-dining room below.

The bedroom had a door to the outside, locked by a spring-loaded dead bolt. You could open it from inside, but not from the roof. Or so they had assumed. The lock hadn't been changed. It was still the same substandard mechanism that had been there six years ago. She was inside within thirty seconds. There were three steps down to the bedroom floor.

Looking down the spiral stairs from the darkness above, she evaluated both occupants. The girl was the lighter, she would be the one to be taken alive. Miriam watched the man. He fit her personal needs very well. The last time she had been here all had been as now: a young couple, dinnertime. The only difference was that John had been with her then, and they had shared their meal on the bedroom floor.

Miriam used the same ploy she had before: she hissed. Dinner stopped downstairs. She did it again, louder.

"Is that a cat?"

She repeated the sound.

"Frank, there's a cat upstairs."

"Goddamn it."

She did it another time, imagining herself to be a cat in pain.

"Frank, go see. It sounds like it's hurt."

His chair scraped. Instantly, Miriam stepped back into the bathroom. A moment later the bedroom light came on and Frank's heavy tread sounded on the stairs. She watched him from the shadows, tensing for the kill. He did exactly the same thing his predecessor had done: looked around and, seeing nothing, bent to peer under the bed.

Miriam had no need of a scalpel. Nature had given her race a tongue proper to its uses and she penetrated the flesh instantly. He sucked in his breath, kicked once against the floor, and was dead. In ten seconds she filled her body with the fire of his life.

"Frank? What's that sucking?"

Miriam removed her chloroformed rag from its Ziploc bag and once again withdrew to the bathroom. She took with her the loose bundle of clothing that had been the male.

"Frank?"

She made the hiss of the cat again. Then she stomped on the floor.

"Are you killing that animal? Frank, that's probably Mrs. Ransom's cat, you realize that!" Another strangled hiss. "Frank, don't!" The scrape of a chair, patter of feet.

Miriam knew the type very well. With this one she would step out into the light, stunning it into momentary immobility. She got to the top of the stairs. "Fra-ank? Oh!" She stood, mouth gaping with surprise, eyes darting in confusion.

"I'm a policewoman," Miriam said, crossing the room with one bound. "It's perfectly all right."

The girl lurched and mumbled in the chloroformed rag, but soon went limp. Miriam put the remains of Frank in the usual black plastic bag. The unconscious girl was more of a problem, but Miriam had thought carefully about that. Getting her home would be the riskiest part of the procedure. If anybody came out of one of the other apartments while they were on the staircase, she would have to kill again.

She went downstairs quickly. Nobody appeared. There were a few people on the street, but women in the human culture are shielded by their position from any expectation of violence, so she was only mildly concerned that she would raise suspicions by assisting her woozy "girl friend" into a cab.

They got home without incident, Miriam alternately comforting the half-conscious girl and threatening her. But until the girl was locked in the bedroom closet Miriam remained vigilant. With the turning of the key in that lock, all was at last prepared. It was now nine-thirty. Miriam herself was fed and once again able to be among human beings without the constant temptation of the hunger. And Sarah's first victim awaited her.

Tom sought Sarah with increasing desperation, in her office, then in her lab, then in Geoff's lab where the blood wash was to have been done. Geoff was there and he had all the fresh blood he needed.

But he did not have Sarah.

Tom finally had to accept the truth. She had left Riverside in spite of her condition. "How much time does she have?"

Geoff's expression said it all.

"I was afraid of that."

"I did all I could, Tom. I practically had to rob the Red Cross to get this stuff."

Tom rushed down the halls, blind with sorrow and terror. How could she have done this? The thought crossed his mind that Miriam might have kidnapped her, but he dismissed it. Even Miriam could not have negotiated the drop from her window with Sarah on her hands.

He came to the conference room, saw Hutch slumped in a chair. Phyllis was nursing him with wet paper towels. "Hutch," Tom said, "any idea at all where she might be?"

"As soon as I tried to stop her she hit me so hard I was stunned."

Tom bolted from the room, went to the elevators, hammered at the button. He felt nauseous, he was shaking. But he knew now where she had gone. The only place she would have gone.

Sarah. Please, darling. *Please!*

The night air was damp and sharp as Sarah ran down First Avenue. Never had she experienced such a wild sense of freedom. Her body felt incredibly *capable*. She was moving fast, not even breathing hard, enjoying the wind in her face.

For a brief moment she had embraced Miriam in the Psychiatric Ward. In that instant she was filled with gladness and wonder. She had seen into Miriam's mystery. How dense they all had been. Not one of them had noticed the ecstasy that could be drawn from Miriam's gaze, or the joy of her touch.

These feelings could not be explained by science. The effect Miriam had on her was beyond measurement. How could you weigh the difference between a spirit imprisoned and a spirit free?

A thrill went through her. Two blocks ahead a lone figure had come out of a coffee shop. She increased her pace, her feet drumming on the pavement. There was a delicious sense of precision about her movements.

That figure seemed so delicate as it strolled along. It would be like digging into a honeycomb and tasting its hot, secret sweetness.

Did she want to hit that man? No, it was worse than that. She imagined his head flying like a melon beneath the wheels of a passing bus, saw the blood spurt from his neck.

She stopped running.

These were not her thoughts, could not be.

The man stopped at a corner and lit a cigarette. Sarah saw the white neck exposed as the head bent forward, then the profile in the glow of the match.

The man straightened up and stared back in her direction, seemingly aware of her sudden change of pace. His bland, haggard face regarded her with the mildest curiosity and then he went his way.

His very gentleness enraged her. She took a few strides toward him, then stopped herself. A radio was playing in a passing car. Two children came out of an apartment house lobby and dashed off into the night.

There was no reason to be enraged at the old man.

Miriam. She would know, she would understand. The thought brought all the glee back and Sarah started running again. It was wonderful to feel so free in the streets like this, so utterly unafraid.

She found herself passing Carl Shurz Park. Why exactly she had come this far east she could not say. Mist was starting to fall, blowing like smoke in the streetlights, making the park's paths glisten as they had last night. Sarah slowed to a walk.

The little park had lost all its mystery and terror. A Baby Ruth wrapper clung to a gatepost, a dismal loop of kite string hung from a tree. In the distance the East River muttered with the rising tide and tires hissed on FDR Drive.

This was the real world, Sarah's world. She came to the gate she had entered last night, saw the path leading up into darkness. If she went in, what would she find?

Empty benches and silence. Nothing more.

Last night had been a bad dream. She moved on, going more slowly toward Miriam's house. She was left with a single, practical wish: find out what she could do about this awful craving. It was beyond an appetite.

As she went down East End Avenue and turned west to York she passed the exhaust fan of a restaurant. Cooking odors poured into her face.

She was revolted.

People were willing to eat garbage these days. Her mind seized on the familiar image of the peaches they used to get from their backyard tree down in Savannah. They had been rich and yellow-red. She wished she had one now.

"Please, Miriam," she said aloud. "Help me."

By the time the house finally appeared she was livid with need. Try as she might she could not discover what it was she wanted. It was as if life itself was the food she required. But what nutritional need could possibly translate into such a desire?

Sarah rang the doorbell. Instantly the lock clicked and the door swept open. Miriam stood in the dark hallway. Arms outstretched, Sarah ran forward, attaching herself with a gasp of relief. Miriam made no sound closing the door, her own arms coming around Sarah. Miriam could be so very tender.

When Sarah calmed down enough to talk she began
to babble thanks, to explain that she understood now
what Miriam had given her, she knew that it was the
very longevity she had been trying so hard to achieve in
the laboratory.

"That isn't all it is."

No, that was true. Despite her relief and happiness
there was still this awful, cloying need—and with it a
growing revulsion for normal food. Until now she
hadn't thought about Miriam's diet. Her confusion
must arise out of the fact that she had no instinctive
craving for what Miriam ate, and what must now also
be her own food.

"Come." Miriam took her by the arm, led her
upstairs. The stairway and hall were brightly lit. Miriam
opened a door to a dark room. "This is my bedroom,"
she said, "you were here yesterday." Sarah allowed
Miriam to lead her in, close the door. The darkness was
absolute. It would be a few moments before Sarah's
eyes adjusted to the rapid changes in light intensity.
Miriam pushed her by the shoulders, sitting her down.
"Wait. I am going to relieve your hunger. Be prepared,
Sarah. This is going to be quite unexpected." Sarah
obeyed the calm reassurance of the voice. She thought
with childish delight, 'she's glad to see me.' There was a
high-pitched sound, like the scream of a dying rabbit.
"Open your mouth!" Miriam's tone was now strident,
demanding that Sarah do as she was told. A hot stream
sluiced down her throat, hot and pumping, while the
reedy little scream got lower and lower and finally died
away. For a horrible instant Sarah had thought that this
was a stream of urine, it was so hot and saline, but the
effect it had on her dispelled that fear almost at once.

Sarah and Tom had occasionally taken a little cocaine. It lifted one, in the first instant, to what had up
until now seemed the pinnacle of pleasure. It was
nothing compared to this.

Sarah kicked, threw her head back, lost the stream,

then lunged forward in the dark, seeking more. A fleshy something was thrust into her mouth. "Suck!" More came when she did, better than what had come before. Each time a new swallow of it entered her mouth stars exploded in her mind. Angels were singing around her, singing the most glorious euphonies.

Then the pulsing hotness was withdrawn. Sarah lurched forward, sobbing, trying to find it again, her body and soul blazing with pleasure beyond intensity. In her mind she felt the cool clarity of spring rain, but it was in her heart that the greatest pleasure rested. "Welcome to the kingdom," Miriam said. She turned on the lights.

Sarah screamed. The sound was like exploding bells in her own ears, not a shriek of fear, but of delight wild beyond words. Miriam did not look a thing like a human being, but she was *beautiful!* "I thought I would take off my makeup." This was the Goddess Athena, Isis—Sarah could not find a word, a name . . .

The eyes were not pale gray at all, but shining, golden, piercingly bright.

The skin was as white and smooth as marble. There were no eyebrows, but the face was so noble, so much at peace that just seeing it made Sarah want to sob out the petty passions of her own humanity and have done with them forever.

The hair, which had been concealed by a wig, as gold as the eyes, was soft, almost like smoke, finer than the hair of a baby. Angel's hair.

The majestic being that had called itself "Miriam" now spoke. "You shall learn secrets," it said in a new tone, the voice of authority absolute. Sarah had to suppress an impulse to shout with delight.

Suddenly, Miriam's face seemed to jump at her. She heard words, quavering, concentrated with effort, inside her head. "Sarah, I love you." Then they were gone, as if the speaker had released a desperately difficult effort.

"Oh my God! You—"

"Projected my voice telepathically. Yes, I can *touch* your heart."

Sarah wasn't so sure. There was little scientific grounding for notions of telepathy.

At this moment, however, she didn't much care. As her stomach digested the mysterious new food extraordinary perceptual changes were taking place. First, she became aware of a new sensation in her body, one she had never felt before. It was strength, the profound wellness that must be experienced by powerful animals. She found that she could also call upon a sense of smell so improved that it was virtually a new addition to her body. The room, in fact, was a maelstrom of odors. She could smell the cool scent of the silk coverlet on the bed, the mustiness of the carpet, the faint sharp-sweet odor of the beeswax that had been used to polish the furniture.

And there was something else, something familiar and yet not familiar—a terrible odor, meaty and strong, but also by far the most exciting scent in the room. It was under the bed. She bent toward it.

"Not yet," Miriam hissed. In an instant she was beside Sarah.

"It smells wonderful." Childishly, she felt petulant at being denied access to whatever was hidden there. Miriam drew her close, pressed her face to her white skin. This diverted her. The new sense of smell drew in an aroma that brought music to mind. As befitted someone so beyond the stunted nature of man, Miriam's scent was more than addictive. Sarah rested her head there, vowing that never as long as she lived would she move, never would she be denied this—this heaven—again.

Miriam heard pounding at the door below. If Sarah had seen the look in those golden eyes she would have thought no further of angels.

Gently Miriam detached herself. Obviously, Haver

had sorted things out sufficiently to come here. Sarah moaned as Miriam laid her on the bed. Sleep would soon overwhelm Sarah after the relief she had just experienced. It was well that she Sleep. There was no need for her to see the events that were about to occur. John, hiding in the attic, was about to make the move against her that Miriam had anticipated.

And Tom Haver was about to take the full force of it in her place.

12

John waited until he was sure he heard two voices, then he put his hand on the lock. He closed his eyes. When he turned that lock his life was going to come to an end. He would never, by his own free will, move again.

But at least he would be able to take this magnificent revenge with him—for as long as he must remain aware.

The lock clicked. The door slammed open, smashing John against the far wall. He fell to the floor, his dry skin tearing like paper. Dark shapes tumbled out into the attic. There was a dry, old odor, like the smell of ancient leather.

For a long time only faint rustling sounds were heard. John had not known exactly what they would be like, but he had assumed that they would move faster than they did. Miriam must not—

Something touched his foot, came slipping up his leg. He kept his eyes shut tight, he did not want to see it.

There was a tiny sound, the remains of his own voice, crying.

They soon discovered that he was useless to them. He heard the scraping as they pulled themselves toward the door to the lower part of the house, the thuds as they went down the attic stairs.

"Open up!" Tom pounded on the front door. He hadn't expected to be ignored. All the more it confirmed to him that Sarah was in there and his presence was not appreciated. "I'll kick this damn door in!" His voice echoed up and down the street but he didn't care. Let somebody call the police. He would welcome the help. He stepped back and gave the door a hard kick—and almost fell into the hallway. The door had opened on its own.

The entrance gaped black. A whispering sound abruptly stopped. Tom could see somebody back in the shadows, crouching low. "I want to see Sarah Roberts," he said as he strode across the threshold. He had intended to leave the door open to get some light from the street, but it closed as soon as he was inside. The smoothness of its motion and the decisive *chunk* of the lock made him suspect that it was being controlled from elsewhere in the house. "All right, Miriam, enough is enough!" He flailed, seeking the wall, then began to slide his hands along its smooth surface trying to find a light. He pressed an old-fashioned button switch but no lights came on. "Oh, for God's sake!"

The whispering began again, closer this time. He recoiled. There was something awful about it, something avid. He pressed back against the front door. The handle would not turn. "Get away from me!" He kicked, met air. The whispering grew louder and louder, becoming a frenetic chatter. It was not a voice at all but rather the sound of movements, as if a swarm of insects were crawling down the hallway.

Tom twisted the handle of the door, threw his weight

against it, hammered on it. It might look like wood but it felt like steel.

To his left was an archway leading into a living room. Windows.

He stepped forward. Something came around his right ankle. He yanked his leg free but now it attached itself to the other ankle. He stamped his feet but it was no use. Both ankles were grasped. *"Sarah!"* The pressure became pain, searing, excruciating, forcing him to his knees. He clawed the darkness before him, grabbed toward his agonized ankles, and fell forward into a tangled, ropy mass. His legs kicked, his arms flailed. Every movement seemed to entangle him further with whatever it was. Thin fingers groped in his hair, slipped around his neck. He screamed and screamed, pulling at the ropy substance as best he could. A fingernail popped into his cheek and cut through all the way down to his chin. The pain made him bellow, but he managed to move so that it missed the critical blood vessels behind the jaw. "Sarah!"

Tom's hands connected with something solid—a head. He pushed back with all his might. There was a crackling sound and the fingers released his hair. Again and again he smashed at the thing, feeling it break like glass beneath his blows.

He pulled himself to his feet and lunged past it into the living room, rolling across the floor, brushing the stinking dust it had left on him to the floor.

His cheek, his ankles and his hands screamed in pain. He stared into the darkness. Had he killed it?

What the hell was it?

"Sarah, it's me! Come back! You've got to get out of here!"

He saw the shadow of somebody standing at the far end of the room, a tall, thin individual with a bobbing head. It did not look any more human than the thing that attacked him had felt. Its outline was dim in the light from the street.

He didn't understand at all what was happening in this place. Only Sarah was here—somewhere. Every fiber of his body screamed at him to jump out a window, to escape, to get away from whatever monstrous evil had infected this house—

But Sarah was here.

"You! Where is she?" He took a step toward it. Another. Its head stopped moving. Abruptly it dropped to the floor.

Another one appeared in a doorway that led into the rear part of the house. He could see it marching like a man whose knee joints had been fused. Then it too dropped to the floor.

The scrabbling sound began again.

"Sarah Roberts!"

The sound rose as the things crossed the floor. Tom's hand went to his cheek, touching the open wound. In that instant he knew that he had to leave this place. If they reached him again he was going to die.

To his left was a sun porch with French doors leading to a garden. He stumbled toward the doors, grabbed the handle and jerked at it. Locked.

He didn't try to unlock the door, but took a chair and hurled it through.

He ran wildly across the garden, flailing in the shrubs, seeking some kind of a fence. At last he came to the edge of the property and climbed the brick wall he found there, cutting his fingers deeply on the shards of glass embedded in the top.

Atop the wall he paused, looked back at the house. There were no lights. Not far behind him the shrubbery was waving madly as something struggled through it.

He jumped six feet to the sidewalk.

Back in the world again. A woman walked toward him leading a dachshund. He brushed past her to the corner and hailed a cab.

"Riverside emergency," he gasped out.

"You bet."

They stitched him in the brightly lit emergency room and bandaged his hands. He told them a window had fallen out at his apartment.

What had actually happened he did not know. Perhaps it had been real, perhaps some kind of complex illusion designed to frighten him away.

He had them call over some detectives from the Twenty-third Precinct. Half an hour later he met them in his office.

"So you want us to go to this house and get out your girl friend?"

"That's right, officer. I have every reason to believe she's there against her will."

"Kidnapped?"

"Psychically kidnapped. Influenced."

"It doesn't sound like a crime. She's not under age—"

"Of course not! You're telling me I can't get help."

"Doctor Haver, you haven't reported a crime."

He let them leave. When the door closed he could contain himself no longer. In his defeat and loss he wept, muffling his face in his hands to deaden the sound.

Sarah had been at peace until she heard somebody call her name.

Tom?

She was drifting on the softest of waters, in the moonlit sea. . . .

He screamed.

She opened her eyes. In her mind was a vivid image of Tom. "I love you." The screams pealed again and again, so frantic that Sarah clapped her hands over her ears.

Abruptly it was over. After a moment Miriam's voice drifted through the door. "It's all right," the voice said, "sleep now."

"Thank you," she replied. But she thought, 'please

don't let him be dead.' She had to go to him. For that she somehow had to get out of this bed. She swayed when she sat up, shook when she put her feet on the floor, had to grab the bedpost for support when she tried to move.

Helpless, almost overcome with sleep, she sank to the floor.

She lay her head down, wishing she had never left the bed. It was so cold! Her eyes opened, she tried to gather enough energy to pull herself back up.

It was some time before she realized that she was staring into a face. Somebody was lying under the bed, still and silent. Sarah sighed, all that escaped of a scream.

It was not a peaceful face, but a sad one.

So this was Miriam's "food." Sarah gagged with the memory of it. And yet it sang in her veins. Slowly she extended her hand. Her own eyes closing as if she were under the influence of some opiate, she stroked the forehead of the person whose life she had taken.

She Slept.

Miriam moved about the house struggling with her failures. The body of Tom Haver was nowhere to be found. She was not really surprised at his escape. His attackers were fierce but they had little real strength. Poor man. All his survival had gained him was a harder death. He could not be allowed to survive, not with what he now knew. If she was clever, his death could be arranged in such a way that it served a purpose.

She followed a trail of broken plants to the garden wall. There was Eumenes, arms outstretched, mouth lolling open, lusting toward food he could never swallow. Astonishingly repulsive.

She remembered lying with her head in his lap on the slopes of Hymettus.

She returned them all to their resting places, forcing

their remains into the chests. At last there was John, slumped against the wall of the attic. She picked him up, holding the wrists together with one hand, carrying him with the other. "I know you can hear me, my love," she said as she placed him in his container. "I'll make you the same promise I made the others. Listen well, because you must hold this in your memory forever. John, I will keep you beside me until time itself comes to an end. I will neither abandon nor forget you. I will never stop loving you."

She pressed him down into his steel tomb until his knees were against his chest and slid the cover closed. Weeping, she spun the bolts one by one.

Tom lay in their bed alone. Each time he had dropped off, shouting terrors had jolted him back awake. His face was a dull haze of throbbing pain, his left eye was swollen closed.

He kept trying to understand what had happened to him. No matter how he worked it out, however, there just wasn't a satisfactory explanation.

He thought of Sarah and cried aloud. She was in the hands of a monster. It was as simple as that. Perhaps science would never explain such things, perhaps it couldn't.

And yet Miriam was real, living in the real world, right now. Her life mocked the laws of nature, at least as Tom understood them.

Slowly, the first shaft of sunlight spread across the wall. Tom imagined the earth, a little green mote of dust sailing around the sun, lost in the enormous darkness. The universe seemed a cold place indeed, malignant and secret.

Was that the truth of it?

Something tickled his unwounded cheek. Tears again. He threw back the covers and got out of bed. All at once he froze. This room was the only one with any sunlight in it. The rest of the apartment was still dark.

He was frozen with terror. He could not move from the place where he stood.

It came at him shrieking, tearing with its long knives of fingernails, its jaws snapping—

And was gone.

He shook his head, went to the bathroom, splashed his chest and neck with cold water. He must not let the image of that thing creep into his mind again. It was not outside the realm of possibility to be driven catatonic by fear. That had to be guarded against if there was to be any hope left at all.

He looked like hell. One eye was an angry purple mass of flesh. The other was black. He badly needed a shave but the bandages were going to get in the way.

Suddenly, the sound of the intercom broke into his thoughts. How long had it been buzzing? Turning on lights as he went, he moved to the foyer and answered it.

Three minutes later Geoff and Phyllis stood at the door. They had food and coffee and they didn't buy any stories about broken windows. They wanted to know what Miriam had done with Sarah.

Miriam stood beside the bed watching Sarah, waiting for her to wake up. The transformation was working well. Miriam touched Sarah's cheek, feeling the cool dryness of the skin. That was another good sign.

It was a happy moment.

The only barrier left to complete transformation was the emotional one. Loyalty was, as always, the issue. Sarah must be made to realize the truth of her situation. She now belonged to a new species and must leave the values of the old behind.

Miriam turned her thoughts to Tom Haver. She could see a good way to use him to further Sarah's change of allegiance. He would be the medium.

A slight variation in Sarah's breathing pattern alerted Miriam to the fact that the Sleep was about to end. Very well. When Sarah awoke, she would find love waiting for her.

An ugly dream receded. Sarah opened her eyes. The thing looming over the bed startled her for an instant. Miriam, of course. Her eyes were glaring, the stare avid. Sarah's impulse was to run.

She thought of the body under the bed, the dead skin dull and dry.

"Don't," Miriam said. "You can't change the past."

"You're a murderer!"

Miriam sat on the edge of the bed. It made Sarah shudder when Miriam stroked her face, but she was afraid to turn away. As a child in Savannah she had captured a baby rabbit. She remembered how it had huddled so quietly in her hand, and she had thought, 'I've tamed it with my touch.' But it wasn't tame at all, it was in a rapture of fear. She had cuddled it to her face and, giving it a friendly snuffle, found that it was dead.

Sarah almost wished something similar would happen to her. But it did not. Instead she remembered last night. "Tom—"

"He's quite well."

"I've got to call him!" Some of her old self was returning, it seemed, as she recalled Tom's screams. "Where's the phone?"

Miriam's expression was hard to read. She seemed at once angry and curiously at peace. "I don't think you should phone him. Go to him instead."

Sarah hid her amazement. She had assumed herself a prisoner. "Can I go now?"

"Certainly. You're no prisoner."

At once Sarah got out of bed. She could stand up easily. The hunger, the grogginess, were gone. Her body seemed unusually light and healthy. The sense of physical well-being was remarkable.

Then the image of the dead girl swam into memory again. Her own experiences crowded out all happiness. She remembered the blood hot in her throat, the delicate sadness of her victim's face. She moved away from the bed.

"The room is clean," Miriam said. "We remove evidence very quickly, you'll find."

Sarah couldn't stand to hear it. She clapped her hands over her ears.

"You took a life. That's what you feel in you now. Her life. She was a healthy young woman of about twenty-five, about your size and build. She was wearing jeans and a brown sweat shirt when I captured her."

"Shut up!"

Sarah's heart had started pounding, her temples throbbing. She longed somehow to expel what was in her. All she could do was escape. She ran from the room, down the hallway toward the stairs.

Miriam's strong hand grabbed her shoulder, spun her around. "Get dressed," she snapped. "You can't go out like that."

"I'm sorry."

"Your clothes are in the bedroom closet."

Sarah hesitated. She didn't want to go back in that bedroom. Miriam pushed her. "Face it, Sarah. You killed. *You.*" She pushed again. "And you'll kill others. You'll keep killing." Another hard shove and Sarah stumbled through the door. Miriam rushed past her, strode to the windows and swept back the heavy drapes.

Dawn was spreading up from the east, the red sun gleaming on the East River, sending a spear of light across Miriam's garden. Such beauty hurt.

"You haven't got any reason to cry," Miriam said. "You should be rejoicing."

"You said I could go." How small her voice sounded.

In answer Miriam swept her clothes out of the closet. Sarah threw them on, thinking only of Tom and the salvation she would find in his arms.

In a few more minutes she was setting out into a magnificent spring morning. The door of the house swung shut behind her. As Sarah walked down the street she was conscious of Miriam's face at the window of the library. Only when she was able to turn a corner and get out of that line of sight did she begin to feel free.

Never, as long as she lived, would she return to that house.

She was actually going back home. She felt all the delight of one who escapes from an unjust imprisonment. She was going back to her place as part of humanity. She was resurrected.

Tom shared as much of his tragedy as he dared with Charlie and Phyllis. He could not tell them of the things he had seen. They might have thought he was hallucinating, which would only confuse matters. Phyllis wept a little when Tom told her that he did not know what had happened to Sarah. She was Sarah's closest associate and a good friend, and she shared some of Tom's anguish.

Tom didn't know if he would ever see Sarah again. He suspected she might be dead. This black thought was in his mind when the lock clicked and Sarah came in.

She burst in. Tom was astonished and glad, and yet somehow assaulted. There was something about the total surprise of the arrival and the quickness of her movements that made him want to retreat.

He refused to accept such a feeling. Her poor, small frame was shaking with tearful joy and he was afraid of her. Or was it joy that moved her? What was that look in her eyes?

"Sarah!" Phyllis' voice rang through the silence.

Sarah glared. Tom had never seen such an expression on her face before. For a moment he was afraid she might strike Phyllis.

"Tom, please hold me!" She came toward him, then paused. He did not understand her hesitation. Her expression became almost desperate.

"You're home now," was all he could think to say. "You made it home." His emotions were beginning to overwhelm him. He wanted to sob. Never again would he let her go. They circled one another, a slow dance.

He recalled their past: lying on a beach in Florida, Sarah holding forth on age vectors in the baking sun. He had laughed aloud at her intensity. Sarah in her lab, her voice strident, the atmosphere charged with her energy. Sarah in bed, loving.

As the shock of her arrival wore off she became more real to Tom. He kissed her. Her mouth was sour and he drew back. Tears appeared in her eyes. "I have a confession—"

"Not yet."

Her eyes widened. Her fingers came up to his bandages. "She hurt me," he said.

"Don't call her 'she.' Miriam isn't a 'she.' That's a human word."

"What, then? Woman?"

"A female of another species. A woman is a human being. Miriam is a mockery of humanity. Women stand for life. Miriam stands for death."

"You're pale," he said. He didn't want to pursue any conversations about Miriam right now. Not until they both felt a lot better.

Phyllis and Charlie had drawn close, instinct making them seek the comfort of the group. Tom could not blame them. He felt it too: something black and cold was in this room.

"I may look pale but I feel good," Sarah said. "I wish I didn't feel like this." Tom detected more than a little desperation in her voice. He began to wish Phyllis and Charlie would leave. He wanted Sarah alone.

"We didn't understand how dangerous she was," Phyllis said.

Sarah turned to her. "I failed, Phyl. You believed in me, but I failed." She was starting to back away, as if their closeness disturbed her.

"We got a lot of data, Sarah."

"Not enough. You don't know the half of it. She didn't let you have anything of real value."

Sarah kept backing away. Tom made a gesture to Phyllis and Charlie, nodded toward the door. "Yes," Sarah said, "it's best if they leave."

"Sarah," Phyllis said, "I don't want you to think you failed."

"Please, Phyl."

"I'll go, but just don't think you've failed. It isn't over yet. Remember that. We haven't even begun to work on that data."

"Yes, Phyl."

"I think you'd better cut it short," Tom said at last. Sarah looked as if she were about to explode. When the door closed behind them at last, Sarah took a ragged breath. She was now on the far side of the room, poised like a cornered animal.

Sarah had known from the moment she entered the apartment what Miriam had done to her. Another trick.

They smelled so good.

She wanted to handle them, to caress their warm, moist skin, to draw them close to her.

How accommodating Miriam had been. And why not, when she knew what this was going to do to Sarah. She wanted to run . . . and then again she didn't. There was something very pleasing about them, about Tom especially, the slow way he moved and the trust in his eyes. This odd feeling isolated her from them, forced her into a kind of loneliness she had never known before.

When the door closed behind Charlie and Phyllis, Sarah knew that Tom was endangered. He should not be alone with her. Not when she was like this.

She strove for control. "Stay on that side of the room," she said.

He looked across at her, a question in his eyes. The

wall was directly behind her. She could not get farther away from that wonderful scent. If she opened her arms, called to him, he would come. She must not allow herself to do that.

"Darling?"

"Tom, don't come any closer!"

"You're joking."

"I am not."

"Didn't you come here to be with me?"

There was such hurt in his tone. She wanted to go to him, but she did not dare. He took a step closer. Her flesh crawled, but her arms came up. Another Sarah, mean and evil, smiled, another voice welcomed him. She could hear his pulse as he approached, hear the whisper of his breath, the faint liquid sound as his lips parted.

"We had good times. Don't you remember?" She did remember, as he had no doubt intended she should. Sweaty hours banging away at one another. Such innocence and pleasure.

"Tom, *stop!*"

Thank God it had finally come out. The shout stunned him. He stood still, his smile fading. "Why?"

"Just do it. Don't come a step nearer. Not one step!"

He bowed his head, remained motionless.

"Go into the bedroom and close the door. I made a major error coming here. I've got to get out and I can't possibly make myself do it unless you leave the room."

"What are you talking about?"

"Tom, I can't stand it much longer! Please just do as I say, even if you don't understand."

"I think we ought to talk about it."

"No! Go away!"

He was moving closer again. In a moment she was going to open her arms once more and this time she would not be able to stop.

Miriam called it hunger. A mild word.

"Please!" She cast her eyes down, felt her muscles tensing for the kill. Her body was preparing to spring at

him. Hot, anguished tears poured out of her eyes. Very softly, she made a last plea. "Don't touch me."

"You're serious. You're absolutely serious!"

She looked up at him. He was four feet away. She could not warn him again.

"OK, I get the point. But why, Sarah?"

"Just do as I say. Do it now."

At last he began to move toward the bedroom. For a horrible moment she thought she was following him, but she managed to go out the front door instead. Her movements were sinuous and quick. She reminded herself of a rat questing through a maze. There was another person in her, powerful and evil, and she was losing control.

The hallway was empty. That was a small miracle, and Sarah was grateful. She could smell them all around her, behind the doors of their apartments. The moan of need that came out of her mouth was hardly human.

Sarah knew where she had to go, where it was intended she go. There was only one place that did not smell human, only one being who did not tempt the hunger. Miriam had made her point. For Sarah the only thing that now mattered was getting back to that house. Doing it through the crowded Manhattan streets was going to be hell. She clung to the notion that she would not kill another human being.

As the elevator descended, she tried to prepare herself for her ordeal. She had moved in the streets before, after all, and hadn't eaten at all the last time. She remembered the man on the sidewalk whom she had nearly killed, the apartment balcony she had climbed.

That was with the streets empty. Now they were going to be jam-packed. 'I am a human being,' she thought. 'I will not harm my fellow man.' With all the willpower left to her, she resolved to remain a human being. The hunger she felt, after all, was not her own. It belonged to the creature's blood. The need to kill was not her need, it was Miriam's. She resolved to keep telling herself that. Then the elevator doors opened and she saw Alex at his post. 'Miriam's hunger,' she repeated, 'not mine.'

She managed to slip past him, get through the front door and out onto the sidewalk.

Madness. People everywhere, more even than she had imagined. She made an involuntary lunge at a passing businessman, managed to dash past him into the middle of the street. Brakes squealed, horns blared. A cab swerved, slurred to a stop. The driver was cursing, the passenger staring terrified from the backseat.

There was no time to waste, no opportunity to miss. She got in. "Whassamatter with you? I got a goddamn fare in here!"

"Emergency!"

"Call a cop, lady. You nearly got yourself run over. Now get outa here."

"Somebody's about to die. I'm a doctor."

The driver rolled his eyes. "OK," he said, "where to?"

Sarah told him Miriam's address and opened the window. The fumes from the street would perhaps mask some of the smells within the cab. She listened as the driver reassured his passenger that all was well, the detour wouldn't take long. Many drivers would have refused to budge, she knew that. But she had gotten lucky. This guy had a heart.

As soon as the house appeared Sarah leaped from the cab, raced up the steps and began hammering the knocker, pressing the buzzer, trying the door.

She could feel Miriam standing just the other side of the door. "Please," she said softly, "please open it." She did not want to shout. Attracting the attention of the neighbors was dangerous.

After the longest thirty seconds of Sarah's life the door clicked and swung open. She staggered in and slammed it shut behind her, on all the bustle and beauty, and the hideous temptation, of the world of man.

Miriam knew at once that Sarah's will had proved stronger than her need. She sighed with displeasure, let the poor thing into the house, waited for the inevitable recriminations.

Sarah's hunger would eventually break her will, but until it did Miriam would have to endure this annoying independence. She hardly heard Sarah's wails of anguish, her roaring anger, hardly felt the clawing and the pummeling as she pulled the girl up the stairs and back into their bedroom.

"I'll return when you're feeling more reasonable," she said. "Try to calm yourself." There was little point in saying more. Sarah was stronger than the others, a lot stronger. Too bad. It was going to make things that much more difficult for her. She had a romantic vision of herself as the great healer. A fool's vision. The world has forgotten that romance has two aspects, that of love and that of death. Sarah didn't know it, but she had moved to the side of death.

The walls of the apartment were closing in on Tom. He stood in the foyer, his mind racked with indecision. He should follow Sarah, go back to that house again.

But he could not. That pretty little house held nothing for him but terror. Pink brickwork, window boxes, romantic white shutters, all seemed evil and grotesque, like makeup smeared on some sneering face. The screaming terrors of last night seemed to come close to him. His hand touched the bandages on his face. Had they been demons? Were such things real? His belief in science had evaporated. All the grand procession of knowledge now seemed nothing more than smugness and ignorance.

In the face of something such as Miriam had a man any power at all? There was no place to turn. Prayer meant nothing to him. His childhood prayers had gotten only silence in reply.

If that silence was sacred, he had not known it until now, and he felt it was too late to challenge the rock of his disbelief. He could not turn to God for strength.

There seemed nowhere to turn. He just didn't have the courage to break the spell of Miriam. Or did he? He imagined taking Sarah in his arms and shouting out his love so loud it would penetrate to the depth of her soul.

That love, that was truth.

That was his weapon.

He took a step toward the door. One step, no more. He remembered the look in Sarah's face as she had pleaded with him not to come near her. "I love you, Sarah! I love you!" His voice echoed. Sunlight spread across the living room. He saw little clouds beyond the window, white and fluffy. He screamed the scream of nightmare.

Miriam decided to wait a bit before telephoning the victim. It would be best if he could get up the courage to come on his own. That way she could let him force his way to Sarah, to succeed where he had failed last night. It was doubtful, however. Human courage had its limits.

She went to the garden to pick flowers. It was a soothing pastime and it would be best if the house appeared as cheerful and sweet as possible. The windows must be opened, the curtains drawn back. There should be music on the stereo, something soothing, perhaps Delius' *Florida Suite,* or the overture from *The Land of Smiles.* Perhaps there should be some fruit and wine set out. No, just wine. Fruit was too much trouble. She didn't even know if they still sold natural fruit, it had been so long since she had noticed.

Carefully avoiding even a glance at her destroyed rose arbor, Miriam clipped until her basket was heavy with marigolds, snapdragons, iris, all the wealth of her garden. She loved the exuberant life of the flowers. Nature demanded nothing more of them than that they open each morning to the sun. Miriam's race was not so lucky. From her and her kind much more was demanded. Not all that nature wants from its children is innocent.

She carried the cut flowers onto the sun porch, laid them on the table which contained the portrait of Lamia. She looked into her mother's eyes, rendered by the artist as pale blue. Before the invention of contact lenses and shaded glasses Miriam's species was marked as having the evil eye. The artist had not wanted to offend his client by giving her eyes their true color.

The portrait was a source of peace and reassurance to Miriam. The eyes said to her, 'Go on, never stop. For me, be immortal.'

Tom had managed to get as far as Miriam's front door. The house stood before him, the vortex of a deadly whirlpool. He was reminded of the flowers that eat flies, using their nectar and their beauty as bait. Tom hated most the beauty of the place. It should have foreboded somehow of the danger within. Must Miriam always smile?

It was a sunny morning, the sky now clear blue. Before him the house glowed in sunlight dappled through budding trees. The green shutters were open. Behind them silk curtains billowed in the fresh breeze. He heard music and saw shadowy movement in the living room.

For an instant he was ready to run, but the music seemed at odds with danger. It was happy, rich music, the kind of thing he might have heard drifting up from the bandshell on a summer night of his boyhood. He supposed that he had been seen, and the music was meant to make him feel just as he did.

He had imagined how life was going to be without Sarah, and had wound up here, telling himself how he loved her. Still, it was going to be hard to get to that front door to ring the bell. If anything the obvious musical attempt to soothe him made him more uneasy than ever.

Either he go in that house now or face the fact that he would never see Sarah again.

How desperately she needed him. When somebody you loved has nowhere left to turn, you help. If there was such a thing as a human compact, that was part of it.

Sarah had to be gotten out of there and taken by force to Riverside. And as for Miriam—she belonged in a specimen container.

A face appeared at a downstairs window. Miriam smiled at him.

In a moment she opened the front door. He mounted the steps and went in. It was as simple as that. She stood before him, blond and beautiful, smelling of flowery old-fashioned perfume, her expression welcoming. As the door closed she regarded him with concern. "I'm so glad you came. I was just going to call you. Sarah needs help."

"I'm aware of that. I came to get her."

"I had hoped she would stay with you this morning. When she came back I just didn't know what to do."

"I want to take her to Riverside."

"That would be best. Tom, I'm afraid I'm at my wit's end. Sarah's reactions have been all wrong. I—I never intended to harm her." The gleam of a tear appeared in one eye. "Now she's up in that bedroom and she won't unlock the door!"

"Upstairs? What room?"

"First door on the right at the head of the stairs."

"You lead the way." Tom had absolutely no intention of wandering around this house on his own. Miriam walked ahead of him, down the very hall where he had been attacked the night before. It was nothing but beautiful now, with flowers on the tables and a cheerful coaching print on one wall. The room's innocent appearance only intensified his caution.

Miriam seemed aware of his feelings, as if the act downstairs had been little more than a formality. "Sarah," she said, "please let me in. I have a surprise for you." She turned to Tom. "I've got a key, but I hate to open a door somebody else has locked."

"Why don't I just bust it down," he said caustically.

She used her key.

It was the most beautiful room Tom had ever seen. The windows opened across a magnificent garden. He could see thousands of flowers, and there were more arrangements of cut flowers on the desk and night-stands. There was something a little obscene about the profusion of flowers. They were a kind of overstatement of an innocence that did not exist, and Tom was beginning to see them as the exact opposite of what they were obviously intended to suggest. They seemed to confirm Miriam's guilt.

The breeze blew past gossamer pink curtains and sunlight poured in the windows. Tom found himself estimating the distance to the ground, and then saw in the garden something that chilled him. There was a path of broken shrubs and upturned earth right across to the brick wall at the garden's far edge. He could see from here the brown scuff marks his shoes had left on the wall.

Sarah lay in a magnificent rosewood bed. She was not asleep, but in a sort of trance-state. Her eyes followed him from beneath half-closed lids. She looked languid, but he had the impression that she was far from it. The eyes hardly blinked.

A fly came in the window, buzzing energetically. Tom watched it spiral up to the ceiling. For a moment he was stunned. He had not noticed that the ceiling was magnificently painted to resemble a blue, cloud-flecked sky. Clouds billowed and larks soared in that magical, ineffably romantic air. The fly, crawling across the painted birds and clouds, was the only thing that disturbed the perfection of the illusion.

Sarah moaned. Tom went beside the bed. Gone were the protests he had heard in the apartment. Her face, beaded with perspiration, became almost sensual. Her eyes were dreamy, softened by desire. Her arms opened wide. He bent close to her, kissed the tears that stained her cheeks.

The next thing he knew her arms had come around him and he was lying beside her on the bed, drawing the delicate silk sheets away from her body. She was more beautiful now than he had ever remembered her.

He was vaguely aware that Miriam had retreated to the hall and pulled the door closed behind her. He feasted his eyes on Sarah's body. It was smoother, softer. He touched her cool breast, felt the heart beating there beneath the firm flesh. Only her eyes told him that she was conscious of his touch. What turmoil was in those eyes. They looked at once delighted, avid with need, and as deeply troubled as any eyes he had ever seen. He tried to comfort her with soft sounds, soothing caresses. This was what he had longed to do at home. This was the truth of love. Surely this would reach her.

Sarah was anguished. She could not even speak, much less cry out. Her body screamed with silent need, her mind hummed with excuses and justifications.

She had determined to lie here until she died. Then Tom had appeared. She hoped at first that it was a hallucination. Then their eyes met and she knew that he was real.

How could anyone be so foolish.

She hadn't the strength for both of them, not anymore. Every cell of her being demanded action. This hunger was not the slow desperation of starvation, it was something far worse. Where starvation was dreamy and sad, this was quick and cunning and frantic.

"Sarah, we can conquer this thing together."

He lay close to her, unendurably close. She let her arms twine around him. It felt so good to give in. So very good. "Yes," she said, "we'll do it together."

His body was growing tense with passion. She noticed his eyes flick to the door.

"Miriam won't bother us," she said. "This is exactly what she wants."

She ran her hands under his shirt. She knew just what Tom liked. Deep within, a voice shrieked at her to warn him, to drive him away once again. She purred and arched her back, offering herself to him.

She knew just how to excite him and he found himself responding to her more passionately than ever before. The beauty of the surroundings, the quiet, the warm sunlight combined to encourage him to forget the horrible problems that were besetting them, to forget for just a few minutes. He caressed her breasts, her thighs, sought her lips with his own. 'It'll help,' he told himself, 'it's healthy and normal and positive.'

She unbuttoned his shirt, touched his nipples with her deft little hands. Their delicacy had always delighted him, and he kissed them now. He felt himself growing erect and guided the hands to his zipper.

"Yes, Tom," she said. She was smiling now. He burst out of his unzipped pants.

He hugged her. "We'll be free again," he said, "you'll see."

"Oh, Tom, I hope so!"

He entered her. Every tiniest move brought intense pleasure. This was what they had needed. They should have trusted love more.

Tom closed his eyes, heard her whispering his name to the rhythm of their movements. Her voice merged with the hypnotic buzzing of the fly on the ceiling. He nuzzled close behind her ear and buried his face in her hair, where it was as soft as the fur of a rabbit.

A new feeling entered him, one that hurt like the

contemplation of great beauty. He held her to him, riding her.

With every bit of concentration remaining to her, Sarah tried to resist her need. He lay atop her in his disheveled clothes, sweating out his passion. Beads of perspiration glittered on his forehead. His cheeks were red, as if he had been running.

She was emptied of hope.

Tom's passion rose. She loved him, she realized, as she might love a child. His sexual significance, in the past few days, had dwindled to nothing.

Bang-slap, his body went as it plunged against her. She felt his heat, smelled his breath, tasted the salt of his hot flesh as she waited.

She knew perfectly well what Miriam wanted. And that she wasn't going to do. She couldn't, even if she wanted to. Miriam had forgotten one simple thing. There was no weapon in the room, and without one she could not make Tom's blood flow.

She had almost called out to Miriam for one. But now she was sure she wouldn't do that. Her suffering became a kind of hypnotism. She was lost in it when a flash of light on her face made her open her eyes.

Miriam stood at the foot of the bed, holding up an object so bright it dazzled Sarah.

Tom went on making love, his human senses oblivious to the silent drama being enacted around him.

Miriam was closer now. The object in her hand was a gleaming knife.

A scalpel.

Miriam placed it on the bedside table and departed at once.

Sarah touched the sharpness of it with her fingers.

"Oh, Tom, Tom!"

"Sarah! I love you, love you! Oh, *God!"*

His pumping shook her. The scalpel dazzled in her hand. So light, so strong.

His face, melting with love, gazed down into hers.

She closed her eyes, held her breath. 'No, I will not,' she thought, a chant within her. 'No no, nono, no no.'

It came rolling up from the depths, the *thing* within her.

The scalpel belonged to it. Had always belonged to it.

No no no no.

This was her truth. She pushed it into him.

"SARAAAAAH!"

She took it out, shoved it in again. It whispered through his flesh and all at once the purple miracle of his life was pouring into her.

Alive again. She heard a song that hurt like a memory. Somebody was sobbing. She was sobbing.

Why? She was happy.

His head bobbed, his jaw went slack. To escape his collapsing weight she wriggled out from under him, slipped from the bed. He shook horribly, huddling in the sheets. Blood spread. Then she touched him, bent to him, made believe she was kissing him. She took his life out of him.

She twirled slowly around and around, her whole body rapturing with a fine pleasure. She spread her arms in the warm air. The world had become dream-golden, touched with every beauty she had ever known. She could feel everything—the gentle movement of air past her body, the slow warmth of the sun, the secret pumping of her own blood.

She could feel Tom.

Feel him!

Her eyes went to his dead body. Something extraordinary was happening. Emotions almost seemed to pour from him like some healing water: sorrow, pity, peace.

Such peace.

She heard his voice in the air around her, saying her name in the rhythm of their lovemaking. It got fainter and fainter. More than anything she had ever wanted, she wanted the sound of that voice.

She was desolated.

Miriam cringed at the scream that pealed in her ears. It was an incandescence of grief. She could not remember measuring such sorrow as this before. The intensity was too great, much too great.

Miriam went to Sarah. As she hurried through the silent halls to the bedroom she felt a twinge of concern for her own safety. Anguish such as Sarah's could turn easily to anger. Killing anger. Miriam could be endangered.

She paused at the bedroom door, listened to ascertain Sarah's position. The long, ragged sounds of her breathing came from the far side of the room. Miriam fitted her key into the lock. After an instant the mechanism made a soft *chunk* and the door swung open. Its weight of steel faced with ordinary wood panels was perfectly balanced, and it moved silently.

A glaring pillar of sunlight dazzled Miriam's eyes. Sarah was standing near the window, staring into the dawn-lit garden. The remains of her lover lay in the crumpled sheets of the bed.

Miriam put all her affection into her voice when she called to Sarah, trying to speak as a mother to a child, as lover to lover and as friend all at the same time. Sarah gave no indication that she had heard. Miriam began a slow approach, aware that Sarah might at any moment lunge at her.

"Sarah, I know exactly how you feel."

"You have no idea."

"You may not believe me now, but you've got more to live for than you ever did before."

"Miriam, I just killed the man I love! You don't seem to understand that. I haven't got more to live for. I have nothing to live for."

"Don't say that! You have me, Sarah."

Sarah looked at her, then bowed her head. Her shoulders shook. She wept silently.

"All you've done is trade one way of life for another."

"You're obscene, do you know that? Obscene!"

"You've joined a new race. We have our rights too. And we never kill more than we need."

Sarah tossed the scalpel aside as if it had burned her. Miriam took the opportunity to get closer. They needed physical contact.

"Stay away!" Sarah twisted away from her. "Don't you dare touch me." There was warning in the tone. Sarah was unarmed now, but still capable of inflicting an injury.

Miriam circled her, trying to maintain contact with her eyes. "You're more than human now. You've acquired the right of life and death over human beings."

"You disgust me!"

Closer and closer Miriam moved. From the depth of such despair, Miriam felt sure a new Sarah would soon emerge. Tenderly, Miriam spoke again. "You're alone without me. All alone. Come to me."

The look of revulsion that crossed Sarah's face hurt Miriam more than any blow. She guarded the kindness in her own face carefully. In a moment Sarah was going to break. No matter what her feelings might be, instinct would take her to loving arms.

Until now Sarah had not realized how unpleasant Miriam smelled. She was revolting, sweet and touched with rot. Sarah kept edging away from her, thinking only of what a fool she had been to toss that scalpel aside, wishing she could cut Miriam open exactly the same way she had Tom.

Miriam kept coming closer, her movements swift and obsessive. On her face was an expression that made Sarah long to kick it, to feel her foot connecting with that condescending smile.

Although she tried not to look at him, Sarah's eyes returned again and again to Tom. His face was half-hidden by the sheets but she could see the staring eyes, filled even yet with surprise and sorrow.

He had died in agony. Her heart beat hate for the one who had so corrupted her that she would have done that to him.

"You don't deserve to live, Miriam."

"But I *will* live. And so will you."

Sarah did not reply. 'Oh no we won't,' she thought. 'No we won't.' Her eyes searched for the scalpel. Miriam stiffened slightly, stopped moving toward her.

"Sarah, please try to understand me. I've given you a new life, and it's worth living. Believe me when I say that. It's a better life than you could ever imagine."

Sarah stilled her urge to scream insults, to howl out her rage. Her whole soul concentrated on one thought: how good it would be to cut into that evil being, to push the knife deep and feel the heart shake the blade.

"I love you," Miriam said. "Love is beyond price."

That was too much. Sarah could not restrain herself in the face of such overbearance. "You love only yourself! You're worse than a monster. Much worse!" Her words reverberated in the small room. "You can't love me or anybody else. You're incapable of it!"

Miriam's arms opened and she once again came close. Sarah slapped wildly, connected with Miriam's cheek. As if shot, Miriam leaped away. On her face was a look of raw fear.

Then control reasserted itself. She stood near the door, nursing her cheek. "You surprised me," she said. "You have no idea how dangerous it is to do that."

Nor did Sarah care. All she knew was that before the hunger came over her again she would be dead. And so would Miriam. She swore it to herself and the memory of Tom.

That slap had hurt. Miriam's cheek was burning. It had been a long time since a human being had success-

fully struck her. Before this, none had done it and
lived.

What spirit this woman had. Life with such a person
would be fascinating. Sarah would become an equal in
every sense of the word. She had all the needed
attributes. The next feeding, Miriam would be most
careful to make sure all the life was absorbed. Unless
she did that Sarah could not obtain enough energy to
feel the true wonder of her new life. Sarah must touch
the glory.

"The hunger has to be served very carefully, Sarah.
You need to learn the technique—"

"Technique! You talk about it like it was a sport or
something. You're barbaric." She tossed her head,
proud, her conviction unassailable. Miriam admired
such control, but it was time Sarah broke down and
vented her rage. That would make it much easier for
them both.

"In some ways it is a sort of a sport." She tried to
make herself sound happy. "And it does indeed have a
technique."

"I don't want to hear about it!"

"But you must! Don't you understand that you're
going through the process again? You'll Sleep and then
you'll feed. There's no way out, Sarah. It's going to
happen."

Sarah clapped her hands to her ears as if to deaden
the sound of the truth. A low moan started in her
throat and rose to a wail of anguish. She grabbed wildly
at Miriam, tried to claw her. But Miriam was not to be
surprised again. She took Sarah's wrists in one hand
and forced her head back by grasping her hair with the
other.

Sarah's eyes were wild, her mouth flecked with foam.
Her wail broke to hoarse growling. Lunging and twisting, she tried again and again to reach Miriam. Miriam
kept her arms extended, bearing Sarah's weight easily,
letting the rage spend itself. In every silence Miriam

spoke softly. "I love you," she said each time, "I love you."

Finally Sarah hung limp in her arms, sobs trembling through her body, her head bowed. Slowly, carefully, Miriam drew her close. "Sleep," she said, stroking the brown curls. "Sleep and all will be well."

She carried Sarah across the hall to a little-used bedroom. The door was stout enough to contain Sarah when she awoke, and the window was barred.

Sarah had not realized that she was losing consciousness until she felt Miriam pick her up. She tried to pull away, but experienced a wave of dizzy stupor. Dimly she was aware of Miriam's soothing words. Although her heart rebelled, her body accepted Miriam's embrace.

She tried to keep her eyes open, was only dimly aware of being placed in a clean bed.

She plunged into a new reality. It was worse than the worst nightmare, more realistic than the most perfect dream. Tom was sitting on the foot of the bed. His expression was rigid with anger. With a jerk of his head he turned and stared into Sarah's face. "YOU KILLED ME! KILLED ME! KILLED ME!" His voice scratched high and desperate notes.

Then he looked at her with such sadness she wanted there and then to be dead. "I forgive," he said.

Suddenly it was high summer. They were in Vermont together. It was last summer's vacation again. Sarah was lying in the grass. So happy. She knew that this remembrance was a gift from Tom. So very happy.

When she opened her eyes she saw into the sparkling leaves of the tree they were sitting under. A breeze rustled the grass beside her ear. There was a sudden pop and a froth of champagne splashed her. She sat up laughing. "You did that on purpose."

"Of course. Lunch is served."

They ate, enjoying themselves enormously. Sarah

watched the day soften and fade along the distant range of the Green Mountains. Soon they made love and lay naked in the rich air of summer.

They witnessed the westward march of the sun, the appearance of the first stars, and cuddled close in the night wind.

"YOU KILLED ME!"

She ran. The summer hill became dark and cold, the grass congealed into stones.

His voice echoed and re-echoed behind her, lost and far away.

Miriam watched Sarah Sleep, evaluating her state. She felt the pulse, then opened one eye and looked long at the pupil. As a last test she ran her fingertips carefully along the skin of Sarah's cheek. The Sleep was true.

Sarah was transformed.

"Welcome," Miriam said, "welcome home."

When awareness returned everything was changed. Sarah sat up. She was in a bed in a dark room. The day had become night in the time she had been asleep. Beyond the window she could see a crescent moon gleaming over the East River.

She wasn't alone.

Miriam stood at the foot of the bed, a shimmering being. Sarah could not take her eyes off that strange, radiant figure. Miriam was exceedingly beautiful without her disguise. The moonlight made her skin seem white, made her eyes gleam golden. For an instant they shone like an animal's eyes, then she turned her head.

"You've Slept eight hours," Miriam said. Her voice was song.

Something moved in Sarah's stomach. She must have gasped because Miriam smiled. A tickling sensation in her throat made Sarah momentarily nauseous. Then her whole body began to tingle.

Hunger slammed into her with a force that made her cry aloud. The fiery pain of it caused her to jump from the bed. She had to have help! Unbalanced by the suddenness of it, she bellowed need, clawed air. Miriam stepped deftly away from her, was at the door in an instant.

The lock clicked with a heavy sound of steel and Sarah was alone. She rushed at the door, grabbed the knob, shook it with all her might. It didn't even rattle, it was so strong.

Despair washed over her.

Just when she thought she would lose her mind with the need for food the lock clicked again. Miriam entered the room, carrying a limp human form.

Sarah hardly even noticed the sex. Never before had she wanted so much to touch something, to caress moist skin, to possess.

Miriam laid the body out on the bed. "Control yourself," she said in a clipped tone. "And listen to me. You've got a few things to learn before you start."

Sarah watched a hand slip off the edge of the bed and dangle. She saw the face in the moonlight, grave and pretty, a common-enough young woman's face. Her lips had an almost humorous cast to them.

Sarah could imagine this girl dancing.

"She's been stunned and she'll come to in a couple of minutes. You've got to be ready for her." Miriam spoke matter-of-factly about inserting the scalpel and popping the vein, opening one's mouth over the wound, letting one's body absorb all the life. "All of it," she said. "That way you'll need to feed only once a week at most."

Miriam's every word was a harmony, her every gesture purest grace. What a beautiful form evil had assumed. Standing there, frantic with hunger, Sarah did not think there could be hatred greater than the hatred she felt for Miriam. It was a white fire.

The girl moaned, then gasped and coughed herself

awake. Her eyes opened, looked with longing at the moon, then turned to the two figures standing over the bed. Miriam stepped back, not wanting, Sarah supposed, to frighten the girl with her undisguised presence.

'You killed me,' Tom had said in another world.

In this world Sarah was about to kill Miriam. "Give me my scalpel," Sarah said.

"It's on the night table."

So clever. To reach the night table Sarah had to put the bed between herself and Miriam.

She had to get that blade into Miriam, had to feel it deep within her. She imagined herself ramming it home with the heel of her hand.

The scalpel was light between Sarah's fingers. Such a delicate instrument. The girl made a miserable little sound in her throat, clutched the sheets.

"Don't move," Miriam said to her. "Don't you dare." Sarah felt Miriam's eyes on herself. "Straddle her and make sure your knees pin the arms." The girl groaned miserably when Sarah came onto the bed. Her eyes followed the knife.

Sarah thought only of Miriam. Now she was just a few feet away. Sarah raised the scalpel. Miriam leaned forward. "Don't jab, just slip it in." The girl began shaking her head. "Hurry up, Sarah!" Miriam snapped. The girl screamed. Her eyes were bulging now, her mouth wide.

With a single motion Sarah slashed out to her right, toward Miriam. She lost her balance on the writhing girl and fell to the floor. The scalpel hadn't connected. Miriam was now across the room. Sarah's heart sank. It was hard to understand how she had missed. Miriam was so fast.

The girl jumped up, scrambled from the bed and made for the door. Almost indifferently Miriam slammed her against the wall so hard the whole house shuddered. The girl slid to the floor.

"You have a great deal yet to learn," Miriam said to Sarah. "Perhaps you ought to starve for a few hours." She picked up the girl, moving quickly to the door. Sarah was coming toward her, trying for another chance with the scalpel.

Miriam was through the door and had it locked before Sarah had taken three fast steps. Unless Miriam was completely surprised there was no hope.

Sarah hurled the scalpel at the door and snarled the rage that consumed her.

She grabbed at the door handle, yanked angrily, knowing in advance that Miriam's doors were all of steel.

Her heart weighted with disappointment, Miriam took the victim across the hall and stuffed her into a closet in her own bedroom. The girl's skull was crushed so there was no need for caution. The coma would last perhaps three hours. Sarah would have to feed before death occurred or the girl would be wasted.

Drawn by her concern for poor Sarah, Miriam went back to the locked door and listened. The sounds within were hideously reminiscent of those made by her own kind in the dungeons of Paris. Sarah's will was quite extraordinary. There were howlings and screams on the other side of that door, but not a whisper of a plea. Here was one whose will was great enough to do battle with the hunger.

But not forever.

Sarah shrieked out her suffering. Miriam was unkillable! So fast and so strong. If only there was a telephone in this damnable room, even a tape recorder.

She opened drawers, searched the closet. There was nothing except ancient, rotting clothes and a stack of theater programs from the last century.

The room grew stifling. Sarah's whole body hurt. She felt as if she had a blood infection, which in a sense she had. Her tongue was hard and dry, her eyes watering. Her guts churned and she was momentarily doubled over by the pain.

Her medical background told her that Miriam's blood, finding no other nutrient, was beginning to feed on its host body. She was literally being eaten alive from within. Her mouth jerked open. A spasm choked her until darting black shadows filled her eyes and the room seemed far, far away.

When the spasm passed she found herself lying on the floor, the weave of the carpet crawling beneath her as if she were lying in a mass of worms.

She managed to get to her feet. Somehow she had to reach Miriam. Her mind screamed at her, 'last chance, *last chance!*'

If only she had told Tom earlier. There had been time back in the apartment. Just a few words and he would have known the whole truth.

He would never have come here then, not without help. Perhaps even at that late hour Geoff's blood wash would still have worked.

Sarah could have saved herself, she saw it clearly.

'Why not, you fool?'

Even this morning she was still half-convinced she wanted Miriam's "gift." She remembered well the thought that had revealed her truth: 'I could live forever. Actually live forever.' And she had tried to imagine it. 'Me. Still alive in a thousand years.'

Or two thousand.

What was death but a disease, she had asked herself. And she had told herself she would break the secret of death from within the shelter of immortality and give the secret to humanity. What a lie that had been!

That was before she killed Tom. Not until her victim was someone she really loved had she come to her senses about the evil of it all.

She longed for hot life in her throat, for the salt of deliverance to fill her belly. The scalpel gleamed in her fingers, waiting.

Astonished, she dropped it. "My God, look at my *hand!*"

It was a claw, withering before her eyes. "Oh my God!" She darted to the dressing table, stared into the mirror there. By moonlight she saw a sunken thing, eyes black sockets, cheekbones stark in a famished face, teeth prominent behind shrinking lips.

Malnutrition, sped up beyond the wildest nightmare. "MIRIAM! BRING HER! BRING HER!!" She clasped her hands in her hair, threw back her head and screamed. "FOR THE LOVE OF GOD!"

The scalpel. The scalpel. She looked wildly across the floor, saw its gleam, pounced on it.

The door clicked.

No.

'You've failed at everything else. But don't you feed the hunger again.'

She drew the scalpel across her wrist, drew it deep to the bone. Bright red blood poured out. Instantly she was staggered by an overwhelming weakness.

As the door swung open she fell to her side. 'Tom, I love you.' Her heart rattled and shook her whole body, then stopped.

Silence.

Miriam was bending close to her. "You can't die!" she said in a high, frantic voice. "Now that you've let out your blood you can't live either!"

Can't die? I must die. *I am dead!*

Miriam was cradling her head in her lap, crying bitter tears. "You've gone right to the end of my world," she said, "and missed all the beauty that comes before." She stroked Sarah's head again and again, a sorrowful gesture. "My poor, dear Sarah." She breathed sharply, as if trying not to cry. "What an evil irony."

Sarah became aware that Miriam had picked her up. With slow steps Miriam was carrying her up a stairway, to an attic.

Miriam took her to a tiny room, one wall of which was stacked with chests of various ages. Sarah writhed when she realized that she was being put in a similar chest that lay open in the center of the room. Her mind rang with pleas but she found she could not speak. The top of the chest came down and a heavy latch was closed.

Sarah was in total darkness.

"It was futile, my darling. You were too much changed for mortal death, and now you've got eternal death. Sarah, you missed it all! It's so beautiful and you missed it all. You poor woman. I'll make you the same promise I've made all the others. I will keep you with for all time. I will never abandon you, and you will always have a place in my heart."

'God help me.'

Even the hunger was still here, tormenting her. The least movement resulted in minutes of weakness.

Time began to pass, but in a different way than it had in life. She knew only that it was passing, not how much was gone.

Little rustlings and sighs filled the air around her, coming from the other chests. So Miriam had done this before. The thought of what must be in the other chests terrified Sarah. How many were there?

Some of them must be hundreds of years old. Some thousands.

Thousands of years like this.

No. Impossible.

She pushed as hard as she could at the top of the chest. She clawed at its sides. 'I have to get out. I'm so hungry.'

The chest was unyielding.

She remembered what she had done to Tom and what she would do if she did get out. She was glad she was here. At least she could count herself a human being still. No matter what she must suffer, this was better than being Miriam's thing.

So much had been at stake. She found she could look within herself and even in this hell find riches of peace and love she had never known were there. She was full of grand memories, and she possessed a great love as well. Tom was with her in spirit. No matter how long she must remain here, she came to realize that in the end there was going to be a place even for her, where Tom had already gone, on the far side of the river of life, where the lost of this world are found.

Epilogue

MIRIAM ABANDONED NEW YORK. She dared not remain in her house or in her old identity. The disappearance of the two doctors would be investigated.

She wept for Sarah. The poor woman had not known the pleasure of her new estate, only the pain. Before this experience Miriam had never imagined the heights that could be reached by a human being who was groping toward the truth of love.

She went often to Sarah. The boxes were kept in the coal cellar in her new house, and she would speak softly to her lost friend in the cool and dark.

Such a person would have been a grand companion, more than worthy. But Miriam now realized that the gift she could confer was not above one such as Sarah, but beneath her.

"I miss you," she said into the darkness. It was the hour after evening and the shadows were deep in her new living room. A fog was rising out on the bay, and she heard the buoys sounding. She enjoyed the beauty and the safety of the fog in San Francisco.

"Did you say something, my dear?"

Miriam smiled up at her new companion, who had appeared with glasses of Madeira for the two of them. "Only that I love you. I've never loved anyone but you."

He sat down, sipped reverently at his glass.

"That's an 1838 Madeira," Miriam said. "I hope you like it."

He kissed her, putting his glass down near the portrait of Lamia that was framed in the table before them. It was like him not to cover the portrait. His devotion was total, to Miriam and to all she had revealed of herself.

She had sought him carefully, looking for loyalty and intelligence and the old hunger for life that she understood so well. She closed her eyes, welcoming his excited kisses.

She would always miss the courage of Sarah, and the nobility. But he would bring contentment, and she doubted Sarah would ever have offered that. As in the past she would dream her dream of his immortality and tell herself that here at last was her eternal companion.

Time would pass and nature would come and shatter the dream. So she would find another companion. And another. And so on until time itself slipped away.

No matter how her loneliness tempted her to find one who would last forever, she resolved never to attempt the transformation of another like Sarah, not this time or the next time, or for all time.

196